Acclaim for Cathy Bramley:

'It's impossible not to fall in love with Cathy Bramley's
feel-good stories'
Sunday Express

'Heartwarming and positive . . . **will leave you
with a lovely cosy glow**'
My Weekly

'Books by Cathy Bramley are brilliantly **life affirming**'
Good Housekeeping

'This is **delightful**!'
Katie Fforde

'As **comforting** as hot tea and toast made on the Aga!'
Veronica Henry

'Thoroughly **enjoyable**'
U Magazine

'This book **ticks all the boxes**'
Heat

'Reading a Cathy Bramley book for me is like coming home from
a day out, closing the curtains, putting on your PJs and settling
down with a huge sigh of relief! Her books are **full of warmth,
love and compassion** and they are completely adorable'
Kim the Bookworm

'Full of **joy and fun**'
Milly Johnson

'Perfect **feel-good** loveliness'
Miranda Dickinson

'I **love** Cathy's writing and her characters –
her books are **delicious**'
Rachael Lucas

'The **perfect** tale to **warm** your heart and make you smile'
Ali McNamara

Cathy Bramley is the author of the best-selling romantic comedies *Ivy Lane, Appleby Farm, Wickham Hall, The Plumberry School of Comfort Food* and *The Lemon Tree Café* (all four-part serialized novels) as well as *Conditional Love, White Lies & Wishes* and *Hetty's Farmhouse Bakery*. She lives in a Nottinghamshire village with her family and a dog. Her recent career as a full-time writer of light-hearted romantic fiction has come as somewhat of a lovely surprise after spending the last eighteen years running her own marketing agency.

Cathy would love to hear from you! Find her on:

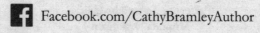 Facebook.com/CathyBramleyAuthor

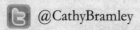 @CathyBramley

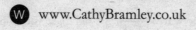 www.CathyBramley.co.uk

Cathy Bramley

A MATCH MADE IN DEVON

CORGI BOOKS

TRANSWORLD PUBLISHERS
61–63 Uxbridge Road, London W5 5SA
www.penguin.co.uk

Transworld is part of the Penguin Random House group of companies
whose addresses can be found at global.penguinrandomhouse.com

First published in Great Britain as four separate ebooks
in 2018 by Transworld Digital
an imprint of Transworld Publishers
First published as one edition in 2018 by Corgi Books
an imprint of Transworld Publishers

A CIP catalogue record for this book
is available from the British Library.

ISBN
9780552173933

Typeset in 11.5/13pt Garamond MT by Jouve (UK), Milton Keynes.
Printed and bound in Great Britain by Clays Ltd, Elcograf S.p.A.

Penguin Random House is committed to a sustainable future
for our business, our readers and our planet. This book is made from
Forest Stewardship Council® certified paper.

1 3 5 7 9 10 8 6 4 2

For Gregory Carven, Hans van Eenennaam
and John Dulos. We owe you everything.

PART ONE

The First Guests

Chapter 1

Maxine Pearce, the director, shoved her glasses to the top of her long charcoal-grey curls and clapped. 'Okay, folks, quiet please.'

In *Victory Road* Studio Two, on the outskirts of east London, everyone fell silent.

We were about to shoot my final ever scene in the show. This bit was so absolutely top secret that Maxine had insisted on the minimum number of crew on set. No one else knew what we were doing. It was all very exciting.

And I was part of it. The thought sent a rush of adrenalin swooping through me. Acting was my life. My dream. There was a sort of magic that happened to me when I took on a role. I ceased to be forgettable, plain old Nina Penhaligon with hamster cheeks, freckles and impossible-to-style hair, who on a good day would be classed as curvy, and on a bad day really needed to lay off the peanut-butter Oreos, and I became . . . anyone, anyone I wanted to be. And I loved every second of it.

Not much magic required today, however, because my character, Nurse Elsie Turner, was lying dead under a collapsed beam.

It would be heart-breaking for fans of the show; the first death of a character.

'Okay, Nina?' Maxine asked before giving final instructions to Mike behind the camera.

3

'Yep.' I tried to keep the tremor from my voice; never mind the viewers, my heart was breaking too. I was going to miss this lot.

Victory Road was a weekly drama set in the east end of London during the Blitz. Think *EastEnders* with gas masks and victory roll hair-dos. It had been my best part to date by far. I'd earned proper money and hadn't had to work for the temping agency for months. I detested office work, but needs must when you're a jobbing actress.

But after today it would be over; I squeezed back the tears, mindful of my make-up.

This morning we'd shot the cliffhanger ending to an episode in which I, Nurse Elsie, had been hurrying to take cover during an air raid when I'd heard a cry for help coming from a nearby house. I'd gone in to rescue the old lady who lived there just as a bomb exploded and the house collapsed around me. As the credits roll, the audience would be left on the edge of their seats. Will Elsie survive? Will she still be able to meet her boyfriend, Constable Ron Hardy, in the square where he's waiting with an engagement ring in his pocket? Will they be the first couple on the show to marry?

And only the people in this room knew the answers: no. I wasn't even allowed to tell my best friend on the show, Becky Burton, who also played a nurse. I understood the need for discretion but I felt bad about leaving without saying anything.

'And action,' murmured Maxine.

The atmosphere in the studio was crackling with tension. The ratings had dipped a bit recently and the management was hoping that a death would revive them. I was their sacrificial lamb. Apparently that was an honour because it meant my character was popular.

The sound effects began and we were transported to bomb-scarred London as the distant bells of fire engines and the wail of sirens filled the little studio.

Lamplight illuminated the wreckage of 33 Victory Road and two air-raid wardens, Ray and Godfrey, picked their way over the rubble looking for casualties.

'Over 'ere,' shouted Ray.

Ray, played by actor Lee Harwood, was the male lead. Drop-dead gorgeous. Shame I was playing a corpse and couldn't gaze up adoringly at him.

The beam of his lamp found my face. He dropped to his knees beside me and I managed not to blink under the glare. Godfrey leaned over us both as Ray checked for my pulse.

'Cor blimey,' Ray groaned, rocking back on his heels. 'It's Nurse Elsie. She's dead.'

Ninety minutes later it was all over. I'd packed up my bits and pieces and said farewell to the crew who'd filmed my last scene. Maxine, her stiletto heels tapping on the marble tiles, accompanied me through the revolving doors and out into the April sunshine. We squinted as our eyes adjusted to the brightness. It was the first of the month today; I wondered briefly whether the end of my contract had just been an April Fool.

'What an exit!' Maxine said as we stepped towards the bus stop.

Not an April Fool, then.

'So this is it,' I said, fighting the urge to grab her hands, fall at her feet and beg her to let Nurse Elsie live.

'You were marvellous today. Very professional.' She gave me a brisk smile. 'The reaction from the audience is going to be dynamite. It was a shame to kill you off but—'

'Maxine!' I warned as two teenage girls strutted towards us.

'Oh gosh, yes.' She tutted, folding her arms across her chest. 'Here I am enforcing an embargo on the storyline and then five minutes later blabbing it.'

'Ask her, ask her,' hissed the shorter of the two girls, pushing her friend towards me.

'Can we have your autograph?' The tall one shoved a scrap of paper and a pen at me.

'Of course,' I said, surprised to be recognized in public. I signed the back of what appeared to be a note excusing her from PE.

The two girls stared at the piece of paper.

'Oh.' The small one's face dropped. 'It's not her.'

'Told you.' The big one elbowed her sharply.

They screwed up my autograph, dropped it on the pavement and sashayed off.

Maxine and I exchanged wry smiles.

'At least they didn't hear what you said,' I said, scooping up the paper.

'Thank heavens. More than my job's worth if we had a story leak now.'

'Ditto,' I agreed. 'Not that I've got a job any more.'

Maxine smiled sympathetically. 'Sorry. But it's testament to your talent that you've lasted this long. The writers had originally only scripted you in for six episodes but you proved yourself worthy of more.'

I nodded, not sure how to respond other than to do the begging thing.

'When will you tell the rest of the cast that Nurse Elsie is . . . dead?' I said, lowering my voice on the last word.

'Not until the last possible moment. Can't risk the press getting hold of it. We'll let the rumour mill work its magic as long as we can: is she dead or alive? The love story between Elsie and Ron has captured the nation's hearts; the bookies are already offering odds on a wedding. This could really put *Victory Road* on the map. And you, too, Nina.'

'I hope so; it's such a good show.'

Maxine checked her watch. 'I'd best press on. You'll be at the party later?'

Jessie May, who played the flirty pub landlady, was having a birthday party in Soho.

'Of course,' I replied.

The press would be out in full force for this one; there was no way my agent Sebastian would let me pass up such an opportunity. He had recently told me that whilst I hadn't got star quality, there were plenty of parts out there for Miss Average (he was nothing if not brutally to the point), but that I had to show my face at showbiz parties, on the basis that someone might remember me and cast me in something. So that's what I did.

'Good.' She exhaled with relief. 'I was worried you might not feel like partying now that we've killed you off.'

'Actually, I . . .' I bit my lip, wondering whether to confide in her even though it hadn't been confirmed in writing yet.

'Go on.' She waited, one eyebrow cocked.

I couldn't resist; the opportunity to impress her was too great to miss.

'Strictly off the record, I've got a part in the new BBC period drama: *Mary Queen of Scots*.' I tried to look cool about it but my excitement was impossible to contain. 'So I'll be celebrating that.'

'Brilliant news!' Her angular face softened into a smile. 'Queen Mary?'

I blinked at her. 'The lead role? Gosh, no! My agent didn't put me forward for that.'

'He should have. Sebastian Nichols is your agent, isn't he?' Maxine furrowed her brow. 'Prince Charming himself.'

I nodded. Sebastian wasn't all that charming to me; ruthlessly ambitious, he only turned it on when he needed to.

'So who are you playing?'

'Eve, lady's maid to Queen Mary herself,' I said. In the distance I spotted an approaching bus and felt in my bag for my Oyster card. 'I'm just grateful to still be acting.'

Maxine took her phone out as the driver pulled up to the stop.

I jumped aboard and waved to her. 'Thanks for everything. It's been a joy working with you.'

'Likewise. But, Nina, hold on; something's niggling me.'

She rested the tip of her shoe on to the platform of the bus, thus preventing the driver from pulling away. I shot him a nervous smile while Maxine tapped at her phone screen.

'Ah. Thought so. Cecily Carmichael.' She pulled a face. 'Not a name I'd forget in a hurry, more's the pity. I had a brief fling with her father – awful man.'

It struck me that that was the first personal piece of information she'd ever revealed to me; Maxine was notoriously private.

'Thought what?' I said, conscious of a chorus of tutting passengers behind me. 'What is it?'

'Nina, dear heart,' she held the phone out to me, 'that part is already spoken for.'

'What? Who?' I took the phone from her and stared at it. Somebody's Twitter profile filled the screen and it took me a second to take it in. 'No way!'

Maxine was right: another actress, Cecily Carmichael, had announced that *she* had got my part. The part I had set my heart on. The one that was going to keep me in acting and out of temping. Her Twitter feed was full of it. Disappointment trickled through me like iced water.

Soooo thrilled to announce I'm to play Eve in new @BBC drama #QueenMary #excited #perioddrama MORE news at 6pm!!

Cecily's timeline was full of congratulations. Even Benedict Cucumberpatch had wished her well, as had . . . Sebastian – *my Sebastian*? – had sent her his love.

'I don't understand.' I stared at Maxine in disbelief. 'And she says she has more news to come? This can't be right.'

She pursed her lips thoughtfully. 'Darling, they must be barmy to pass you over for her. She auditioned for us once; she had about as much facial expression as Big Ben.'

My heart was pounding so much I couldn't even absorb

the compliment. I needed this job; it was the only thing that had been keeping me going. It could be ages before something else came along.

'Is she getting on or not?' the bus driver grumbled.

'Not,' I replied. 'Sorry.'

Just then a young mum with a double buggy huffed up to the bus stop and Maxine and I helped her on to the bus.

'You need to be aiming higher than Eve the lady's maid,' said Maxine. 'And if your agent can't see that, he's a fool.'

'But it was better than nothing and if I don't act I'll never become famous and—'

She held a hand up to stop me. 'Fame is completely overrated and totally unnecessary for a serious actress. Which I know you are. I'll see you at the party and don't forget in the meantime . . . Nurse Elsie's story.' She mimed zipping her lips.

'Absolutely. Bye for now,' I called as the bus doors closed in my face.

The bus joined the stream of traffic and I waved through the window and tried to make sense of my thoughts. I had every respect for Maxine, but she was wrong about the fame thing.

My need to be famous wasn't driven by vanity, it was fuelled by fear. A fear of being forgotten.

Because when you've been forgotten by the one person you thought loved you most, the world became a much scarier place.

Chapter 2

There *would* be an explanation as to how another actress had stolen my part in *Mary Queen of Scots* from right under my nose; I was sure Sebastian would be in touch, I just needed to be patient. I plucked my book from my bag and tried to distract myself by reading as the bus trundled towards the city.

But it was no use; my thoughts kept turning to Cecily.

She was the daughter of Campion Carmichael, the famous landscape artist. I knew Sebastian had been trying to woo her from a rival agency for months: she'd bring such a wealth of contacts with her. Not, I'd noted at the time, because of her incredible acting talent. In fact, to my knowledge, she'd only appeared in a documentary and even that had been about her father.

Two bus journeys later I was in Knightsbridge and striding towards Harrods to meet my flatmate Trudy. She worked behind one of the make-up counters and she'd offered to give me a makeover before tonight's party.

I checked my phone as I got to Harrods' doors. Still no call from Sebastian. This was all very odd. At my audition, the casting director had said that I was perfect for the role of Eve: I was the right age, build, colouring, even my slight northern accent would give the role just the right twist. So why had blonde, twiggy, plummy Cecily-bloody-Carmichael been given the part instead?

Somebody behind me huffed at me for blocking the doors. I murmured my apologies, stepped to the side and gazed at a window display of expensive handbags. A text flashed up on my screen from Trudy telling me to hurry up.

It was nearly six o'clock, Sebastian would be leaving the office soon. Suddenly, I couldn't wait; I absolutely had to hear from him tonight or I'd never be able to relax.

I leaned against the window and called his number. It rang for ages before he answered.

'Nina,' he said flatly. 'I'm with someone, can I call you back?'

'Let me just quickly ask . . .' I heard him sigh softly, but I soldiered on. '*Mary Queen of Scots*?'

He cleared his throat. 'Yes?'

'Have you heard from the casting director?'

'Not exactly.' There was a giggle in the background and I could tell he wasn't concentrating on what I was saying.

'Are you in your office?' I asked.

'Yes, and as I say I'm with someone, so—' He coughed lightly and prepared to end the call.

'I'll come over. I need to talk to you.' I was already marching to the tube station; it was only two stops to his house-cum-office in Kensington.

'Nina, no.'

'It's no bother; I can be there in no time. Bye.'

Within minutes I'd completed my tube journey and was heading away from Gloucester Road station. Discussing this in person would be far better. And Trudy wouldn't mind. I'd already sent her a text cancelling my six o'clock appointment. Something else was happening at six, what was it?

Oh yes – more news from Cecily.

I slowed down to open the Twitter app on my phone and clicked on her profile. My stomach flipped, my jaw dropped and some extremely uncharitable thoughts whirred through my brain.

Drinks with NEW AGENT @SebastianNicholsTalent
Exclusive interview on Entertainer's News coming
soon #actressgoals #livingthedream

The tweet came with a selfie of her and Sebastian in his
office, chinking champagne glasses, a huge bouquet of
flowers at the edge of the shot. All at once things began to
make sense. Cecily had got *my part* because Cecily had also
got *my agent* and was consequently living *my dream*. Sebastian
must have persuaded the casting director to offer the part to
her instead of me. The total, absolute slimeball.

I flounced through the gate of the little mews house where
Sebastian lived and up the path. It had been a long and stren-
uous day and my hair, which had looked amazing this
morning, curled and fixed into victory rolls, was itchy from
fake bomb-blast dust. I punched the number into the secu-
rity pad at the front door to let myself in and ran up the stairs
two at a time to the first-floor office. The sound of male and
female laughter rang out; they were both in there.

I curled my hand around the door knob, drew myself up
to my full height and threw open the door.

There they were, exactly as Cecily's selfie had shown
them: glued to each other on Sebastian's side of the desk,
champagne flutes in hand, the bottle nestling in a bucket of
ice and the flowers perched next to it.

'Nina!' Sebastian ran his tongue over his lips. 'That *was*
quick.'

'Well, this is cosy,' I said tightly. 'I hear congratulations
are in order. To both of you.'

He glanced at the iPad on his desk and gave a bark of nervous laughter.

'She can't come in here,' Cecily said through gritted teeth
whilst still managing to maintain a dazzling smile. 'This is
my moment.'

'Of course, of course. Nina, give me two ticks, old thing,

and I'll be right with you.' Sebastian got to his feet, giving me his best crinkly-eyed smile.

In three strides I reached the desk and prodded him in the chest. He wasn't a tall man and as I'd caught him off guard he plopped back into his seat.

'When were you going to tell me?' I folded my arms and glared at him.

'Whoops,' Cecily murmured, sipping her champagne. 'Do I smell sour grapes?'

'Tonight.' Sebastian ran a finger around his collar. 'Honestly. It all happened so fast, my hands were tied – look, can we talk about this outside?' He jerked his head towards his desk, or Cecily, I couldn't be quite sure.

Perhaps if Cecily hadn't been looking at me with such smug satisfaction I might have done as he suggested, but suddenly the emotional tension and disappointment of the day got the better of me.

'Why do this to me, Sebastian?' I said with a trembly voice. 'Isn't it bad enough that Nurse Elsie is dead? Without my whole acting career being dead too?'

Overreact? *Moi?* Possibly, but I had been banking on the *Mary Queen of Scots* thing. It had been in the bag. Even Sebastian had said so. And now I'd have to face the pitying looks when I turned up to my first day as temporary receptionist somewhere. *An actress? Would I have seen you in anything?* I could have wept.

'For pity's sake, Nina, be quiet!' He sprang up again and clapped a hand across my mouth.

I bit his finger and he yelped. Cecily swung her silky hair around dramatically and gasped.

'I will not!' I cried, dodging away from him. 'I loved being in *Victory Road* and the only consolation was that I'd be moving straight on to the role of Eve, and now mysteriously that part is Cecily's. It's just not right.'

Cecily glared at me. 'Look, darling, you're rather raining

13

on my parade; can't you have your tantrum somewhere else?'

At which point I lost it totally, picked up the ice bucket and dumped it on her head.

Cecily screamed. So did I; I couldn't believe what I'd done.

'Sorry, so sorry,' I stammered, flicking ice cubes from her lovely blonde hair.

'Get off me,' she yelled, batting me away.

'Ladies, please!' Sebastian begged.

'This is meant to be MY exclusive for *Entertainer's News*!' she fumed. She scooped up her bag and flounced, dripping wet, from the room, shouting over her shoulder, 'Daddy is not going to be pleased about this. Not at all.'

'Wait! Come back!' Sebastian darted to the door but Cecily's heels continued to stab their way down the wooden stairs.

'She's forgotten her flowers,' I said, looking at the pretty bunch of scented stocks and roses.

'*Your* flowers,' Sebastian muttered darkly, pressing a hanky to his clammy face. 'Arrived this afternoon. You have made a big mistake, Nina, why you couldn't—'

I tuned him out and plucked the card from the centre of the arrangement, holding my breath that this time the sender had revealed their identity.

Congratulations on the episode of *Victory Road* when you saved the little girl's life, you were brilliant!

My heart squeezed. How lovely! It was a good episode, I had to admit, and the little ego boost was so timely too. Anonymous again, sadly. I wished I knew who was sending these mystery bouquets. I turned the card over in my fingers, looking for clues. The first had arrived a year ago at Sebastian's office after he'd announced to the press that he was representing me. Since then flowers arrived every time I had something to celebrate: a new role, a tiny mention in the press, even my birthday. But never with the sender's name.

A deep-throated chuckle filled the room and I dragged my gaze away from the card.

'Well, well, well,' came a voice from Sebastian's desk. 'I think it's my lucky day. Nurse Elsie is dead, is she? Do I smell a spoiler, Miss Penhaligon?'

The blood drained from my face as I peered at Sebastian's iPad propped up on the desk; a man's face grinned back from the FaceTime screen.

My mouth was completely dry but I managed to squeeze out some words. 'Ross! Hello.'

Ross Whittaker was the editor of *Entertainer's News*, a man who'd sell his firstborn child for a scoop. He was licking his lips and edging closer to the screen.

It was April the first, I remembered. Please let this just be some sort of April Fool's prank. Maybe I hadn't lost two acting jobs, tipped ice over Sebastian's new client and leaked *Victory Road*'s most cliffhangery storyline to a journalist all in the space of one day? I looked at Sebastian. His face had gone so white his skin was translucent.

Okay, maybe I had.

'So, Nina Penhaligon, tell me more—'

I didn't get a chance to tell him anything because Sebastian lurched forward and ended the call with a jab of his finger.

'Do you realize what you've done?' He paced the office, raking his hands through his limp brown hair. Patches of sweat appeared under his arms. 'You have broken the sacred code of acting. Actors *never* reveal plotlines. To anyone. You know that.'

I dropped into Cecily's chair and pressed my hands to my face.

'I don't know what came over me; attacking her like that!' I said shakily. Only an hour ago Maxine was praising me for being professional. I shuddered. 'Maxine is going to do her nut.'

'So is the entire cast and crew.' He sank into the other chair and swore under his breath.

'What are we going to do now?' I said hoarsely.

He leaned forward, resting his arms on his thighs, and fixed me with very fierce eyes.

'I'm going to tell you to do something that I can truly say is a first in all my years of agenting.'

'I'm listening.' I nodded. He might have just morphed into the most disloyal agent ever, but he still knew more about dealing with a crisis than I did. 'Thank you.'

'Firstly turn off your phone. Secondly talk to no one.'

'Right, good idea.' I did as I was told. 'What else?'

'Go away.'

I blinked uncertainly at him. 'Go where?'

'Somewhere. Anywhere that's not London.' He shrugged impatiently and then got to his feet and walked to the door, holding it open for me. I followed him on autopilot, trailing the bouquet behind me. 'Frankly, I don't care. Just keep a low profile, okay? I've got a feeling your name could be mud for a very long time.'

Me? Low profile? And not London? How could I hope to land another part if I wasn't around to audition? Also, what happened to all publicity being good publicity?

I gulped. 'Don't you think you should issue a press release, apologize on my behalf?'

He laughed. 'Nope. You've put me in a very difficult position. Cecily's father is not a man to be crossed. I need to rescue the situation immediately.'

'What about me?' I said in a small voice.

'I've done my best with you, but let's face it, you're not exactly leading lady material. Cecily might not have your experience, but she has potential. I think I've taken you as far as you're going to go.' He looked down at me pityingly and I felt my eyes burn. There was one thing not having total confidence in myself, but it was quite another to have the news confirmed by the person supposedly responsible

16

for bigging me up. 'You're toast, as far as I'm concerned. You'll have to fight your own battles.'

'I think I just did that, don't you?' I folded my arms and looked him squarely in the eye.

He exhaled impatiently. 'You did. Very publicly. Ross Whittaker will have tweeted the hell out of your *confidential* storyline already. The news will circle the earth quicker than the International Space Station. And isn't it Jessie May's birthday party tonight? Guess what everyone will be talking about, or should I say *who*?'

I shuddered, imagining the disappointment on Maxine's face. 'I feel sick at the thought.'

'Hard cheese.' The phone on his desk started to ring and he shot me an admonishing look. 'See, word has already spread. I'm afraid you have to roll with the punches in this game.'

It was that final comment that tipped it for me; I was officially livid.

No apology for giving my part to Cecily. No accepting responsibility for his part in my downfall. He was washing his hands of me, feeding me to the lions. The absolute snake.

'Thank you for the advice; you're absolutely right,' I said with a tight smile. And I swung my fist as hard as I could into his stomach.

The flicker of satisfaction I'd had at seeing Sebastian winded lasted as far as my walk to the tube station. So now I could add assault to the list of my crimes of the day. There was no way I could attend the *Victory Road* party in Soho; I dragged my sorry carcass home instead. I spent the evening in the flat with Trudy and after I'd told her the full story and left a wobbly apology on Maxine's answerphone and sent a cryptically repentant text to Becky Burton, I turned off my phone for the rest of the night and we formed a plan: I would follow Sebastian's orders and leave London in the morning, in disguise. That last bit was Trudy's idea.

17

This fiasco was going to take a few days to blow over. My best option was to disappear, lick my wounds and wait for some other poor unfortunate to make an even bigger mistake than me, at which point the media would have something new to talk about.

Which was why the next morning, after dying my caramel hair black and shoving as many clothes as I could into a case, I was standing in the ticket line at Paddington Station with Trudy.

'Are you totally sure about doing what your agent says and running off?' said Trudy, yawning; she wasn't a morning person. 'I mean, Exeter is, like, miles away.'

'I'm not really sure about anything, but his is the only advice I've got,' I said in a low voice. I had my hood pulled up and was trying to avoid eye contact with anyone. To be perfectly honest, I wasn't often spotted, but today I wasn't willing to take any chances. 'And right now being miles away and having a few days with my big brother is just what I need.'

Trudy nodded. She knew how close I was to Archie, my only family. I'd spoken to him last night, asking if he'd put me up for a while. I'd been a bit light on the truth, just saying I'd got a break in my schedule. The details could wait until he met me from the train later today.

I caught sight of myself in the plate-glass window of the ticket office and recoiled with shock. Trudy had volunteered to do my face for me this morning so that I could travel incognito. She'd been a bit heavy-handed with the fake tan and I looked like the love-child of Donald Trump and a satsuma.

She tapped my forehead with a long nail. 'Stop frowning, you'll get permanent wrinkles.'

Make that an old satsuma.

'I'll try.'

'Come back soon, won't you?' she added. 'I love having an actress as my lodger. You're my claim to fame. I'll miss you.' She blinked her heavily kohled eyelashes at me and I felt a rush of warmth for her.

'Thank you, Trudy, I'll miss you too,' I said, giving her a hug. 'But after last night's mammoth mistake, I'm just hoping I'm not your claim to infamy.'

'Also, my customers love gossip,' she continued blithely.

There'd be plenty of that, I thought with a pang.

'Next please!' yelled someone from behind the ticket counter.

I moved towards the cashier.

'A ticket to Exeter please.'

The cashier tapped at his screen. 'Single or return?'

London was where I needed to be: the flat, the press, future auditions . . . not to mention the *Victory Road* cast to whom I owed a massive apology. Was I doing the right thing by running away? Sebastian's angry words echoed through my head: *keep a low profile . . . you're toast, as far as I'm concerned . . .*

I handed over my credit card and sighed. 'Single, please.'

Chapter 3

As the train pulled away from the platform, I waved until I couldn't see Trudy any more and then settled back against my seat. A couple of teenagers sat opposite, heads touching and sharing a set of earphones and a tube of Pringles. I reached into my bag for my phone automatically and then dropped it again.

I mustn't turn it on; if I looked at it I'd only feel worse. There'd be texts and messages from other cast members, not to mention umpteen Twitter and Facebook mentions from the entertainment media. I'd have to face the music at some point, perhaps issue a statement – my first one without Sebastian's help – but now was not the time. First I needed to put some serious miles between me and my problems. The journey to Exeter would take about three hours; I closed my eyes and tried to visualize my next move . . .

I must have nodded off because when I opened my eyes the teenagers had gone. The sprawl of London had given way to motorways and towns and fields and villages and the chalky blue sky had expanded to fill the gaps. It was the colour of hope and happiness and I felt my spirits begin to lift. This was more like it. It was Sunday, spring was starting to bloom and I was going to visit my brother Archie, who I adored. Things would work out fine. Probably.

I bought a bottle of water from the snacks trolley and took a sip.

I'd always acted. As a little girl, I'd loved making up plays and stories, putting on shows for my mum. It was my way of securing her attention for a few minutes. Joining a drama club had opened even more possibilities; those two hours were the highlight of the week. I took to the stage like a swallow to the sky: soaring higher and higher as my dreams got bigger and bigger, spending every spare minute with the drama teacher, Mrs Figgis. I loved everything about acting, from rehearsals to set-design to selling tickets. Acting was my escapism; a world away from my cheerless Manchester home.

That home wasn't there any more. Mum passed away after a series of strokes when I was nineteen while I was studying drama at The Arts University in Bournemouth. Clearing the house she'd rented for years was one of the most depressing things I'd ever done and I was glad to have Archie to share the task with. When I left university a couple of years later, I moved to London, determined to make it as an actress. The last seven years had been tough going, and I'd supplemented my income with office temping jobs, but gradually my roles had been getting bigger and more frequent, my résumé more impressive. And when Sebastian rang me to confirm my role as Nurse Elsie on *Victory Road*, I thought all my Christmases had come at once.

The train was slowing down again and we pulled into a tiny station. The stop after this one was Exeter.

'These seats free?' said a woman breathlessly. The man beside her was wheezing too.

I nodded. The woman set her bag down on the table. I couldn't take my eyes off her cardigan; it depicted an entire Lowry painting – a woolly reminder of the streets where I grew up. Her husband took an unlit cigarette from his lips and tucked it in his breast pocket.

They stowed their luggage and sat down opposite me.

'What a palaver,' said the woman. 'Bus was late and we nearly missed the train.'

I pulled a sympathetic face from under my hood.

'Had to run, we did. Pass us the paper, love,' said the man, taking a pen from his pocket.

She tugged it from her handbag and smacked him playfully with it. 'You and your blinkin' newspaper.'

The man pretended to cower and winked at me. 'I haven't missed the *Daily News* crossword for six years. It's my claim to fame.'

He flapped it to smooth out the creases and then opened it to page three.

'Look at her!' The woman tapped the paper and tutted. 'What behaviour. *Celebrities*. Worse than animals, some of them.'

'Who is she?' her husband asked.

'Nina Penhaligon from *Victory Road*.' The woman scanned down the page. 'Almost didn't recognize her pulling all those faces.'

My chest tightened and I surreptitiously tugged my hood further over my burning face. Firstly: awkward. Secondly: how on earth had my tiny faux pas made the national press?

'Says here that she assaulted her agent and Cecily Carmichael, and Cecily's dad's considering pressing charges.'

So, that was how. I bit back a squeak.

'Blimey,' said the man. 'She looks like butter wouldn't melt in her mouth.'

Would Campion Carmichael really take me to court? I'd only tipped ice on his daughter's head. She'd probably be angrier about me gate-crashing her interview with Ross Whittaker. This must be a stunt to eke out as much publicity from the incident as possible. I wondered if Sebastian was behind it. That thought made my head spin.

'Could I see dat, please?' I said, putting on the world's worst Irish accent. I don't know why; it was just a spur-of-the-moment thing.

The man lowered the paper to the table with a sigh.

'*Tank yew*,' I said, channelling Marian Keyes.

Oh no . . .

My heart battered against my ribs. Even looking at it upside down I could see it was bad. The headline had managed to sum up all my sins in one sentence: *Penhaligon drops the bomb on Victory Road and commits ice attack on rival Cecily Carmichael!*

A lump appeared in my throat; until yesterday afternoon everything had been going swimmingly. How had my life taken such a nosedive?

'May I?' I murmured distractedly, forgetting to do the accent as I tweaked the paper out of his hand.

He tutted, but let me keep it.

'That's really *koind* of you,' I said with a big smile.

Maxine Pearce, director of TV show Victory Road *wasn't available for comment, but Freddie Major, who plays Nina Penhaligon's love interest, Constable Ron Hardy, says, 'She always had a chip on her shoulder about my acting pedigree, but to ruin the show for our millions of viewers is a hollow victory indeed.'*

Oh harsh, very harsh. I did not have a chip on my shoulder; so what if he'd attended a posh West End drama school? My course in Bournemouth had been brilliant. The article was illustrated with screenshots from Ross's FaceTime interview with Cecily: me shoving Sebastian in the chest, me mid-yell, upending the ice bucket . . . I looked demented.

Sebastian Nichols, Penhaligon's former agent . . .

Former. My *former* agent. Now I was seeing it in black and white it was all starting to feel real in a horrid nightmarish sort of way.

. . . commented from his London headquarters: 'Nina is a talented actress but the pressure of being

in a hit TV show had begun to show and she is
clearly suffering from stress. We wish her well.'

I couldn't read the words any more; they'd gone blurry. That wasn't me, I never behaved like that. I mean, it *was* me, but it was so out of character. It wasn't the normal me. And what did he mean about pressure? Being in *Victory Road* had been challenging, but I'd thrived on it, so I thought.

'Much *obloiged*.' I pushed the newspaper back across the table. This was a gazillion times worse than I'd expected. And that was in print; imagine what the trolls were saying in the online comments, or on Facebook . . . I shuddered, sinking low in my seat.

The woman shook her head. 'I can't believe Nurse Elsie is being killed off. I thought that nice policeman boyfriend might propose to her. No point watching it now. I'm so cross with that girl for ruining the story.' She folded her arms across her matchstalk men and matchstalk cats and dogs.

My eyes were hot with shame and my face was burning underneath Trudy's orange make-up. I probably looked like a crème brulée by now.

'I'm ferry, ferry sorry,' I said gravely. Doing a sad Irish accent was much harder than a happy one.

The couple stared at me.

'It's not your fault,' said the woman.

'After that performance,' said the man, chuckling, 'I doubt she'll be in anything else for a while. No one wants to work with a diva.'

I lowered my voice to a whisper. 'To be honest wit ya, oi actually know her and she's a luvly girl, really, really luvly. And happy. Not at all diva-loike.'

The pair of them blinked at me.

'You *know* her?' The man leaned forward, all ears.

I nodded. Why had I said that? Now they were staring at my hot face. Any minute now they'd recognize me.

'Well, she's made an awful lot of people very *un*happy.' The woman pursed her lips. 'So I'd lay low for a while if I were her.'

Just then the train hissed to a halt at Exeter station. I got to my feet, collected my suitcase from the rack and knocked my hood back.

'You're not the first person to say dat,' I said, instantly realizing my mistake as confusion gathered on their faces. 'Oi imagine.'

A smart four-wheel drive with blacked-out windows swished into the drop-off zone just as I appeared from the station. My brother got out and pulled a sausage roll from a paper bag. He took a gigantic bite, chewed, swallowed and popped the rest in before finally doing a double take and seeing through my disguise. He held up a hand and smiled. I felt my own smile growing wider at the sight of him.

Archie, at thirty-two, was three years older than me. He didn't look it. He was like Peter Pan, he never entertained the idea of growing up, or settling down, he had more energy than Usain Bolt, and more drive than a Ferrari.

'Hey, it's the famous actress!' shouted Archie, deliberately loudly. 'Nina Penhaligon.'

A few people looked round and I tried to pull my head in like a turtle.

'Shush,' I murmured, kissing his cheek. 'Don't draw attention to me.'

'I thought you wanted to be a celeb?' He studied my face. 'If you don't mind me saying, you're looking very . . . orange?'

I might have known he wouldn't have read the newspaper or seen any rumours on social media; my brother was too busy to absorb the world around him.

'I'm travelling incognito.' I brushed pastry crumbs from his chin. 'Nice healthy lunch.'

He swiped a hand across his mouth before patting his

lean stomach. 'Are you mad? This isn't lunch. I had that hours ago, this is a snack to keep me going; I have been working since the crack of dawn.'

He was always working. That was what Archie did. He worked and made money.

'Archie,' I said loudly, forcing him to look at me, 'I need a hug.'

My brother didn't really do hugging, but he made an exception for me and complied. For a moment neither of us spoke and then Archie murmured the motto we'd adopted years ago.

'You and me against the world, Neen.'

'Yeah, you and me against the world,' I repeated.

It had been that way since I was five. Right from when Mum became a single parent. We soon realized that she might be there to feed and clothe us, dust us down when we fell, make sure we got to school . . . in other words, do her duty, but anything else, we'd have to supply ourselves.

He straightened up and checked the time. 'Right. Come on, places to be.'

I smiled; emotional display over and on to the next thing. He slung my case in the back of the car and within seconds we were off.

'So what's new in the crazy world of television?' he said, as we joined a stream of traffic. 'And what's with the disguise?'

'I made the national papers today,' I said.

'Fantastic! That's great!' He shot me a look of such pride that I felt tears prick at the back of my eyes. 'Are we celebrating?'

He nosed the car into the left-hand lane and held a hand up in thanks to another driver.

'No,' I said, in a small voice as I recalled the accusations in the *Daily News*. 'I've broken every rule of showbiz, alienated my co-stars, lost my agent and physically assaulted two people. I've blown it, Archie. Totally blown it.'

He stared at me, a smile hovering at his mouth while he waited for me to say I was joking. I looked down at my lap and swallowed the lump in my throat.

'Oh Neen, that doesn't sound like you. Tell me everything.'

His total faith in me made me feel worse; I heaved a sigh and shared my tale of woe.

'Isn't your agent paid to help you out of this sort of mess?' Archie curled his lip in disgust. I stared out of the window and shrugged. He was right; Sebastian hadn't stood by me, or even offered any practical help. I'd thought he cared about me but he'd abandoned me in my hour of need.

'I suppose,' I conceded. 'In fact, thinking about it, all this might have been avoided if Sebastian had tried to salvage the situation rather than cut Ross off, not to mention being honest about Cecily in the first place.'

'Hey, it's not that bad.' He patted my knee, then leaned across to the glove box, took out a bag of peanuts and handed it to me to open.

'Archie, it couldn't be any worse!' I tipped a handful of nuts out for him.

'You know,' he said kindly, 'I think a break from London will do you good. Hardly a week goes by without getting a selfie from you at some event or other, it seems very full-on to me.'

I stifled a sigh. Archie had never liked me working in London and was always trying to tempt me down to the south-west; he didn't understand how important it was to my career to get my name out there. It had been one of Sebastian's conditions when he'd taken me on: I was supposed to maximize my exposure at all times. But before I could challenge Archie, he slapped his hand against the leather steering wheel.

'I've just had a thought: some of my customers are *Victory Road* fans. If you've upset them, they might turn against me too. It might even affect business.'

I snorted. 'Archie, you run a laundrette and a cleaning business; you basically air dirty linen for a living.'

He bristled for a second and then lapsed back into his usual grin. 'I like what you've done there, but it's a very sophisticated business, I'll have you know.'

My brother had entrepreneurial spirit running through his bones. He'd started at school selling illicit chocolate bars in the school playground during Lent when sweets were banned. At fourteen he had a job sluicing down the fishmonger's counter every evening and worked as a barman as soon as he was old enough. At university, he invested his student loan in a top-of-the-range washer-dryer and then charged his fellow students five pounds a load. Within two months he'd bought two more machines and taken a lease out on a lock-up. By the end of his time at uni, he'd got an honours degree in business, four staff and a brand-new Porsche. Now he offered a range of services to restaurants, hotels, stately homes and even some medical practices.

'And how *is* Exeter's answer to Richard Branson?' I teased. I was immensely proud of him really, I just wished he'd let up occasionally. He put in such long hours and I couldn't remember him ever taking a holiday.

'I'm . . .' He hesitated. 'Under a lot of pressure.'

I waited, assuming there was a punchline on its way. Archie never admitted any weakness. 'Go on.'

'My blood pressure's on the high side.' He cleared his throat. 'The doctor told me I need to work less and play more.'

'Oh, Archie.' I placed my hand over his and gave it a squeeze. The doctor might as well have suggested Archie should lie naked in a bath of cold custard. 'So what else did the doctor say?'

He gave me a sheepish look. 'Get a hobby and relax.'

'Haven't I been saying that for years?' I raised an eyebrow. 'Do something other than work?'

'Have you set up a pension fund yet like I told you to?' he retorted.

'Fair point.' I was as bad at following advice as he was.

'Just as well I've set one up for you.' He winked and I felt a rush of warmth for my generous only relative.

'Hey, this isn't the way to your house,' I said, suddenly realizing that we'd left Exeter behind.

'We're making a detour,' he said, his eyes glinting in the sunlight. 'I've decided to follow the doctor's orders. I've found a hobby; I'm going to buy a classic car and do it up.'

'Good for you!' I said. 'Tinkering with an old car sounds the perfect way for you to unwind, take your mind off business once in a while.'

'I know.' He puffed his chest out. 'A friend's old Triumph TR6S popped up for sale and I couldn't resist it.'

There was a look in Archie's eye that made me think there was something he wasn't telling me.

'And that's where we're going now?' I asked.

'To check it out, yes.' He rubbed the back of his neck. 'If I buy it, I'll have to get it towed up to Exeter, but the fantastic thing is that it will be worth double what I'm paying for it when it's done.'

I rolled my eyes in despair. 'I knew it! I knew you were looking shifty, everything you do revolves around money.'

Archie opened his mouth to argue, but then seemed to think better of it. Probably because I was right.

Half an hour later, the roads had become more like footpaths between the blossoming hedgerows, at some points so narrow that we'd had to reverse to allow passing cars to squeeze by. I wound down the window and filled my lungs with air. After London, the smell was intoxicating: sweet hawthorn petals and new grass mixed with the salty tang of the sea. The worries of this morning already felt a bit hazy.

Suddenly we reached the brow of a hill and ahead of us, down a steep incline, was a handful of cottages either side of the narrow lane and beyond them was a wide expanse of cerulean blue.

'The sea!' we cried at the same time and then laughed.

'Brightside Cove,' I read out as we passed the village sign. 'What a lovely name.'

We hadn't had many holidays as kids. Mum hadn't had the money to take us anywhere fancy and anyway she didn't like the sea, she said. It wasn't until Archie moved to the south-west that I'd ever even ventured into Devon and I'd loved the coast so much that I'd chosen a seaside town for my own university course.

'Brightside Cove,' I read out as we passed the village sign. 'What a lovely name. I've never heard of it.'

'Me neither before getting the address from Th-thing.'

'Can't you remember the guy's name?' I said with a smirk.

'Shush, I'm concentrating on the directions.'

Archie's satnav directed us around the back of the village, past a clutch of isolated stone cottages and then up and down a few single-track lanes before finally taking a steep hill away from the centre of Brightside Cove. The two of us had begun to bicker over where it was actually leading us when the robotic voice announced that we'd reached our destination. Which appeared to be in the middle of nowhere.

Archie pulled on to the grassy verge and consulted Google maps while I absorbed the view. We were right on the clifftops overlooking a rocky bay. Far below us was a crescent of golden sand and a cluster of youthful figures were racing towards the waves with surfboards under their arms. To the left a patchwork of fields edged with purpley gorse led away to a headland disappearing out into the sea, and down far away to the right was a harbour dotted with boats marooned by the tide and beyond that, a slipway and what looked like a pub, a couple of shops and a row of sherbet-coloured cottages.

It was so beautiful and after the soot-tinged terraced houses in Clapham it felt surreal. In fact, it felt like a film set.

'I know what this reminds me of.' I turned to Archie, a

huge smile on my face. 'You know at the beginning of *The Wizard of Oz*, when it's in black and white and then Dorothy wakes up in Munchkin Land and everything's in full Technicolor and she thinks she's dreaming?'

'Hmm?' Oblivious to my musings, he pointed to an open five-bar gate bordered on either side by a prickly gorse hedge. It was set a little way back from the road and had what looked like a piece of driftwood hanging from the middle bar at a jaunty angle.

'Aha! There's the entrance. Thank God for that.' He restarted the engine and gave a sigh of satisfaction. 'I thought I was going have to phone Theo and ask him to come and find us.'

That name made me pause for a second, but I shook it off; the Theo I knew lived miles away from here.

'Theo who?' I asked, already a bit envious of whoever lived here.

'Um.' Archie flicked his eyes shiftily to mine.

A prickle of dread ran down my spine.

'You can't mean . . . *The* Theo? Theo-and-Kate Theo?' I stared at him, my jaw hanging open in horror.

'Sorry, didn't I say?'

Chapter 4

'I can't come in. I just can't. I'll wait here for you.'

My hand fumbled for the door handle to escape but Archie quickly pressed the central locking.

'Don't be daft. That business is water under the bridge and—'

Before he could finish, a lorry whizzed by so fast and so close to us that it clipped the wing mirror and shook the car. My heart, which was already pounding, nearly leapt out of my chest.

'Blimey, mate! Where's the fire?' Archie yelled.

The lorry pulled off the road and sped through the open gate.

Archie whistled. 'If that was Theo, he and I need to have words about dangerous driving.'

He opened his window and adjusted the wing mirror.

'And I need to have words with you!' I pressed my hands to my hot face. 'I haven't seen Theo since his . . . the . . . you know, wedding. I can't see him now. And what about Kate?'

My mouth had gone dry; I couldn't even swallow.

'Calm down. Kate won't be there.'

'How do *you* know?' Panic rose in my chest like a tidal wave. 'What if she comes back while we're here?'

'She won't,' he said in a tone that put paid to further questioning. He put the car into gear and pulled off the grass verge. 'Come on, let's find out what's going on.'

OhmyGod ohmyGod ohmyGod. Just when I thought my day couldn't get any worse.

I gripped the door handle, noting the words *Driftwood Lodge* carved into the piece of wood dangling from the gate as we glided past. Archie steered the car along the unmade road, avoiding the worst of the potholes, unlike the lorry, which was crashing up and down like some sort of comedy get-away vehicle.

Seconds later we came into a courtyard in front of a gorgeous house, a little tired at the edges perhaps, but the overall feel was quintessentially English-cottage perfection. It was long and low, painted the colour of clotted cream, and topped with a thick thatched roof. The windows were glazed with tiny leaded-glass panes and the deep window sills on the ground floor had pretty wooden window boxes on them (actually, most of the plants had died, but there was still a hint of colour from the pansies). At right angles to it was a row of cottages that looked like someone had started to paint and abandoned the task halfway through. And over the gate between the buildings I could see sheds, garages and acres of green.

A skinny man in a suit jumped out of the passenger side of the lorry clutching a clipboard and began hammering on the wooden front door. The driver reversed as close to the door as he could and then sprang out and opened the doors at the back of the lorry. This man was enormous, with Popeye-sized biceps, a gleaming bald head and a barrel for a belly. His jogging bottoms hung so low that even from twenty metres away I could see the writing on his underpants . . . Correction: not his pants, he had 'Mam and Dad' tattooed just above his bum. Nice.

'What the hell?' muttered Archie, slowing down.

'Delivery drivers,' I said, dragging my eyes away from the man's inked behind. 'All the same.'

Although my nerves were jangling at the prospect of seeing Theo again, I couldn't help being curious. There was an

33

air of decay and neglect here that was at odds with the image I had of Theo and his new wife Kate at their wedding five years ago, so loved-up and gorgeous that the aura of happiness surrounding them had almost been tangible. If a collection of singing woodland animals had formed a procession behind them as they kissed everyone goodbye and left for their honeymoon, no one would have batted an eyelid.

How did Archie know that Kate wouldn't be home? I thought, shaking the picture of Theo and Kate from my head. Plus, I could have sworn Kate and Theo lived near her parents in Birmingham.

Archie parked the car next a rusty white van and I examined the large gravelled courtyard. It had probably been quite beautiful at one time. Now it was scruffy: broken plant pots lay on their sides, weeds had sprung up, broken pallets had been piled up bonfire-style in one corner, there were abandoned tyres, bits of farm machinery, and at the far side a huge pothole had filled with water and a clutch of hens and two ducks were scratching around it.

The front door remained resolutely closed but Suit Man wasn't giving up easily and continued to thump on it. 'Mr Fletcher, open up!'

'He should be in.' Archie looked puzzled as he released his seatbelt. 'He's expecting me.'

Suddenly the front door opened and almost as quickly began to close again. But not quickly enough. Suit Man forced his foot through the gap and Baggy Trousers came to assist.

'I don't think they are delivery drivers, you know,' I said as both men pushed their way into the house.

Archie swore softly under his breath, opened the car door and climbed out. 'I don't like the look of this. Stay in the car, Nina, this could get nasty,' he said before slamming the door.

Yeah, right.

I opened the door but before I'd even got out the men reappeared. Baggy Trousers was carrying a television set under one arm and a DVD player under the other, the cables trailing on the ground. Suit Man was scribbling on his clipboard closely followed by a third man who had to be . . . *Theo*?

All of a sudden my heart was in my mouth. I rubbed my eyes, doubting what I was seeing . . . He looked bloody awful. What a transformation!

Last time I'd seen him he'd been broad and muscular, his wedding suit straining at the shoulders. His raven-black curls had been shiny and glossy, his jaw square and strong and his chest proudly puffed out. Now he looked stooped and thin, his jeans hung off him, he had a straggly beard threaded with grey and his hair looked lank and greasy under an unflattering blue cap.

'Theo?' Archie ran over to him. 'Mate? What's going on?'

I got out of the car quietly and tiptoed softly across the gravel so as not to draw attention to myself. I needn't have worried; Theo didn't even look up. He sank down on to the low step outside his front door and dropped his face into his hands. He might even have been crying. Archie squatted beside him and reached out awkwardly to give him a manly pat.

Meanwhile, Suit and Baggy were loading a second television, a laptop, two telephones and a coffee machine into the lorry. I crept up behind them and tapped the one in the suit on the arm. Close up he smelled of mothballs and mildew. He had wispy hair and deep-set wrinkles in his forehead, reminding me of the dogs who have all those folds of skin.

'Excuse me?' I said.

'Hold on.' He scribbled something on his clipboard.

'You've spelt Nespresso wrong,' I pointed out.

'Makes no difference where this lot's going,' he said with a harsh laugh.

'And where *is* it going?' I asked.

He peered at me and then checked his clipboard again. 'Do you live here?'

'No but—'

'None of your business then, is it?' He wiped his nose on the back of his hand and went back inside the house.

Baggy Trousers met my eye. 'Sorry about him, he's having a bad day. We always hope someone's going to pay up; so far today, all we've done is repossess.'

'So Mr Fletcher owes you money?' I resisted the temptation to hike his trousers up to a less offensive level. He had huge sweat patches under his arms and the smell was even worse than his colleague's suit. Goodness knows what it must have been like in the cab of the lorry with the pair of them.

He gave a wary look. 'Don't give me any aggro please, miss. Look at this.' He pointed to the side of his head where a lump glowed vivid red.

'That does look sore.'

'Clobbered with a mobile phone in Brixham,' he said, prodding the lump gingerly with a meaty finger. 'I was only doing my job.'

'Look, I'm sure there's been some sort of misunderstanding. Theo – Mr Fletcher – is a businessman.' As I recalled, he'd studied engineering at uni and had gone on to set up his own consultancy.

Archie caught my eye as he handed Theo a handkerchief and made a slicing gesture in front of his neck.

'I think,' I added faintly.

'Everyone is given a chance to pay; this is a last resort.' Baggy Trousers nodded towards the mass of loot in the back of the lorry. They must have been to half the homes in South Devon this morning. 'Our clients would much rather have the cash.'

Archie always carried a lot of cash. I wondered if now would be a good time to mention it.

'Of course they would,' I said. 'And if you don't mind me

saying, you look like you need a coffee, especially after that bump to the head.' I gave him my Nurse Elsie caring frown. 'Why don't I make us all a drink and between us we can try and sort something out?'

Baggy Trousers sighed with longing. 'Would you really? I could murder a brew.' He nodded towards the coffee machine on a teetering pile of used household gadgets. 'Better make it tea.'

Five minutes later, Norman and Warren, the bailiffs, were slurping mugs of tea in the cab of their lorry and Theo, Archie and I were sitting at the scrubbed-pine kitchen table. I use the term 'scrubbed' loosely. What the kitchen needed, like everywhere else I'd seen so far, was a thorough clean and someone to care for it. But through the muddle and mess the potential was there to be a warm and comforting hub of the cottage. I dragged my eyes away from the lovely blue and white Dutch tiles around the cream Aga and tipped a packet of biscuits I'd found on to a plate.

Nothing had been said yet about my behaviour at Theo's wedding. Possibly because Theo was too embarrassed about his tears to even think about the past. When I'd said hello, he'd just mumbled that it was nice to see me and that was that. Thank heavens.

'We moved down here, you know, after the . . .' Theo paused to swallow and his Adam's apple bobbed up and down. 'Ivy.'

The Ivy? My eyes slid to Archie's questioningly; he looked away quickly and gave Theo an encouraging nod. I was confused and dying to ask about Kate but no one had mentioned her and I didn't want to make matters worse, so I held my tongue.

'Driftwood Lodge was meant to be a fresh start,' he added two sugars to his tea and stirred distractedly. 'Trouble was I couldn't. Start, that is. I couldn't seem to think, or do anything. Still can't, truth be told. And then when Kate left, I—'

37

'She's left?' I said with a gasp and then instantly blushed, hoping I didn't sound pleased. Because I wasn't. Truly. I'd moved on years ago. I covered my embarrassment by biting on a biscuit. It was soft and powdery and too stale to swallow. I discreetly spat it out and tucked the rest of the biscuit in the pocket of my hoody and when I looked up Theo was blinking at me.

'Yes, she left me last month. Didn't Archie say?'

'No.' I managed to squeak. 'He did not. I'm so sorry.'

I reached across the table and touched his arm. We continued to stare at each other, and I looked again at his haggard features, the unkempt curls escaping from underneath his cap, the dark shadows under his eyes . . . It was all starting to make sense. The poor lamb.

Archie stood up abruptly and began rummaging in the cupboards. 'Sorry, mate, must have slipped my mind. Got any crisps?'

I glared at him. 'I wonder you've got any friends left at all, you are useless when it comes to anything personal.'

'Men aren't good at talking.' Theo heaved a sigh that seemed to come from his boots. 'There's no crisps. No food. Nothing edible, anyway. Even the tinned peaches have gone.'

'Ah ha, bingo!' Archie said, from the depths of a cupboard. He reappeared brandishing a packet of prawn-flavoured crisps, tore them open, stuffed a handful in his mouth and instantly spat them out again. 'Eugh, how old are these? You weren't even this bad when you were a student.'

The men had met at university in Exeter. Archie had brought Theo home during that first long summer holiday. I must have been fifteen, full of hormones and desperate to fall in love. Theo was nineteen, tall, dark and nice to me. Predictably I'd formed a crush of colossal proportions on him, which, despite me having various boyfriends through the years, never quite went away. Archie had teased me mercilessly about it. Theo, of course, didn't notice. It had been quite a shock for him to discover my feelings nine years later on his wedding day.

'Sounds like Theo's been having a tough time.' I gave my brother a disappointed look. 'Alone.'

Archie cleared his throat. 'I'm here now and the important thing is—' His eyes widened suddenly. 'Hey, Theo, they aren't taking the Triumph, are they?'

I glared at him.

'Not that it matters,' he added hurriedly, but relaxed when Theo confirmed that his classic car was hidden under canvas at the back of the house. 'The important thing is getting you out of immediate trouble.'

Theo stared wordlessly into his tea while Archie explained to me that Theo had confessed to using loan sharks to cover his maxed-out credit-card repayments, mortgage and utility bills. But the interest had spiralled and Theo now couldn't repay the loans and after ignoring the demands had no choice other than to let in the bailiffs.

'I'm the world's biggest loser,' he muttered.

He looked so dejected that I almost pulled him into a tight hug before remembering that the last time I did that I almost stopped his wedding.

'Don't talk rot,' said Archie, punching Theo's arm. 'You've just had, er, a run of bad luck.'

I suppressed a smile; that was as close to a display of love as my brother got.

'How much are you offering Theo for the car?' I said, deciding to get the ball rolling. The bailiffs might have been happy to have a short tea break, but Warren (Baggy Trousers) had already told me they were due at a hat shop in Salcombe before long.

Archie named a figure and Theo looked so grateful that my heart melted.

'Add another five hundred quid and it's a deal,' I said briskly. 'Now hand me your wallet.'

Archie opened his mouth to say something but thought better of it and did as he was told.

I took five hundred pounds out of it and went outside.

'Will this buy Mr Fletcher some more time?' I said, shoving the notes through the window to Norman.

Norman licked his fingers and counted the money. Some of the wrinkles in his forehead softened and he looked far less hound-like. 'Better unload Mr Fletcher's gear, Warren, and then we'll be on our way.'

In no time, everything was back inside and the lorry hurtled back out of the courtyard in a cloud of dust.

Theo sagged against the doorframe and lowered his gaze to the ground. 'Until next time, lads,' he muttered.

Archie jerked his head meaningfully at Theo.

'Nina, why don't you two catch up on the news, ' he said, rubbing his hands together briskly, 'while I nip and have a look at the car.'

Behind Theo's back I was shaking my head frantically, but Archie strode away, jingling the coins in his pockets. I studied Theo for a few seconds. He was lost in his own thoughts and I wondered what could possibly have gone so wrong between him and Kate to have brought him so far down. It seemed I wasn't the only one to have hit a low point.

I took a deep breath and tucked my hand through his arm. 'Archie's right. We probably need to talk.'

Chapter 5

Back inside the kitchen, I filled the sink with hot soapy water.

'If we're going to clear the air, we might as well clear the dirty pots at the same time,' I said, pulling on some rubber gloves.

He took off his cap and rubbed a hand distractedly through his hair as he surveyed the mess. 'What must you think of me?'

I grinned. 'That you're a slob?'

'The kitchen has got on top of me.' He frowned, acknowledging the truth. 'I suppose everything has got on top of me. Kate would be so disappointed . . . Oh hell.'

The thought of his wife seemed to make his legs go weak and he reached for a chair to sit down again.

'No you don't.' I pulled him back towards the sink. 'I have had the most awful twenty-four hours during which I have let down the world *and* his wife. If I only achieve one thing today it will be to sort out your kitchen. Believe me, we'll both feel better for it.'

'Thanks, I miss someone bossing me about.' Theo's face brightened. 'I suppose I still think of you as Archie's kid sister. Well, I did right up until—'

'I prefer to think of myself as determined rather than bossy,' I jumped in quickly, not quite ready to address the elephant in the room. I handed him a tea towel and plunged my hands into the water. 'Now, as you look like you need a good laugh, I'll tell you what I've been up to since I last saw you.'

'I'd like that,' he said with a sigh, leaning against the draining board. 'I'm completely sick of my own company.'

'So,' I began, 'do you ever watch *Victory Road*?'

While I brought him up to speed with my acting career over the last five years we dealt with about twenty mugs, most of which looked like abandoned chemistry experiments in how to grown penicillin, three frying pans of varying degrees of encrusted egg, numerous baked bean pans and countless plates and cutlery coated with old food that had dried to the consistency of concrete. I embellished all my showbiz anecdotes for maximum entertainment value and by the time I'd finished telling him how I'd single-handedly screwed up *Victory Road*'s big cliffhanger, potentially lost my agent his newest client and revealed myself to be a vicious diva to the UK's media, even I was beginning to see the funny side. And Theo . . . well, I was delighted to say, he had almost begun to look like the Theo I'd fallen for all those years ago.

Suddenly the sound of an engine revving reached us through the kitchen window.

'Good grief!' said Theo. 'Archie's managed to get the engine to turn over. It hasn't run since we moved in.'

We.

'And when was that?' I asked, seizing the opportunity to turn the spotlight from me to him.

'Eighteen months ago,' he said, instantly deflating again.

'It's a lovely place,' I said encouragingly. 'What's the village called again?'

'Brightside Cove. We even joked that looking on the bright side might be just what we needed. Therapeutic, Kate said.' He glanced down at the floor. 'That backfired.'

'Well, we could all do with a bit of therapy now and again,' I said with a laugh to lift the mood.

'Tried that too.'

The feeling I'd had at the table moments earlier came back to me: the urge to take him in my arms and hold him tight. I could sense a sadness deep within him which permeated everything, every word, every movement, every breath.

I watched as he slowly dried the soap suds from a cheese grater and then carried it to the table. I picked up a scrubbing brush and began to tackle the last item – a wooden spoon with caked-on egg – and turned my gaze to the view out of the window. Immediately outside was a strip of wilderness where dandelions bloomed riotously amongst the long grass. A pretty stone wall, about four feet high, ran along the edge of the garden and was covered in star-like pink flowers. Beyond that was the coast road and in the distance, a line of shimmering sea met the sky. Even the air of neglect couldn't stop Driftwood Lodge from being heart-stoppingly beautiful.

'I bet you get a good view of the sea from upstairs?' I said, taking off the rubber gloves, slipping my thick hoody off and hanging it on the back of a chair. I was only wearing a skimpy vest underneath, but needs must. The sun shone directly through the window above the sink and with the effort of washing up I was beginning to melt.

He nodded. 'All the bedrooms face the sea. I'll show you.'

I hadn't noticed the warm sand-coloured flagstones when I'd arrived, or the worn rugs in gold and pale blue which ran down the length of the hall, or the burnished-wood window sills that looked big enough to curl up on to read, or the shafts of sunlight that filtered down the stairs from above. I'd been too busy trying to remember how the bailiffs took their tea, but now as we made our way to the bottom of the staircase, these tiny details began to add up and I could see the homeliness of Driftwood Lodge that must have appealed to Theo and Kate as well as the cheerful name of the village.

'Your home is gorgeous,' I said.

'Kate thinks so.' He gestured for me to go ahead. 'Or did. But it has never felt like a home to me.'

I frowned at that but said nothing.

'I take it this is the spare room?' I said, peering into a bedroom full of junk. There was a double bed in there somewhere but it was piled high with clothes and surrounded by cardboard boxes. There was hardly any floor space left for us to stand on, but Theo forced his way to the window, which was set low into the wall and only came up to his chest.

'Yeah,' he said, yanking back the curtains. 'I wouldn't take you in our . . . my room; it's far too messy.'

He scratched at his skin through his shirt. 'And the sheets probably want washing.'

Quite possibly so did he, but I'd lost interest in the state of the room because the view from the window was completely breath-taking. I stepped over a crate and bent down for a better look. I could see the underside of the thatched roof from here and it looked like a big bushy eyebrow framing the view. A view that made my heart sing. Downstairs only a narrow ribbon of sea was visible, but up here you could see everything: the cliffs, the headland and white-crested waves crashing against distant rocks.

'Oh, smell that sea air!' I said, throwing the window open and inhaling the fresh tang of salt in the breeze. 'Doesn't that make you feel alive?'

'Sometimes.' Theo shoved a heap of jumpers aside and sat down on the bed. 'Other times it makes me feel like I'm living on the edge of the world. One false move and I could be over those cliffs and whoosh. Gone for ever.' His eyes dropped to his lap. 'Like everyone else in my life.'

I crouched in front of him and took his hands, forcing him to make eye contact briefly before he lowered his eyes again.

'Look, Theo, I'm your friend, let me help you, whatever it is . . .'

44

He withdrew his hands from mine. 'You don't know me any more. You haven't seen me for five years.'

'I know,' I said, making room for myself on the bed beside him. 'Hardly surprising, given my behaviour.'

One corner of his mouth lifted in a smile. 'I didn't know what had hit me. One minute I was having a quiet moment by myself outside the church, the next you appear from inside, throw yourself at me and beg me not to marry Kate.'

I winced, glad that he hadn't mentioned the kissing part. 'Talk about drama queen. I'd had a silly crush on you for years. And seeing you about to marry someone else brought it all to a head.'

'It was a bit of a shock, but I must admit, I was flattered.' Theo's eyes glazed with the memories of his big day.

'Archie was furious with me, saying he wished he'd never brought me. I'm so sorry.'

Archie had been Theo's best man. He and his girlfriend had split up the week before the wedding and so I'd stepped in at the last minute to be his 'plus one'.

Theo shrugged. 'Apology accepted, as indeed it was at the time. You were young.'

'I was twenty-four,' I said, still mortified at the memory.

'It could have been worse; you could have stood up in church at the crucial "does anyone have just cause or impediment" moment. I probably wouldn't have forgiven you for that.'

I bit my lip; the idea had crossed my mind, but I hadn't wanted to make a spectacle of myself. As it was, Kate's wedding car had pulled up at the church gate at precisely the worst time and she had caught me with my arms around her husband-to-be, kissing him for the first and only time.

Footsteps crunched across the gravel outside, breaking the moment, and I stood up to go back downstairs to Archie. I'd be glad to be on our way. I was looking forward to settling in at Archie's house and tackling what I was going to do about the remaining shreds of my career.

'Theo's in the kitchen, do come through.' Archie's voice travelled up the stairs.

Theo frowned. 'Who's he talking to?'

He launched himself off the bed and descended the stairs and I followed.

Archie turned to see us both coming from upstairs and I suddenly felt very underdressed in my vest top.

'What were you doing upstairs?' he muttered in my ear as I pushed past him to retrieve my hoody from the kitchen.

'Nothing!' I replied, my cheeks aflame.

'Mr and Mrs Fletcher?' A short man stepped from the shadows of the hall and held out his hand to Theo. He was dressed in long linen shorts, a soft-knit jumper and deck shoes. 'Joe Bird.'

Theo shook the outstretched hand and dropped it again. Joe perched his hands on his hips and looked around.

'I say, this place certainly lives up to the website description,' he said with a whistle. 'You're not kidding when you say "off the beaten track"; the kids are going to love it. Oh, by the way, your sign's hanging off the gate.'

'What kids?' Theo looked confused. 'What sign?'

'I think Joe means the carved driftwood on the gate,' I said with a growing sense of doom. Whoever Joe was, he certainly wasn't expected, although something told me he thought otherwise.

'That's the one.' Joe rubbed his hands together and stepped out into the courtyard. 'Right, better get back to the pub or Mary will kill me. Feeding our brood in public would test the patience of a saint.'

'Joe and Mary? Tell me your real name's not Joseph,' said Archie with a chuckle.

'It is. I had to stop her arriving on a donkey for our wedding – great sense of humour, my wife.' Joe shook his head, grinning to himself. 'Happy days.'

'So . . . ?' I smiled encouragingly at him. 'Did you call in for something in particular?'

He slapped his forehead. 'Silly me. Must be all this fresh air after Surrey. Yes. I wanted to apologize for arriving so late when I did promise you we'd be here for our welcome afternoon tea at three.'

I thought back to the stale biscuits that had been the only edible thing in the kitchen; perhaps there was a secret stash of fluffy homemade scones lurking in a cupboard somewhere. But judging by the blank look on Theo's face, I doubted it.

'I tried to call,' Joe continued, 'but I haven't been able to get a signal since leaving the motorway.'

'Sounds about right,' Archie agreed. 'I've been trying to organize transport for the Triumph, but the only signal I did get was so weak, the guy on the other end thought I was ringing from a call centre in Mumbai and hung up.'

'And I called the landline from the phone in the pub but it just rang out,' Joe continued. 'So Mary asked me to pop up in person.'

Theo scratched his head. 'Damn. Don't tell me I haven't paid that bill either?'

Joe, probably thinking Theo was joking, gave a bark of laughter. Archie's shoulders sank.

I spotted the pile of small electricals that the bailiffs had piled up on a velvet chair under the stairs. There were two phones amongst them, and no one had got round to plugging them back in.

I laughed heartily and tucked my arm through Theo's.

'Oh, darling, you are funny.' Adding to Joe, 'We've just had our electrical appliances checked, and the phone is unplugged, that's all. Sorry you couldn't get through.'

'Not at all,' Joe beamed again. 'All part of the charm.'

'Unless you're trying to run a business,' Theo muttered. 'Not so bloody charming then.'

'Oh, do look on the bright side, Theo, for goodness' sake,' I burst out, suddenly frustrated, confused and quite frankly tired of whatever game it was that we were playing.

'Bright side! Ha!' Joe pointed at me delightedly. 'Good one. And talking of business . . .' He paused to remove his wallet from his back pocket. 'We didn't get a reply to our email so we haven't paid the balance yet. Here it is.'

He counted out several fifty-pound notes from his wallet and handed them to me.

'Er . . . ?' I looked at Theo, who made a noise somewhere between a yodel and a groan. 'Thank you.'

'As I say, we're having an early supper at the pub,' Joe continued, 'and then we've promised the kids a play on the beach. So should I collect a key now or will you be in later?'

'Oh crap,' Theo whispered, having turned an odd shade of yellow. 'Oh Kate. Oh crap.'

Joe's worried eyes flicked from me to Theo and back again.

'Later is perfect,' I said, plastering on a smile. I steered him back through the front door and into the courtyard. 'You go and enjoy yourselves. Take all the time in the world. I'd even stop for ice cream if I were you.'

He beamed. 'Good idea, where would you recommend?'

I looked to Theo for guidance. After all, how would I know? But he looked like he might be on the verge of throwing up.

'They're all good, you can't go wrong,' I said, vaguely. 'See you later.'

Or at least Theo would; Archie and I would be off. I watched Joe jog off towards a family estate car complete with a roof rack and over-stuffed boot and then went back into the house to find the men in the living room, Archie perched on the edge of one sofa and Theo lolling on another, his feet dangling over the edge.

Another lovely room, I thought, taking in the open fireplace, low beams, squishy buttery leather sofas piled high with fluffy cream cushions and windows that let light in from both sides of the building.

'What was that all about?' I asked, sitting on the arm of Archie's sofa.

'Which bit?' Archie asked drily. 'That bloke asking for a key or you two disappearing upstairs the moment my back was turned?'

'Nothing to worry about on that score, mate,' said Theo, pointing at his crotch. 'This soldier hasn't been into battle for months.'

'Oh, please,' I said, resisting the urge to jam my fingers in my ears. 'We were just looking at the sea, that's all. Well, I was, Theo was just staring at his lap . . .'

Archie coughed pointedly.

'Anyway, Theo,' I continued. 'You look about to be sick, what's going on?'

'For weeks I've thought life couldn't get any worse. Then the bailiffs arrived and I just thought, well, I've finally hit rock bottom.' He lay back and clamped a hand to his forehead.

'But we've fended them off,' said Archie encouragingly. 'Theo Fletcher lives to fight another day. And with the money from the car, which I'll transfer just as soon as I've got an internet connection, you'll be solvent again.'

But Theo wasn't listening. He hugged a cushion to his chest and gave a shuddering groan. 'Turns out rock bottom is lower than I thought.'

'You're not making sense,' I said. 'Whatever Joe Bird wants—'

'A holiday,' said Theo, cutting me off. I could hear the tremor in his voice. 'Joseph and Mary must have booked to come here on holiday.'

'Bloody HELL, Theo.' Archie pinched the bridge of his nose and looked incredulously at me.

'I suppose there's no way we could tell them that there's no room at the inn?' I said faintly.

Archie snorted at my joke and I looked down at the wodge of notes that Joe had given me; Theo needed an injection of cash. But did he need it enough to put up with holidaymakers?

'Let me get this straight,' said Archie, pacing the living room. 'Joe is descending on you in a couple of hours with his entire family. For a holiday?'

Theo swallowed.

'It was Kate's idea; we were going to run a self-catering cottage business. That was what attracted us to this place. To keep us busy after . . .' He pressed his hands into his eyes and groaned. 'Brightside Holidays, we were going to call it. She threw herself into it, started having renovations done to the cottages, making plans and so on. But I couldn't get motivated and she got fed up of waiting and left me. I didn't realize she'd already taken a booking.'

'Are we talking about those buildings across the court-yard?' I asked, nodding to the window.

'Yeah,' said Theo woefully. 'They could be quite nice but . . .'

His voice tailed off and he sighed as if the effort of all this talking had worn him out.

I caught the gleam in Archie's eye. He'd love this sort of challenge, converting a row of run-down buildings into chic little holiday cottages. But Archie and Theo were not cut from the same cloth, at least not any more, and if Theo couldn't even manage to put clean sheets on his own bed, I doubted he'd be up to running a holiday business.

'There you go, then,' Archie said, springing to his feet. 'A ready-made revenue stream. You're on the up, Theo.' He glanced at his watch. 'I'll nip to the loo and then Nina and I had better get back to Exeter. I'll be in touch about collect-ing the Triumph.'

He strode from the room and began trying doors until he found the downstairs loo. Theo sat up and looked at me with fear in his eyes.

'I can't do it,' he whispered. 'I can't look after a family of holidaymakers. They'll be all jolly and I'll want to punch them. They'll want directions to places and tips on restaur-ants and stuff like when the tide is in. Or out.'

Personally, I thought the most pressing issue was whether the cottages were habitable. I leaned forward to take his hand.

'Can't you call Kate? Perhaps she'll come back and help out?'

'She won't, she—'

'Right.' Archie came back in, drying his hands on his trousers. 'Nina, hand Theo that cash from Mr Bird, that'll put a smile on his face.'

Honestly, sometimes he could be so dim. 'Money doesn't always solve everything, Archie.'

He shook his head affectionately as if to say, Of course it does.

I hustled him back out of the door and into the hall. 'We can't leave him like this,' I whispered. 'Not until we've at least spoken to Kate and found out what this family are expecting.'

Archie made a big show of looking at his watch again. 'Fine.'

'You can't speak to Kate,' came Theo's muffled voice from the sofa.

Archie and I popped our heads back round the door.

'Why not?' we both said together.

'She's gone to South America, a tour of Chile, Argentina and Brazil.'

'Perverts,' said Archie and I at the same moment and then smiled at each other.

Theo blinked. 'What?'

'Private joke,' I explained. 'Mum saw the Rio Carnival on TV once with all the thongs and nipple tassels and branded all Brazilians perverts.'

'I hope Kate will be wearing more than that where she is; she's near the South Pole.'

Theo went to the mantelpiece and retrieved a postcard from behind a framed wedding photograph. He handed the postcard to me. It was from Chile with a picture of penguins on the front.

'She gave me an ultimatum.' He shoved his hands in his pockets. 'To set up Brightside Holidays ready for the school holiday season. If I haven't done it by the time she gets back at the end of June she's calling time on our marriage.'

Archie and I exchanged looks. It didn't exactly look like he was steaming ahead with it.

'Right well, first things first, Archie and I can't help you set up the business, but we can help you sort out your immediate problem,' I said firmly, 'and that's getting one cottage ready for your imminent guests. Joe Bird mentioned a website. Do you know anything about that?'

Theo scratched his head. 'Kate set one up. I can look at it on my laptop, but I haven't got any administrator log-in details, so I can't see any messages.'

'Well, can you at least go and find out how long they're staying?' I suggested, trying to stay patient.

Theo nodded numbly and left the room.

'No wonder she left him,' Archie tutted. He grabbed a footstool and stood on it near the window, waving his arm in the air trying to get a signal on his phone. 'He's wetter than a mackerel's bikini. I know he's having a tough time, but he needs to get a grip.'

'Archie!' I chided. 'Be nice.'

He was right; Theo was being a bit pathetic and I couldn't help but wonder what had gone so wrong for him and Kate to cause her to run away to the other side of the world and for him to have had all the life sucked out of him?

'According to the availability calendar on the website,' Theo announced, coming back in, 'someone – the Birds, I presume – have booked to stay in the largest of the three cottages for six nights. Which could be worse, I suppose.'

'So,' I clapped my hands briskly, 'we've got about two hours to make it a holiday haven for them. All hands on deck.'

'Whoa.' Archie jumped down from the footstool and held both palms up. 'No can do. Sorry, mate.' He turned to Theo. 'I need to get back to Exeter.'

'On a Sunday evening? Why?' I said, folding my arms.

'Work,' he replied. 'We're under a lot of pressure at the moment and I've got spreadsheets to do for the accountant by tomorrow. But you could stay, Nina – you wanted a break from London.'

Theo grabbed my arm, a look of panic in his eyes. 'Nina, stay for the whole week. You can do all the talking. Please. Mr Bird already thinks you're my wife. You're an actress, you can fake it. I can pay you? Well, sort of.'

A week in Devon . . . I looked at Archie for advice.

'Could you pose as a holiday cottage owner?' Archie said. 'How are your domestic skills?'

'I did once have a non-speaking part as a chambermaid on *Downton Abbey*,' I said thoughtfully. 'I was highly commended for making beds.'

I'd had high hopes for that role, but the next episode had been about the family tightening their belts and I'd been 'let go'. The cast were lovely on that show. I'd even been invited to the National TV awards with them that year, but it had clashed with the filming of a corpse scene on *Silent Witness*. One day, though, one day . . .

'Please stay.' Theo swallowed hard, his Adam's apple doing that bobbing thing again.

I chewed the inside of my cheek, mulling it over. I didn't have to get back to London immediately and I did want to keep a low profile for a while. Maybe if I was here to gee Theo up a bit, give him a few pep talks about throwing himself back into life, he'd soon be back to his old self. Now that I thought about it, staying here had an awful lot going for it.

And as for acting the role of Theo's wife . . . I glanced at him, his dark brown eyes blinking hopefully at me. He looked so desperate and, as hard as I tried to deny it, adorable. I could think of worse jobs.

Chapter 6

'Okay,' I relented. 'I'll stay. But—'

Before I could finish, Theo scooped me up and held me so tightly that I could almost feel the bruises forming on my ribs.

'Thank you, Nina.' He pressed a forceful kiss to my forehead. 'Thank you so much.'

'But on one condition. I can't do everything by myself, so you'll have to get your backside into gear and help me.'

'Of course,' he said meekly. 'Anything you say.'

'Go and get the keys to whichever cottage we're putting the Birds in.'

He nodded and sloped off to the kitchen.

'Archie, before you disappear, I need you to go and buy some food, restock the cupboards. A girl can't live on stale biscuits alone and I think it might be nice to have a welcome hamper for the Birds too.'

'That's two conditions,' said Archie with a grin.

'Or you can stay here and help get the cottage ready.' I eyed him beadily. I knew my brother, given half a chance, he'd buy his way out of a situation every time.

Archie took his car keys out. 'What shall I get?'

'Everything,' I said, bundling him out of the door. 'Find a big supermarket and get everything.'

I found Theo at the kitchen table tipping out an old tin full of keys, string, magnets and foreign coins. 'These belong to the cottages,' he said, separating three key rings from the rest of the jumble. 'But I've no idea which is which.'

I picked them all up and stuffed them in my pocket and then rummaged around under the kitchen sink until I found a duster. 'If you fetch clean bedlinen and towels, I'll open up, let some fresh air in and flick this round.'

Theo chewed his lip. 'I'm not sure where we keep the bedlinen.'

'Then go and look!' I said, not wanting to dwell on how long it had been since his own sheets had been changed. I shooed him upstairs and headed outside towards the outbuildings – ahem, I mean, luxury holiday cottages.

Their location itself, perched on the clifftops with the soundtrack of waves breaking on the south Devonshire coastline was enough to warrant a hefty weekly rental. Their interiors, I imagined, would only add to their desirability. I didn't know Kate well, but well enough to know that she had impeccable taste.

Three hens spotted me picking my way past the debris in the courtyard and scurried over, clucking loudly. The Birds' three children were going to love the ducks and hens, I thought, scattering pieces of stale biscuit for them from my pocket. Collecting fresh eggs could be a lovely activity for children to join in with. And if I could locate some now, I could add them to the welcome hamper.

I was humming by the time I reached the largest of the three cottages and automatically touched the space between my eyebrows. Smooth. Totally smooth. Trudy would be proud. I took a deep breath. Despite the drama of the last twenty-four hours, despite the obvious distress that Theo was in, and despite the fiasco of holidaymakers arriving soon to take up residence, I felt less stressed than I'd felt in a long time. I felt ... useful, and it was a lovely, heart-warming feeling.

This sensation of gooey warm happiness remained as I admired the lovely soft china-blue colour of the freshly painted window frames, it lasted through having a giggle at the signs Kate had erected outside each cottage – Beaver's Barn, Kittiwake's Cabin and then the final one, which the Birds were due to occupy, Penguin's Pad – and it even lasted through me juggling and trying every key until I finally found one to fit.

And then I opened the door.

Any vestige of hope I'd had that all we'd need was a bit of elbow grease and a stack of clean sheets evaporated in the sea breeze. Penguin's Pad reminded me of *Victory Road* Studio Two: a bomb site. I felt sweaty suddenly. This was a nightmare.

I stepped inside on to the bare concrete floor. It was open plan in design and if I closed my eyes I could picture how it would all look when it was finished. It would be a haven of happiness and tranquillity.

But right now the fitted kitchen had carcasses but no doors, a sink but no taps and several gaps where I guessed the appliances would go. The splashbacks had been tiled, but that was it. The other half of the room: a large living room with double doors leading into a scrubby bit of garden had a log burner and . . . nothing, nothing else at all. Not that there was any point going any further, but I jogged upstairs anyway.

The three bedrooms were actually the most habitable out of all the rooms, painted, carpeted and relatively clean. All they needed was furniture. And doors. The bathroom did have a roll-top bath, I was pleased to see, but the shower consisted of a plastic tray on the floor and a cable sticking out of the wall and no taps anywhere.

Joe Bird might have said his wife had a sense of humour, but I wasn't sure she'd see the funny side if we told her this was to be their home for the next six days.

My heart was racing as I ran downstairs and back outside to try the other cottages. You never know, I told myself optimistically, the other two could be showroom perfect. But if they weren't, we were in trouble.

I was fitting the key into the lock of Kittiwake's Cabin, the smallest cottage, when Theo came striding towards me, looking pleased with himself.

'I found these,' he said, holding up a paltry pile of shabby-looking sheets and pillow cases. 'Shall we make the beds?'

'There are no beds,' I said, putting my shoulder to the door and giving it a shove. 'Goodness me, this is stiff.'

It was stiff because behind the door was a pile of builders' rubble.

'So far there are no holiday cottages, Theo, only one big building site.'

'Ah.' Theo scratched his head once we'd stepped in and looked around the room, which if anything was in an even worse state than Penguin's Pad. 'That rather scuppers our plans.'

We stared at each other for a long moment, the horror of the situation getting more and more vivid. The Birds had paid handsomely for a holiday; I had visions of them appearing on that consumer complaints TV show weeks from now talking about their holiday from hell.

Kittiwake's Cabin smelled of damp plaster and dust and I could feel a sneeze forming. I dragged Theo back outside.

'We need a new plan,' I said firmly. 'The Birds are expecting a holiday and I have every intention of giving them one.'

'Righto.' Theo looked at me expectantly.

I cast about for inspiration and my eyes alighted on the little wooden plaques next to each door. 'What's with the names of the cottages, by the way?'

'Kate thought it would be nice to call them after indigenous wildlife.' He pressed his lips together firmly in an attempt at loyalty but I could see the humour dancing in his eyes.

'Indigenous? Penguins?'

'She's a city girl.' He cleared his throat to stifle a chuckle. 'What can I say? Also, she loves penguins.'

'Well, naturally,' I said, feeling a bubble of inappropriate laughter about to explode. 'Who doesn't love a Devonshire penguin?'

Just like that the ludicrousness of the situation rushed up at me. The two of us, out of our depth, attempting to prepare a building site for imminent occupation, Theo with a pathetic supply of bedlinen, and me with a duster. And I began to laugh, a little refined giggle at first, followed by a snort and then a proper full-on hoot of laughter. Theo met my gaze, a bit taken aback, and then to my complete joy, he joined in. Soon the two of us were falling about, helpless with laughter, clutching our sides, tears running down our faces.

'We could always try to wing it?' Theo wheezed, wiping tears from his face. 'Say we've mixed urban decay with coastal minimalism?'

'And who needs an oven, when you can have a barbie on the beach?' I said, pressing a hand to the stitch below my ribs.

'And blow some inflatables up and call it a beach-themed holiday!' Theo grinned.

'Yeah, like lilos and those chairs with the holes in the arms for beer . . . Ooh!' I gave an almighty gasp. 'That's it! That's what we can do! Got it!'

'What?' Theo looked at me, startled by the change in direction.

'Come on!' I yelled and dashed back into the house as fast as I could with a bewildered Theo jogging behind me.

Back in the hall I called Archie from the landline.

'Twenty miles to the nearest proper shop,' he grumbled. 'I've only just arrived.'

'I hope it's a superstore because we're going to need a lot of stuff,' I said urgently. 'Are you listening?'

'What shall I do?' Theo was hovering at the door, listening. I wafted him upstairs.

'Go upstairs and strip the beds,' I ordered. 'Even the ones you can barely see.'

I gave Archie a huge list and sent up a silent prayer of

thanks for giving me a brother with a generous heart and a big enough car to put everything in.

I must have burned off about two thousand calories in the next two hours. Between us, we vacuumed, scrubbed, bleached, washed and polished everything in Driftwood Lodge. We carried packing boxes down from the spare room to the shed, made up the little camp bed in the box room and emptied all of Theo's belongings from the master bedroom down into the garages. The bathroom was given the same treatment and was now sparkling. We aired the living room, refilled the log basket and plumped up all the cushions. When Archie returned with more cleaning supplies, food and most importantly bedlinen and towels, I stripped them from their packets, tumble-dried them with a bit of fabric freshener and hung them outside on the washing line to give them that fresh just-washed aroma. Meanwhile, Archie took a heap of new camping furniture, airbeds and a barbecue over to Penguin's Pad while Theo took a scythe to the long grass in an attempt to transform the jungle into a more guest-friendly garden.

By the time the Birds called from the village phone box to tell us they were on their way, the three of us were completely shattered. Archie had stayed to help in the end, thank goodness, and he and I had collapsed on to a bench in the courtyard while Theo made us a pot of tea on our new little camping stove. The sun had already sunk behind the thatched roof, but I was so hot and exhausted that the cool air was delicious against my skin.

The amazing thing was, we were ready. My last task had been to hunt amongst the borders and hedgerows for flowers and I'd managed to fill four jugs with blossom and foliage. Now the master bedroom, living room and hallway were filled with the fragrance of spring.

Brightside Holidays was open for business.

'I do hope the Birds won't mind staying in the house

rather than the cottage,' I said, leaning back against the bench and allowing my eyes to close for a blissful few seconds. 'I'm going to pitch it to them as an upgrade.'

'Nina Penhaligon,' said Archie, nudging me with his elbow, 'I bloody love you. You have quite literally saved Theo's bacon.'

Theo handed me a mug. 'And I think you're a brick for agreeing to camp out in Penguin's Pad with me.'

'You're welcome.' I felt my stomach fizz. After starting off the day so disastrously, it was lovely to be in someone's good books again.

'I think Kate'll be really proud of me for achieving all this,' Theo added. He caught mine and Archie's bemused expressions. '*Us*,' he said hurriedly. 'Proud of us. Perhaps I could try to track her down, call her parents and find out her exact whereabouts . . .' His face took on a wistful look.

'You must miss her,' I said softly.

He sighed. 'I miss the sound of her voice, the smell of her perfume, the feel of her—'

I cleared my throat. 'If you do speak to her, ask her for the number of the builders, you need to get them back here asap to finish the job.'

'I've got their number; they ring me most days.' Theo rubbed his fingertips and thumb together. 'We owe them money.'

'There's plenty we can do ourselves,' I suggested, determined to maintain his positive mood at least until the guests arrived. I'd never attempted any DIY in my life, but how hard could it be? 'Isn't there, Archie?'

'Count me out. Too busy.' Archie got to his feet, taking his wallet out yet again and peeled more notes from the never-ending cash supply. 'But I'll help financially. Here.'

Theo shook his head. 'You've done enough.'

Archie tucked the notes into Theo's jacket pocket. 'You'd be doing me a favour. Look at my sister's rosy cheeks! Being here is as good as therapy for her; she needs you as much as you need her. Besides, you promised you'd pay her, remember?'

Theo tapped his pocket. 'I'm glad to help.'

'Archie!' I retorted indignantly. 'You make me sound like some sort of care in the community case.'

He kissed my cheek and grinned. 'Enjoy your stay at the seaside. And try to stay out of trouble.'

The sound of tyres bouncing along the bumpy lane made us all turn to look as Joe's car made its way gingerly around the potholes.

'Oh crikey, they're here,' muttered Theo.

'Don't panic, follow my lead,' I said briskly, setting my mug down. 'You can do this.'

I stood and took Theo's big warm hand in mine and we walked towards the car, smiling and waving.

Archie took advantage of the distraction to slink off to his car. 'Speak soon, good luck!' he yelled before jumping in, starting up the engine and making a hasty retreat.

Mary Bird got out of the car first and clasped her hands together. 'Oh, heavenly! What a lovely place!'

I liked her instantly. She was a mumsy mum, with hair pulled back into a no-nonsense ponytail, a large stain from what looked like chocolate ice-cream dribble down the front of her white T-shirt and thighs that wobbled in her leggings as she darted forward to say hello.

'Thank you!' I shook her hand. 'I'm Nina, you must be Mary!'

'I am indeed.' Mary's eyebrows lifted in surprise. 'But I thought your name was Kate?'

I had a sudden flash of panic. Theo and I hadn't thought this through properly. Of course I was Kate. Also, the real me was meant to be lying low. I'd have to hope Mary wasn't a *Victory Road* fan. I was going to have to up my game if I wasn't going to blow my cover. I contemplated faking a faint Birmingham accent to match Kate's before realizing that Joe had already met me.

'It is! Nina is my middle name,' I said, improvising rapidly. 'Which I prefer. But Nina or Kate. Whichever. I answer to both.'

'I see.' Mary looked confused and then narrowed her eyes. 'Have we met before? In Surrey?'

My stomach fluttered nervously. People did this sometimes. They ran through the places we may have met like the dentist or gym or hairdresser's until eventually realizing they were watching *Victory Road* last night . . .

I shook my head. 'Never been to Surrey.'

Just then two small children jumped from the back excitedly and immediately gave chase to the hens.

'What lovely children!' I said gaily, keen to change the subject. 'They are going to have such fun, aren't they, darling?'

Theo nodded weakly.

'Hi there!' Joe waved and lifted a baby seat containing an even smaller child from the car.

'Hello again,' I called.

Theo stared at him like he'd seen a ghost. When he asked me earlier to do all the talking I didn't think he actually meant *all* the talking. I pinched him discreetly.

'Ouch.' He gave me a wounded look. I sent him some stern eye signals to make an effort.

'Welcome to Driftwood Lodge!' he said, clearing his throat. 'I hope you, er, have a lovely stay with us.'

'Oh, we will!' Mary, seemingly oblivious to Theo's less than effusive greeting, bent over the car seat, unclipped the straps and lifted out a tiny infant with dark-blue eyes, a gummy smile and sand between his toes. 'Come on then, Thomas, let's go and explore our cottage.'

Joe slung a casual arm around her shoulder, kissed the top of his son's fluffy head and studied the row of cottages.

'The end one, isn't it?'

I looked at Theo, assuming he'd explain. He looked pleadingly back at me.

Oh, for goodness' sake.

'Actually,' I said, stepping into my role as hostess-with-the-mostest, 'good news! In honour of the fact that you're our first guests, we've upgraded you.'

'Really, we're your first guests!' Mary gasped. 'But upgraded to where? I thought we'd already booked the biggest of the three?'

'Ta dah!' I made a sweeping gesture towards the house. 'Please allow us to give you the grand tour of Driftwood Lodge!'

'An upgrade, Joe, wait till our friends hear about this,' Mary said, her eyes shining with glee.

'This way, please,' said Theo, attempting a gracious smile. He strode purposefully towards the door.

Mary and Joe smiled delightedly at each other and scampered after him.

'Jolly decent of you.' Joe beamed at me. 'Kids! This way.'

Theo, to his credit, actually did a thorough job of showing the Birds the ropes, from how to handle the stiff doorknob in the pantry, to how to find the children's TV channel for the two older ones (Darcy and Leo) to lighting the log burner, and he even helped referee a dispute between the children as to who would get the biggest room.

Mary was thrilled with the welcome pack we'd assembled on the kitchen table and when she joined us upstairs she was carrying a glass of the nice Beaujolais Archie had chosen. Joe was holding the baby while Theo was demonstrating the thermostatic valve on the shower.

'Cheers,' she said, taking a big slurp. 'This is fab, Kate – *Nina* – and Theo, really fab. Now if you could just point us in the direction of the travel cot, we'll let you get on.'

'Travel cot?' I echoed, with a sudden rush of unease. If Kate hadn't got round to buying any guest beds for the cottages, the chances of having a baby's cot stashed away were less than slim.

'For Thomas.' She shot me a look of panic. 'I did mention

it in the email. We didn't have room to bring ours. You said it was fine.'

A hundred different ideas ran through my head: like how we could possibly knock up a cot from the pile of old wooden pallets outside and a few cushions to whether we could fob them off long enough to tear off to the nearest shop and buy one.

'It is fine, isn't it?' Mary chewed her lip.

I looked at Theo. And then did a double take. His face had turned green.

'Kate said that?' he said in a hollow voice.

Mary nodded.

Theo scuffed his toe against the skirting board and exhaled shakily. 'In that case, the travel cot is, the cot is in the, er, little . . . room under the eaves.'

Thank goodness for Kate's foresight; I let out a breath of relief.

'Of course it is. Brain like a sieve,' I said, rolling my eyes at my apparent memory lapse. 'Theo, perhaps . . . Oh.'

I looked at the space where Theo had been. Mary, Joe and I stared at each other awkwardly as Theo's footsteps thundered down the stairs and out across the gravelled courtyard.

Through the open bathroom window, we watched him charge off down the lane and eventually out of sight towards the cliffs.

'Migraine,' I said weakly. 'A terrible affliction. The only cure for it is to, er, do that.'

Mary and Joe nodded earnestly.

'I'll just find that cot,' I said, sidling out of the room. And then I'd better find Theo . . .

Chapter 7

Twenty minutes had passed by the time I was free to look for Theo. I didn't have a clue where I was going but I followed my instincts down to the coast road. I crossed over to the path that ran along the cliff edge and leaned on the stone wall, taking in the view down to the rocks on the other side.

There was no sign of him.

The wind whipped the ends of my newly black hair into my face and I pulled Theo's huge padded jacket around me, glad I'd grabbed it at the last minute. The heat had disappeared from the sun altogether now and the air was damp with salt spray. It was so bracing that my skin had already begun to tingle. Just being here was probably as good for me as one of Trudy's fancy exfoliators, I thought, trying to secure strands of hair behind my ears.

Far below me, the beach looked almost deserted. To the left, waves were lapping at rocks and a dog was jumping in and out of the water. To the right of me, a set of steps, carved into the rock, led down to the shore and although I couldn't see him, I had a hunch that Theo was hiding somewhere down there.

The steps were steep and zigzagged through gorse bushes, but with the rocks behind me, I was sheltered from the wind and I warmed up as I jogged down to the sand. Seagulls squawked as they circled over the sea and the waves made a perfectly rhythmic whooshing and dragging sound as they broke on the pebbly part of the beach. At the far end of the beach someone whistled to their dog, and two children playing in the frothy surf in their wellies shrieked with laughter. There was plenty of noise and yet there was a peacefulness surrounding Brightside Cove that felt like balm to my soul.

I tipped my head up to the sky and breathed deeply, inhaling the smells of the seaside. I needed this. Right now, I was in exactly the right place.

Water oozed over the edge of my trainers as I squelched along the shoreline. A wet springer spaniel bounded up to me, dropped a rope toy at my feet and waggled its bottom in the air hopefully, its tongue lolling out of one side of its mouth.

'Sorry!' someone shouted in the distance, just as I bent to pick the rope up. 'Mabel, come here!'

The dog snatched at the toy and scampered off again, showering my face with wet sand.

'Yuck.' I spat the sand from my mouth, laughing. 'Thanks, Mabel.'

'Made a friend already?' A familiar voice reached me on the wind.

He was sitting high up on a rock like a long-legged gnome, facing out to the sea with his arms clamped around his knees.

'For goodness' sake, Theo,' I said with a mix of relief and frustration. 'You just abandoned me! What was I supposed to think?'

I marched to the base of his rock and stared up at him.

'That I'm not cut out for hospitality?' He jumped down and landed with a thud beside me.

'In case you hadn't noticed, nor am I.' Honestly, this man was the limit. I was beginning to have sympathy for Kate. 'Last time I looked I was an actress.'

To be totally accurate, the last time I looked I was a dangerous diva. My stomach roiled at the thought. At some point I was going to have to contact someone from my proper life and find out what was going on. The gnawing feeling of guilt

I had about not speaking to Becky before I left was getting worse. But that could wait; right this minute I needed to find out what had caused Theo to bolt for the door.

'Look,' I said, patiently, 'if I'm to help get you through this week, you're going to have to try a bit harder.'

'Yeah, I know,' he said wearily. 'I'm sorry. Again. All I seem to do is apologize.'

It was on the tip of my tongue to tell him to stop being such a drip and pull himself together but there was something in the forlorn set of his shoulders that held me back.

'No worries,' I said, looping my arm through his. 'Besides, I've been dying to get on the sand since I arrived. I miss the sea so much when I'm in London. I used to spend half my life on the beach when I was a student. Let's walk along the edge.'

I thought he'd protest, but we fell into step and carried on across the bay towards the harbour. My feet were getting soaked, but I felt like a little kid watching my footprints getting washed away by the foamy sea as we dodged the waves.

'I love watching the tide come in and out,' said Theo, nodding ahead of us to where a dozen or so little fishing boats were grounded in the harbour. 'In a few hours all these will be bobbing about again, the beach will be half this size and the rock pools over near the sea wall will be teeming with hermit crabs. After eighteen months living here, it still amazes me how quickly things change.'

'Ooh, a big shell!' I said, pointing to a spot just in front of him. He picked it up and handed it to me and I cupped it in my palm. It was light brown, coarse on the outside and a bit rough round the edges but when I turned it over it revealed its softer side: a whorl of beauty, shiny and smooth, and shimmering in iridescent shades of pink.

'Look what it was hiding.' I held it up to show him and he stroked the smooth surface with the tip of his finger.

'Who'd have guessed it had all that going on inside it,' he said with a soft smile and began to plod onwards.

67

Ahead of us was a manmade slope which led away from the sea and up to a cluster of shops and cottages and I could just make out a pub sign swaying in the breeze. Theo's pace began to slow as we approached the slope and I could feel his reluctance to leave the beach.

I had to know what was going on and what had caused him to run and it felt like now or never. I stopped in my tracks causing him to stop too.

'Theo, what is it?' I searched his dark eyes for clues. 'What's going on inside you?'

He stiffened and looked out to sea above my head and refused to meet my gaze. 'I feel calmer down here, like I'm using the whole of my lungs to breathe instead of just the top ten per cent. So this is where I come when it gets too much.'

It wasn't exactly an invitation to probe further, but it was probably as good as I was going to get.

'You and Kate loved each other, you still love her, I can tell, so what went wrong?'

And then he did look at me and the pain in his eyes almost made me weep. He raked a hand across his stubble.

'You know that cot?'

I nodded.

'It was Ivy's. Our daughter, Ivy.'

'Oh, Theo,' I murmured.

My heart squeezed as a rash of goose bumps slithered down my spine.

To the left, at the top of the slipway, was a weather-beaten wooden bench in front of a small whitewashed building. Rows and rows of lobster pots were lined up outside and a handwritten board advertising fresh lobster caught daily by Big Dave had been nailed to the door. I quietly took Theo's hand and led him to the bench.

I learned the power of silence in drama school. Staying quiet when the audience was expecting you to speak built dramatic tension, had them on the edge of their seats, eyes glued to the stage. Now the moment was prickling with tension. And the stage was all Theo's.

'She would have been two and a half now,' he said, easing his wallet from the pocket of his jeans. Tucked into the flap were a handful of photographs. 'If she'd survived.'

My throat ached with sorrow as suddenly everything began to make sense.

'Here she is at five months old.' He handed me a picture of a smiling Kate holding a tiny child. My breath hitched; Ivy was the most perfect little thing I'd ever seen. Even though the baby only had the merest wisp of fine blonde hair, and was wearing cream rabbit-covered dungarees, she was unmistakably a little girl.

'Beautiful,' I said, clearing my throat to banish the lump in it.

'She was,' Theo said gruffly. 'Our little angel.'

My heart skipped a beat as a tear slipped down his cheek.

'Tell me about her,' I whispered, blotting his tear with my fingertip.

And against a backdrop of sea and sky and immeasurable beauty, I listened as he talked me through the photos and told me of the joy that Ivy had brought to him and Kate from the moment they'd learned they were going to have a baby. Her arrival had been simple: a fast labour and a water birth and Theo had fallen in love with his daughter instantly and with Kate all over again. A love more fierce and precious than he could have imagined.

'She left us as quickly as she arrived.' Theo held up a picture of Ivy and him, her little hands on his face, beaming with an adorable smile. The Theo in the picture was the one I remembered. His open smile, his eyes dancing with happiness.

'One minute she did her first roll-over, the next, it seemed, she had a temperature and an infection and before we knew it she was fighting for her life in a hospital crib.'

'What a nightmare,' I said, my heart swelling with sadness, unable to process what the two of them must have gone through. I slid closer to him and pressed my shoulder to his.

'By the time the medical team diagnosed sepsis, it was too late. She wasn't strong enough to fight it. She was six months old when she died.' He rubbed his thumb tenderly over Ivy's face in the picture. 'And a piece of me died with her.'

'Oh Theo, I am so, so sorry for your loss.' My eyes brimmed with tears and I slipped an arm around him. 'And Kate? How did she cope?'

His shoulders sagged. 'Without Ivy, we ceased to be a family, but we'd forgotten how to be just *us*. At first we clung to each other. Our grief was so sharp that everyone and everything else faded from view; she and I were the only ones who understood the other's pain. But before long, the cracks started to show and we began to disintegrate.'

He told me how they'd struggled through bereavement counselling, which had only led to tension between them, each of them sinking under the weight of their own despair, battling with feelings of guilt and uselessness until one day Kate had seen Driftwood Lodge for sale. A fresh start, a chance to reconnect and heal. As Theo didn't have any better ideas, he'd agreed. He'd more or less abandoned his business as a lighting consultant but he could start it up again anywhere. And so they'd moved on.

'Or should I say Kate moved on.' He hung his head miserably. 'To a degree, at least. She made Driftwood Lodge our home, bought some ducks and chickens, came up with the idea for the holiday cottages. But I couldn't move on. I couldn't think straight, let alone work. I couldn't bear the fact that some of Ivy's things, like her cot, were sitting redundant in that little room under the eaves. In the end, Kate gave up on me. I don't blame her; I gave up on myself. Devon was supposed to be our second chance at happiness and I threw it away. And I miss her, I miss Ivy, I miss our family, I miss the life we had.'

My heart ached for the two of them. How cruel fate can

be. Instead of bringing up their daughter, and surrounding her with love, Kate and Theo had been plagued by sadness and loss.

Theo shivered. I was growing cold too, sitting on this draughty bench facing a sharp breeze blowing in with the tide. The sound of laughter made me look round at a group of people gathered outside a pub, called The Sea Urchin.

'Wait here a minute.'

I dashed off to the pub and came back with two takeaway coffees and some extra sugar packets for Theo. I tipped the sugar in and gave it a stir before handing it to him. He mumbled his thanks but his eyes were fixed on some faraway place, a memory perhaps of a happier time.

When Theo had spoken about Kate's ultimatum, I'd been indignant on his behalf, but now I understood a little better. I had to do something. I *could* do something.

'Let me help you,' I said.

He looked down at his coffee as if surprised to find it there and took a tentative sip. 'You are helping. And so is Archie. Goodness knows what state I'd be in if you two hadn't turned up when you did.'

'I can do more,' I said with a burst of energy. I turned to him, my eyes shining. 'Let's do it. Let's take on Kate's ultimatum. We can get the holiday cottage business up and running properly like she wants. It's doable.'

My mind was racing. I could take an extended break from acting and by the time Kate came back, all the brouhaha about my *Victory Road* blunder would have disappeared and I could go back to London and pick up where I'd left off. Onwards and upwards.

'Is it?' Theo eyed me doubtfully.

'Yes!' I cried. 'We'll finish the cottages off just as Kate would have done with beautiful interiors and all the little luxuries that make a holiday special. Proper outside space, fluffy towels, beach equipment to borrow, fresh eggs, home-made cakes . . . I can see it all now!'

'All I can see is a lot of work.' Theo blinked at me.

'Exactly! This is the perfect way to win her back!' I got to my feet and began pacing along past the lobster pots and back again. 'Show her you want to make a go of life. She will be so proud of you.'

'I was a failure at being a dad and a husband.' He swallowed a mouthful of coffee, and tears sprang to his eyes. 'I want to win her back but I don't think I deserve her. All I've done recently is let people down.'

'Been there, got the T-shirt.' I thought of the trail of disaster I'd left in my wake in London. I stood up and held out a hand to him. 'But tomorrow is a new day. Let's go home and make a plan.'

It may have been my imagination but there was a new lightness to Theo's step on the way back. And the thought that I might have put it there made me feel very happy indeed.

Back at Driftwood Lodge, the Bird family were having a whale of a time. After a hunt for freshly laid eggs around the garden and courtyard, the two oldest children had begged to be allowed one last walk to the beach before bedtime. As soon as they'd gone, we'd sneaked in to have showers and while I was drying my hair, Theo checked his emails and found one from Archie. He had transferred the money for the car into Theo's account and was sending a tow truck to collect it next week.

Theo had money again, for the moment at least. We drove to the nearest cashpoint, withdrew as much as we could and took it straight round to Vic, the builder. As luck would have it, Vic had got some of his mates round for a poker night, one of whom was Geoff the plumber who'd half completed the cottages' bathrooms. The men were wary of restarting work at Driftwood Lodge, but after Theo paid them what they were owed and I explained that he hadn't been too well after Kate left suddenly, they promised to be back at work on Tuesday morning.

We celebrated our success with fish and chips on the way home and ate them on our bench by the lobster pots straight from the paper. The batter was crispy and light, the fish melted in my mouth and the chips were cooked to perfection. Theo hoovered his up and then finished mine, declaring it to be the best meal he'd had in weeks. I was glad to see him eating properly. Hopefully his appetite for life wouldn't be too far behind.

The Birds were already settled in for the night when we got back to Penguin's Pad. There was scarcely any light pollution in Brightside Cove and of course no electricity at all in our cottage, but the moon was full and with a couple of candles and a camping lantern each, there was plenty of light in our makeshift sleeping quarters – Theo in one bedroom and me next door. The air was chilly, though, and I was glad of the extra-thick bedding that Archie had bought. After a trip to the outside loo tucked away next to one of the garages, I settled into my airbed with a book. I'd scarcely got to the bottom of the page when my eyes began to droop. I tucked my bookmark into the pages and put it down, straining to hear any noises from next door.

'How's your luxury mattress?' I called softly to Theo.

He didn't reply. I rolled off my airbed and tiptoed towards his room, worried in case he was feeling low again. There were no internal doors up here and so it was easy to spy on him. To my relief, he was fast asleep, his breathing slow, his black curls glinting in the pale moonlight, dark lashes brushing his cheeks and the ghost of a smile playing at his lips. In his hands, relaxed in sleep, was his wedding photograph, and on top of that, a picture of Ivy from his wallet.

I crept away and back to my own bed, a steely core of determination strengthening my resolve to do my best for him and Kate. I'd almost ruined their wedding five years ago and now fate had presented me with the chance to redeem myself. I might have cocked up my own life, but I was determined to try to salvage theirs.

Chapter 8

On Monday morning I was up with the larks, or should I say seagulls. They'd woken me up with their squawking and I'd unearthed some buckets and spades and a tatty-looking bodyboard from a shed for the two oldest Bird children and watched as they'd run off to persuade their parents to take them surfing.

As soon as they'd gone, I snuck into the house and made myself some toast, took another quick shower and just made it out in time before Mary came back with a wet and howling baby after an incident involving a bucket of cold sea water and a very repentant big sister.

Theo still hadn't surfaced so I hunted down the code to the WiFi and decided to finally make contact with the outside world. Luckily the internet signal reached across to the cottages from the main house so I took a coffee up to my bedroom and logged on. I ignored all the notifications from Facebook and Twitter, cast only a cursory eye over the new emails including one from Sebastian and another from that dreadful gossip-mongering journalist Ross Whittaker requesting a follow-up chat, and began a WhatsApp message to Trudy instead.

Have found the perfect place to lie low for a while: indoor camping, all meals al fresco, and salt scrub facials for free! Xx

She replied in a nano-second:

> **WHERE are you??? My Harrods customers would go WILD for this. Also, get you! There's a video of you tipping ice on Cecily on YouTube and it's had over 20,000 hits already. You're famous! Xoxo**

My pulse raced and I almost went online to see what she was talking about. But I resisted. Being able to step away from my real life for a while was one of the most precious things about being in Brightside Cove; the longer I could stay off social media, the better. Instead, I replied that I couldn't say quite yet where I was, but promised that she'd be the first to know when I could. Trudy's wealthy clientele could be very useful to Theo and Kate when they were properly ready to start taking bookings.

Next I began browsing interior design websites for ideas, and a couple of hours later I'd drawn up a simple scheme for furniture and soft furnishings which would work in all three of the cottages and I couldn't wait to see what Theo thought of it. Someone had already bought paint; there were tins of it stacked up next door – a soft chalky white, which was exactly the same colour as the crest of a wave. Penguin's Pad had been mostly decorated but the other two cottages hadn't been touched. And as painting was something even I felt qualified to tackle, I planned to spend all afternoon sloshing emulsion about in Kittiwake's Cabin.

At noon I heard movements coming from Theo's room so I nipped downstairs to make some fresh coffee.

'Fine,' said Theo, a bit bleary-eyed, when I'd run through my ideas and showed him one or two online retailers who fitted into the category of cheap but gorgeous. 'Whatever you think's best.'

'Haven't you got anything to add?' I said, slightly disappointed by his lack of interest in my endeavours.

He passed me his credit card. 'Nope. Just go ahead. See if they can deliver asap.'

'What about the lighting, Theo? I read that lighting can make all the difference to a design.' I eyed him steadily. 'Or is that wrong?'

He looked at me for a long moment, and I could see his brain clicking into life. I'd guessed he wouldn't be able to let that comment slide. Eventually he conceded defeat and smiled.

'A good lighting scheme can do many things, from highlighting key features to giving the illusion of more space – or less – and can be used to alter the mood of a room too.'

'I don't want a good lighting scheme; I want a brilliant one.' I handed him a notepad and pencil. 'And more to the point, so would Kate.'

'You're right,' he said with a lopsided grin. 'She would.'

Five minutes later I found him sketching in the pad, it looked like a series of tiny spotlights hidden along the beams that ran the length of the downstairs in Penguin's Pad.

I pressed a kiss to his cheek.

'What was that for?' he said, alarmed.

'This time yesterday you'd given up hope, now look at you.'

He didn't reply but as I walked away he was humming cheerily to himself. Busy hands and a happy heart, that was what my old woodwork teacher used to say. Theo might not have a happy heart yet, but we were working on it and mine was beginning to sing a happier tune too. Being banished from London had turned out to be much less arduous than I'd thought.

'Ketchup with that?' I said, the following morning, holding the bottle over Vic's bacon roll.

'Please.' He beamed as he added an extra sugar to his tea and slurped at it. 'This is more like it.'

True to their word, the builders, Vic and his apprentice,

76

Hayden, and Geoff the plumber had turned up bright and early to work on the cottages. I was still in my pyjamas and dressing gown, braving the chilly morning sun with a strong coffee and Theo was laying more bacon neatly in lines on the barbecue.

After a hearty breakfast and mugs of strong tea, the men walked around the project making a list of the most pressing jobs and were soon unloading generators, tools and materials from their vans while I stacked dirty crockery, trying to pluck up the courage for a cold-water wash in the outside facilities.

'Is that your cooker?' said a small voice.

I looked around to see little Darcy peering at me over the wall that divided the back of the cottages from the rest of the garden. She pointed to the barbecue.

'It is.' I smiled. 'Cooking outside is a lot more fun than in a kitchen.'

She was dressed like me in pyjamas and there were creases in her left cheek from sleep. She eyed up the last piece of bacon on the griddle. 'You're lucky. We've only got Shredded Wheat for our breakfast.'

'Hello,' said Theo gruffly, appearing from inside Kittiwake's Cabin. 'What's that about lucky?'

'Darcy's envious of our cooking arrangements,' I said lightly, hoping his less than welcoming frown didn't reduce her to tears. 'And our bacon.'

'Is she?' he said, raising an amused eyebrow. 'Let's see what we can do about that.'

Theo added yet more rashers to the barbecue and I left them chatting about the things she'd found in the rock pools yesterday and went to get dressed. He'd be fine, I thought fondly, listening to him chuckle as Darcy explained the difference between a girl crab and a boy crab. He just needed to come out of his shell . . .

I threw on my jeans and a soft linen shirt and padded back downstairs. The noise from the workmen had well and truly broken the peace and Theo and Darcy were having to shout to each other over the racket coming from Beaver's Barn.

'We're going to an island today,' Darcy announced solemnly. 'Iceberg Island. Except Thomas can't swim. And Daddy says sometimes you have to swim across if the sea is too deep.'

'Burgh Island, darling,' said a voice with a laugh. 'And no one will have to swim, I promise.'

I turned to see Mary hovering at the gate. She was still in her dressing gown, her fair hair piled up haphazardly.

'Mummy, look!' Darcy held up her bacon roll gleefully.

Mary came through the gate into the cottage garden and kissed her daughter. 'There you are! Your cereal is going soggy.'

'Tea?' I said, holding up a clean mug. 'We're breakfasting outside today as it's sunny.'

'No, no—' Mary tried to protest but then gave in with a sigh. 'Actually, yes please, I haven't had one yet and we've been up with Thomas for hours.'

'Teething?' Theo busied himself scraping incinerated bacon off the barbecue and studiously avoided her eye.

'Yep,' said Mary, taking a mug from me gratefully.

'Poor thing.' I dropped into the camping chair beside her. 'Can you do anything for him?'

'There are some bananas in the fruit bowl,' Theo said gruffly, 'freeze one, it'll soothe his gums.'

'Good idea, thank you,' said Mary.

I shot Theo a look of admiration. He was full of surprises; I bet he'd been a brilliant dad. I felt a pang of sadness well up. Poor Theo. Poor Kate.

'Bye,' shouted Darcy, handing her mother the last tiny piece of her breakfast. 'I'm going to find the ducks.'

'They're hiding this morning,' said Theo. 'I don't think you'll find them.'

Her face fell momentarily, but he held his hand out to her. 'But you're in luck, because I know all their secret places.'

Mary and I exchanged warm smiles at the sight of them disappearing off together on their quest.

'Your husband is a darling,' said Mary, through the steam rising from her mug. 'So good with the children.'

All at once I knew where this was going. I shifted uncomfortably in my chair. Sure enough, Mary turned to me.

'Are you two planning a family?' She paled instantly at the look of horror on my face. 'Oh gosh, I'm sorry! I shouldn't have said anything. I never learn. Please ignore me.'

'No, it's fine,' I said, arranging my features in a wistful gaze. 'It just hasn't happened yet for us.'

Vic popped his head out of Beaver's Barn with two empty mugs. Never had I been so glad of an interruption. 'Any chance of a top-up, Nina?'

'Of course!' I sprang to my feet and picked up the teapot to see if there was enough in it.

Vic leaned on the doorframe and nodded a greeting at Mary.

'Theo's like a different man since you arrived. You've cheered him up no end,' he said to me, folding his arms. 'I don't think he got out of bed at all for the first week after his wife left him.'

Bugger. I felt my mouth dry up.

Mary frowned 'His wife?'

'Kate.' Vic nodded. 'Lovely girl.'

'I'm so confused.' Mary gave a gentle laugh but she was staring at me questioningly. For the longest second I couldn't think of a single thing to say. My hands shook as I handed Vic two full mugs of hot tea and he disappeared back inside, oblivious to the hot water he'd just landed me in.

I licked my lips. 'It's complicated.'

'Oh, of course.' She got to her feet and set her empty mug down on the table. 'None of my business.'

I couldn't bear to see the disappointment on her face. She thought badly of me and I felt awful. Theo and I were just trying to make the best of a bad situation; I couldn't afford to have a setback now.

'Mary, I'm sorry we misled you.' I grabbed her arm. 'Come and have a look inside Penguin's Pad and I'll explain everything. Please. Besides, I'd like your opinion on kitting it out, from a guest's perspective.'

Mary bit the inside of her cheek and considered for a moment. Her face broke into a tiny smile. 'All right then. And I don't suppose you've got any more bacon?'

'We have,' I said with a sigh of relief. 'In fact, we've got enough for everyone.'

'I'll go and give Joe a shout.' Mary's lips twitched. 'Don't tell Darcy but we both detest Shredded Wheat.'

And just like that, my role as Theo's wife ended. So that was the third acting job I'd lost in less than seventy-two hours. Perhaps someone was trying to tell me something?

By Friday the littlest of the three cottages, Kittiwake's Cabin, had hot water and an almost finished bathroom. All the kitchen appliances for the three properties had arrived the previous day on one big lorry, which had sent the hens into a flap as it attempted a three-point turn in the courtyard. And now all three of the cottages had fridges, cookers and dishwashers.

I'd never classed myself as much of a cook, but I christened the new oven in Penguin's Pad by making a batch of brownies, which we shared with our guests and the man who came to collect Theo's classic car for Archie. Mary had asked for the recipe and suggested that I make cakes every week for our guests. Then she'd remembered I was only Theo's temporary wife and wouldn't be here to bake every week and we'd had a good laugh about it.

She and Joe had been brilliant about our unusual circumstances in the end and had invited us over for dinner on Wednesday night and insisted that we come and go as we pleased to use the proper shower in the house.

Vic and Hayden were making good headway with the joinery in Kittiwake's Cabin too. The air outside the cottages was thick with sawdust, and the smell of freshly sawn wood mingled with the salty tang of the sea. My senses had been on full alert since arriving in Devon: the colours seemed brighter, everything smelled potent and full of life. And waking to the distant tinkling of the sailing boats, the call of the sea birds and the gentle roar of the waves made my heart sing every morning.

Saturday soon came around and the Bird family reluctantly began gathering their belongings. By lunchtime they were nearly ready to leave. Theo and I went out to see them off. The sun hadn't made an appearance yet today and the soft grey sky seemed to match the children's moods as they dragged their bags despondently from the house to the car. Joe was alternately tapping his watch and checking the latest traffic news to plan their return route and Mary was dashing around, packing enough food and activities for the trip to prevent boredom. Theo offered to hold the baby while the other two children got themselves comfortable in the back and when he thought no one was looking he pressed his cheek to the top of Thomas's downy head and murmured his goodbyes. I thought my heart might break.

Finally, everything was in the car, including Thomas in his car seat and a bucket of Darcy and Leo's seashore treasure, which had begun to pong and had been consigned to the boot.

'Goodbye, Nina,' said Mary, flicking a tear from her eye. 'Thank you for such a lovely family holiday.'

'Thank *you*,' I said, giving her a hug while the men shook hands formally. 'For not minding about the whole Nina/ Kate issue and for being such good sports about the cottage not being ready.'

'And dear Theo,' Mary said, taking hold of his hands.

Theo let out a small breath and I could see how much he

wanted to avoid an emotional conversation. I willed him not to bolt like he had at the mention of Ivy's cot.

But all she said was, 'You have a lovely home at Brightside Cove; thank you so much for sharing it with us.'

'You're welcome,' said Theo graciously.

And then Joe and Mary climbed in and Joe started the engine. As he turned the car round to face the driveway, Mary wound down her window and smiled. 'And I'll be sure to leave a glowing review so you get lots more bookings.'

'Thank you!' I called, pretending to wipe my brow. 'But there won't be any more bookings until the cottages are ready.'

'Oh hell,' muttered Theo through gritted teeth as the Birds disappeared down the lane.

'You have checked that there are no other bookings, haven't you?' I said.

I'd been so busy all week that I hadn't even spared a thought to the possibility of more guests. What if the Birds were simply the first of many? What if today was change-over day and another family was right now heading our way? Or worse, three families – one for each of the cottages!

'Not exactly,' said Theo, scuffing his toe in the gravel.

'Theo!' I exclaimed.

'As soon as I saw the Birds' booking, I panicked and didn't look at anything else on the calendar . . .' His voice faded away sheepishly. 'Sorry. Shall we go and check Kate's emails?'

I rolled my eyes at him. 'No, I'm taking the rest of the day off. You can manage that job on your own.'

I wished him luck, reminded him that the furniture delivery was due any minute, and I set off to visit the little gift shop I'd seen in the village by The Sea Urchin pub at the edge of the harbour. Other than a couple of early-morning walks along the beach and our two visits to the lobster-pot bench as I now referred to it, I'd barely strayed from

Driftwood Lodge all week and now that the Bird family had gone and I had nothing pressing to attend to, I was looking forward to having a little explore.

I took the long way across the beach and along the harbour. I walked as far as a little supermarket called Jethro's General Store, stopped to read the menu outside The Sea Urchin and finally arrived at the Mermaid Gift and Gallery. The shop was set at the end of a row of whitewashed cottages right next to the pub. It had two large planters filled with frothy grasses flanking the doors. The door itself was painted a deep sea green and the wide shop window was brimming with the types of objects that I found impossible to resist.

I pushed open the door and stepped inside. The interior didn't disappoint; it was a real treasure trove. Pretty objects covered every surface including the ceiling: driftwood carvings, seascapes in every shade of blue and green, shell sculptures, pottery ships in bottles, pretty glass storm lanterns and candles in every shape, size and aroma.

I stood at the threshold, mesmerized.

'Hey, beauty!' said a creamy Devonshire voice from the counter.

She was round-cheeked, with shoulder-length blonde hair, dip-dyed pink at the ends. A blue and white striped T-shirt strained over her plump arms and buxom chest and one strap of her faded dungarees had slipped off her shoulder.

'Hi there,' I replied.

Before I knew what she was doing, she'd grabbed her phone and pointed it at me. 'Smile.'

'Oh!' I blinked as the flash went off and stumbled into a rack of hand-painted pebbles. 'I think I've gone blind.'

The girl giggled. 'Sorry, I should have warned you.'

'Why did you take my picture?'

'Hold on. Two ticks.' She poked out her tongue in

83

concentration as her thumbs tapped at the touchscreen. She finally looked up. 'Sending it to my brother. He's had no luck with internet dating so I'm on a mission to find him a match myself, see?'

'By showing him pictures of your customers?'

'Only the pretty ones.' Her phone beeped and she winked a sapphire-blue eye at me. 'A reply from my bro. That was quick.'

'Actually,' I said, a bit taken aback, 'I came in for a postcard, not a partner. So please tell him to ignore my picture.'

She screwed up her face and dumped her phone down. 'Just as well, he says no. No offence. Are you staying nearby? What's your name?'

Good grief, who'd trained this girl for customer service – the KGB?

'Nina,' I blurted, without thinking. 'And I'm staying at Driftwood Lodge.'

'Really?' She came out from behind the counter and folded her arms. 'Has his wife left him? Apparently Molly Asher knows, because she was friendly with his wife, but she's not telling. I feel sorry for him; he always looks so sad. I'm Eliza, by the way.'

'Pleased to meet you,' I said, edging towards the rotating postcard display unit.

'That's funny you being called Nina,' she said, chuckling. 'I was reading on Facebook this morning something about an actress called Nina who . . . Hold on.' She narrowed her eyes suddenly and shoved her face closer to mine.

Damn. I was rubbish at this lying-low thing.

'Your shop is lovely,' I said swiftly, selecting a couple of postcards and marching to the counter. 'I'll take these please.'

Eliza scurried behind the counter and grinned.

'I know who you are,' she said. 'Nina Penhaligon, the missing actress. I'd never heard of you before but everyone's looking for you. Didn't you do the ice bucket challenge on Cecily Carmichael? And blab a confidential storyline?'

'Shush.' I glanced automatically over my shoulder.

'So it is you!' Her eyes lit up. 'Is there a reward for turning you in?'

'No!' I yelped. At least I hoped there wasn't. 'And I don't need *turning in*; I'm not a criminal, I just needed to get away for a while.'

Eliza's face softened sympathetically. 'Oh, beauty, I get it. Hey, I know what you need.'

To be left to shop in peace? I eyed the door, already regretting my visit.

She shoved a leaflet in my hand. 'To be a mermaid for a day. You dress up, get a photo shoot on the rocks or in the water, depending on the weather. And we focus on body positivity and stuff like that. Ooh, can I take a picture of you in one of my mermaid tails? It would really help launch my business. They're not here yet but—'

'Actually, Eliza,' I lowered my voice, 'I'm keeping my stay here low key. So, if you don't mind?'

'Oh, but you'll love this!'

I looked down at the leaflet, which had clearly been cobbled together on a home computer.

Brightside Cove Mermaid School – Be a mermaid for a day!

'I love mermaids. So much. I've got a website,' she said, 'and I'm getting authentic mermaid tails from the USA.'

'*Authentic?*'

She nodded.

'Let me show you a picture of them on the American website,' she demanded.

'No signal,' I said, holding up my phone.

'Come behind the counter by me and you can log on to the pub's WiFi for free.' She demonstrated by holding her phone up to the wall between the shop and the pub and beckoned me behind the counter. 'And mind the kittens.'

I gave her a puzzled look; mermaids and kittens? Was she right in the head? But sure enough, there was a basket on the floor with four tiny sleeping kittens in it.

'Oh, cute!' I bent down to stroke them. 'May I?'

'Sure,' said Eliza. 'You can even take one as your fee for posing as a mermaid for my website. Give me your phone; I'll log in for you.'

'Thanks. But no thanks.' I'd only brought it out with me so that I could take some photos. I was still avoiding contact with the outside world as far as possible.

I took a picture of the kittens and laid my phone down before picking up the biggest one with long black fluffy fur. It mewed crossly at me.

'Hello, grumpy. You are just like Theo.' I laughed, pressing a kiss to its little head.

Driftwood Lodge had chickens and ducks, but no cat. And a cat would give Theo something to care about round the house other than himself. Maybe giving one a home might not be such a bad idea.

'So he is depressed, then. Here you go, WiFi connected. And I've texted your number to my phone so I can ring you about—'

'Oh no!' I whirled round to grab it out of her hand but before I could even wrestle it from her grasp it beeped with a text. She read the screen and sucked in air before handing it to me.

'Poor man.'

It was from Theo.

Managed to get in touch with Kate. There's good news. And there's bad news. Please come back.

A second text followed immediately from Becky Burton, my best friend on the cast of *Victory Road*.

Jesus, Nina, where are you?? Everyone is going ape-shit. CALL ME!

Oh God. My fingers fumbled as I grappled to turn off my phone. Should I call? Or should I follow Sebastian's instructions and talk to no one? Staying silent seemed a bit cowardly. But I felt safe and cocooned from the mess I'd left behind me here. If I spoke to Becky, I'd have to face the world again. Whereas if I simply put my phone away and didn't look at it again, it would be problem solved . . . and I could sort out Theo's bad news. I blew out a calming breath. I'd do that.

I shoved my phone in my pocket.

'I'll get back to you about the kitten,' I said, putting the ball of fluff back in the box.

'Oh good,' she said, stuffing the postcards into my jacket pocket. 'And don't worry; I'll have another bash at my brother for you. He might reconsider once he knows that you're famous.'

'We can but hope,' I said drily. I halted at the door. 'No really, thanks for the confidence boost, but please don't mention I'm here to anyone. Mum's the word, okay?'

'Okay.' She saluted her compliance.

'Phew.' I grinned. 'Thank you.'

'Bye, Nina, bye!' Eliza yelled and waved as I set off on the coast path back towards Driftwood Lodge. 'And remember: always be yourself, unless you can be a mermaid, then always be a mermaid!'

That had to be the most surreal shopping experience of my life, I thought and I laughed to myself all the way home.

Chapter 9

Brightside Holidays was expecting another guest.

Just one. Someone called B. Nutley. Arriving on Monday. Which gave us approximately forty-eight hours to finish off one cottage completely. According to Theo this was bad news. I didn't know what he was moaning about. Beaver's Barn could be ready by then; it would be a piece of cake.

'It's just so vague,' he'd complained as we stuffed the Birds' bedlinen into the washing machine. 'We know nothing about this person.'

'I remember this about you.' I grinned, handing him the fabric softener. 'Archie used to say you were a bit OCD, which is what made you such a good engineer. He said you needed to gather every piece of information on a subject before you'd even contemplate starting work.'

'True,' said Theo, bending down so that the detergent dispenser was at eye level. He poured the liquid in precisely up to the line on the display. 'You can't fight with the facts. Case in point,' he said, twisting the dial and switching on the machine. 'That load weighs eight kilograms and therefore requires fifty-six millilitres of detergent.'

'Phew,' I said, 'imagine if you'd calculated that wrongly.'

'Details matter in business,' he insisted. 'The only thing Kate's email reveals . . .' his eyes softened at the mere mention of her name, '. . . about this Nutley person is that they live in Windsor and plan to attend a local art festival. Apparently they want to stay close by but not too close.'

I'd spotted a poster in Eliza's shop about a festival. It started tomorrow and completely took over the little seaside town of Shapford, where the light was meant to be unique and it was therefore a mecca for artists.

'So? He or she is probably an artist. What else do you need to know?' I picked up the laundry basket full of freshly washed towels and handed it to him, then found some pegs and set off outside to the field where Theo had strung a lengthy washing line. 'It's a self-catering holiday, as long as they pay up and adhere to your rules, nothing else matters, does it? Get pegging.'

'I've emailed him or her directions and our bank details. Perhaps the response will shed some light on the matter,' he grumbled.

The sky had cleared and was back to being bright blue and breezy. The washing would dry in no time, which was just as well as we had several more loads to get through and I wanted to crack on with painting Beaver's Barn if we were to get rid of the smell of wet emulsion by Monday morning.

The Nutley booking had only been half of what Theo considered bad news. The other half was that evidently before leaving, Kate had contacted Coastal Cottages, an internet bookings agency for upmarket self-catering properties in the south-west. She had arranged for a representative to come and vet Brightside Holidays next Friday with a view to being featured on their website. I offered to pretend to be Kate for the meeting, but Theo was reluctant.

'I want Kate here for that appointment,' he said with a sparkle in his eye as he looped a large bath towel over the washing line. 'The real Kate. Coastal Cottages is the crème de la crème of holiday rentals. She'll be delighted if Brightside Holidays secures a listing on there.'

So we agreed that he would contact them on Monday

during office hours and postpone the appointment. Fine by me; our immediate goal was to complete the cottages and get Brightside Holidays properly open for business. Then Kate would come back to Devon, retract her threat of ending their marriage and the two of them would live happily ever after. Meanwhile, I would go back to London and pick up where I left off.

Back to my dream of becoming an Oscar-winning actress. I tilted my face to the sky, feeling the sun on my skin and the clean air in my lungs and I felt a niggle of disquiet. If I really did want to be a famous actress, then why did I feel so happy hanging laundry in a Devonshire field?

'Tell me again what the good news part of Kate's email was,' I said later on when we went back inside to make ourselves a sandwich.

Theo popped the caps off two beers and handed me one and tried desperately to keep the grin off his face.

'She apologized for forgetting to tell me about the Birds and she was delighted that I managed to accommodate them. She said . . . some nice things.' He slurped his beer and looked down at his feet shyly. 'I think I've earned lots of brownie points.'

'Did she say anything about me?' I said, sitting opposite him at the kitchen table and sliding the plates on to the table.

'Um.' He bit into his sandwich. 'I didn't mention you.'

I felt a tweak of concern that she might somehow find out and be annoyed with him for keeping secrets but quickly brushed it away. Theo didn't seem to have made any friends here and Eliza obviously didn't know where Kate was so it seemed unlikely that that would happen.

'To you and Kate,' I said, clinking my beer bottle against his.

'To me and Kate,' he echoed. 'And to you for helping.'

'You're welcome. Do you think we can forget about that kiss at your wedding now?'

'What kiss?' He raised his dark eyebrows innocently.

We both drank to that.

With the help of Vic and his team, Theo and I finished Beaver's Barn by the skin of our teeth. It was a triumph and just how I'd envisaged it: warm and welcoming but at the same time contemporary and fresh in tones of chalky white, soft sea-glass green and natural oak. I'd cleaned and hoovered every inch of the cottage and Theo had ironed the sparkling new bedlinen so thoroughly that the creases would probably never drop out. We'd made up both bedrooms, to give our guest a choice, and left a pile of soft fluffy towels and a selection of toiletries from the Mermaid Gift and Gallery in the bathroom. There was a lovely seascape above the tiny log burner and a row of pretty green and white mugs hung from hooks above the kitchen worktop. I could happily move in there myself, I thought, recalling the cramped little flat I shared with Trudy.

Theo peered into the cottage one last time and whistled. 'Vic and his crew have worked wonders. Hard to imagine that this was a building site a week ago.'

'And by the end of this week, the others will be habitable too,' I said, swishing the mop from left to right and backing my way out of the kitchen. 'There. Done.'

Vic wandered over and handed Theo an envelope. 'Here's my invoice. Cash most appreciated.'

After securing a promise from Theo not to keep him waiting for his money this time, Vic and his apprentice left for the day.

'Just in time,' said Theo, as the builder's van trundled away in the distance. 'The email said they'd be here any moment now.'

We set off back to the house to put the kettle on in

readiness for the arrival of our guest. We didn't have to wait long; I hadn't even had the chance to drink my tea before the purr of an engine and a crunch of gravel had us heading to the door.

A sleek blue Mercedes came gracefully to a halt beside Theo's van and we walked out to greet our latest arrival. Definitely an artist: the legs of an easel were sticking out of the boot, which had been secured with a stretchy luggage strap.

'It's an AMG,' murmured Theo, eyeing up the badge on the car. 'Expensive motor.'

'*OMG* more like,' I said, squinting to see through the blacked-out windows. I'd been to a red-carpet do last month with Sebastian and I'd had a driver to collect me in a car like this. I half-expected a celebrity to climb out.

'Businessman, at a guess,' said Theo.

'Or woman,' I countered.

The driver's window slid down with a luxurious buzz.

'Hi there!' I bent down so I could peer into the car.

A buxom woman in her fifties with poppy-red bobbed hair and matching lipstick lifted her sunglasses to the top of her head and boomed, 'Heavens to Betsy! How gorgeous are you and your little house!'

'Kind of you to say,' said Theo, failing to hide his surprise with an open jaw and wide eyes.

She started to open the car door and then hesitated. 'You don't have dogs, do you?' She grimaced. 'I don't really do dogs.'

'No,' I confirmed, 'although we might be getting a kitten.'

'Might we?' Theo gave me a look of surprise.

'Part of your emotional therapy,' I said out of the side of my mouth while the woman clambered out ungracefully.

'We guessed you might be an artist,' I said, nudging Theo to close his mouth and remember his manners.

'An artist!' She pressed a hand to her quivering cleavage

as if I'd just paid her an enormous compliment. 'I paint, therefore I am!'

There was no questioning that; she had paint ingrained under every fingernail and her neon-green Crocs were speckled with a rainbow of colours too.

'Welcome to your Brightside holiday.' Theo stepped forward, ready to shake her hand. I mentally cheered; his hospitality skills had improved a hundredfold since last week.

'Thank you!' She ignored his outstretched hand and threw her arms around him, inhaling so deeply that her bosom reached perilously close to Theo's chin. She then retrieved a fold of banknotes from her bra and handed them to me. They were warm.

'This air, the light!' she cried, exhaling as she tossed her purple pashmina over her shoulder. 'I can tell already this is going to be perfect. Over here, are we?'

She pointed at the row of cottages and without waiting for a reply, stomped off towards them. I was about to set off after her to show her the facilities when she twirled round and flapped a hand at Theo. 'Bring my easel, would you?'

'She seems fun,' I whispered with a giggle.

'What did her last slave die of?' Theo chuntered, battling to pull the huge wooden easel wedged between a crate of red wine and a box of paints from the boot of her car.

'He was crushed,' I murmured, 'under the weight of her personality.'

Afternoon tea, it transpired, was something that Kate had promised to all guests. The Birds might have arrived too late, but I didn't want to disappoint our artist. Ten minutes after she arrived, I sent Theo over with a pot of tea, a plate of homemade scones, jam and clotted cream. And strict instructions to find out B. Nutley's first name.

He quickly returned none the wiser.

'She was in the loo,' he said. 'I didn't feel I could ask.'

93

'Fair enough,' I said, helping myself to a scone and piling it with jam. 'I'll ask her later.'

We'd just demolished the rest of the batch when we heard raised voices outside.

'What on earth?' muttered Theo, dashing for the door.

The Mercedes had been joined in the courtyard by a mud-splattered Land Rover. The heated voices – and a very insistent yap – were coming from the rear of Beaver's Barn.

Theo and I dashed over. A middle-aged man in camouflage trousers, a beige gilet covered in pockets and a khaki hat resembling an upturned plant pot was scrambling around the newly laid terrace trying to catch a small excited dog. Meanwhile, our lady guest had flung one leg over the wall, presumably to escape the dog's advances, and appeared to be stuck.

'I could have been naked!' she said indignantly, pointing at the man.

'Thank heavens for small mercies,' muttered Theo, furrowing his eyebrows as he helped her unstraddle the stone wall.

'Can I help you?' I turned to the man, who by now had the little dog under his arm. 'Are you lost?'

'I'm Bruce Nutley,' he said, and patted the dog's head. 'And this is Tiger. She's not dangerous. Her name is ironic.'

'Bruce?' I looked from him to Theo. 'Nutley?'

He nodded. 'You were expecting me . . . Here's the confirmation email.' He pulled a folded sheet of paper from one of his many pockets.

'Hello, Bruce,' I said with a gulp. I extended a hand but the dog's head lunged at me so I retreated. 'I'm Ni—'

'Kate,' said the woman from behind Theo, whom she was using as a shield from the dog. 'You're Kate Fletcher, we spoke on the phone when I enquired whether the cottage was available, remember, and you said it was free? I'm Penelope Jensen. But when I called to confirm my booking you didn't pick up. Hence me paying cash when I arrived.'

Theo gave a low moan and my heart sank. Just when everything was going so well . . .

'Double-booked, are we?' Bruce chuckled. 'Never mind, no need to make a fuss, I'll just take the cottage next door.'

'It's not ready,' said Theo.

'Neither is the other one,' I added.

'Ah. In that case,' said Bruce, looking Penelope up and down, 'maybe you and I could bunk up?'

Penelope's nostrils flared. 'What sort of a woman do you think I am?'

Bruce sneezed and put the dog down to take a handkerchief out of his pocket to blow his nose. Tiger instantly lunged at Penelope, who gave a yelp and leapt on to Theo's back piggy-back style.

The heavy sort, Theo mouthed to me with a wince.

Having obviously decided there was nothing worth barking at, Tiger came and sat at my feet and offered me her paw.

'She's quite safe,' said Bruce, trumpeting into his handkerchief. 'She doesn't have any teeth.'

I bent down to pet her and she licked my hands gently. Penelope slid slowly to the floor. Tiger trotted meekly over to her and leaned against her leg affectionately.

'You are quite a dear little thing, I suppose,' Penelope conceded.

Theo and I looked at each other; it was like *Groundhog Day* – yet more confusion over bookings.

'Penelope, Bruce, there has been a terrible misunderstanding . . .' began Theo heavily. He went on to explain that only one booking had been recorded but that Beaver's Barn did have two double rooms and although it was highly unorthodox, and he totally understood if they said no, would they consider sharing the cottage?

'And allow us to refund—'

'Half of your money,' I put in quickly before Theo gave away all the week's earnings. 'And dinner tonight is on us.'

'Deal,' said Bruce, grinning happily. 'Every little helps. Now let me get my easel out of the car.'

'Hold on a minute, this was meant to be a personal retreat for me, a chance to commune with nature—' Penelope interrupted herself with a gasp and her eyes lit up. 'Wait! Did you say easel? Are you an artist too?'

Chapter 10

They say love conquers all. In this case, a mutual love of art was able to overcome Penelope's resistance to sharing a cottage with Bruce and Tiger, and they were getting on like a house on fire. Mind you, it wasn't entirely plain sailing to begin with.

For one thing, Bruce was a vegan while Penelope wasn't keen on vegetables, which made our dinner menu a challenge. And they quickly found out the next morning when they set up their easels that they had quite a different approach to painting: Bruce laid out all his oil paints neatly and chose a quiet spot near the trees with the gentle strains of Classic FM in the background. In fact, dressed in his signature khaki and beige, we could neither see nor hear him. At the other end of the scale, when Penelope decamped to the centre of the field directly behind the cottages, everyone knew about it. Guns N' Roses blared out from a wireless speaker while she swirled bright slashes of turquoise, red and orange paint on anything that dared to stray into her vicinity, including a duck, two hens, Theo's trainers and, most unfortunately, Tiger.

But after Penelope apologized, bathed the dog and cooked Bruce a chilli non carne for supper, and uncorked a couple of bottles of her red wine, they seemed to reach an *entente très cordiale*, if the hoots of laughter we heard coming from Beaver's Barn were anything to go by.

After that we didn't see too much of them, they sped off together to the art festival in Penelope's car in the morning with Tiger poking her head out of the window and then wandered off either to the beach or to the village to paint. Theo and I both thought we'd got off rather lightly.

Most of the week passed uneventfully. The builders turned up on time and finished off Penguin's Pad and Kittiwake's Cabin so at least all three cottages were now habitable.

However, the grounds of Driftwood Lodge, which were huge, still left a lot to be desired. And in spite of Theo's insistence that holidaymakers liked the wild look, I decided to get a bit green-fingered and tidied up the courtyard, pulling up weeds and replanting some of the pots with geraniums to add a splash of Penelope-like colour to the place. I barely scratched the surface but at least the courtyard now created a better first impression when guests arrived. Theo concentrated his efforts on cleaning up thoroughly after the builders, who by Thursday had packed up and left for good, and he and I had celebrated with bottles of local Devon Dreamer beer by the old lifeboat house at the far end of the beach. It was absolute bliss.

On Friday morning I found Theo at the kitchen table on his laptop looking very industrious.

'I've been making a list of items we still need to complete the cottages,' he said, leaning back in his chair. 'Visitor information packs, leaflets, maps, and so on.'

'Don't forget we still have only one set of cutlery, crockery and pans and stuff,' I reminded him, taking a seat next to him. 'And they're in Beaver's Barn.'

Theo, sensibly, had been mindful of the money side of things when we'd ordered furnishings. Consequently, the kitchen cupboards in the other two cottages were empty.

'Oh yes.' He tapped at the keyboard to add items to the list. 'And I've been thinking about Kate's ultimatum. She only wanted me to get the cottages habitable and ready for the season, she wasn't expecting me to actually take new bookings. But what if I did? What if I started advertising, taking advantage of the summer trade? And Christmas! Imagine spending Christmas here!'

I could, I thought wistfully, and I bet it would be gorgeous.

A thought struck me. 'Didn't you spend Christmas here last year?'

'Yes, and the year before that, but it was awful.' A shadow passed over his face and I could have kicked myself for spoiling the mood.

'But this Christmas will be totally different,' I said, pouring us both a fresh coffee. '*You're* totally different.'

Theo smiled. 'You're right. I am. And with any luck, we could be fully booked by the time Kate gets home.'

My heart squeezed for him. Two weeks ago he'd told me that Driftwood Lodge had never felt like home. I wondered if he realized just how much he had achieved. Not just the cottages, but in his outlook on life.

'I like your thinking,' I said, chinking my mug against his.

His dark eyes met mine.

'I couldn't have done any of this without you, you know,' he said, as if reading my mind.

'Happy to help.'

I added a drop more milk to my mug to break eye contact. It was true, I'd enjoyed being here, but the doubts I'd had about running away from London were getting stronger.

'I'm going to collect the eggs while you finish your coffee.' He got to his feet. 'Then I'll cook us both some breakfast.'

I nodded, glad to have a moment to collect my thoughts. I loved it here but I could only hide away for so long. I owed it to my fellow cast members of *Victory Road* to give some sort of statement of apology and much as it grated on me, I should really apologize to Cecily too. Besides, could I really keep a low profile in this tiny seaside village until June and still expect to have a career to come back to? I just didn't know . . .

Theo was chuckling when he came back in. 'Looks like our guests are getting on well, I just heard Bruce calling her Pen-Pen and she replied with a Brucey-darling!'

'Those two are a match made in heaven.'

'Or Devon.' Theo elbowed me, pleased with his joke.

'Ha ha, very good.' I glanced at the time. 'And haven't they usually left for the art festival by now?'

He popped a clutch of speckled brown eggs into the wire basket on top of the fridge and took out the frying pan. 'Apparently they were inspired by a skin workshop yesterday, whatever that is, and they're going to do a joint creation as it's their last day. They're setting up on the grass at the back later to make the most of the sunshine. Fried okay?'

'Theo.' I took a deep breath, feeling my throat thicken at the thought of what I was about to say. 'About what we were just saying, I don't think—'

Theo held up a hand. 'Hold that thought; I just heard an engine.'

'Sure.' I let out a breath, relieved at the interruption. It could wait.

Theo turned to look through the open front door as a car crunched to a halt on the gravel.

'Oh hell,' he muttered. 'I completely forgot to cancel the appointment.'

'Theo!' I groaned, as a man climbed out of a car stickered on its sides and rear with the Coastal Cottages logo.

'Nigel Rees, and I am in LOVE with your house!'

'Thank you,' I said, showing him into the hall. There was no mistaking who he worked for: his polo shirt, briefcase and even his watch sported the logo too.

'Thatched roof, my favourite!' he exclaimed, pausing to look at the underside of the thatch. 'It is literally THE chocolate-box Devon property. My, oh my, Mrs Fletcher, you lucky lady!'

'Very lucky,' I agreed. By now I was so used to masquerading as Kate that I didn't bother correcting him and Theo seemed to have temporarily lost his voice. But Nigel didn't notice, he was so effusive in his praise of Driftwood Lodge that he totally dominated the conversation.

'Gorgeous spot, Brightside Cove,' he said, setting his slim briefcase on the kitchen table. 'A real find, as we say in the holiday business. If we did take you on, you'd be our first property in the area.'

'Really? That would be great, wouldn't it, Theo?' I said, trying to bring him into the conversation.

'I really wanted Kate to be here for this bit,' he replied glumly as Nigel wandered to the window and peered out at the garden. 'This was her dream.'

'Look on the bright side,' I whispered, 'this way, you'll have bookings coming in much sooner.'

'True, and I suppose Nigel need never know you're not really Kate.'

'Exactly,' I said firmly. 'So let's do Kate proud.'

'I like the fact that the outside space isn't too fussy,' Nigel continued enthusiastically. 'It feels very authentic.'

That's one word for it, I thought, catching sight of a discarded patio chair that Penelope had broken yesterday by standing on it.

'Beaches, bathrooms and barbecues,' he turned from the window and smiled. 'Those are the things our holidaymakers comment on the most. And a warm welcome, but I see you've already got that bit covered.'

I made a fresh pot of coffee and Theo hurriedly shoved the frying pan away while Nigel arranged his brochures on the table. I tipped the last few vegan cashew shortbread fingers I'd made specially for Bruce on a plate and set it in front of him.

'So what do you need from us today?' I asked, finally getting a word in while Nigel attempted to remove some shortbread from the roof of his mouth.

'A tour of the cottages and lots and lots of photographs,' he said after swallowing. 'But first a discussion about our services, which should take about an hour.'

I shot Theo a look of panic. The properties were clean and tidy, but not exactly photo-shoot ready and I had no idea what state Beaver's Barn was going to be in.

'Perhaps you could take photos on your next visit?' I suggested.

Nigel chuckled. 'There won't be a next visit. We represent two thousand properties; there aren't enough hours in the day to see them all twice.'

'We have guests in one of our properties,' said Theo, finding his tongue at last. 'But no worries, we can take some pictures for you and send them on.'

Nigel pulled the corners of his mouth down. 'All our properties have to be photographed and verified by us. Company policy.'

'In that case,' I said, scooping up various sets of keys and my bag, 'I'll leave you in my husband's capable hands and I'll see you in an hour.'

I had sixty minutes to do . . . whatever needed doing.

My first stop was Penguin's Pad; it looked lovely. The smell of plaster and paint still hung in the air, but when I thought back to how it had been that awful Sunday when the Birds had arrived I could scarcely believe the transformation. I walked around the living room, adjusting the picture frames, straightening the rugs and picking up a stray feather from one of the cushions, wondering what else I could add . . .

Flowers. That was it, fresh flowers would give it the lived-in touch I was after. Not the little wild ones I usually picked from the garden but big bold blooms which would look good in the photographs. There weren't any florists in Brightside Cove, but I was sure if I headed inland I'd come across one. But I'd have to hurry.

I ran from the cottage, jumped in Theo's van and drove

off as fast as I could. Most of the lanes around here were so narrow and the hedges so high that it took all of my concentration to squeeze past oncoming cars. And junctions were scary too, particularly when cars appeared from nowhere. I was approaching a T-junction now and would have to give way and hope nothing was coming as I couldn't see round the corner. I couldn't remember whether I had to turn left or right here. I headed towards the left of the junction. Or was it right? Yes, I remembered now, definitely right. I changed direction at the last second and aimed the car to the right.

BEEEEPPPP!

I yelped and automatically stamped on my brakes as the loudest horn in the world sounded behind me. I wound the window down, heart pounding.

I stuck my head out to see a man in a navy-blue van doing the same. His front bumper was a hair's breadth from the rear of Theo's van.

'You frightened me to death!' I yelled.

'You cut me up, changing your mind at the last second,' he shouted back in a thick West Country accent. I could just make out his stubbly chin, a big grin and a flash of hazel eyes under his baseball cap. He leaned a tanned, muscular arm out of the van. 'You should use your mirror more often.'

'You should use your brakes more often!' I retorted. My hands were trembling after our near miss, and the fact that he found it so amusing wasn't helping to calm my nerves.

Just then a brown and white dog bounded on to his lap and blocked its owner's face from view.

'Get down, Mabel,' he laughed, a spontaneous rich, warm giggle, which if I hadn't been so cross would have made me join in. He tugged her out of his line of vision. I still couldn't see him properly because of his cap but I recognized that dog. It was the friendly springer spaniel from the beach.

'Listen,' he said teasingly, 'why don't you apologize nicely and we can all move along?'

'*You* apologize. For beeping at me.'

He tipped his head back and laughed again but before he had a chance to reply the dog dived at his face.

'Urrggh. Mabel, don't lick my mouth; how many times?' He pulled a face and managed to push the dog back to her own seat.

I smirked as the man rubbed at his mouth in disgust.

'Okay then, *I'm so, so sorry*,' I said insincerely, pulling my head back into the car. 'See you around in Brightside Cove.'

'Wait,' he yelled as I put the van into gear. 'How do you know I'm from Brightside Cove?'

But his question blew away unanswered on the wind; I had urgent floral business to attend to.

The rest of the journey was incident free and back at Driftwood Lodge I collected some lovely Devon slipware jugs from the kitchen, refreshed Nigel's coffee (he was explaining cancellation fees; Theo was trying to stay awake) and zoomed over to place hand-tied bouquets in the two empty cottages. Then there was just Beaver's Barn to tackle.

I knocked on the door. There was a lot of laughing going on inside but finally Bruce opened the door in a very short red satin dressing gown.

'I am so sorry to disturb you,' I said, averting my eyes, 'but can I come in?'

Bruce made a sweeping gesture with his arm and stood back to let me in as I explained that we'd got an inspection and asked if we could possibly take some photos.

'Who is it, Brucey-darling?' Penelope called from upstairs.

I suppressed a smile as he yelled up to her, 'Kate wants to take some photos.'

Kate? Oh yes, that was me. 'Sorry, I'll be as quick as I can.'

Penelope trotted down the stairs, also in a very short satin dressing gown, only this time in green, with Tiger clutched to her chest.

'Of course you can!' Penelope's face looked flushed, and as she lowered the dog to the floor I caught a glimpse of bare boobs beneath the robe. 'We're just off outside to paint. Sorry about the mess. We had a bit of a party last night.'

'It's fine,' I said weakly, taking in the state of the cottage. Dirty dishes, empty bottles, goodness knows how many wine glasses ... A party? A full-on rave might be more accurate; how two people could have created this mess was beyond me. 'Absolutely fine, you go and enjoy yourselves. Theo says you're working on a joint piece today.'

'Yes,' tittered Penelope, 'we've entitled it *Crescendo of Passion*.'

'Sounds amazing.' I nodded as if I knew about these things and they ran barefoot outside, giggling like teenagers, followed more sedately by the long-suffering Tiger. I quickly got to work stacking the dishwasher, filling bin bags, plumping the cushions and wiping the kitchen surfaces. Finally, I shoved the lovely flowers in water and ran upstairs.

In the bathroom, I arranged the towels and folded the end of the toilet paper into a little triangle like I'd seen in hotels. As I went through to check on the bedrooms I heard Nigel's incessant voice and two sets of footsteps crunching across the gravel towards me.

My time was almost up. I quickly smoothed the bed covers in the front bedroom and kicked a pile of shoes under the bed. I flung the door of the second bedroom open and did a double take – it was precisely as we'd left it on Monday morning. The bed was untouched and pristine, the covers turned down at the corner. Only the pile of towels had gone.

Pen-Pen and Brucey-darling had clearly been getting on even better than we'd thought.

'You go, girl.' I smiled to myself as I ran downstairs to greet the men.

Theo looked browbeaten and bored when I appeared from inside; Nigel was still talking.

'Here she is!' Theo interrupted him with a sigh of relief. 'Kate will show you round. I'll leave you two to it; lovely meeting you, Nigel.'

He shook Nigel's hand and scuttled off before he could talk at him again.

'Let's start in here, our middle cottage,' I said brightly as Nigel took the lens cap off his camera.

He was a thorough photographer but he knew exactly the shots he was looking for and all I had to do was point out the various features.

'So what type of customers use Coastal Cottages to book their holidays?' I said, leading the way up the staircase.

'Upmarket professionals,' he said, pausing on the landing to take a wide shot of the bedroom. 'And families. Our standards are high and our prices reflect that so we . . .'

His voice drifted off and I assumed he was concentrating on taking the picture.

'The bathroom has a separate shower cubicle and a heated towel rail,' I said, flattening myself to the wall to make sure I wasn't in shot. 'And the views are truly unique.'

'That's one word for it,' said Nigel faintly.

I turned to find that he was no longer behind me but leaning on the bedroom window sill.

'I've never seen anything like *that*,' he said in a choked voice.

I joined him at the window. 'Oh heavens!'

Our two guests were butt naked and bent over a row of paint pots. A large canvas was spread out on the lawn and pinned down with a rock at each corner. I looked at Nigel, weighing up whether to shield his eyes, yell at the artists to put some clothes on or brazen it out.

'Shall we go next door and photograph Kittiwake's Cabin?' I said, tapping Nigel's arm gently. 'You must need to get back?'

Nigel for once was lost for words and simply shook his

head, rooted to the spot. Side by side we watched as Brucey-darling and Pen-Pen daubed each other with green and blue paint and then both dived head first, body-surfing across the canvas, finishing by jerking their arms starfish-style. Then Bruce pulled Penelope on top of him and began kissing her, much to her audible delight. At which point I dragged Nigel from the window.

'That,' he stuttered, visibly shaken, 'is an image I'm unlikely to forget.'

'No,' I agreed, dabbing a line of perspiration from my forehead, 'me neither, let's move on. Did Theo tell you about our rainwater-harvesting?'

Nigel let out a sigh of relief. 'No, tell me about that. Please.'

After our tour of the properties, I left Nigel taking photos of little details, like the cottage signs, and a couple of eggs I'd pointed out to him under the hedge which Theo must have missed and the new plants in their pots, while I went to find Theo, who was refreshing the hens' water trough.

'He's slightly traumatized.' I explained how Bruce and Penelope had achieved the impossible and shut Nigel up. 'But I think he likes it. He says Brightside Holidays definitely has a place on the Coastal Cottages website.'

'Really?' Theo's face lit up.

'Yes.' I beamed. 'You are officially in business.'

'Thank you; you made this possible,' he said, his eyes sparkling.

'Look at you,' I said, patting his cheek affectionately. 'I feel like we've got the old Theo back.'

'I know, I know. If only I'd been more like this before, Kate might never have left.' He sighed. 'She hoped leaving me would shock me into action and it did.'

'Don't beat yourself up,' I said, conscious of the thud of

his heart through the fabric of my T-shirt. 'You were bereaved and overwhelmed with the thought of starting afresh.'

'So was she. But she managed to keep going.'

'You got there in the end,' I said with a grin. 'And I'm so pleased for you.'

I hugged him, pressing my cheek against his. Reminding myself as I did so that Theo was someone else's husband and I was only supposed to be acting the part.

'Lovely!' The shutter clicked on Nigel's camera and he stuck his thumb up. Neither of us had heard him approach. 'That's me done. Thanks, both of you. I'll be in touch with contracts, etc., in the next few days.'

He walked back to his car, stowed his camera in the boot and climbed in.

I waved politely but Theo frowned.

'He just took a picture of us.'

'Don't worry, you look fine,' I said with a laugh as we waved Nigel off. 'You've brushed your hair and everything today. Oh look, someone's coming!'

'Not another visitor,' Theo said as we squinted through the midday sun to see who was walking towards us, waving madly.

'It's Eliza from the Mermaid Gift and Gallery,' I said, recognizing the pink hair as she got closer. 'Perhaps her brother wants a date with me after all.'

Theo's mouth opened and closed in astonishment.

'And look happy,' I added, 'she seems to think you're very miserable.'

'What?' He looked horrified.

'Hey there!' Eliza looked from Theo to me slyly. 'Am I interrupting something?'

'No!' I said hastily. Although we were standing very close. I took a step back. 'Theo, you know Eliza?'

She beamed at us both and shifted a wicker basket from one arm to the other.

'Sort of. Hi.' He pulled his lips back in the scariest smile I'd ever witnessed.

There was a hoot of laughter from where Penelope and Bruce were creating their *Crescendo of Passion* followed by a squeal and the crash of paint pots.

'Ooh, sounds like you two are not the only ones having fun.' She giggled, wagging a finger at us.

Theo turned pink. 'Please excuse me, I'm going to go and email *my wife*. Who's in South America.'

'Ah, poor thing,' she said in a stage whisper as Theo strode away. 'Anyway, ta dah!'

Her eyes twinkled and she reached a plump hand under the wicker flap of her basket. 'I think this was the one you wanted.'

She brought out the kitten I'd fallen in love with last weekend and handed it to me. It was still tiny and fluffy and adorable.

'Oh hello,' I cooed, kissing its head.

'It's a boy,' she said confidently. 'I think. What are you going to call him?'

'Gosh, Eliza, it's very good of you, but I haven't confirmed it with Theo and I'm not allowed to have animals in my flat in London—'

'I insist,' she said, adding shiftily, 'it's the least I can do.'

'What do you mean?' I asked cautiously.

'I'd better get back to the shop.' She bent over the kitten and tickled his head. 'Bye-bye, little one.'

'Stop right there, Eliza,' I said sternly. 'Out with it. What have you done?'

'I'm really, really sorry.' She stared down at her canvas pumps, which looked like she'd hand embellished them with bits of shell. 'I couldn't help it; last night I told my brother, Danny, who you are. I've done well, really; I've lasted almost a week without letting on to anyone that you came into my shop.'

My heart began to thump and I stroked the kitten for comfort. 'And? Has he kept it a secret?'

Of course he hadn't. Stupid question. The cat was quite literally out of the bag.

She fiddled with the strap of her dungarees. 'He couldn't help it. Neither of us has met a proper celebrity before, unless you count Big Dave. Well, we wouldn't, would we, living down here?'

'So who has Danny told?' I asked. Perhaps he'd just mentioned it to the lads at the pub. Perhaps I was worrying about nothing. And wasn't Big Dave the name of the local lobster man?

'Just Facebook.' Two pink spots appeared on her cheeks. She twirled a strand of hair around her finger nervously.

'*Just?*' I spluttered. I made that about 1.8 billion people.

'His timeline went bonkers. He's had five hundred friend requests overnight. He can't keep up with the comments.'

'Oh God! Eliza! This is crazy.'

I stared at her numbly. Okay, so I'd mistakenly blabbed the *Victory Road* storyline and tipped ice on Cecily Carmichael's head before disappearing. Get over it, people; move on.

She bit her lip. 'But then the press got in touch and asked where you were.'

'Did he tell them?' I demanded. 'Do they know I'm staying here, with Theo?'

Eliza squirmed. 'I think so. In fact, yes. Theo was tagged by someone. Sorry. Has anyone called you yet?'

I shook my head. To be honest, I'd hardly looked at my phone for ages. There was no signal here and even when I went out I rarely took it with me.

'Well, that's that,' I said resignedly. 'My period of lying low is well and truly over.'

At least that was the decision made for me. No more prevaricating. I had no choice now but to go back to London and face the music . . . Oh hell.

'I need to leave Brightside Cove. Immediately.'

'Oh no!' Eliza pouted. 'I wanted you to help me with my mermaid school. Now you're no longer incognito.'

Just then Theo appeared from inside. 'There's a call for you on the landline, Nina . . . Oh,' he groaned. 'Now who's this? It's like Piccadilly Circus today.'

A car was trundling up the drive towards us. A camera lens was poking out of the passenger window and I could hear the shutter whirring. My stomach began to churn.

'Nina Penhaligon?' the driver shouted. '*South Devon Echo*. Are we the first?'

'First what?' muttered Theo, folding his arms.

'Journalists,' I said, swallowing hard. 'I hope Bruce and Penelope have put their clothes back on. Who did you say was on the phone?'

'A lady called Maxine Pearce and she sounded quite agitated.'

Maxine. Oh God. My legs turned to mush.

'I'd better take it.' I handed the kitten to Theo. 'Wish me luck.'

'I'll go and talk to the press!' Eliza offered.

'Okay,' I agreed, against my better judgement, 'but just say "no comment" or something, just . . . just keep it simple.'

'I'm on it,' Eliza shouted and scampered up to the car.

My pulse was racing as I stumbled inside and I genuinely thought I might be sick. 'Nina Penhaligon speaking.'

'For pity's sake, Nina! What the hell do you think you're playing at?'

'Hi Maxine,' I stammered, 'I'm lying low. Sebastian told me to.'

'He what? The bloody idiot. He said he didn't know where you were.'

'He doesn't. Didn't. He banished me from London.'

'Arrgghh! Unbelievable. You do realize what a completely bloody trail of disaster you left behind you?'

'I'm beginning to.' I cringed.

'If you'd stuck around, given a statement and come to see me, all of this could have been sorted out within twenty-four hours, but disappearing made it worse, apparently

111

Cecily Carmichael is baying for your blood, the *Victory Road* PR team is chomping at the bit to put this story to bed and the producers are foaming at the mouth like rabid dogs.'

That was ironic because right now mine was as dry as a bone.

'So,' I said tremulously, 'what shall I do?'

'Get back to London! We need you on set.'

'But . . . Nurse Elsie is dead.'

'Not any more, she's not.'

I screwed up my forehead in confusion. 'How can that be?'

'See you tomorrow. Noon sharp for a press briefing. We film on Monday.'

I stared at the receiver. She'd gone.

I slumped against the wall and looked up to see Theo standing under the porch stroking the kitten. Judging by the serene look on his face, he hadn't heard a word of that exchange.

'Eliza was very forceful with the press,' he chuckled. 'Told them you'd gone to fetch your gun. They left pretty smartish.'

Great, so now I'd be able to add *crazed markswoman* to my list of crimes.

'I'm keeping the kitten,' he said brightly. 'I think it will show Kate that I'm ready to love again . . . Nina, what on earth's the matter, you look like you've seen a ghost?'

'Almost; it appears Nurse Elsie has come back from the dead.'

He looked bemused. 'What do you mean?'

'It means I can't stay and help you, after all; I've got to go back to London. Today.'

'I see.' His shoulders slumped and the look of disappointment etched into his face broke my heart.

'Theo, I'm sorry.'

'Of course,' he said, finally meeting my eye. 'It's selfish of me to keep you here any longer; I'm sure you want to get back to London.'

'I do,' I said. 'I really do.'

And if that wasn't worthy of a BAFTA, nothing was.

I couldn't think of anything else to add, so I ran upstairs to pack. Now the decision had been made, I wanted to leave as soon as possible.

My brain was skittering all over the place as I stuffed my things into my case. What sort of reception would I get in London? How on earth were they going to bring Nurse Elsie back to life? Would there be a wedding in *Victory Road* after all?

Of course I had to go back, I told myself, resolutely not looking out of the window at the shimmering sea. I was an actress; London was my home. So why was I already counting the days until I could come back to Brightside Cove . . . ?

PART TWO

The Hen Party

Chapter 11

All my life I'd secretly yearned to one day put on such a poignant performance that the audience was so blown away, so *in the moment*, that it was incomprehensible to them that I was only acting. It would be the turning point in my career, the role that propelled me into household-name status, an actress people remembered. So that maybe, possibly, the person who'd long since forgotten me might feel compelled to seek me out.

Never once did I daydream that a video of me blurting out *Victory Road*'s cliffhanger, tipping ice on Cecily Carmichael's head and punching my ex-agent Sebastian in the stomach would make me famous. The quarter of a million views on YouTube, the internet memes and the 10,000 new followers on my Facebook page were not a source of pride; I was mortified.

'So, Nina, thank you for agreeing to talk to *Entertainer's News*.' Ross Whittaker stared wolfishly at me. 'Again.'

I was back in London. It was Saturday lunchtime in the middle of April and outside the skies were blue but inside Ginny Walsh's office the atmosphere crackled as if there was an electric storm on its way. My insides were feeling pretty stormy too. This press interview, organized by Ginny – who clearly despised me for several reasons, including being hoiked back into work at the weekend – was an exercise in damage limitation. If I managed to pull this off, I really did deserve an Oscar.

'My pleasure,' I replied, inclining my head. 'It was the least we could do given the prank we pulled on you.'

I hoped he couldn't spot the line of perspiration on my forehead from the other side of the table.

'So you're sticking to the April Fool line, then?' Ross sneered, as if the whole thing was a farce.

Which incidentally it was. But Ginny, the head of publicity for *Victory Road*, was adamant that the only way to get me out of this PR fiasco was to lie. And because I was firmly in everyone's bad books, Maxine, the show's director, had advised me to toe the party line.

Ginny batted her eyelashes. 'Now, now, Ross. Let's all play nicely.'

She passed an official statement to him across the desk; he ignored it. I didn't blame him; it was pure fluff.

'Nina, please tell Ross what you told me,' said Ginny in clipped tones. 'And then we can put these silly rumours to bed once and for all.'

Ross leaned his elbows on the table and fixed his eyes on me as I cleared my throat.

'Sorry, Ross,' I said, my tone contrite, 'but Cecily and I played a joke on you. The whole thing was a set-up.'

'I've seen Cecily act.' Ross rubbed his nose as if hiding a smile. 'She's not normally that good.'

I sucked in my cheeks, trying not to react. 'I bet her she wouldn't go through with it.'

Ginny coughed.

'When I say, *bet*,' I corrected swiftly, 'I mean that I offered to make a charity donation if she let me tip ice over her.'

I had sent her a message via Twitter to this effect last night, offering my sincere apologies and offering to donate money to her nominated charity. No reply so far.

Ross narrowed his eyes. 'So you did it for charity?'

'Exactly,' Ginny beamed. 'So, moving on—'

Ross held up a hand to silence her. 'But Cecily has got the part you went for in *Mary Queen of Scots*? Aren't you annoyed about that?'

'Not at all.' I frowned, feigning confusion. 'I could never have taken that part because of my . . . other filming commitments.'

His eyes locked on to mine. 'But not for *Victory Road*?'

I licked my lips, not breaking eye contact. 'Yes. In fact, I'm due in the studio next week.'

'So,' he leaned closer, 'Nurse Elsie is *not* dead?'

The beads of sweat on my forehead were surely the size of golf balls by now. I glanced at Ginny, who shot me a pinched look. Ever since I'd arrived in her office this morning she'd adopted this martyred expression, as if I was making her life impossible. She wasn't fooling me. Her pupils were dilated and there were two pink spots on her cheeks; she might hate me but she was loving the drama.

'I can confirm that Nina still has scenes to shoot, Ross,' she said, making cow eyes at him. 'You'll have to draw your own conclusions from that.'

Ross thumped his fist on the table. 'So what can you tell me, then? You disappeared to,' he glanced at the press release for the first time, 'Devon? What were you doing there, rehab? A love tryst?'

My eyebrows shot up at that. The last thing Theo needed was to be romantically linked to me in the press. That would get Kate back from South America quicker than you can say *divorce settlement*.

'I was resting,' I said hastily, 'I was overdue a break.'

'So it was rehab?'

'No!' I stammered. 'I was staying with a friend. Friends. Of my brother.'

I glanced at Ginny for help. She was picking her nail.

'A man? So there's a man involved?' Ross raised an amused eyebrow. 'You're blushing.'

My jaw opened and closed pathetically until Ginny finally

stepped in to rescue me. 'We're not dealing with Miss Penhaligon's private life today, Ross,' she said primly. 'Now let me give you this DVD of exclusive *Victory Road* content. I'm sure we can trust you with the embargo . . .'

I slipped away and left them to it, exhaling with relief. One ordeal down, next my meeting with Maxine . . .

'I'm so sorry,' I said, pale faced, as Maxine opened her office door. 'I've made a huge mistake.'

Dressed in her habitual black wrap dress and heels even on a Saturday, Maxine pushed her mass of grey curls off her face and scowled at me for what felt like an eternity. She had good skin, I noted absently, a bit sallow from spending too much time at work, but very few wrinkles around her eyes. I knew she must be about sixty, but she could pass for much younger. She was taller than me and had a sturdy matronly figure, and right now, with her arms folded and her eyes trained on me, she was absolutely terrifying.

'We're all allowed one mistake,' she said finally, standing aside.

I heaved a sigh of relief and entered her office. It was full of clutter: a wilted pot plant, piles of papers on every surface and a teetering in-tray marked 'scripts'. Was there a part suitable for me in amongst all of those? I wondered. Probably not the time to ask, all things considered.

'Made an almighty one myself once,' she continued. 'I lived in fear of the consequences for years before life went back to normal.'

It was hard to believe that Maxine Pearce, so totally in control, could ever have made a mistake. There was a misty look in her eye and I was tempted to ask what she'd done; whatever it was, it obviously hadn't held her back. But she waved me into a seat at her meeting table and carried on talking.

'Shame you followed Sebastian Nichols' advice and decided to hide in Devon,' she said, switching on a coffee machine in the corner of the room. 'It must have been awful for you.'

'Hmm,' I said noncommittally.

I thought of Theo and me drinking coffee on his garden bench, the tang of sea in the air, watching the hens pecking amongst the grass; I remembered the shells I'd collected on the beach and splashing through the foamy waves getting my jeans wet. *Awful.*

'And no mobile phone signal, you say?' She pushed a cup of coffee in my direction.

'None,' I said, trying to keep the wistfulness from my face. Not being contactable had been very liberating once I'd got used to it, although I'd soon got back into the habit of checking my mobile every five minutes in case I was missing something. I'd be back at Brightside Cove in a heartbeat, given a chance. Especially as giving autographs to the small crowd gathered outside the studio doors this morning hadn't been half as thrilling as I'd imagined. All they were interested in was where I'd been and whether Cecily really was going to press charges.

'Maybe not all bad, then.' Her brow furrowed as her own phone began to buzz. She grabbed it and turned it off. 'As far as your ex-agent goes, I think he's been blinded by Cecily Carmichael's sexy image and forgotten that actresses need to have talent too. Have you spoken to him?'

'Only via email,' I admitted. 'I'll be looking for new representation. Sebastian has made it quite clear that Cecily is his priority from now on.'

'He'll regret having anything to do with that family eventually,' she said darkly. 'I know I did. Anyway, that's his problem. But ask someone else for advice in future.'

'There isn't anyone else,' I said, blowing on my coffee. 'My brother is lovely, but he's a businessman with no idea about acting. And I have no parents; my dad—' I cleared my throat. I rarely spoke about him and don't know why I'd even mentioned him. Maxine cocked an eyebrow. I carried on. 'And my mum died a few years ago.'

Although *she* would have been the last person I'd ask for advice about my career. She'd told me once in no uncertain terms that acting was a sordid profession. Adding in the next breath that anyway, with my physique, the best I could hope for was the chubby and cheerful best friend. It had been a relief to leave home for university at eighteen and be away from her negative vibes. I supposed I should have been grateful that she used the word 'cheerful'. Within eighteen months she had died and never got to see me on television. I think she'd have loved *Victory Road* and would have been proud of me. That was all we really ever wanted from our parents, wasn't it? Love and pride, a place in their hearts.

Maxine was still regarding me intently and I held my breath, hoping she wouldn't probe about my family.

'I could never confide in my mother,' she said with a shudder, echoing my own thoughts. 'She had very set ideas on what one should and shouldn't do. I had to wait until she'd passed away before I could truly be myself. Anyway, in future, if you're ever in need of a mature ear, ring me. I'll listen.'

'Really?' A lump in my throat appeared from nowhere. 'Like a mentor?'

She gave me a brief but genuine smile, which transformed her usual steely face. 'Exactly.'

'Thank you. So much.'

She gave a quick nod to end the discussion and picked up a slim stack of papers. 'Now would you like to know what Nurse Elsie has been up to while you've been away?'

On Monday I was back on set. I'd spent the morning apologizing to everyone on the cast and crew as I'd encountered them and it was a relief to get down to work. In Studio Three it was the middle of the night, during the Blitz in February 1941, and I was in a hospital bed. I was in a white gown, with a white face and my head was swaddled in bandages. I had to look ill because I was in a coma. Which meant all I had to do in this scene was lie still.

Handy really because I hadn't got much sleep last night. Trudy had rented my room out to two male Korean foreign language students for a month, which meant I was having to share a bed with her. She had talked until midnight and then even talked in her sleep. But I was grateful to have a bed at all given my emergency flit from Devon on Friday. It was odd being back; Trudy's flat no longer seemed like home. With one Korean making a huge spicy mess in the kitchen and another Skyping his entire family at full volume in my old bedroom, it felt cramped and stuffy.

Even having a bath had been difficult; someone had draped their wet washing over every surface and a row of misshapen T-shirts hung damply from the shower rail. I thought longingly of the big bathroom at Driftwood Lodge with its roll-top bath and its little window carved into the thatched roof with the view of the harbour in the distance . . .

'Hey!' Freddie Major, the man who played my boyfriend, Constable Ron, had arrived.

My stomach flipped. I'd seen him across the canteen earlier but we'd not spoken yet. He, more than any other character, had been affected by me leaking the plot and I wasn't sure what sort of reception I was going to get.

'Nurse Elsie, as I live and breathe,' Freddie said, bouncing on to my bed and rucking up the blanket.

'My darling Constable Ron,' I said casually. 'Have you missed me?'

'I have, actually. You're not looking too hot, though,' he said, peering at my white face. 'You're like that Lazarus from the Bible. Back from the dead.'

I raised an eyebrow. 'Maybe. Or maybe I *am* dead and we're just shooting this scene to throw people off the scent.'

'What?' He gave me a quizzical look. 'I just meant back from Devon. It's gotta be dead there. You must be relieved to be back from exile.'

'Um . . .'

I didn't get a chance to argue with him because someone shouted, 'Quiet please,' and I took some deep breaths ready for shooting to commence.

Was I relieved? I'd always loved London: the energy, the bustle, the noise of it all and the feeling of being part of something exciting. And I loved my job, no doubt about that. But after two weeks with Theo at Brightside Cove, where the light was clear and the air was pure and the constant restlessness of the sea gave a different sort of energy to the rhythm of the day, the city had lost a teeny bit of its sparkle. Plus, now I was allegedly famous, I spent my time scurrying around behind my sunglasses. I knew it wouldn't last; someone else would do something outrageous next week and I'd soon be forgotten, but right now, for someone used to a quiet life, it was exhausting.

Maxine shoved her phone into her back pocket and blew her curls out of her eyes. 'And action,' she called.

I lowered my eyelids, keeping them slightly open so I could still make out what was going on.

'Elsie, sweetheart, can you hear me?' Freddie as Constable Ron pleaded softly. He slid further along the hospital bed towards me. Fake tears glittered in his eyes.

'She's had a serious blow to the head, Constable,' whispered Becky Burton, from the other side of the bed. Becky played flirty Nurse Marjorie and was my best friend in the *Victory Road* cast. Or had been – she was a bit frosty with me because I hadn't returned her texts when I was in Devon. She took my pulse and checked it against the fob watch pinned to her apron. 'But the sound of your voice might bring her round. You can touch her, too.'

I kept my arm heavy and lifeless as he clasped my hand in his.

'If you can hear me, squeeze my fingers,' he breathed over me.

I stayed resolutely unresponsive.

'Keep talking,' said Nurse Marjorie, replacing a clipboard on the rail at the bottom of my bed. She paused to rest her hand on his shoulder, adding breathily, 'Imagine how wonderful it would be to wake up to find you on the bed.'

She batted her eyelashes at him and they shared a long

look. Poor Elsie. How could Marjorie do that to her, they were supposed to be friends? The audience would be shouting at their TV screens.

As soon as she had gone, Ron took a ring box out of his pocket. He held up a slim diamond engagement ring to the light and then slipped it on my finger, wiping a glycerine tear from his eye.

'I love you, Elsie,' he murmured, pressing a kiss to my nose. 'You're my girl and I'll wait for you. As long as it takes. One day I *will* make you my wife.'

He dropped his chin to his chest and shook his shoulders to make it look like he was overcome with grief.

'And cut. Nicely done.'

I opened my eyes as Maxine stepped from the shadows and into the scene.

'If that doesn't get the tears jerking nothing will,' she said briskly. 'Right, off you go, Freddie.'

'Cheers, boss.' He grinned and hung an arm around her neck casually. She gave him one of her stares and he immediately removed it.

'Yes, well done, Freddie.' I propped myself up on my elbows. 'And I'm really sorry if my behaviour has caused you any problems.'

Freddie punched my arm. 'No worries, you've done me a favour, as it turns out. My agent got straight on the case as soon as you leaked the story. I've landed the role of Buttons in *Cinderella* in panto in the West End, my Instagram followers have passed the half-million mark and now that my girlfriend's in a coma, all the female viewers will adore me. And all because of you and your big mouth.'

'Glad to be of use,' I said through clenched teeth.

He winked at me and sauntered off.

His agent sounded a damn sight more proactive than mine had been. Sebastian, rather than take the opportunity to strike while my name was hot, had struck me off his list and sent me away to hide.

I let out a breath of relief at having got that conversation out of the way.

'Smug little whatsit.' Maxine rolled her eyes as Freddie left the studio for the day. 'Right, we need some close-up footage showing you unconscious to splice into future scenes so we don't need to call you in, and then tomorrow we'll re-shoot the bomb explosion scene.'

'I think I can manage that,' I said with an awkward smile.

I felt at a distinct disadvantage, lying prone under a hospital blanket with her looming over me. Despite her offer to mentor me when required, she could still turn me to stone with her icy glare.

'The reaction to Nurse Elsie's rumoured death was far bigger than we'd expected, probably fuelled by your disappearance,' she continued. 'So the writers have ramped up the next few episodes accordingly. We've got so much conflict and heartstring tearing that the audience won't be able to leave their sofas.'

'I can't apologize enough for all this extra work I've created,' I mumbled.

'I'd noticed,' she said flatly and then her lips twitched. 'Although that clip of you tipping ice over Cecily Carmichael's head was the funniest thing I've ever seen. All my friends have watched it.'

My stomach lurched; being an internet sensation had never been on my agenda. I wanted to be known for my acting prowess not my tantrums. 'Don't remind me.'

'What's done is done and in the long run you may even have done the show a favour.'

'That's something, I suppose.'

If I could turn the clock back, I would. Some people might relish this sort of publicity but I was much happier being in character than being a YouTube sensation as myself.

Chapter 12

The following morning, I was back at the studios bright and early. It was a rerun of the scene where the two air-raid wardens, Ray and Godfrey, discover my body amongst the ruins of the house. Only this time, they find a weak pulse, whip me on to a makeshift stretcher and stumble out from the wreckage over the rubble to get me to safety. I'd also had to wear a wig to cover my dark hair. I'd repeated my apologies again, and they appeared to accept them, although they plonked me on the stretcher quite roughly and I was glad when I made it off set in one piece.

By eleven o'clock my scenes were done, another strand to my storyline was in the bag and I wouldn't be needed again for the foreseeable future. At least not until Maxine decided whether or not Nurse Elsie was going to recover from the coma.

Downstairs in the canteen, I bought myself a cup of coffee and a slice of toasted fruit loaf and took it outside to the courtyard. As gardens went it was a bit manmade but miniature willows, red-leafed acers and cherry trees helped to soften the look of a modern metal water feature and stark concrete benches, and two symmetrical rows of copper urns looked very smart filled with lavender bushes.

It was the closest I had come to peace and quiet in four days. Bliss.

The silence lasted about ten seconds until my phone

began to buzz. I looked at the caller ID. It was Eliza. I grinned, imagining her in her shop, cuddling kittens and chatting about mermaids.

'Hey!' I said, brushing toast crumbs from my chin. 'How are you? How's Devon? Have your authentic mermaid tails arrived from America yet?'

'Fine, good and almost, stuck in customs. I owe two hundred dollars in customs duty, that's my next job. But that's not why I'm ringing.'

I narrowed my eyes. 'If this is about Danny . . .'

Eliza's brother was the reason I was no longer in Brightside Cove helping Theo out.

'It's about Theo.' I heard the wobble in her voice and my heart began to pound with dread. 'I'm worried about him.'

'What's happened?' I sat up straight, ears pricked; I'd called Theo last night and he hadn't picked up.

'Raquel from the pub saw him at the doctors collecting a prescription yesterday. She said he looked awful and his eyes were all puffed up from crying. She thinks he was getting anti-depressants.'

'Really?'

I'd only been gone for a few days and he'd seemed okay before then. He'd been disappointed that I was leaving but he'd driven me to the train station and promised to keep me posted on the plans for marketing the cottages. Could he really have sunk so low in such a short time?

'And that's not all,' Eliza continued. 'He went into Jethro's General Store and had an argument because he was only allowed to buy thirty-two paracetamol and he wanted more. Jethro tried to explain that it was the law, but Theo just stomped off in a rage.'

How odd: why would Theo need more than thirty-two tablets so urgently?

'Perhaps he's got a really bad headache?' I suggested weakly.

'And then last night, I was locking up the shop at sunset and it was almost high tide.'

'Yes?' I could picture it vividly. The boats in the harbour would have been bobbing up and down in deep water, their masts tinkling, and the beach would be nothing more than a thin golden ribbon curled between the rocks and the waves . . .

'And I looked out at the sea wall, and there was a tall figure silhouetted against the red of the setting sun. Would have made a lovely photo,' she added as an aside.

I frowned. 'Actually on the sea wall at high tide?'

'Yes. And it was Theo.'

My eyebrows were knitted together with worry. I'd scrambled up there once myself. The sea had been like a mill pond at the time but the wall was narrow and jutted straight out from the beach towards the west. When the sea was rough, huge waves arced high above it and during high tide the water would be deep and unforgiving. I shuddered to think what would happen if someone fell in.

'What on earth was he doing out there?' I murmured.

'Depression, prescription drugs, excessive pills, erratic behaviour . . .' Eliza listed. 'You tell me.'

He couldn't be contemplating . . . what she was suggesting. Things were beginning to pick up for him, the cottages were ready, the holiday business was on the cusp of taking off. Unless . . . A sudden wave of panic hit me. Had Kate found out that I'd been staying with him and put two and two together and made five? If so, he might feel as if he had nothing to go on for.

'Did you call the police, or the coastguard?' I asked.

'No, I ran down the beach myself and shouted at him to get down. He was very rude, actually,' she added. 'Told me I'd frightened the life out of him. But at least he climbed down. He went home after that, as far as I know.'

I let out a breath of relief. 'Thank you. I'm glad he's safe.'

'Till next time,' she muttered ominously.

Maybe Eliza was making a mountain out of a molehill. But maybe she wasn't. I wished he'd answered my call last night.

'Perhaps I should come back,' I said.

'Definitely!' I could almost see her punching the air. 'And that's perfect timing because on Friday, Danny is doing a photo shoot of the new mermaid tails, assuming they've arrived by then, to say sorry to me for revealing your whereabouts to the press. You can be in it.'

'He's apologizing to *you*? What about me?' I said.

'Hold on, he's here, I'll ask him.'

I swallowed my last mouthful of coffee as, with a muffled voice, Eliza relayed my message to her brother.

'Danny says there's a two-for-one offer on mussels on Saturday night at The Sea Urchin. He'll take you if you don't mind going Dutch.'

Despite my worries about Theo, I couldn't help smiling. No surprise that Danny was single if that was the best he could do. 'Tell him he's all heart.'

I vowed to be back as soon as I could and extracted a promise from Eliza to go and check up on Theo straight away and then I ended the call. I was about to ring Archie to see if he could get down there when Maxine entered the canteen and my heart nearly beat its way out of my chest.

Had I really just agreed to run off again? What was my director going to say about that? Also, I hadn't actually told Eliza that I didn't want to be in her mermaid photo shoot. The sensible thing would be to call Theo and put my mind at rest. I tried his number but it just rang out and when the answerphone eventually picked up I couldn't think of anything to say that wasn't 'please don't do anything foolish'. So I hung up.

I had to go back to Brightside Cove. It was what any decent person would do. And actually a tiny part of me acknowledged that it was what I wanted to do more than anything. I might not be needed on set this week, but what if Maxine decided that Nurse Elsie should wake up and I ended up with a full filming schedule next week? I couldn't let the cast down again. I bit my lip, watching as Maxine helped herself to bottled water from the fridge and selected a banana from the fruit display. I needed advice. If only I had a . . . mentor.

'Maxine!' I called, barging my way back through the glass doors and towards the table where she'd settled down alone to peel her banana. 'Can I talk to you?'

'It would seem you already are,' she said, slicing the banana into circles.

I sat opposite her.

'I have a dilemma,' I began.

And I told her how acting had always been the most important thing in my life. That being part of a hit TV series like *Victory Road* was a dream come true and that I honestly couldn't imagine another career for myself.

'But . . . ?' Maxine posted a piece of banana into her mouth without taking her eyes off me.

'I'm worried about a friend of mine. The one I've been staying with in Devon. He's been very down recently and his neighbours are concerned about his state of mind. He lives alone and I honestly don't know what he might be capable of.'

Maxine's eyes met mine. 'And you want to go back?'

My heart thumped and I nodded. 'But I also care about *Victory Road*. I don't want to leave you in the lurch.'

'So I guess it would have been easier if we had killed off Nurse Elsie?'

'No, no!' I exclaimed selfishly, and then squirmed when Maxine raised a knowing eyebrow. 'Yes, I suppose so, but the coma idea is such a good one and puts the suspense back into the storyline which I so idiotically threw away.'

Her eyebrow was still up. 'So. Any ideas?'

'Perhaps she could stay comatose for a long time?'

Maxine unscrewed the top of her water bottle and took a sip without breaking eye contact. 'How long is *long*?'

I felt a surge of hope. This might actually work. I might be able to get a stay of execution as it were and still keep my job. I wet my lips. 'Well, I could be back on set by, say . . . the end of June?'

My mind was forging ahead, thinking of everything we could do by then: Brightside Holidays would be up and running on the Coastal Cottages website; we could have taken some bookings, produced brochures, put together a fabulous marketing plan and Kate would come back from South America to a successful business, make up with Theo and live happily ever after.

Maxine sucked in air and took out her notebook, flicking through the pages. 'Let me see. The episode where you fall into the coma will air next week. So if we couldn't film a new scene with you until June, it wouldn't air until July. That's a long time to string out a coma plotline.'

'But just think of the tension,' I urged. 'Freddie and Becky can start an affair right under my nose. Literally. The viewers will be horrified!'

'True.' She stared at me and I could almost hear the whirring of her brain. 'That could be a ratings winner. While Nurse Elsie lies there fighting for her life, Ron grows closer to Nurse Marjorie until they begin an inappropriate affair behind the closed curtains of your hospital cubicle.'

I nodded eagerly.

'And one day your eyes flicker and you raise a hand but no one notices because they're too busy snogging and then you wake up just as Ron yanks the engagement ring off your finger and pops the question to Marjorie. You go into cardiac arrest and die. Cue credits!'

She sat back in her seat, eyes glittering with ideas.

'You are brilliant,' I said, full of admiration. 'But evil.'

'And that's why they pay me the big bucks,' she said in an

American accent and mimed reloading an automatic machine gun.

'Isn't that from a film?'

She nodded shiftily. '*The Holiday*. My favourite film.'

I coughed to hide my surprise; I hadn't been expecting that. Some foreign, subtitled arthouse film, yes, but not Cameron Diaz and Jude Law frolicking in the snow.

A spot of colour pinged on to her cheeks and she gave her papers an unnecessary shuffle as if already regretting that momentary glimpse of a softer side. 'Don't bandy it about or my reputation will be ruined.'

'My lips are sealed.'

I felt honoured, as if she'd unzipped her coat on a cold day and let me share her warmth.

'There are lots of things about me you don't know,' she continued. 'That no one knows.'

Her features took on a brief mask of sadness but in the next second she blinked and when she met my gaze her eyes were as clear and perceptive as ever. 'You care about him a lot, don't you? This man.'

'Yes,' I said in a gruff voice.

I did care about Theo. What he and Kate had endured, losing their precious baby daughter, broke my heart every time I thought about it. And on that last day in Brightside Cove he'd been so enthusiastic about his plans for the holiday business. He could do it, he could survive this pain and start afresh, and not just for Kate, to win her back, but for himself. Because Theo deserved a bright future too.

Maxine reached across the table and grabbed hold of my hand.

'Then go. Be there for him,' she urged. 'Let him know that you care, because if you don't, you'll regret it for the rest of your life. Take it from one who knows.'

I could hardly believe my luck. 'For two months?'

'Yes, now go before I change my mind.'

Impulsively, I darted around the table and held her tight, muttering my thanks.

'If you fancy getting away from it all,' I said, hoisting my bag on to my shoulder, 'we're taking bookings for the holiday cottages. Come and enjoy the peace and quiet of Devon.'

And right on cue her phone buzzed into life.

'Don't tempt me,' she said, stabbing the phone with an impatient finger. 'Maxine Pearce?'

And while she barked instructions to the caller, I ran for the exit, hoping that whatever was going on at Brightside Cove was not as drastic as we thought.

Chapter 13

Six hours later, I was hefting my suitcase over the potholes towards Driftwood Lodge. I'd called Archie to fill him in on Theo's odd behaviour and he'd promised to get down here too as soon as he could get away from work.

'He's your friend,' I'd reminded him sternly, 'don't leave it too long.'

I stopped in the courtyard to catch my breath, anxious and hot from the journey, but despite my worries about Theo, my stomach swooped with joy. The late afternoon was warm, the sky was cornflower blue and the smell of the sea mixed with the sweet scent of yellow gorse flowers was as heady and beguiling as any perfume.

I knocked on the door and tried the handle. It was unlocked as usual.

'Hello?' I called, pushing it open.

'Nina?' Theo appeared at the kitchen door, typically dishevelled in scruffy jeans and a holey jumper. His curls didn't look as if they'd been brushed since I'd left on Friday evening and his chin was bristly with stubble. And his eyes . . . red-rimmed and puffy.

'Oh Theo!' I dropped my case and ran at him, throwing my arms round his neck. 'I'm here and everything's going to be okay.'

'Glad to hear it.' Theo looked at me, alarmed, and tried to fight me off. 'You're back sooner than I expected. Are you on the run again? What did you do this time, pick a fight with the Queen?'

'I came back to be with you.' I gave him a watery smile.

'You don't look too happy about it, if you don't mind me saying,' he said, passing me a tissue from his pocket. 'It's clean.'

'I am,' I confirmed, keen to make sure he didn't think he was a burden. 'I'm very happy. I've arranged time off work. All above board this time. I won't leave you alone for a second. And between us, you and me, we're going to take the ultimatum from Kate and we're going to smash it . . .' My voice petered out. That was insensitive of me; the ultimatum may well be off by now. 'If that's what you still want?'

I peered up at him. His eyes were red, but there was no sign of any recent crying. In fact, if anything he seemed more confused than upset. I stepped closer to check.

'I do want. Careful,' he warned, 'you'll squash Mittens.'

He bent down and scooped up the kitten that was sitting on his foot and showed me the little white mittens on his paws.

'Although I should have called him Limpet: he clings to my leg all the time. I've even taken to walking with a straight leg to avoid flicking him off. I started doing it automatically when I was out yesterday and he wasn't even there. People must have thought I was a right weirdo.'

They thought far worse than that.

He kept the kitten at arm's length and rubbed a finger under its chin until it purred. 'You're ticklish under there, aren't you, little fella?'

The sight of this big hulk of a man cradling the tiny creature in his hands made me want to cry again.

Theo sneezed and I rubbed his arm.

'I'm glad you've bonded,' I said.

'Yes, in spite of—' He broke off and waggled his eyebrows.

I raised my own eyebrow questioningly. 'In spite of . . . ?'

He gave me a stern look that I couldn't quite interpret. 'I nearly gave up yesterday. It's no good, I thought. I can't go on like this.'

'So Eliza was right,' I said sadly, rubbing his arm.

'She saw the state I was in?'

I nodded, biting my lip.

He frowned, set the kitten down and walked into the kitchen. 'Eliza keeps turning up here like some sort of phantom door-knocker. Except she doesn't actually knock, she presses her face against the window, and when I catch her, she runs away. Clearly doesn't trust me to look after one of her kittens. Cup of tea, or something stronger?'

It was on the tip of my tongue to ask for a glass of wine. Until I remembered that taking anti-depressants with alcohol was probably forbidden and I didn't want to make him feel awkward.

'Tea would be lovely.'

I followed him into the kitchen. It was amazingly tidy and my heart swelled when I noticed two tiny silver cat bowls and a little tartan cat bed in front of the Aga. Mittens tiptoed over to it and immediately curled up into a contented ball.

'The doc said the tablets would take a couple of days to kick in,' he said, rootling around in the cupboard for mugs.

'And you'll feel so much better then,' I assured him. 'You did the right thing going to the doctor. I only wish I'd been here to support you. We're all here for you: me, Eliza, Archie, even Raquel from the pub and Jethro have been worried.'

'That's thoughtful of everyone.' He gave me a bemused smile, dropping teabags into two large mugs. 'But I think I can manage an allergic reaction by myself, even if it has made me a bit tetchy.'

He motioned towards a box of tablets on the kitchen table. Antihistamines.

'That's what the doctor gave you?'

He nodded and sneezed again and the penny dropped: the puffy eyes, the sneezing, Theo holding the kitten at arm's length.

'You're allergic to Mittens?' A smile crept across my face.

'Apparently so. It started almost immediately. Why did you think I had beetroots for eyeballs?'

I let out a giggle of relief; he wasn't on Prozac at all. Theo folded his arms and leaned back against the Aga.

'Hey, don't mock the afflicted.' He grinned. 'It's very uncomfortable, you know.'

We gave up on the tea and opened a bottle of wine and I confessed that Eliza had put him on suicide watch and he laughed, but I could see he was quite touched that she had cared enough to keep an eye on him.

Then he showed me how hard he had been working in my absence. He'd started collecting leaflets from places of interest to make visitor packs, he'd been busy in the garden and was building a brick barbecue for the cottages to share and he showed me the neat little first-aid boxes he was compiling for each cottage with antiseptic wipes, bandages, plasters, tweezers and . . . paracetamol.

'Although Jethro wouldn't sell me enough tablets for a whole box for each cottage, which was a nuisance,' he said, pointing to the gap in one of the boxes.

Mystery solved.

'So you weren't stockpiling pills in preparation for a suicide attempt.'

'Definitely not.' He ran a hand through his hair and blinked incredulously. 'No offence, but if I can survive losing my child to a cruel illness and endure my wife flying to South America to get away from me, I think I can cope with you going home after a two-week stay.'

'Well, if you put it like that,' I said, feeling a bit silly, 'perhaps I was over-reacting.'

He reached across the table and covered my hand with

138

his. 'Nina, I'm grateful, really. I don't have any family of my own and relations with Kate's parents are strained at the moment, to say the least. Apart from Archie, I lost touch with most of my friends when Ivy died, and since moving down here ... Well, let's just say I haven't been very sociable. So thank you. For caring.'

We looked at each other then and his dark eyes were warm and brimming with gratitude. There was still one thing that bothered me.

'Eliza said you were on the sea wall last night?'

Theo broke eye contact and shifted in his seat. 'That was embarrassing. It sounds ridiculous, but I was talking to Kate. It was a clear evening, a glorious sunset and I wanted to feel close to her. The sea wall faces west, which is where she is. Argentina now, I think, and I just ... I miss her.'

I nodded and squeezed his hand.

'Have you heard from her since Danny posted my whereabouts on Facebook?'

He shook his head. 'Not a word. I'm not sure if that's good or bad.'

I smiled sadly and for a moment neither of us spoke until I picked up the wine bottle.

'But you're okay, that's the main thing, which means that basically,' I said, topping up our glasses, 'I've just managed to get two months' leave of absence because you have itchy eyes.'

'Yep.' He slurped his wine and smacked his lips together with satisfaction.

'Then we'd better make the most of it. Cheers.' And I chinked my glass against his.

'Well, there's plenty to do,' Theo replied. 'So not too much wine, I don't want you comatose before bedtime.'

'Good point,' I agreed. 'One coma a day is quite enough for anyone. Now I should really go and let everyone know you're all right. And there's someone else I need to speak to too ...'

*

I settled myself into a little button-backed velvet chair by the window in the hall and after making quick calls to Archie and Eliza to update them on the good news I dialled a mobile number I knew by heart.

'Hello?' Sebastian answered immediately.

I could hear the burble of conversation and chink of glasses in the background. A faint voice shouted, 'Over here!' and another yelled at someone to give them a wave. It sounded as if he was at a press event. I glanced out of the window. Dusk had settled over Brightside Cove and the sky was a patchwork of purple and pink and, almost within touching distance, the perfect sliver of a new moon glistened above the cottage rooftops. I was so glad I was here and not there.

'It's Nina. I'm calling to thank you for sorting out my new *Victory Road* contract,' I said gaily. 'And to say I won't be bothering you again.'

'What?' he demanded. 'Why not?'

I blinked in surprise. I'm sure his last words to me were that I was toast?

'I've moved back to Devon and I won't be in London for a while.'

'So you won't want to know about the work I've secured you,' he said, sounding sulky.

'An audition?' I said, surprised. (And hopeful. A girl can't live on fresh air and moonlit views for long, after all.)

'Not exactly,' Sebastian backtracked. '*Vanity Case* magazine wants to do a "What's in your make-up bag?" feature. Urgently. As in tomorrow. And someone from *Horizons*, the online travel mag, wants your recommendations for your top getaway. Seeing as you're fond of a quick getaway,' he said slyly, 'they thought you'd be perfect. No money, but it's all good exposure.'

'I've had plenty of exposure recently,' I reminded him, biting back my disappointment. 'I want to act and earn money.'

'There is one paid thing.' He paused.

'Go on.'

'A voiceover for ladies' . . .' He coughed. 'Incontinence products.'

I was speechless.

'Hello? Damn. I've lost her.' Sebastian muttered into the phone.

He *had* lost me. For the last two years I'd followed his every instruction. Auditioned for small acting roles because he'd said I didn't have the gravitas to handle anything weightier. And now this: I bet he hadn't asked Cecily to be the voice of weak bladders. Even if I didn't manage to get another agent, Sebastian Nichols would never represent me again. I'd seen the light.

'The media attention I accidentally created for *Victory Road* has worked out well for other members of the cast. Freddie Major's agent has even landed him a job in the West End. You, on the other hand, have decided to align me with nappies for nans. So thanks, but no thanks. It's time to part ways, Sebastian.'

There was a terse silence for a few seconds.

'I've renegotiated your contract on *Victory Road* and got you two PR slots today. You're hot property at the moment, you might never get this attention again, you've got to use it. You need me.'

'*I* renegotiated the contract,' I argued. 'And I'm only famous for that clip on YouTube! I want to be known for my acting skills, not a one-off tantrum.'

'Good luck with that,' he scoffed.

I took a deep breath, determined not to sink to his level. 'Thank you. And thank you for the press opportunities, but I'm afraid I can't help.'

Sebastian began whinging that he'd have to find someone else now at the last minute and leave the Odeon in Leicester Square just as Johnny Depp had arrived on the red carpet.

I stayed silent.

'Fine,' said Sebastian. 'But if you're serious about your career then you need to think about where your loyalties lie.'

'If I ever want a lecture in loyalty, Sebastian, the last person I'd come to is you. Enjoy the party.'

I put the phone down. I wouldn't be taking advice from him ever again. From now on I was going to run my career my way.

Next morning after breakfast, Theo and I wrapped up warm and took the coastal path towards the village for the last packet of tablets for his first-aid box. I'd only been away for a few days but it felt good to breathe in the briny fresh air again. Fluffy clouds scudded boisterously across the blue sky, and here on the cliffs the wind was keeping the temperature low. But breezy or not, there was no escaping the sublime scenery of this little Devonshire hideaway.

'I honestly think this might be my favourite place in the world,' I said happily.

'For eighteen months I regretted moving here,' Theo admitted. 'But since I started my marketing plans for Brightside Holidays, I'm beginning to see the attraction of the place myself. I even managed to take a booking while you were away. Brucey-darling and Pen-Pen have booked again for next year.'

The swelling in his eyes had begun to go down; if you didn't know better you'd think they were just a bit watery from the wind. In fact, he looked a completely different man to the defeated and depressed Theo I'd found when I'd first arrived in Brightside Cove. He looked like a man who was looking on the bright side.

'That's brilliant!' I bumped his arm with mine affectionately. 'And what are your marketing plans?'

We'd reached the end of the path and joined the pavement that led into the village. To the left of us was the pretty little row of cottages I'd seen when I'd first arrived with Archie, painted in ice-cream colours of cream, pink, pale green, yellow and lavender, and opposite them stood the Mermaid Gift and Gallery. Perfect. Utterly perfect. Shame there wasn't a proper job for me here, or I'd be tempted to stay for ever.

'I thought perhaps you could persuade some of your celebrity friends to visit.' He grinned boyishly at me. 'You know: golden sunsets, beautiful beaches, luxury accommodation endorsed by the cast of *Victory Road*, or whoever. What do you think?'

We walked past the Mermaid Gift and Gallery and I looked for Eliza inside. She was with a customer and didn't see me. I'd called her last night; she'd been mortified to hear about the cat allergy and had even offered to take Mittens back. Theo wouldn't hear of it.

'I love it here, you know that,' I said diplomatically.

'I detect a but.'

'But my friends are . . . different. They like the idea of the seaside, but when they're not on the beach they want hotels and restaurants owned by celebrity chefs, they want to be able to peruse little boutiques. I'm not sure a crab sandwich at The Sea Urchin followed by a shopping spree in the Mermaid Gift and Gallery will really do it for them.'

We passed an elderly couple in deckchairs sitting outside one of the cottages with blankets across their knees. The man had his binoculars trained on the gulls swooping overhead while the woman was lost in her knitting. A pot of tea sat between them. Theo and I exchanged affectionate looks.

'I take your point,' he said with a chuckle. 'It's hardly London-by-the-sea, is it?'

'Which is exactly what I love about it,' I said, looping my arm through his and giving it a squeeze. 'And so will others. We just have to tap into the right market.'

We walked down the hill past the cottages and shops until we reached Jethro's General Store. A small fruit and vegetable display stood next to a rack of faded maps and nautical tide tables. Inside the door it had a motley assortment of buckets and spades, beach shoes and sunhats, aisles of household essentials in the middle, a mini post office desk in the front corner and next to it, a small ice-cream counter.

An elderly man with a fuzz of grey hair escaping from under a New York Yankees baseball cap jolted awake from his snooze as we entered. He struggled to get out of his chair and waved away Theo's offer of help while I waited at the counter.

'Just one packet of paracetamol today please, Jethro,' said Theo.

The old man screwed up his face into a scowl. 'More drugs? T'aint normal, that.'

'They're for first-aid kits to put in self-catering cottages,' I explained. 'Not personal consumption.'

'Yes. We've kitted out the three little cottages at Driftwood Lodge,' said Theo, leaning his elbow casually against a pyramid of boxes of washing powder. 'Hopefully regular bookings will mean more customers for you.'

I felt a tinge of pride; Theo striking up conversation was a huge improvement. He'd be actually making friends with people soon.

'Tourists?' Jethro said morosely. 'As if I wasn't busy enough.'

I cast my eyes over the layer of dust on the shelf of tinned peas and managed to smother a smile.

'We probably won't attract many visitors,' said Theo, hastily backtracking.

'Probably not.' Jethro's face relaxed a bit.

'It looks as if not everyone shares our vision for boosting tourism,' I whispered to Theo when Jethro turned away to get the tablets.

I added a scoop full of fudge to our purchases and we left the shop and headed down on to the beach. The tide was on its way in and we kept to the dry sand away from the approaching water. Children pored over the rock pools at the far side of the bay with nets and buckets, and at the water's edge, two adults were swinging a little girl up over the waves and she was shrieking with joy. Theo noticed them too and I saw a look of grief flash across his face. My stomach twisted for him and Kate; that could have been them playing in the waves with their daughter.

I offered him some fudge and we fell quiet as we chewed on chunks of it.

'So when we do start this marketing campaign, then?'

Theo's face lit up. 'You'll help drum up business?'

'Yep. In fact,' I said, suddenly recalling that awkward conversation with Sebastian last night, 'I've got a travel website who might be interested in covering Brightside Holidays. That would be brilliant publicity. I can ring them, if you like?'

While Theo gushed over how fantastic I was and how he was going to pay me a percentage of all the bookings I helped him attract, my mind was racing ahead.

I would do anything to help him, I decided. Because if Kate came back and liked what she saw, then maybe they could be a family again. And what was the point in having well-connected friends if you couldn't take advantage of them now and again?

Chapter 14

Theo and I spent hours the next day at the kitchen table drawing up a marketing plan.

'The key to being famous is to put yourself out there,' I'd said when he'd laid out a large blank sheet of paper.

Theo tapped a pen against his mug. 'What happened to simply being the best at what you do and letting your customers find you?'

'Very funny.'

'I'm serious. Word of mouth is way more effective.'

'Name me one successful brand that doesn't spend a fortune on advertising.'

'Krispy Kreme Donuts,' said Theo smoothly. 'The world's number-one doughnut brand. But I take your point. It took them seventy years to get there. Time isn't on our side.'

For the next few hours we brainstormed. And by the end of it we had ideas for promotions, discounts, newsletters, competitions, social media . . . you name it.

The subtle approach was out; the hard sell was in.

It had to be: we had three empty cottages, zero budget and we wanted plenty of bookings to show Kate when she returned at the end of June.

There was no time to lose, no opportunity too small to pass up.

According to Nigel Rees from the Coastal Cottages bookings website, Theo's page was due to go live in the next day or so, which should give the cottages a boost, but in the meantime there was still plenty we could do. So while Theo designed a Facebook campaign advertising Brightside Holidays as the ideal destination for a painting/reading/yoga holiday location, I swallowed my pride and called Sebastian for the email address of the travel journalist at *Horizons*.

'And while you're on, don't broadcast this,' I said to Sebastian in a low voice, knowing he'd do exactly the opposite, 'but Brightside Holidays will be *the* coolest place to stay this summer, I guarantee it. It's undiscovered. So far. You and I are literally the only ones in the know. That travel website will love it, I promise.'

'What makes it so special down there?' he said with a sneer. 'Good restaurants, quaint little shops, plenty of nightlife?'

'Oh yes,' I said airily, crossing my fingers. 'All that. And there is no other holiday accommodation here. Very exclusive. Our three cottages will be booked up in a flash.'

Sebastian loved being first. I knew he wouldn't be able to resist.

'Send me the link to the website,' he said, feigning disinterest. 'It's not my bag, but it always pays to keep ahead of the pack.'

'Of course,' I said sweetly. 'And if you do get any interest from anyone, I'm sure we can sort out some commission . . .'

By five o'clock, I'd given an interview to the editor at *Horizons*, and sent him some photographs, and Theo, with a sleeping kitten on his lap, had put the finishing touches to the visitors' welcome folders complete with a map of the best beaches, a copy of the local tide tables and a list of places to eat in a five-mile radius.

'Fancy a walk to The Sea Urchin?' I stood up and stretched my spine. 'All this office work has made me thirsty.'

'I've got a better idea.' Theo carefully put Mittens in his basket and fetched a bottle of champagne from the pantry.

'This has been here for ages. I haven't had anything to celebrate. But now I think I do. We can have it outside.'

I approved wholeheartedly of both the champagne and his celebratory mood and while he ran the bottle under the cold tap to chill it a bit, I went out to water the geraniums I'd planted last week. I found a watering can and filled it from the outside tap and when I turned round, there was a woman in the courtyard holding a bicycle, staring at me.

'Arrghh,' I said, sloshing water on my feet. 'You startled me.'

'Sorry about that.' She leaned the bike against the wall and pulled off her cycle helmet. A shimmering curtain of stunning red hair fell to her shoulders. She was a bit older than me at a guess and she had long athletic legs and a slim boyish figure, both accentuated by tight-fitting sportswear.

'I'm Nina.' I put the watering can down and walked across to her, my hand outstretched.

'Yes, I know.' She ignored my hand. 'You were at Kate and Theo's wedding. Also you were in the newspaper at the weekend.'

'I was,' I confirmed, racking my brains to remember who she was. I drew a blank. 'I'm sorry, I don't recall meeting you at the wedding.'

'I didn't know them then.' She lifted a cake tin from the basket at the front of her bike and took her handbag out of the child seat at the back. 'But I've heard about you from Kate.'

I was guessing from her pinched expression that what she'd heard hadn't been entirely good.

'Champagne!' Theo cried, appearing from the front door carrying two glasses and a bottle. 'For my favourite actress! Without whom—' He caught sight of our visitor mid-sentence, turned bright red and began to splutter. 'Molly! What are you doing here?'

The name rang a bell; this must be the friend of Kate's who Eliza had mentioned. So if Kate didn't already know I was here, she probably would soon . . .

'Interrupting a celebration, by the look of it,' Molly

replied. In contrast to Theo's flaming cheeks, she had gone as white as a ghost. 'I heard from Eliza that you hadn't been well, so I brought you a cake, but I can see that I needn't have worried. I'll be off.'

She rammed her helmet back on.

Theo hurried over to her. 'Wait! Please, join us for a drink in the garden.'

After a bit of juggling he managed to force a glass of bubbly on her and ushered us towards the gate to the garden at the back of the house.

'Sorry about this,' he murmured, catching my arm. 'Her husband left her for someone else last year at her thirtieth birthday party and she's a bit prickly.'

'Don't worry, we'll soon sort out any misunderstandings over a drink,' I replied and sent him inside for an extra glass.

I went through the gate and couldn't believe my eyes. I hadn't ventured into the garden since I'd witnessed Bruce and Penelope rolling around on the grass creating their *Crescendo of Passion* canvas. But in the last few days, Theo had clearly been very busy.

There was a new fire pit surrounded by wooden seating made from old pallets, and a long wooden table. Molly and I both took a seat at it.

She regarded me suspiciously.

'It was kind of you to come and check on him,' I said. 'And bring cake. I'm glad he has friends looking out for him. Other friends, I mean, besides me. Because that's all I am. A friend.'

'Men. They're all the same.' She tightened her grip on the cake tin and turned her face away.

Luckily, Theo reappeared just then with a third champagne flute.

'You approve?' he said, nodding at the new garden additions.

'Massively,' I said. 'You must have spent a fortune!'

He shook his head smugly. 'Free to a good home from a hotel that was closing. Just paid for delivery.'

'So.' I smiled brightly. 'Are you going to introduce us properly?'

Theo ran a hand through his curls. 'Yes. Sorry. Nina, this is Molly, a friend of ours.'

'Of *Kate's*,' Molly corrected. 'Whereas Nina is obviously a friend of yours.'

'Theo and I have known each other for years,' I said lightly. 'My brother Archie was Theo's best man.'

'Yes.' Molly's nostrils flared. 'Kate told me. So what are you celebrating?'

'Brightside Holidays,' said Theo, chinking his glass against hers. 'Nina's been helping me get it off the ground.'

Molly slurped at the bubbles but didn't raise her glass. 'So Kate knows she's here?'

'Ah, well . . .' Theo began.

'Typical.' She thumped her glass down. 'As if Kate hasn't been through enough, as soon as her back's turned—'

'There's absolutely nothing going on between Theo and me. This is a surprise for her,' I said, jumping in quickly. 'Kate has given Theo an ultimatum to have the cottage business up and running by the time she gets back and I've offered to help. And let's not forget,' I said quietly, 'that Theo has been through just as much as Kate.'

'I know that.' She huffed indignantly. 'But I would have helped, Theo. Kate asked if I'd keep an eye on you, so I came round every day for a week offering to help. But you wouldn't let me in.'

'She really asked you to do that?' he said.

'Really.' Molly tucked her hair behind her ears.

'Sorry,' Theo mumbled. 'I went to pieces for a while. I only let Archie in because . . . I had no choice.'

He met my eye and I remembered that awful day with the bailiffs and the surprise arrival of the Bird family and the state of Driftwood Lodge. The coffers still weren't exactly

150

overflowing, but the recent bookings, plus the sale of his car to Archie were currently keeping the wolf from the door. And I had every confidence that he'd stay on top of his finances from now on.

'Whatever.' She knocked back the rest of her champagne and stood up. 'You've got an *actress* to help you so obviously my professional services aren't required.'

I willed Theo to say something to smooth her feathers.

'Okay. Cheerio.' He tipped up his glass and swallowed. 'And thanks for the cake.'

Give me strength.

'Molly, please don't rush off.' I touched her arm. 'It seems to me that we all want the same thing. To give Theo and Kate the happy ending they deserve. I'm going to be here for another few weeks and I'd like us to be friends. Plus, there's still some fizz left in the bottle.'

She bit her lip. 'It's tempting.'

I felt a twinge of hope until I realized she was contemplating another drink rather than being my friend.

Then she lifted her bag on to her shoulder. 'But I've got to pick my son up from my neighbour's soon.'

'How is little . . . ?' said Theo, topping up everyone's glasses regardless.

'Ellis,' said Molly with a flicker of amusement. 'His name is Ellis and he's fine. Thanks for the offer of another drink, but I'd better not or I'll fall off my bike.'

'Okay, another time?' I began to walk her back to the courtyard.

'Sure. Listen, I email Kate regularly,' she hesitated. 'I'm guessing you don't want me to mention to her that you're here?'

'It's up to you,' I said. 'She's your friend. If you think that she needs to know, when she's seven thousand miles away, unable to do anything but worry about it, tell her. But please believe me, my only reason for being here is to get Kate and Theo's marriage back on track.'

151

She thought about it for a moment and, with a curt nod, handed me the cake tin and put her helmet back on. 'I believe you.'

I was so relieved I pulled her into a hug just as a car roared up the drive and curved into a skid sending a shower of gravel towards our legs.

'What on earth . . . ?' Molly gasped.

It was Archie in Theo's old Triumph, which was unrecognizable. The red paintwork was glossy, the chrome gleamed and the engine sounded rich and throaty. Archie grinned at us through the driver's side window and revved the engine. And then the passenger door flew open and Eliza jumped out.

Molly went over to greet her. She must have been a few years older than Eliza, but it seemed they knew each other well.

Archie got out, jingling his keys proudly. 'What do you think of my new hobby?'

'That depends whether it's helped lower your blood pressure.' I prodded his chest.

'Ah, doctors,' said Archie, waving a hand. 'What do they know?'

Theo slapped him on the back. 'Can I have my car back please? I'll return all your money.'

'Ha, not likely. It's worth a fortune now. Look at this.'

In an instant Archie had the bonnet up and the two men stuck their heads under it.

'So how did you end up in my brother's car?' I asked, joining Eliza and Molly who were whispering. Probably about me.

'Hey, Nina,' Eliza said in a high voice, her plump cheeks turning as pink as her hair.

Definitely talking about me.

'He saw me struggling with my bag at the bottom of the drive and gave me a lift,' she said, fanning her face. 'And you've met Molly, that's nice, now we can all be friends.'

152

I looked at Molly, who also looked flushed.

'Eliza's just told me how you gave up your job and rushed back from London to look out for Theo,' she muttered. 'I'm sorry I doubted your motives. They've been through so much as a couple and I really want them to have the happy-ever-after I didn't get with my marriage. I'm afraid recent events have left me a bit suspicious of men and attractive single women.'

'Mine and Theo's relationship is completely above board, I promise,' I said with a grin. 'Friends?'

'Sure.' She smiled. 'I've never met a celebrity. I feel a bit star struck.'

I laughed. 'You hid it very well.'

'Yay, now we can all be mermaids together,' cried Eliza. 'The tails have arrived from America just in time! Let's go and try them on!'

Molly and I pulled faces at each other as she scooted round to Archie's boot and pulled out a big nylon zipper bag.

'More drinks, everyone?' Theo held up the bottle.

'Not for me,' said Archie. 'I'd rather have a cup of tea.'

'Me too,' said Molly, whipping off her helmet. Archie looked at her properly for the first time and obviously liked what he saw.

'Molly meet Archie, my brother. Archie, this is Molly, a friend of Kate's.'

'Wow,' said Archie. 'I mean hello. Pleased to meet you.'

'Hey,' she said, coolly holding out her hand for him to shake.

'Sorry, I'm a bit sweaty,' he said with a grin.

'You are,' agreed Molly, wiping her hands on her leggings – a gesture that also wiped the smile off his face.

'Molly has a little boy,' I added. 'Called Ellis.'

'He'd like your car. He's only four but he's car mad,' said Molly. 'Unfortunately I can't drive, and since my husband left me for Tess the Tart, he's reduced to riding on the back of my bike.'

'I am rather proud of the Triumph,' Archie said. 'Spent a fortune on it to get it running again. Treated myself to a deluxe mohair hood. Top of the range.'

'Sounds like a waste of money to me,' said Molly, doubtfully.

Archie swallowed. 'Well, I—'

'Who wants cake?' I said, whipping the lid off the cake tin. 'Molly made it.'

'Yes please,' said Archie, patting his flat stomach. 'What sort is it?'

I had never seen my brother eat cake in his life. He was a savoury snacker through and through.

'Oh, nothing special,' she shrugged, 'just a banana loaf.'

'My favourite,' said Archie goofily, gazing at her.

He hated bananas.

'Then it's your lucky day,' she said drily, pulling her phone from her pocket.

I went in to fetch a knife and some plates while Molly phoned her neighbour to check on Ellis. This afternoon was turning into quite a party.

Chapter 15

Before I got as far as the kitchen the phone in the hall rang.

'Brightside Holidays, how may I help?' I said.

'Maxine here,' said my mentor bluntly. 'How's the friend in need?'

'Apart from being allergic to his own cat, he's fine, thankfully,' I said, explaining about the series of unfortunate events that had led Eliza to suspect Theo was suicidal. 'Bit of a wasted journey, really.'

'On the contrary,' she argued. 'Now your friend knows he can count on your support when he *does* need it; we all want someone who'll drop everything for us. Bravo.'

'That's a lovely way to put it, thank you,' I said, with a rush of warmth for the usually no-nonsense Maxine.

'So now what?' she said.

'Technically, I could come back to London,' I said. My mood dropped a notch at the thought.

'No need. The writers are raving about the "long coma" storyline you and I concocted. Ron and Marjorie will soon be conducting a clandestine affair right under Nurse Elsie's nose. The cast is thrilled. It's going to be very uncomfortable viewing.'

She said this last bit with relish and I couldn't help smiling.

'I'm so glad the show hasn't suffered too badly after I leaked my own death,' I said. 'What a relief.'

'Told you,' she said blithely. 'And the PR team thinks the new thread is strong enough to make the cover of *Sensational Soaps* magazine. So all in all you've probably done us a favour.'

'In that case, I'd like to stay here and get Theo's business properly established.' I paused. 'But two months away from London is a long time, do you think my career will suffer?'

'Don't be ridiculous,' she scoffed. 'You're still on screen in *Victory Road* and even after the episode in which you're injured airs, you'll still appear comatose under the bed sheets.'

She was right but it wasn't quite what I meant. I didn't have an agent any more, and I was worried if I wasn't seen out and about that people in the business would forget about me.

'But London's where it's at,' I said. 'I should be seen, I should network. Build my profile.'

Maxine clicked her tongue. 'I think you've done enough of that for the time being.'

I sighed. 'You're right. All I really want to do is be a better actress. But I can't even work on that if I'm down here.'

'Not true. Laurence Olivier once said that an actor should be able to create the universe in the palm of his hand. And to do that, dear heart, you need to experience the universe, the world, life. Use your time away from London wisely: feast on life, observe, interact, soak up the emotions of others, get high on new experiences. It will add new depths to your craft. Something you'll never get from flirting with the gossip columns. Whatever that agent of yours says.'

'Ex-agent,' I said. 'And yes, I'll do just that, I promise.'

Just then Eliza dragged her huge bag into the hall and pulled out a long strip of iridescent fabric in shimmering tones of blue and another of orange and pink.

'Sorry to interrupt,' she said, 'but do you want to be Peacock Mermaid or Tropical Mermaid? I've already bagged Bahama Blush Mermaid.'

'What was that?' Maxine demanded. 'Did someone just say mermaid?'

'Got to go, Maxine,' I said with a giggle. 'Looks like I'm going to be very busy experiencing life.'

Ten minutes later, Molly, Eliza and I had been transformed.

'Oh my word,' I laughed, adjusting my realistic-looking scallop-shell bra. 'I like it. I really am a mermaid.'

The full-length mirror confirmed it. From the waist down I was encased in a tight spandex tail which changed through a spectrum of blues as I moved. Eliza added the final touch: a stiff piece of plastic which she stuffed into the fin-shaped bottom section. She pulled me up to standing and turned me round on the spot.

'Amazing. And this is just on dry land,' she beamed. 'Wait till you get into the water.'

'That water, out there?' I pointed through my bedroom window to the sea. Even from this distance I could see the frills of white, indicating how rough the waves were.

'It's the most incredible experience,' she confirmed. 'And free, that's what I love about it: the freedom. Kicking powerfully through the water so fast it feels like you're flying. You feel magical.'

'And totally freezing, I should imagine,' Molly put in.

'Pah,' Eliza said, as if hypothermia was beneath the concerns of a mythical sea-creature, and tugged at her own tail, which was straining a bit over her generous curves.

'You've been obsessed with mermaids since primary school,' Molly said, wriggling her legs into a very tight orange and pink Lycra sheath. She looked incredibly sexy in hers. If anyone was going to lure men on to the rocks with a siren song, it was Molly. 'I'm so happy you've made this happen.'

'I know. Remember how jealous I was of Madison when I realized she'd been named after the mermaid in that film *Splash*?' She turned to me to explain. 'Molly's little sister Madison was in my class.'

Molly snorted. 'And on careers day Madison said you got in trouble because you filled in your career form saying you wanted to be a mermaid and your key skills were keeping your eyes open under water and holding your breath.'

'That horrible Mr Norton had no imagination. He wanted me to learn touch-typing.' Eliza pulled a face.

The pink in her hair matched her tail perfectly and her bikini top, which was doing its best to protect her modesty, had tiny shells knitted together with silver thread. She looked ethereal and beautiful and completely elated.

'I definitely couldn't see you cooped up in an office, typing all day long,' I said.

'There was no chance of that. I had a vision, I knew I could make it happen. I had a job in an underwater-themed restaurant in Australia for two months. They had a tank behind the bar and I used to swim backwards and forwards and wave at the customers. Best job ever.'

'That was a real job?' I said, never having considered that there was such a demand for mermaids before meeting Eliza.

'She's a brilliant swimmer,' said Molly proudly. 'Very powerful legs.'

'So how did you end up running a gift shop?'

'Oh, you know, parental commitments,' Eliza said.

No, I thought wryly, not having experienced much in the way of commitment from mine.

Eliza hopped in front of the mirror and pulled us either side of her and while we gazed at our reflections, preening and twisting from side to side, she told us how she'd taken over the shop for her mum, who'd gone to live with her sister in Wales. Her first task had been to change the name from *Seaside Tackle* to *Mermaid Gift and Gallery*. Her second had been to turn a profit for the first time in a long time and only then could she start working on her own plan to open a mermaid school in Brightside Cove.

'And this summer, I will,' she said, tilting her chin up. 'With the help of you two, my Siren Sisters.'

'Isn't that a town in the Cotswolds?' Molly sniggered, nudging Eliza.

'I should send that teacher a picture of us dressed up,' said Eliza. 'Prove him wrong.'

'As long as I can do this.' I sucked in my stomach and turned sideways.

'No!' Eliza gasped in mock horror. 'Being a mermaid is about having the body confidence to say this is who we are, we're real!'

Molly and I exchanged amused glances but the irony of mermaids being 'real' was lost on Eliza.

'I want women to come and have the most amazing day, to feel beautiful, to celebrate their bodies whatever they look like and to connect with their inner beauty. And I want to put Brightside Cove on the map as having its very own mermaid school.'

'That's really inspiring.' I looked at Eliza afresh; her ambitions might have been different to mine, but there was a steely determination behind those vivid blue eyes that I'd not seen until today.

'Says the famous actress,' Eliza retorted.

I shook my head. 'I'm only famous for my mistake, not my acting. Normally, I get people coming up to me and saying, "Have we met? Do I know you?" But one day I plan to be famous for my talents.'

'Your goals make mine look a bit dull,' said Molly, wrinkling her nose. 'All I want is for my business to be successful so I can support my boy and never let him down like his dad did.'

'Aww.' Eliza hugged her. 'You could never let Ellis down.'

Molly's words transported me back to something Archie had said when he was little. That he wanted to be a successful businessman when he grew up, so he could look after Mum and me and never let us down. He'd done it, too. My only regret for him was that he seemed to be so wrapped up in his work that he'd never given himself the chance to fall in love. And he was such a lovely man; he deserved someone to love him.

Molly was still talking, listing the simple things she'd like to do: pay her bills without worrying, learn to drive ready for when Ellis started school in September, save up to take him on holiday to Disneyworld because he was a massive Disney fan . . . Selfless things. Which made my goals feel very selfish.

'What is your business?' I asked, picking up my brush and running it through my hair.

'A bit of washing and ironing for people.' She shrugged. 'Just fitting in around Ellis.'

'Do you do laundry for holiday lets?' I asked, remembering how much washing the Bird family had generated during their week's stay.

'I would if there were any,' said Molly. 'Tourism hasn't quite made it to this part of Devon.'

'Not yet,' I said. 'But I reckon if the three of us work together, it could be quite a summer for Brightside Cove.'

My phone began to buzz and Eliza handed it to me.

'If that's Idris Elba,' she said, 'it's probably for me.'

It was Trudy FaceTiming me. Molly began fiddling with Eliza's hair to make it more mermaidy and I took my phone to the window to talk to Trudy in London. At least I assumed it was London, it was very dark and there were two pale sticks behind her head.

'I wish you had mobile reception in that remote location of yours,' Trudy hissed at the screen. 'So I could phone you like a normal person, I could really do without you being able to see me.'

They were legs behind her, I realized, in high heels.

'Are you kneeling on the floor?'

'Yes, I'm hiding behind the counter at work and I might have a booking for your cottages. Someone special.'

160

'One of your Harrods clients?'

'My *best* client.'

'I love you, Trudy!' My heart tweaked with joy. Having a reservation would be a real boost to our otherwise empty diary and maybe Theo would get his free word-of-mouth advertising sooner than planned.

Trudy pulled a face. 'Hear me out first; you might not be so keen. I told her all about you in your exclusive hideaway, about the sea salt facials and al fresco clean eating last week and she wants to hold her hen party there.'

'That's great!' I said, before registering what she'd just said. 'Oh. You know, I didn't really have a facial, it was just the bracing air and we only ate breakfast al fresco because the kitchen wasn't finished.' And I was no expert but I didn't think bacon sandwiches constituted clean eating.

'I know that *now*!' she said in a panicky voice. 'But I'd already told Sapphire Spencer by then.'

'*The* Sapphire Spencer?' Eliza and Molly immediately forced their faces next to mine to see the screen.

That was what I was striving for, I thought wryly, a reaction like that at the mere mention of my name.

'From *Maidens of Mayfair*?' Eliza squawked.

'She's my favourite,' Molly exclaimed.

Trudy's eyes widened as the women moved closer to the screen. 'Shush! She's the other side of the counter waiting for the go-ahead. Nina could literally save her life. Who are you two?'

I introduced everybody, at which point Trudy noticed we were dressed as mermaids and we had a short discussion about the practicalities of being half woman, half fish, like how to slip elegantly from the rocks into the sea without pulling a muscle and what to do if you need a wee, until Trudy was tapped on the back by her co-worker and forced to serve a customer.

'I'll be right back,' she whispered. The screen went black as we disappeared into her pocket.

Eliza and I flopped on the bed while Molly took out her own phone and texted her neighbour to extend Ellis's play date again.

'I can't leave now, not while we're in Harrods talking to Sapphire Spencer. And just so you're not in any doubt, Nina,' she said solemnly, 'we are definitely friends.'

'And if Brightside Holidays is going to host a hen party, you are definitely going to get the contract to do our laundry too,' I said, feeling more pleased with myself by the second as Molly kicked her tail in the air with joy.

'This is the best day of my life,' said Eliza.

'I met Sapphire at a party once,' I said. 'She's got a doctorate in entomology but the producers make her pretend to be dim on screen.'

Sapphire Spencer was as glamorous and gorgeous as her name suggested. She and the rest of the cast of the reality show about rich girls living in luxury in London had been at the same *X Factor* after party as me last Christmas.

'We met by the vodka luge and Sapphire confided that research had been conducted on ice cubes in public places and had found eleven strains of bacteria including E. coli, listeria and campo-something. I stuck to wine after that.'

Eliza was speechless. I wasn't sure what had shocked her more: Sapphire's brains or ice-cube germs.

'The nearest I've ever been to a celebrity is Big Dave,' said Molly. 'Until I met you, of course.'

It was on the tip of my tongue to ask what his claim to fame was, but just then Trudy FaceTimed us again, still hiding under the counter.

'Right. Down to business. Sapphire is starting to flap and her driver is waiting outside.'

'Then just tell her yes,' I said simply, 'she can come whenever she likes, how many are in her party?'

'Are they filming it for TV?' Eliza whispered, gripping my arm in her excitement. 'Cos that's absolutely fine.'

'No, no, no. This has to be top secret. Total media black-out until after the wedding. Promise?' Trudy wagged a finger at us until we promised. I made a mental note to make sure Eliza's brother understood too.

'Okay, here are the details: she gets married in two weeks to a Canadian called Brad. Her hen weekend has to start tomorrow because her friends are packing as we speak, expecting a stay in a luxury Scottish hotel.'

'Tomorrow?' I echoed, mentally baulking at what still needed doing.

'Yes,' Trudy continued, 'and the location has been leaked to the media and the hotel manager has called to say he can't guarantee her privacy. So she's had to cancel due to a press exclusivity clause with the wedding magazine *My Dream Day*. She needs somewhere else: undiscovered, with a pamper package and excellent food. For twelve guests. I thought of you.'

I exchanged glances with Molly and Eliza. Sapphire's original plan sounded very high end. Driftwood Lodge was lovely, but the potholes in the drive and the second-hand garden furniture and budget kitchen utensils didn't really scream luxury.

'What do you think, girls?' I said to the others. 'Theo can certainly use the money.'

'And Kate would be really impressed.' Molly's eyes shone. 'I can do Indian head massage.' She cleared her throat. 'Sort of.'

'And we can concoct some sort of salt-water facial between us,' said Eliza. 'How hard can it be?'

I didn't answer; I was doing a bed count. We could just about squeeze them in. 'What about the excellent food bit? My repertoire runs to pasta and cakes, and Theo isn't much better.'

'It's two for one on mussels at The Sea Urchin on Saturday, remember,' Eliza suggested.

'How could I forget,' I said.

'There's a company in Thymeford that delivers dinner party food called Deliciously Devon,' Molly said.

That was more like it. We could buy the food in; it would cost more, but at least the quality would be guaranteed. I gave Molly a thumbs-up.

'We can do it but it will cost a lot of money,' I warned Trudy.

'So that's a yes.' Trudy exhaled and fanned her face. 'Hallelujah. I'll put you on to Sapphire.'

There was a flurry of yelps and hair smoothing beside me as Sapphire Spencer appeared on the screen. Her white-blonde hair was styled into a sleek pixie cut and a lace bra strap peaked out from her off-the shoulder top. I held my phone at arm's length to get all three of us in view for her.

'Hey, everyone.' She gave us a little wave.

'Hey, Sapphire!' Molly and Eliza chorused coyly.

'Nina, how are you coping with all the media attention? Takes some getting used to, doesn't it?'

I smiled. 'I'm glad to be away from it, to be honest; I don't know how you do it.'

'Trudy told me all about your secret location,' she said in a low voice. 'And I just knew it would be perfect for us.'

'We'd be delighted to have you and your hens as our guests at Brightside Holidays,' I said. I didn't like to tell her that since being revealed by Danny, it was no longer exactly 'secret'. 'It'll be a bit more rough and ready than your planned Scottish weekend, but the welcome will be warm.'

'Oh, we can do rough, that's no problem,' said Sapphire airily, 'and all we want is a total getaway from the hurly-burly of London.'

'We can certainly offer you that,' I said.

'I shouldn't really say this,' Sapphire leaned closer to the screen and lowered her voice, 'but the magazine is footing the bill, and they're blaming an internal leak for the press intrusion, so money is no object.'

Behind Sapphire I could see and hear the hubbub and the opulence of Harrods, the elegant clientele passing through the beauty department and the glamorous staff wafting bottles of perfume. Then I looked up and caught sight of the three of us in the mirror in our bikini tops and fish tails. The situation was so ridiculous and surreal that the urge to laugh was almost too much to bear.

'I'll bear that in mind when I put the menus together,' I replied.

'I am so grateful.' Sapphire pressed her slim fingers to her chest. A rock almost big enough for a mermaid to dive off glinted from her ring finger and it distracted me so much that the phone in my hand dipped showing Sapphire our outfits.

Sapphire's jaw dropped. 'Are you . . . ? Did I just see . . . ?'

'Yes. You did just see three mermaids.' I began to laugh.

'We're the Siren Sis— Ouch.' Eliza rubbed her ribs as Molly jabbed her.

'My sister loves mermaids; she is going to adore this!' Sapphire squealed. 'This is going to be fabulous!'

Within minutes the deal was done: Trudy had made her best client very happy, the mermaid school had officially accepted its first students, Brightside Holidays had taken its largest, most lucrative booking ever and Molly, thanks to the promise of a significant amount of laundry, was going to have some money left over from paying the bills this month. Theo, who'd never heard of Sapphire Spencer or *Maidens of Mayfair*, was nonetheless blown away by his sudden change in fortune and didn't even notice we were dressed as mermaids when we called the men upstairs.

Archie did. Or rather he noticed how ravishing Molly looked, and I had a feeling we'd be seeing him quite a bit more regularly in Brightside Cove from now on.

My head was still spinning when I climbed into bed that

night. Tomorrow, all three cottages would be full to bursting with twelve women all ready for a good time, all expecting the weekend of their lives. Brightside Cove might be tiny compared to London, but there was never a dull moment . . .

Chapter 16

Dawn at Brightside Cove was my favourite time of day and the next morning I ventured down on the beach to greet it. The air was still and the sea was calm. The tide had washed away yesterday's footprints from the sand and I tiptoed over it to perch on a rock and wait for the sun. There was no one else around but at the far end of the cove in the distance, a dog that could possibly have been Mabel the spaniel sniffed around in front of the lifeboat house, wagging its tail like a rudder. I shielded my eyes and searched for the owner – the man who'd shouted at me for not looking in my rear-view mirror – but the dog appeared to be alone.

I pulled my knees up to my chin and focused on the sound of the waves as the water whispered gently against the rocks. And, as the sun began to rise, I closed my eyes, feeling rather than seeing the start of a brand-new day, of new beginnings and almost certainly the most exciting thing to happen in Brightside Cove for a very long time: the Maidens of Mayfair would be here in less than twelve hours and we were going to give them a weekend they'd never forget.

At eleven o'clock I pulled on a jacket and shut Mittens safely in the kitchen before heading into the village. Theo had been dispatched on a shopping expedition to stock up on thick towels, scented candles and twelve towelling robes, and Molly and I had given all three cottages a thorough clean and made all the beds.

She had strong views on our choice of bedding. We had, it seemed, made several errors from a laundry expert's point of view.

'Better to get larger flat sheets than fitted ones,' she said as we stretched corners under the master bed in Penguin's Pad. 'They take up less room in the linen cupboard because they fold flatter and they're quicker to iron. And quicker,' she added, 'means I charge you less.

'And polyester cotton rather than pure cotton,' she commented about the lovely Egyptian cotton pillowcases that Archie had chosen during that mad dash when we were waiting for our first arrivals. 'It takes less time to dry, and on a wet weekend in November, you'll thank me for it.'

By then, I was hoping that it would be Kate doing the thanking, but I took her point.

Molly had strong views on men too, 'all men are knobs' being a favourite. Her ex-husband, Steve, now lived thirty miles away with the twenty-three-year-old trainee from his architect's practice.

'And thirty miles on Devonshire roads is equivalent to sixty anywhere else. He only sees Ellis twice a month,' she said, flapping towels furiously, adding, 'the knob.'

But at least he did see him, I thought with a pang, wondering for the millionth time why my own father had disappeared so completely from our lives.

Before Molly left, we'd worked out how to make our own beauty treatments using store-cupboard ingredients and she'd given me a quick demonstration of her Indian head massage, which apparently did something to my chakras. Whatever it was, it sent me to sleep and when I woke up she'd gone and had scribbled the number of Deliciously Devon, the catering firm she'd mentioned, on a Post-it note and told me to ask for Angie.

I checked my watch as I headed into the village. The hen party was arriving in six hours but I wasn't worried; everything was coming together, all I needed was alcohol and food . . .

Seafood would wow my sophisticated guests and Brightside Cove had its very own supplier. What could be more delicious than freshly caught crab for our lunch tomorrow?

I found Big Dave inside his shack, mending one of his lobster cages. He was nailing lengths of plastic plumber's pipe into a wooden pallet.

The smell of fish was overwhelming and only my good manners prevented me from holding my nose. I'd only seen him from a distance before. Close up he looked like a grizzly bear with an enormous grey beard and a mass of straggly hair squished under a woolly hat.

'Hi,' I said, not quite knowing whether to call him Dave or Big Dave.

He gave the nail one final bash and looked up.

'Nina Penhaligon.' He eyed me with curiosity. 'I've been hoping to meet you. How are you bearing up under the glare of the public eye? Takes its toll, doesn't it?'

I remembered Molly referring to him as a celebrity, perhaps he'd had his fair share of unwanted attention too.

'I'm feeling a lot better now I'm away from it.'

'Tell me about it. Dave, pleased to meet you.' He dropped the hammer and grabbed my hand to shake it. His hands were rough and warm, his T-shirt bore the slogan 'Catch of the Day' and there were what looked like shreds of lobster shell in his beard. 'Nurse Elsie's not really going to die, is she? I read all the articles but I can't work out whether you're bluffing or not.'

'You'll have to keep watching to find out, I'm afraid,' I said with a grin. 'I'm sworn to absolute secrecy.' And this time I meant to keep my promise.

'Oh, I will watch. So,' he pointed to a piece of blackboard suspended from the door on orange twine, 'what you after – crab, lobster? What is it – romantic meal? Dinner party?'

'Lunch for twelve tomorrow,' I said. 'I've got guests coming who are expecting excellent food. I thought I'd serve crab salad.'

Food for guests in the past had been a takeaway from The Hot Wok in Clapham. This was catering at a whole new level for me. I felt hot just thinking about it.

Big Dave straightened up proudly. 'You won't get better live crabs in Devon. Guaranteed.'

'*Live* crabs?' I baulked, conjuring up an image of a pot of boiling water and a bucket full of innocent crabs . . . I gave myself a shake. I'd be fine. Probably, and Theo could help.

Dave laughed, which made his belly shake and his eyes crinkle.

'I can prepare and cook them for you, if you like? Perhaps garlic and chilli crab salad served with local crusty bread?'

My mouth was watering just thinking about it. 'You could do that?'

He scratched his beard. 'I couldn't do dinner, I'm already booked up tomorrow, but lunch is possible. Pricey but possible.'

I waved a hand; Sapphire had made it clear that money was no object.

'Deal,' I said happily, and we shook hands again. 'So you're a chef as well as a fisherman?'

'Don't you recognize me?' He pushed up the edge of his hat to reveal an extra inch of face. 'Dave Hope? I was a finalist on *MasterChef* years ago. My steamed razor clams with oyster sauce made the judges cry.'

Happy tears, I presumed, given Big Dave's beam of pride. His name was ringing a bell now; I had a vague memory of a winner who opened a fine-dining restaurant, won every culinary prize going but then went bankrupt and lost everything.

'Of course!' I said. 'Didn't you open a seafood restaurant?'

'Yeah. Hope on a Plate. East coast of England. My home turf.'

'And now you're in Devon. Quite a long way from home,' I said.

I picked up an oval stone from his work bench and turned it over in my hands. It was smooth and flat. The perfect skimmer. A sudden memory hit me of a hot summer's day standing ankle deep in foamy water, a large warm hand over mine, showing me how to make stones kiss the surface of the sea. And my eyes, something about the colour of my eyes . . . But as quickly as it came the picture faded and I was back listening to Big Dave's tale of woe.

'. . . so getting away from everything seemed like the best solution. I'd dreamed of opening my own bistro for years. But . . .' He stroked his beard wistfully. 'It turned out to be *Hopeless* on a Plate. I was to blame, of course; I coped really badly with fame. That's why I asked how you were doing.'

'What do you mean by coping badly?' I asked, feeling a pang of recognition.

Big Dave stared out to sea.

'I'm a walking example of how not to deal with success. I'd spent years honing my skills as a chef. It was all I ever wanted to do from being a kid.'

'Sounds like me and acting.' I smiled.

'Winning the TV show propelled me into the spotlight. I opened the restaurant and I was living my dream. But I played up to the cameras, I forgot I was just a chef and I became a man about town, attending every party, rubbing shoulders with the stars. I spent so much time chasing press coverage to keep my profile high that the business floundered.'

'Do you regret taking part in *MasterChef*?'

He shook his head. 'No, but I regret losing sight of what

I loved, which was cooking. I should have remained true to myself.'

'But if your fame was linked to your culinary skills, that was okay, surely? I long for the day I'm an instantly recognizable actress.'

Big Dave pulled a face. 'I thought it was great to begin with. I was the first famous person ever to have come from my town. There was talk of a statue at one point. Everyone was so proud.'

'I'm sure,' I said. Listening to Big Dave was like getting a tutorial on how not to handle fame. 'If you had your time again, what would you do differently?'

'I'd be proud of who I was, what I'd achieved, and I'd let my cooking do the talking. And if I had done that, I'd still have my own restaurant today.'

He heaved a big sigh and looked at me wistfully. 'But that was a long time ago; I don't like to talk about it,' he finished off, pressing his lips together firmly.

'Sorry, I didn't mean to pry,' I said, wondering how long I'd have been here if he *had* wanted to talk about it.

'Now I just cook for myself and special clients.'

'Well, lucky us,' I said with a grin. Having an award-winning chef on tap was another huge plus point to add to the Brightside Holidays website and I couldn't wait to tell Theo about him. 'I am so glad we met.'

'Me too.' Big Dave smiled shyly. 'So crab salad, twelve covers, shall we say one o'clock tomorrow?'

'Deal.' I started to move away and then hesitated. 'Dave . . . my sudden blast of fame has thrown me a bit too. Any advice?'

His wise face softened and he patted my arm. 'Use it wisely and remain true to yourself and you won't go far wrong.'

We swapped numbers in case of any problems before I left him to carry on with his lobster cage repairs. Sapphire

Spencer couldn't fail to be impressed by tomorrow's lunch. This was turning out better than I could have dreamed of. Next stop, The Sea Urchin pub to place an order for enough alcohol to quench the thirst of twelve hens . . .

Thirty minutes later, the bar at Driftwood Lodge had been well and truly stocked. Raquel, the landlady, had recommended wines, given me instructions for a few simple cocktails, suggested a selection of mixers, and had even let me borrow some glasses for the weekend. And after extracting a promise to have it all delivered before the hen party arrived, I left her ordering some extra cases of champagne from her wine merchant.

My final job before returning to Driftwood Lodge was to source some supplies for our beauty treatments.

'Don't get up,' I said brightly, pushing open the door of Jethro's General Store.

'Wasn't about to,' he said, knocking his baseball cap up to make it easier to scowl at me. 'I've got Policeman's heel. I'm in purgatory over here. I'd complain but no one would listen.'

'Sorry to hear that,' I murmured. 'I'll help myself.'

There wasn't exactly a wide range of buckets but there were four yellow ones in the shape of castles so I bought them all plus four washing-up bowls.

'What do you want all those for?' said Jethro, wincing as he got to his feet, too nosy to stay seated.

'The usual,' I said innocently. 'Putting sand in.'

For our Brightside beach sand pedicures. Another DIY beauty treatment we'd pilfered from the internet. Honestly, I didn't know why people bothered going to fancy spas. All you needed was water, sand, coconut oil and salt.

'Heard you got visitors this weekend. From London,' he muttered suspiciously.

'Good news travels fast.' I put the buckets on the counter and handed him the exact money. God forbid I made work for him by having to give me change. 'Don't worry, I'll make sure they don't bother you.'

'They already have. Big Dave has just been in. Cleared me out of lemons. Well, *the* lemon. I was going to have that for my tea.' He gave me a sideways glance. 'On Sunday. Don't know what I'll have now. Still. Don't you worry about me.'

I could see where this was going. I had to get out of the shop quickly or I'd end up inviting him to ours.

'Have you got a bag, please?' I asked.

While Jethro tutted and ferreted about under the counter for something big enough, the door opened and a tall man wearing wetsuit bottoms, sunglasses and flip-flops sauntered in holding a camera followed by Eliza, looking very curvaceous in a full-body wetsuit.

Her face lit up when she saw me. 'Hey, beauty!'

'Only one child at a time,' said Jethro, appearing from under the counter with a black bin liner.

'Ha ha,' Eliza said, pretending to grip her sides with mirth.

'Yep. Very funny,' agreed the tall man. 'As ever.'

'Why is that funny?' I asked, greeting Eliza with a hug.

'He's been saying that to us since we started school,' she said wearily.

'This is your brother?'

It was obvious now that I looked properly. The man was a good head and shoulders taller than his sister but he had identical intense blue eyes, a similar snub nose and blonde hair, although his didn't have pink tips.

'That joke never gets old.' Jethro made a wheezing noise, which I realized was as close as he probably got to a laugh. He pushed the bin liner towards me. 'All I've got, take it or leave it.'

I thanked him for his kindness and put my purchases in it.

'So you're the man I have to thank for blowing my cover last week,' I said archly.

He reached for my hand. 'Danny Tyler, sex god and professional photographer at your service.'

'I've heard it all now,' Jethro muttered.

'And what do you need to say to Nina?' Eliza nudged him.

'I owe you an apology for dobbing you in on Facebook last week.' He lifted my hand to his lips and kissed it. And then ruined it by adding, 'Apparently.'

'Danny!' she cried.

'We-ll,' he said with a casual shrug. 'She probably enjoyed the attention.'

'It was quite annoying, actually,' I said, shaking off his hand.

'Use my shop as a youth club, why don't you?' Jethro piped up, lowering himself with exaggerated care into his chair. 'Don't mind me. I'll just sit here and ponder what to have for my tea on Sunday. While someone eats my lemon.'

'We'll get out of your way, Jethro,' said Eliza, pushing me towards the door.

'Until next time, dude,' said Danny, winking at him. 'Be lucky.'

'At my age?' we heard him chunter as we left the shop. 'Lucky to be alive, you mean.'

I checked the time and prepared to make my getaway. I still had to make contact with Angie of Deliciously Devon and make a shopping list for food for tomorrow's breakfast.

'Bye then—' I began.

'So,' Danny interrupted me by clapping his hands, 'I thought we'd head for the rocks at the far side of the cove.' He took the lens cap off his camera, zoomed into my face and then lowered it to his chest. 'Freckles. Cool.'

'See, I knew you'd like her,' Eliza said smugly.

'The lens likes her,' he corrected smoothly, 'I think we can work together.'

'I'm flattered,' I said drily.

'Great. So if you want to get the clobber on?' he said, nudging me towards Eliza's shop.

I looked at her. 'What clobber?'

'The Peacock Mermaid tail you chose yesterday definitely

suits your colouring,' she said, looping her arm through mine. 'We'll do the pictures for my website in that.'

She began to move but I stayed rooted to the spot.

'But I can't do a photo shoot today!' I shot her a panicky look. 'I've got the Maidens of Mayfair in limos, right now, heading this way.'

'They'll be hours,' said Danny cheerily. 'The motorway is at a standstill. Heard it on the news.'

'It won't take long and you did promise,' said Eliza, increasing the grip on my arm.

'Did I?'

'Quick sticks,' she said, chivvying me forwards. 'You're in a hurry, remember.'

It suddenly dawned on me that the two of them were dressed for the water.

'I'm not going to get wet, am I?' I asked suddenly.

'Absolutely not.' Eliza shook her head solemnly.

'Scouts' honour,' said Danny, tapping his forehead in a two-fingered salute.

'Because that's non-negotiable,' I said sternly.

Chapter 17

I put on the shell-clad bikini and pulled my shirt on over it. The tail would have to go on once we made it down to the rocks.

'This is it. My big break.' Eliza passed Danny the bag containing the mermaid tail while she locked the shop door and stuck a note to it saying she'd be back in half an hour.

'I keep pinching myself. My first proper customers are TV celebrities and I'll have an actress on my website wearing one of my outfits. My dream is coming true thanks to you, Nina. This time next year I'll be famous and people will be travelling from all over the country to be a mermaid for the day.'

'Glad to help,' I said happily. I knew that feeling of euphoria. I'd been the same when I'd landed the role in *Victory Road*, that things were going my way, my dreams were coming true. Not exactly Keira Knightley status yet, but on my way. 'But what about your shop? You won't be able to keep popping out when you've got clients.'

'I shall delegate the shop to another member of my team,' she said airily, 'while I'm busy making a success of the mermaid school.'

'Hmmm. I do want to help you with your photo shoot, Eliza,' I said, checking the time again anxiously. 'But I want Brightside Holidays to be a success too, for Theo and Kate's sake. Do we really have to do this now?'

She nodded. 'The website is ready to launch; all I need are the photographs.'

'And I've only got today off work,' Danny added. 'In demand, me.'

'Okay, let's go.' I followed the pair of them past the harbour and along the path to the far end of the cove.

Danny's dream, he confided on the way, was to work full time as a photographer. He was doing an evening course at college and by day worked in a high-street photographic shop, churning out other people's holiday snaps.

'I need these pictures for my portfolio,' Danny went on. 'My only claim to fame so far is taking a passport photograph for Jude Law. He came to Devon on holiday and had his passport stolen. He let me keep one of them and signed it for me, saying it was the worst holiday of his life. Happy days.'

We walked as far as the old lifeboat house at the edge of the bay. It was a rather lovely brick building; it had a pitched roof topped with a pointed statue at one end, long narrow windows down each side and a quirky bay window just below the front gable. If it hadn't been for the double doors at the front wide enough to fit a boat through and the rough concrete slipway running down towards the water, it could easily be mistaken for a chapel. It was all a bit battered and shabby now, but pretty nonetheless, and I bet it had seen many adventures before it had been replaced by the modern lifeboat station further down the coast.

We went round the far side and set our bags down where we were sheltered from the prying eyes of a group of six surfers who'd just piled out of a camper van and were currently loitering at the shoreline. The sand was soft and warmed by the sun beneath my toes, but the air had a nip in it. Danny walked off to the water to locate the best spot for our shoot and Eliza unzipped the bag containing the costume.

I pulled on the tail over bikini bottoms and Eliza fitted the nylon fin into the end. She brushed my hair until it shone and fixed a tiny circlet of shells on top of my head. All I had to do was take my shirt off and my transformation would be complete.

Danny whistled to us. 'Found the perfect spot!' he yelled, pointing to a large rock jutting out from the water about twenty metres from shore. 'Come on!'

'That's halfway to France.' I looked down at my tail. 'How do I get down there?'

Eliza wrinkled her nose. 'We roll you down the slipway?'

I glanced over at the surfers, who'd now abandoned any pretence at watching the waves and were sitting on their surfboards staring at us. Or rather, at me.

'Like a beached whale? No way. Can't I wade out to the rock and then put the costume on in situ?'

'You'll never manage it without getting the tail wet. Besides, these tails are a devil to get into when your skin is wet. And you might fall over, or snag the fabric on the rocks. Either way the pictures would be ruined.'

'Not to mention me dying of cold.'

Danny came running back up the beach. 'Hurry up, sis. The sun is hitting the rock just right and the sea looks like mercury through the lens and the water is just about shallow enough so I can stand in it to take the shot.'

I whipped my shirt off and tried to ignore the chorus of wolf whistles from the surfers. 'Yes, hurry up, it's not mermaid weather,' I agreed, wrapping my arms round myself.

'You'll have to carry her out,' said Eliza with a frown. 'And plonk her on the rock.'

'Place me down gently, she means,' I added.

'Sure.' Danny swung me up into his arms and immediately staggered. 'Oof. You're heavier than you look.' He lowered me to the sand and pulled an apologetic face. 'No, can't do it. The sea floor is rocky and under that weight, I'm bound to slip.'

My cheeks went pink. 'This isn't quite the magical experience I thought it was going to be.'

'We'll do it between us,' Eliza suggested, giving him a sharp look. 'Danny, you take the tail end to make sure it doesn't get wet. I'll take the top half.'

'*It?*' I said pointedly. 'No, listen, there's a seat lift I had to do once for a scene on *Victory Road*. Let me show you.'

I looped my arms around their necks and they interlocked their hands, grasping me under my thighs and behind my back. Eliza had beach shoes on but Danny kicked off his flip-flops and left them on the sand.

'One two three, go,' Eliza commanded and we set off towards the water.

After only a few paces, I began to list towards her.

'This would be much better if you two were the same height,' I gasped.

'Shut up and concentrate on feeling mystical and powerful and at one with the water,' she giggled.

'Not easy when you're trying to keep your tail dry,' I said breathlessly. It took all of my core strength to keep my legs out of the sea, my stomach muscles were trembling. 'I think I'm getting fin flop.'

'I'll bend my knees, to make myself shorter,' Danny offered.

He crouched a bit, which did help, but the camera dangling round his neck swung forward and hit my head and I cried out in pain.

'I think I should have had a stunt double for this bit,' I said, wincing. 'Or at least be paid danger money.'

Behind us a dog started to bark.

'Mabel!' called a man's voice.

'I know that dog.' And I recognized the man's voice too. I craned my neck to try to look behind me, but Eliza and Danny's grip on me was too tight.

'Wave alert!' Eliza yelled. They lifted me up and I raised my tail as much as I could over the rushing water to stay dry.

'So do I,' said Danny warily. 'It's Jude's. Daft as a brush and doesn't obey a word he says.'

'Keep going!' Eliza ordered.

We were halfway to the rock. Suddenly Danny stubbed his toe on something on the seabed and swore loudly. The pair of them stumbled and I felt their arms loosen round my back.

'Do not drop me!' I yelled, with a laugh. 'I've done some crazy things in my career, but this takes the biscuit.'

Danny winced. 'I'm all right,' he said, 'don't worry about me.'

'That was a close shave.' Eliza exhaled with relief.

'Unlike Nina's armpits,' said Danny under his breath. 'It's like having a cuddle with Harambe the gorilla.'

'I have no idea why you're still single,' I muttered.

The barking was suddenly very loud and awfully close and I screamed as freezing-cold sea water splashed up my back.

'Jeez,' Danny yelped. 'It's nipping at my bum.'

'Nina, that's your fault for saying "biscuit",' said Eliza with a snort.

'Mabel, come back!' yelled a voice in the distance.

'Get off!' Danny yelled. 'Go away, dog. Jude, help!'

'What's happening?' I said, trying to turn round. In my peripheral vision I caught a flash of brown and white fur as the dog leapt up out of the water and Danny's hold on me loosened.

'Moonie!' yelled a voice and a roar of laughter rose up from the surfers who were now all lying flat on their boards and paddling towards us.

'Shoo,' shouted Eliza, kicking out with her leg to splash the dog. 'Danny, do not let go!'

'I've got to,' he shouted, as they staggered in the water, which was now up to Eliza's thighs. 'The bloody dog has pulled my wetsuit bottoms down with its teeth.'

Eliza let out a hoot of laughter.

'Don't make me laugh,' I howled, 'my stomach muscles are killing me.'

'I'm going to have to let go, Nina,' Danny gasped. 'I need to pull my wetsuit up. I've got a reputation to maintain.'

'I want to look,' I demanded.

'No way,' said Eliza, 'both of you. We're nearly there now. Anyway, you do *not* want to look, take it from me.'

'Bloody hell,' said a male voice sploshing towards us. 'That's something you don't see every day.'

'Yeah. *Luckily*,' said Eliza. 'I haven't seen it since we used to have to share a bath as kids.'

'I meant the mermaid.'

'For God's sake, Jude,' Danny cried. 'Grab your dog. And yank my pants up for me while you're at it.'

'All right, no need to get arsey,' Jude shouted back with a laugh.

That rich warm laugh and the West Country dialect took me straight back to that near collision I'd had with the blue van, when he – Jude, apparently – had tooted his horn and criticized my driving. 'She's just trying to rescue your mermaid,' he said. 'She likes fish. Mabel, fetch!'

I heard something plop into the water some distance from us and the dog gave a yelp of delight, splashing me again as she swam away. Then Jude waded towards us. His arm brushed against my skin as he yanked Danny's wetsuit up. I was dying to see his face.

'There you go, mate. All tucked away.'

'About time,' Danny muttered.

'And Mabel's right, I do need rescuing,' I said through gritted teeth, focusing on the rock a couple of metres ahead, my stomach quivering with the effort of keeping my tail dry. 'I need to put my legs down on dry land quickly.'

'Bit of a design fault, isn't it? A mermaid that can't swim?' said Jude, still out of my line of vision.

'We're opening up a new mermaid school in Brightside Cove; tourists will love it,' said Eliza excitedly. 'I'd give you a leaflet but I've got my hands full.'

'A tourist gimmick?' said Jude, wading in front of us to get a better look at me. 'I'll pass, thank you.'

'Rude,' said Eliza.

'Bare-faced cheek, I call it,' I put in, pleased with my own joke.

'Oh. Er . . . hello,' Jude pulled a face. 'Have we met before?'

He was wearing a baseball cap pulled low over his hazel eyes like last time. And he obviously hadn't planned on getting wet: he was wearing jeans and a T-shirt, both of which were now wet and showing off his broad shoulders and muscular physique to full effect. I gave him an awkward smile, waiting for him to recognize me fom *Victory Road*. But he wasn't looking at my face, he was gawping at my . . . I cast my eyes downwards. The shell-clad triangles of my bikini top had swivelled round and both boobs were totally bare.

'Don't look!' I let go of both Danny's and Eliza's necks and attempted to cover myself.

The unexpected manoeuvre unbalanced them both and I slipped backwards towards the water. My head got a dunking in the sea and my tail flipped up catching against something hard.

'Ouch!' yelled Jude. 'That was my chin.'

'Keep your tail up!' Eliza squeaked before all three of us plunged underwater.

The shock of the cold sea water stole the air from my lungs, my legs were trapped inside the tail and my heartbeat started to accelerate with panic. I hit the seabed and flailed my arms about, desperate for oxygen and then suddenly strong arms yanked me to the surface and set me down on the rock. I coughed and panted, swiping my hair from my face. The little circlet had gone. And I was wet, the tail was wet and my make-up was probably in streaks down my face. Eliza was going to be so disappointed. But I was alive. My lungs were screaming with pain but I was alive.

'I don't think mermaids are supposed to drown, are they?'
I said through chattering teeth.

'You okay?'

I rubbed salt water from my eyes.

'That was your fault,' I gasped, 'for staring at my boobs!'

'My fault? I just saved your life.' Jude glared at me.

'Now we've all seen them,' said Danny, cocking an eyebrow, 'we might as well do some topless shots.'

'No way!' I muttered, folding my arms.

Jude was still looking at me. 'So *have* we met before?'

'Actresses hate it when people say that,' Eliza interrupted, staggering towards me to jam the headdress back on. 'Here you go, not that we can actually do the shoot now: you look like a drowned rat.'

Jude opened his mouth to say something but there was a sudden frenzy of barking, accompanied by some strident human yells of displeasure and we all looked back at the beach.

'Whoops,' said Danny, with a grin. 'I think that mad dog of yours is at it again.'

'Jude?' one of the surfers yelled. 'Your dog is attacking the man with the ladder.'

'A ladder?' Jude raised a hand to his eyes and squinted back to the shore.

A small white van had parked beside the old lifeboat house and Mabel seemed intent on preventing a man from climbing a ladder that had been set up against the outside wall.

'You've got to be joking,' he muttered.

'What's going on?' said Danny, using his camera to zoom in on the action.

'If the council think they can sell off our heritage, they're going to have a fight on their hands,' muttered Jude, setting off towards the shore.

'Who is he?' I said once he was out of earshot.

'Jude Trevone,' said Danny, from behind the lens. 'Incomer as a teenager. Reputation as the local bad boy – used to fight with anyone and everyone. No luck with the ladies, unlike me. I'm a lover not a fighter.'

'Hmm,' I said darkly, watching Jude run through the water and up the slipway towards the lifeboat house. 'He certainly brings out the argumentative side in me.'

'Ignore Danny,' said Eliza. She beckoned me to stand up so she could peel off my tail and I tore my eyes away from the skirmish on the slipway. 'Jude's got a heart of gold under that tough exterior. He's just fussy who he shares it with. Which as far as I know is no one apart from his dog.'

Therein lay a tale. I made a mental note to ask her more about him when I wasn't quite so close to freezing. My lips were going numb with cold and my teeth were chattering. Even Danny was starting to shiver.

'What the—' Danny's jaw dropped and he lowered the camera to his goosepimply chest. He stared upwards, back towards land. 'Look at that!'

I jumped down from the rock into the sea and followed his gaze. Two white limousines appeared to be stuck on the narrow road up on the clifftop. All of sudden being a bit chilly was the least of my concerns.

'Got to go,' I yelled, half-swimming, half-running through the water to collect my clothes. 'Brightside Holidays' first hen party is on!'

Chapter 18

A few hours later I was back on the beach. The sun was beginning to disappear from view and the sea glowed like molten gold. It was a glorious evening and Theo's idea to entertain our guests with a beach barbecue was going down a treat. We'd put everything into Theo's van and reversed it down the slipway, setting up the barbecue to the side of the cove in the shelter of the rocks. We'd constructed a bar from a pasting table, and a plastic patio table had been commandeered to lay the food on, both covered with spotty tablecloths I'd found in a kitchen drawer. All the drinks were in cool boxes and a couple of the new buckets I'd bought from Jethro earlier had been filled with ice cubes.

'These are done.' Theo piled some foil-wrapped spicy salmon parcels on to the plate I was holding out for him. 'I thought this cottage holidays lark would be simple. Just take the money and hand over the keys. I've no idea how people can hold down a normal nine-to-five job too.'

'But this isn't a normal booking, is it?' I countered, pointing out a chicken leg that was in danger of incineration. '*Normally* bookings won't consist of guests whose idea of cooking is to pour water on a green tea bag.'

And even then one of them had chewed her lip and asked whether we had an instant boiling water tap. But tiny queries aside, so far, things had gone extremely smoothly. We'd been expecting a party of twelve, but one girl was missing; no one had mentioned her so I hadn't asked.

'True. And normally,' he said, 'our guests won't all be fit women. I must be the luckiest bloke in Devon tonight.'

'It's a good job your wife didn't hear you say that.' I picked up my beer bottle and took a sip.

'Hmm,' he said with wry smile, brushing his raven curls off his face. 'Kate hasn't answered the last three emails I sent her. Even allowing for the time delay she could have managed to reply to at least one of them. So,' he paused to chink his bottle against mine, 'tonight I'm going to say what I like and enjoy myself.'

I wasn't sure how to respond to that but I remembered how badly he'd been coping when Archie and I had first come to Brightside Cove. Archie had described him as wetter than a mackerel's bikini; at least now he appeared to have acquired a stiffer upper lip.

Sapphire and her hens were spread across the curve of the beach, mostly drinks in hand, taking selfies, peering in rock pools and generally chilling out while we cooked the food. Her entourage consisted of five of the other girls from *Maidens of Mayfair*; her best friend Catherine; her younger sister Ruby; two younger cousins whose squeals when they'd seen a real-life chicken had sent the poor birds into a flap and up on to the garage roof and Sapphire's university friend, Virginia, an academic who alternated between being star struck around the reality TV celebs and cross with herself for being impressed.

After they'd arrived and we'd shown them to their cottages, we'd left them to their own devices while we set up the evening's entertainment. Most of the group had opted to soak up the sun on the newly furnished patio with drinks in hand but three of them had set up a pop-up spray tan booth outside Beaver's Barn and had appeared in bikinis to tan each other.

The whole party had looked such fun, and for a minute I

forgot that I was the host and I nearly stripped off, helped myself to a cocktail and joined them.

Finally, the food was ready and I prepared to round everyone up.

'Wait.' Theo caught my arm. 'Before the others join us, I just want to say how much I appreciate your help.'

He smiled – a big face-stretching smile that lit up his eyes. 'Celebrity guests, a full house, more money than I've earned in a very long time . . . You've made all this possible and I am very grateful.'

'Not just me,' I said, waving my beer bottle around awkwardly. 'If Archie hadn't bought your car—'

'I know, I know.' Theo gazed at me, his fingers warm on my skin. 'It *was* lucky that he was able to stump up some cash just when I needed it, but you've done more than that. You've *given* me more than that. You listened to me when I needed to talk about Ivy. That was something I never managed to do with Kate. And you forced me to finish off the cottages even though I didn't want to. And if you hadn't been there when Joe Bird arrived expecting a holiday, I'd have turned him away and then none of this would be happening now.'

He placed an arm round my waist and pressed a kiss to the side of my head. He was just being friendly, of course. And I'd hugged him lots of times before. But this time my nerve endings tingled and I wasn't sure what had just happened.

'You're welcome. Okay then,' I said, matter-of-factly. I stepped away and scanned the beach, conscious of a sudden rise in my pulse. 'Let's get this party started.'

An hour later the food had been demolished and Theo had relinquished his role as chef. There was still enough light to see by as we cleared away and the hens had plenty of energy left too. I'd found some beach games in an outbuilding and brought them down to the beach, half expecting them to turn their noses up. Wrong! So far there had been a game of frisbee which had ended in two falling-over-in-the-sea incidents, a fierce bat-and-ball contest and Catherine, a born organizer, if a little too tipsy to remember the rules, had made everyone play rounders.

I was scraping food in to a bin bag when Sapphire joined me.

'This is just what I needed,' she said, her breathing ragged from laughing so much. 'Just letting our hair down without anyone watching us. I can see why you came here to rest between roles.'

'Such a lovely way of referring to being an unemployed actor, isn't it?' I said with a grin. 'Anyway, you wouldn't call it a rest if you'd seen me making twelve beds this morning.'

'Even though we only needed eleven in the end.' Sapphire winced. 'Sorry about that.'

'No problem.' I shrugged. 'There's always someone who has to drop out at the last minute in a large party.'

'Actually,' Sapphire reached into the bucket for a cool beer and flipped the cap off, 'it was my decision not to let Poppy come. She's the press officer for *Maidens of Mayfair*. I made up some ridiculous reason why she couldn't. But next week I'm going to have to confront her about my suspicions.'

'And what are your suspicions?'

She opened her mouth and hesitated. 'Shall we sit down?'

We flopped into deckchairs and watched the others for a few seconds. Theo was building a fire from driftwood and the girls were cheering Catherine on as she waded into the chilly sea to look for the rounders ball.

'It's the press leak about my hen party. It can only have come from her. Only my hens and I knew that we'd booked to go to that Scottish castle. There's no way any of them would blab. They know how important it is.'

'One of them might have done it by accident?' I suggested.

Like I had done with *Victory Road*. 'Easy mistake to make. An innocent mention on Twitter and pouf . . . suddenly everyone knows about it.'

'Not my girls. We trust each other.' She swigged her beer. 'And if they'd done it accidentally, they'd have owned up straight away. No, I think this was deliberate. To sabotage the exclusive magazine deal with *My Dream Day*. Poppy wanted the show to have exclusive access to every aspect of my wedding; she got quite uppity about it. But some things are private. I know this probably sounds at odds with being a reality TV star, but I didn't want a film crew at my hen weekend, it's bad enough having them at the wedding. I don't understand this need to share my whole life with the media.'

'I know what you mean,' I replied. *Or rather I did now.*

When Sebastian had been my agent, he'd encouraged me to chase every PR opportunity, and each month was deemed a success or failure depending on the number of media mentions I'd had. But over the last couple of weeks I'd begun to question that approach. Perhaps it was better to have just one rave review of my acting than ten 'celebrity spottings' at parties and premieres. Because otherwise, what was I actually famous for?

'It's a mystery to me why people are so interested in my life,' she said. '*Maidens of Mayfair* is essentially about wealthy girls who meet for lunch, argue over cocktails and vie for the most screen time any way they can. I miss my research lab at the university; life was so much more exciting there.'

I raised an eyebrow, wondering not for the first time why someone like her had agreed to take part in the programme at all. 'If that is where your heart lies, then perhaps you should rethink?'

'I rethink every day,' she said with a sigh. 'Anyway, the press hasn't followed us here and that's the main thing. And I'm so glad we came; I've absolutely fallen in love with the place.'

'I'm glad too.'

'And the views aren't bad either, he's rather delicious.' She nodded her head and I followed her gaze to where a man was walking towards us along the shoreline just out of the water's reach. I wouldn't have known who it was if it hadn't been for Mabel running in and out of the waves beside him. She dropped something at his feet and he threw it in a wide arc out to sea, laughing as she splashed out immediately to get it. Sapphire was right, he did look rather delicious.

'That's Jude,' I replied. 'I've only met him twice and both times were a bit of a disaster. But by all accounts, he's more of a dog than a people person.'

'Hmm.' Sapphire narrowed her eyes and stood up. 'He seems to like people now; he's taking pictures of us. And I can't have that.'

Jude did have a camera phone held up to his face, but he wasn't aiming it at us.

'No, look, he's not pointing the camera this way,' I reassured her. 'You're quite safe.'

Sapphire relaxed back down, but kept a beady eye on him nonetheless. Jude was taking pictures of the lifeboat house, specifically, I noticed for the first time, of a new sign that had been erected on the side of the building. But he kept his distance and before long was out of sight again.

The rounders game had ended and the girls were heading back to our makeshift bar.

'You lot cheated,' said Catherine, laughing. 'Ruby hit the ball in the sea on purpose. I demand a re-match.'

'No way!' Ruby held her sides, getting her breath back. 'I demand a drink.'

'I'm on it,' said Theo, dusting the sand from his hands. 'There are cold beers, champagne, plenty of spirits —'

'How about sex on the beach?' shouted a voice from behind us up on the clifftop.

We all turned and I stifled a groan: Danny.

The girls all whooped and Ruby waved her arms. 'You are talking my kinda language.'

Danny began to jog down the slipway towards us and Sapphire dropped her head into her hands with a groan. I'd spotted it too: he had his camera around his neck.

'It's happened again,' she murmured. 'You're not telling me he's not press.'

I jumped to my feet. 'Ah, now he *is* a photographer, but not for the press. So far his commissions have only been seen by the passport office.' I smiled at Sapphire's confused face. 'Don't worry. I'll handle this.'

'Danny Tyler, sex god and award-winning mixologist at your service.' He grinned at the assembled group of women and rubbed his hands together. 'Who's for one of my killer cocktails?'

Theo stepped forward. 'Thanks, mate, but I'm in charge of the bar. Why don't you stick to what you do best?'

Ruby twirled a lock of blonde hair around her fingers. 'And what do you do best?'

'Well, ladies,' Danny crooned, 'where do I begin?'

The girls had formed a cluster around him and he was lapping up the attention. Which gave me the perfect opportunity to creep up behind him.

'By handing this over,' I said briskly, unhooking his camera from around his neck. 'I'll take that for now.'

I put it in Sapphire's lap for safekeeping.

'Hey, that's the key to my future,' Danny protested. 'I was going to do some moody sunset shots for my portfolio. You know, sunlight glinting off the rocks, etc., etc.'

'I'll model for you,' said Ruby, thrusting herself at him. 'I could arrange myself artistically on the rocks.'

'Ruby!' Sapphire glared at her sister incredulously. 'Press embargo, remember?'

Ruby folded her arms. 'It's always about you, isn't it?' she muttered.

Catherine handed him her mobile phone. 'Danny, we'd

love some pictures of all of us, just casual ones to remember the weekend by.' She looked at Sapphire for reassurance. 'That's okay, isn't it, Sapph, if they're on my phone?'

Sapphire chewed her lip and then nodded. 'Of course. Of course it is; I'm being ridiculous. And Danny, that would be really kind of you, if you wouldn't mind.'

Danny bowed deeply. 'No problemo. Okay, come on, ladies, let's have you over the rocks. Blondes at the front.'

'Why's that?' Virginia asked, tucking her short dark hair behind her ears.

Danny smiled sympathetically. 'Gentlemen prefer blondes.'

Virginia's mouth dropped open and Ruby snorted. 'You can't say that.'

'Hey,' said Danny, holding his hands up, 'I don't make the rules.'

'Agreed. Because you're talking rubbish.' Theo had sweetly been Googling the ingredients for sex on the beach cocktails and had concocted a pinky approximation of it in one of the ice buckets. He handed the girls a glass each, Virginia first. 'I prefer brunettes.'

'Like Nina?' said Catherine innocently.

He blushed. 'And my wife.'

'I'm naturally much lighter,' I put in, slightly perturbed by Theo's reply. My hair, which Trudy had dyed black as part of my disguise a few weeks ago, had faded to dark brown, but normally it was the colour of caramel. So not Theo's type.

Ruby peered at me. 'You should go lighter again. It would suit your eye colour.' She squinted. 'What *is* your eye colour? Blue, green, grey?'

I opened my mouth to answer that my eyes were all those colours, but Sapphire jumped in first.

'You look lovely as you are, Nina. And thanks for sorting the privacy thing.' She handed me Danny's camera. 'I'd better go and join in.'

'What are you doing tomorrow?' I heard Danny say to

Ruby, draping his arm around her shoulders as they made their way to the rocks. 'Because there's a two-for-one offer on mussels at The Sea Urchin . . .'

To give Danny his due, he very patiently took pictures with everyone's phone and camera over the course of the next hour without a murmur. I did notice a bit of cleavage zooming at one point when Ruby asked him to take one of her leaning over the fire roasting a marshmallow but I got the impression that she enjoyed it.

And they all listened intently when he showed them how to edit pictures straight from their phones.

'People never make enough use of the filters on their phone cameras,' he explained earnestly, sweeping his blond hair from his face. 'They're only simple but they can elevate a picture to something special.'

The women all cooed. There was a certain appeal to him when he dropped the 'sex god' act. Even Sapphire was won over.

'Danny's cute,' said Ruby, flicking her hair over her shoulder.

'He's single, if you're interested,' I said with a grin. 'We have a good record of matchmaking at Driftwood Lodge.'

She appeared to consider it. 'He did say I'd definitely make it as a model.'

'He's entertaining, that's for sure,' Sapphire agreed thoughtfully, turning to me. 'And it would be lovely to have some good photographs to remember the hen weekend by. Do you think he'd be free tomorrow, if I offered to pay him?'

Danny's ears pricked up and he was at Sapphire's side instantly. 'I'd have to shuffle a few things around,' he said, sucking in air.

I hid a smile. Like his shift at the photographic shop.

'But I think I could squeeze you in.' He dropped his sunglasses down over his eyes and waggled them. 'If the price is right.'

'Complete privacy, though, Danny,' said Sapphire, holding his gaze. 'And you'll have to use one of our cameras.'

She named a figure that made his eyes light up and they made their arrangements to meet tomorrow. The party began to break up soon after that and Theo persuaded Danny to help us load the tables and deckchairs into his van.

It was only when I was stashing the cool boxes into the back that I glanced up and read the sign on the lifeboat house. It was from an auctioneer's inviting interested parties to contact them and collect particulars immediately.

That was sad. Obviously the place was disused but the building itself was lovely and must have been brimming with history. The thought of it being developed or knocked down to make way for something modern was awful. I thought of Jude and his anger when he'd seen the man with the ladder. That must have been when the sign was being erected.

'Danny,' I said, 'why is Jude so upset about the boathouse being for sale?'

'Not sure, but he's a social worker and does a lot of work with the community.' He leaned on the door of the van and shook his head. 'He's never happier than when he's fighting for some cause or other. This will be his latest thing. He thinks we should keep Brightside Cove as it is. Stuck in the Dark Ages. But you can't, can you?' He shrugged. 'Because if you don't move forwards you end up going backwards. And this place is backwards enough, if you ask me.'

'Jethro likes it just as it is,' I said.

Danny smirked. 'I rest my case.'

He had a point.

When I finally climbed into bed in the spare room at midnight my skin was tingling from being exposed to the sun, salt and sand for so long today and my muscles were aching from the mermaid photo shoot earlier. What a crazy perfect day. I had never been as ready for sleep in my life and I hoped I'd manage to wake up in time to cook and serve breakfast for nine o'clock.

I stared through the open curtains, my eyes hypnotized by the glow of the moon, and found myself drifting into a delicious sleep—

DELICIOUSLY DEVON!

The thought propelled me from my pillow as realization dawned. I hadn't booked the caterers for tomorrow night's dinner. I picked up my watch and stared at it. It was too late to ring now; I'd just have to call them in the morning and hope for the best . . .

Chapter 19

I made my morning cup of tea, sifted through the detritus on the kitchen table to find the scrap of paper that Molly had given me and took it to the telephone in the hall.

'Hello?' The voice that answered the phone was so croaky that I wouldn't have liked to guess whether it was male or female. 'Who's this?'

I winced. Okay, so maybe eight o'clock on a Saturday morning was a little too early to be phoning the caterers . . . But I'd woken whoever it was now, I might as well carry on.

'Could I speak to Angie, please?'

'No, she's . . .' There was a cough and a husky male voice continued. 'Excuse me. Angie's not here. Can I help? I'm her, er, partner. In business. A business partner.'

A sleeping partner, by the sound of it . . .

'I'd like to book you to cater for a dinner party,' I said, keeping my fingers crossed for luck. 'Eleven people.'

'Hold on I'll get the diary.'

'Wait—'

There was no need for the diary, I was about to say. But there was a creaky noise, which sounded a bit like someone getting out of bed and then bouncing back in again.

'So when for? Our next available dinner party slot is—'

'Tonight,' I blurted out.

'You have got to be joking?' the man spluttered. 'I was going to say July.'

'I'm not joking,' I said. 'And I apologize for the last-minute-ness. But on the plus side, I have a very large budget.'

'Hmmm.'

I'd hoped money might talk, but there was a very long silence on the other end of the line.

'Look, you're the only catering company in the area, and I have eleven women, several of whom are household names, expecting dinner. You might even get a mention on TV. Imagine what that would do for your business.'

'I'd get even more calls at stupid o'clock asking me to work miracles?' replied the man drily. 'Excuse me for not falling over myself with gratitude.'

I stared at the phone incredulously. It was no wonder tourism had never taken off in Brightside Cove with this sort of attitude.

'So you're turning down my booking?'

The man sucked air in through his teeth. 'I suppose I might be able to get hold of a seafood chef. He does a mean steamed lobster. Locally sourced. Expensive, but very *exclusive*.'

'Big Dave's already busy, if that was who you were thinking of.'

'Ah.' There was a pause. 'Well, as I said, I'm only taking bookings from July so I can't help you.'

'You have to!' My palms had begun to sweat. 'I've promised the guests excellent food, if I don't come up trumps, my friend's business will quite likely fail and I'll blame myself, because it'll be my fault and they'll all end up eating beans on toast and they have specifically said *money no object*. Please!'

The thought of Sapphire et al.'s reaction to one of my home-cooked meals was enough to instil a fear in me worse than stage-fright.

'Oh, for crying out loud,' he muttered. 'Hold on, I'll just flick through some menus, see if I can find something suitable.'

I heard a drawer open, some papers being rustled and a

kettle being switched on. Meanwhile, I waited patiently, sipping my tea. The caterers probably had a folder of set menus and there was more than likely a freezer full of suitable food waiting to be thawed out and served. This man had probably just been hoping for a night off. Some business partner he was. In the background a dog barked excitedly and I heard a door opening and closing and then he was back on the line.

'Okay, I've checked our available ingredients and things and I reckon we can do you a south-east Asian banquet. Six or seven different mains, three choices of rice and a few other odds and sods, I mean side-dishes. That do you?'

I almost choked on my tea. 'That sounds fantastic. Thank you so much! Eight o'clock all right? It's Driftwood Lodge, Brightside Cove.'

'Fine,' he said, yawning. 'Cash on delivery, mind you, I'll work out the price and let you know. Now, I'd better go and . . .' I heard the bed creaking again, '. . . start boiling the lemongrass or something. Goodbye.'

It was on the tip of my tongue to question the boiling of lemongrass but a glance at the time reminded me that I had an immense amount of work to do before the hen party emerged from their cottages – and my bake-at-home croissants weren't going to bake themselves.

By late afternoon the day was going swimmingly and Theo and I were feeling pretty pleased with ourselves. Or at least I was. Theo seemed to be going through the motions a little bit and had made one or two uncharacteristically snide comments about Kate, and I made a mental note to quiz him as soon as we had a moment to ourselves. Whenever that might be . . .

We'd served the girls breakfast in their own cottages while Molly converted the living room in Driftwood Lodge into an oasis of peace and tranquillity. Piles of fluffy white towels, candles scented with cedarwood and chamomile and the 'Sounds of Mother Nature' playlist she'd compiled when she was pregnant with Ellis created the perfect ambiance for our morning of Brightside Beauty. And then while Theo set about making all the beds, and preparing the kitchen for Big Dave, Eliza, Molly and I had buffed, smoothed and polished eleven faces and twenty-two feet with a variety of homemade salt-and-sand treatments. The morning had finished with Indian head massages and Molly had succeeded in sending every one of our hens into a peaceful sleep with her magic fingers.

Lunch had looked and smelled amazing. Big Dave had wowed everyone with his crab salad and he'd even brought a dessert of warm cider apple cake and creamy custard. Goodness knows how much booze was in it, but after a second slice, the hitherto sensible Virginia suggested they head off to the beach for a spot of skinny dipping. Dave, unsurprisingly, was all for it, but Eliza distracted them by bringing in the mermaid outfits, at which point the squeals from eleven women got so loud that the men offered to wash up just to escape the noise.

We'd all collapsed over tea and sandwiches in the kitchen for half an hour while the hens dashed off to make themselves mermaid-body ready. And at three, Eliza led the girls off to the rocks where Danny was due to meet them to do their photo shoot while Theo took the mermaid tails down the slipway in his van to save them having to be carried. I waved them off and went inside to make a start on afternoon tea.

The answerphone was flashing in the hall and I scooped up Mittens and gave him a cuddle while I played the message.

This is Nigel Rees from Coastal Cottages. Check out our website because your page is LIVE! Get ready for your phone to ring and your inbox to sing. Brightside Holidays, here we come!

I'd tell Theo as soon as he got back. That would cheer him up and perhaps give him a positive reason to get in touch with Kate; I was sure she'd be thrilled to see her cottages looking lovely on her favourite website. I gave Mittens a celebratory kiss and skipped into the kitchen to whip up some scones . . .

Afternoon tea was ready to serve. Light, fluffy and golden scones, dishes of bright red jam studded with strawberries and bowls of unctuous clotted cream. I carried the tray across to Penguin's Pad where the girls had asked for their tea to be served and tapped on the door with my foot.

Ruby opened the door, frowning at her phone. 'What's the code to the WiFi again?'

'Elvis lives,' I replied. 'All one word, all lowercase.'

'Sapphire did ask us not to post anything online . . .' Catherine jumped to her feet to help clear a space on the coffee table.

Ruby rolled her eyes. 'Because of course we all know the world revolves around Sapphire.'

'Yes,' said Catherine firmly. 'This weekend, it does.'

She gave me a look of exasperation as I settled the tray down carefully. Aside from the three of us, only the two cousins were in the room and they were sharing headphones and listening to music in a world of their own.

'Where is Sapphire?' I said to Catherine. 'And all the others?'

'Everyone is fast asleep,' she said anxiously.

'Oh, how lovely! It's the sea air and the massage, it knocks you out.'

'It's the itinerary I'm worried about. If they don't wake up soon it'll be shot to pieces.'

'Oh no! Imagine that,' said Ruby in mock horror. 'Cool your jets, sister, this is supposed to be a fun weekend not an army exercise.'

She took a scone and dipped it straight in the cream. Not that I was a purist about these things, I didn't mind which went on first: the jam or the cream. But even I drew the line at dunking.

'Jam?' I said, offering her a plate and a knife.

'I get jittery if we go *off piste*, as it were.' Catherine sighed and pressed a hand to her forehead.

The poor thing; she was the only one who hadn't managed to relax properly yet. I handed her a cup of tea and forced her to sit down.

'So what have you got planned for the rest of the day?' I asked.

Catherine consulted her piece of paper.

'Afternoon tea at five. Right on time, thank you.' She flashed me a grateful smile. 'Brisk clifftop walk at five thirty, back here for six fifteen.'

'Room inspection at six thirty,' said Ruby with a snigger, smearing jam on the top of her scone.

Catherine tilted her chin up and ignored her. 'Then we'll open bottle of champagne number seventeen and start getting ready for dinner at . . . ?'

'Eight,' I supplied. 'A south-east Asian banquet.'

Catherine's eyes lit up.

'Sapphire adores Asian cuisine. Also,' she pressed her finger to her lips, 'don't let on but I've organized some special entertainment for later.'

'I won't say a word,' I promised.

'Hey, everyone. A word about what?'

We all turned to see Sapphire padding down the stairs clutching her phone. Her soft blonde hair shimmered and there was a rosy glow to her cheeks from sleep.

'Hey,' said the cousins in unison, tugging their earphones out.

Catherine shook her head frantically at me.

'About the calories in this cream,' I said smoothly, pointing to the tea tray. 'Besides, you've burned it off on the beach earlier, I'm sure.'

'Correct answer,' she said, yawning delicately. 'By the way, do thank Eliza again. That mermaid photo shoot was the most fun I've had in years. And Danny was such a sweetheart.'

'He said I had real talent,' said Ruby, her blue eyes glinting. 'Out of all the group, he said I was the most photogenic.'

'You certainly posed for the most pictures,' said Catherine pointedly.

Ruby made faces behind Catherine's back and the cousins giggled at her antics until Sapphire's phone made a tinkling bell sound.

'Ignore it,' said Catherine with a groan.

'I can't; that's the sound of an email from a VIP,' Sapphire said, flopping down next to her friend. 'I'd better just read it; it's from the editor of *My Dream Day* magazine. I hope there's not a problem.'

'Let's have some music,' said Ruby, jumping to her feet. She plugged her phone into a wireless speaker and started dancing to some rap music. The cousins quickly joined in.

I walked to the door. 'I'll leave you to enjoy your tea. Shall I knock on the other doors to let them—'

'Oh no!' Sapphire gasped, staring at her phone. 'Apparently there's a picture of us all dressed as mermaids on Facebook. Yet another leak! And *My Dream Day* says because I've breached my exclusivity agreement, they'll no longer pay to feature our wedding.'

My first thought was that thank goodness they'd already paid Theo for the booking. My second was, *who posted the photo?*

'But how can anyone have got hold of the picture?' I said, raising my voice over the music. Ruby was demonstrating to the others how to go low, low, low and gyrate their hips at the same time. 'Was there anyone else on the beach when you were in your mermaid tails?'

'A couple of old dears on the far side, but other than that, just us.' Catherine rushed to her side. 'Let me see.'

Sapphire handed her the phone and dropped her head in

her hands. 'I knew we shouldn't have trusted Danny. Photographers are all the same. Can't resist an opportunity to sell a picture. And wasn't he the one who revealed your whereabouts on Facebook when you were in hiding?'

I looked over Catherine's shoulder at the screen. It was a fantastic picture. All eleven mermaids stood in a row on the sand, one arm in the air and the other around their neighbour's waist. Behind them was the lifeboat house and to the right was the edge of the cliffs. The photographer had timed the shot perfectly to capture a wave crashing against the rocks and a huge arc of white spray like confetti framed the edge of the picture.

I felt a wave of unease. I really didn't want it to be true. Eliza, Theo and Molly had all counted on this booking to go well for their fledgling businesses.

'Did Danny even have his own camera?' I said suddenly. 'Didn't he just borrow one of yours?'

'Let me think.' Catherine gazed up at the ceiling, eyes blinking. 'All the photos he took were on mine or Ruby's phones. He was only wearing a wetsuit. There was absolutely nowhere to hide in that outfit, I'd have spotted any equipment. The only lumps and bumps were . . .' She turned pink and coughed. 'No. Definitely no camera.'

Ruby snorted. 'You *so* checked out his equipment, sister.'

Catherine leapt to her feet and jabbed Ruby with a finger. 'Don't you "sister" me. It's obvious where the leak has come from.'

'Ruby?' The colour drained from Sapphire's face. 'Is it true?'

Ruby snapped the music off and the cousins stopped waggling their bottoms, shuffled back to their seat in the corner and helped themselves to scones.

'Yes,' she snapped, folding her arms and squaring up to Catherine. 'It was me. And I blabbed the address of the Scottish hotel to the press too.'

I sighed with relief; Danny was in the clear. Thank goodness for that. But poor Sapphire – betrayed by her sister . . .

'Poor lovely Poppy missed out on this weekend because I doubted her,' Sapphire said, horrified.

'I should go,' I said, turning towards the door. 'Let me know if I can do anything to help.'

'I know you're judging me,' said Ruby, blocking my way. 'But you don't know how hard it is to get noticed when you're a nobody.'

'I'm still a nobody,' I retorted crossly. 'Most people don't recognize me, even after being in *Victory Road*.'

'But they know you for leaking the plot of the show and dumping ice on Cecily. I'd kill for that sort of publicity.'

I gaped at her. There were no words to deal with that sort of mentality, even if she was right.

'Ruby!' exclaimed Sapphire. 'You're not nobody to me!'

'I'm nobody *because* of you,' Ruby spluttered indignantly. '*I* auditioned for *Maidens of Mayfair* first. *I* should have been star of the show. I'd have been the famous sister.' She looked at me. 'They sent two researchers round to check out my house, to make sure it was suitable for filming, and there was Sapphire in the kitchen flipping pancakes. They were supposed to come and look at my big bedroom with its own dressing room and Juliet balcony and my vinyl collection of Andrew Lloyd Webber musicals. They never even left the kitchen. Two hours later my dreams had gone up in smoke; they dropped me for her.'

'I felt awful about it,' said Sapphire quietly.

'So you always say. But it doesn't change anything.' Ruby's eyes filled with tears.

'I did fight for Ruby to be in the show,' Sapphire explained. 'The producers said that she would get a cameo role as long as I agreed to take part.'

'But I felt like a dog being thrown a bone.' Ruby pouted and I experienced a wave of sympathy for her. I knew only too well what it felt like to be passed over for a job you'd been promised. The Cecily Carmichael incident still had the capacity to make me go hot and cold every time I thought of it.

'I had to take the opportunity to try to raise more awareness of my research project into cleptobiosis in ants,' explained Sapphire, 'but so far I haven't been able to shoehorn it into conversation in the show. So frustrating.'

'Clepto what?' I exclaimed.

Sapphire laughed. 'You know, when members of one species steal food from another. Ants are devils for it.'

Catherine and I exchanged looks and I hid a smile. *Maidens of Mayfair* concerned itself mostly with shopping, eating and partying. I could see her problem.

'Whereas I need the exposure on TV. I *need* to get noticed for me,' Ruby put in.

I felt my hackles rise. This trend of being famous for being famous really got my goat.

'I've met plenty of reality TV stars over the years,' I said steadily. 'They come and go with each new show. But the ones who endure are the ones who have passion and drive and a star quality that attracts others to them. For fame to benefit you, you need to start with your passion. So. What is your passion?'

'Singing.' She stuck her chin up. 'I want to be a singer.'

'Oh.' I hadn't been expecting that. 'That's great.'

'She is a very good singer,' Sapphire agreed. 'Dad's got videos of her singing all the songs from *The Lion King*. Brings a tear to my eye every time. But—'

Ruby rolled her eyes. 'Here we go. But I'm not good enough to make it. Blah, blah, blah.'

'No. You are.' Sapphire's hands balled into fists with frustration. 'But you never turned up for your singing lessons, or practised for your exams.'

'I don't need to. Singing's a gift.'

'Your *voice* is a gift,' I put in. 'I don't sing, but I do know that your voice is a muscle, the same as any other. And you need to put in the training to be the best.'

Ruby frowned and picked at the skin around her thumbnail.

'I just want a chance to shine. It's not easy being in your shadow, you know,' she told Sapphire. 'You've always been the clever one, the good daughter. When I was little I copied you. Then when I got to fifteen I realized I'd never match up, so I stopped bothering.'

'Sing at my wedding,' Sapphire blurted out. 'A solo. Something beautiful. There'll be people in the audience who might be able to help you.'

Ruby looked up, her eyes hopeful. 'I thought you'd got a harpie?'

'Harpist. I have. Catherine, when . . . ?'

'I'll check the wedding itinerary.' Catherine tapped on her phone. 'Got it. Harpist to play Bach solo as played at Kate Middleton's wedding while bride and groom sign the register.'

'Amend it to read Ruby Spencer to sing . . . What do you want to sing?'

Ruby chewed her lip while she pondered. 'Oh I know! "Empty Chairs at Empty Tables" from *Les Mis*!'

Catherine paled. 'The one about death? And loneliness?'

'We'll work on the song choice together,' said Sapphire swiftly. 'And you have to practise. Every day for the next two weeks. Promise?'

Ruby threw herself across the room and into her sister's arms. 'Thank you, Sapph. I won't let you down. I'll go to my room now, find the lyrics and start rehearsing. Girls, you can help,' she said to her cousins who obediently got to their feet.

She kissed Sapphire's cheek and then said in a small voice, 'I'm sorry for posting that picture of us. I should have thought about your magazine deal. You've been so good to me and I've completely cocked things up for you.'

'Forget about it,' said Sapphire kindly. 'What are big sisters for?'

'That is a bit of a bind, though,' Catherine said once the three younger girls had gone upstairs. She squeezed Sapphire's hand. 'What are you going to do?'

Sapphire frowned. 'Nina, you've had run-ins with the press, what do you advise to get them back on board?'

I perched on the edge of the sofa and thought about it. I thought about what Maxine Pearce would say. A month ago I'd probably have come up with a whole list of ideas to get Sapphire's wedding on the front pages of the papers. But things had changed for me recently. I didn't feel the need to grab every photo opportunity any more, and certainly not those that didn't focus on what really mattered to me – my acting career. Right now I was using my limited fame to benefit others and it felt really good. I wondered what was motivating Sapphire.

'Do you really need them there?' I asked.

Sapphire shrugged. 'Brad, my fiancé, is heading up a campaign to protect endangered Vancouver Island marmots. Our fee was heading straight to the charity. And the magazine promised to add a side column about it too.'

Which, if my experience was anything to go by, would be a tiny afterthought and do absolutely nothing for Brad's praiseworthy intentions.

'Wouldn't it be better to ask for donations instead of wedding gifts?' I suggested. 'And ask all the cast of *Maidens of Mayfair* to post a link to his campaign?'

Sapphire blinked at me. 'And have no press there at all?'

'Maybe you could marry in private?' said Catherine.

'Yes, make it about you and Brad,' I agreed. 'Something just for you and your loved ones. Not the rest of the world. There's something precious about that, I think.'

'I could even ban the *Maidens of Mayfair* cameras,' Sapphire said thoughtfully.

'Think how lovely a day without press intrusion would be,' I said.

'Liberating.' Sapphire sighed.

'And you'd get to run the day your own way,' I added.

Sapphire grinned at her best friend. 'Or in my case, how Catherine plans it.'

Catherine went pink. 'To hell with the clifftop walk, let's skip straight to bottle of champagne number . . . Oh, who cares which number we're on.'

The rest of the hen party arrived just as Sapphire was easing the cork out of the bottle and I slipped away to get the table ready for dinner later. There was a whirring noise coming from the garden at the back of the house and I peered round the gate to see Theo in just a pair of shorts with the hedge trimmer. The sight of his bare chest reminded me: judging by the twinkle in her eye I was guessing Catherine's special entertainment must have an element of male nudity involved. Might she have booked a stripper? Or a butler in the buff, maybe?

I'd find out soon enough . . .

Chapter 20

'Please light!' I hovered over the candle with a match, watching as the flame burned ever closer to my fingers while the wick resolutely refused to catch fire. The kitchen was beginning to smell of burned fingernail.

This was the only room at Driftwood Lodge big enough to seat eleven people. As kitchens go it was comfy and cosy, but a bit plain for the elegant dinner party look I was going for. I was trying to make up for that by using candlelight to add some ambiance and simultaneously create a few dark corners to hide the worst of the mess. And I was using Jethro's entire stock of emergency power cut candles to do it. The hens probably wouldn't go in the living room, but I'd put some candles in there just in case and turned off all the lights in the hall to make it look less of a landing strip and more like a dimly lit restaurant.

Theo had gone over to the cottages with some appetizers to keep the women going while I finished off and I'd instructed him to stay over there as long as he could to buy us some time.

Finally, with a few burned fingers and at least one singed eyebrow, all the candles were lit.

There. Done. I stood back to admire my handiwork. I'd raided Eliza's shop earlier this afternoon for anything vaguely eastern to decorate the room with and now delicate paper lanterns in jewel colours of pink, blue and emerald hung from the ceiling, bowls of matching paper flowers adorned the table and candlesticks in the shape of fat little Buddhas sat at opposite ends of the table. Eliza had also lent me some pretty multi-coloured fairy lights and I'd hung them above the Aga. The effect, if not totally authentic Asian, lent a party atmosphere to the otherwise homely room.

What next? I scanned my list. Put plates in to warm in the bottom oven. I opened the cupboard but it was empty. All the plates were still in the dishwasher from lunchtime. But thankfully clean. I dried them off quickly but in my haste, managed to flick the tea towel in my eye, causing my eyes to water and temporary blindness.

Thank goodness I had opted for caterers, I thought, blotting my eye with a tissue, I couldn't even be trusted with empty plates.

When I straightened up from clattering crockery and slamming the oven door, still with one hand pressed to my eye, there was a strange man in the unlit hallway.

'Oh, hello!' I said, startled.

He was wearing a trendy cap pulled low over his eyes, a bright white shirt and a black dinner suit with a satin stripe down the side of the trousers. A lovely smell wafted off him into the kitchen: warm and spicy and totally delicious.

'I wasn't sure where to go,' he said. 'I did knock.'

'I had my head in the oven.' I blinked at him, trying to clear my vision. 'Not for suicidal purposes, you understand.'

'I understand.' His lips twitched. He had nice lips, smiley and full, and lovely white teeth. 'Where shall I set up?'

'Set up?' I stared at him, shadowy and mysterious in the gloom, and it suddenly dawned on me who this was. 'Oh, *set up*.'

Catherine's surprise: the male stripper.

I bet the satin stripes on his trousers were to hide the Velcro; one tug and – whoosh – they'd be off. I wished Catherine had told me he was coming so early. Deliciously Devon would be here any second with the food. What was I supposed to do with him while they were eating?

'Follow me,' I said, squeezing past him into the hallway. I swept an arm towards the living room. 'You can get undressed in there out of the way.'

His hands flew to the lapels of his jacket. 'You have got to be joking.'

'Sorry, what did you expect – a dressing room with lightbulbs around the mirror? This is a Devon long house not the Folies Bergère.'

'I'll keep my clothes on, if it's all the same to you. And I expected a table at the very least,' he said crossly. 'We're talking some very hot stuff, and it could get messy.'

I tried not to look shocked. Perhaps he was one of those strippers who uses fire-eating in their act, or snakes. Where on earth had Catherine found him? And more to the point, why? I couldn't imagine Sapphire being up for anything like this, except maybe the snake part, she did seem to have a thing about animals.

'No way,' I said with a shudder. 'I've heard of people who parade up and down tables waving their pants in the air. Well, not here you don't. You'll just have to keep your feet on the ground.'

'Jeez.' The man backed away towards the door. 'I don't know who your normal caterers are but I've already said, I am not taking my clothes off.'

Caterers?

'Oh my God. Are you from Deliciously Devon?'

'Yes.' He smirked. 'Who were you expecting, *Magic Mike*?'

I blinked my blurry eye and gradually the man's features came into focus. A wave of horror crept up from my toes to my face as he took his hat off. A pair of hazel eyes stared back at me.

'Jude? I'm so sorry. What are you doing here? I'm confused, I thought you were a social worker,' I stammered.

'I am. As well.' He ruffled a hand through his dark hair:

short at the sides and springy on top. He had a long thin scar just above his ear. His face spread into a smile. 'And I thought you were a mermaid. I didn't recognize you with your clothes on. And aren't you the one I nearly drove into the back of, last Friday?'

'Er . . . ?' Was that only last week? I was sure Devon must run on a different calendar system; I felt like I'd been here for ever. Also, I'd never seen Jude's face properly close up. He was strikingly attractive. I pulled myself together. 'For a caterer you seem over-dressed and under-catered. Where's the food?'

'Is the suit too much?' Jude looked down at his suit and rubbed his chin and I regretted making him feel awkward. 'Sorry.'

'You look very smart.' Gorgeous actually. The T-shirt and jeans I'd seen him in previously showed off his muscles, but in a suit . . . my insides were doing somersaults.

'I wasn't sure what to wear,' he continued. 'With Angie being away and me just standing in.'

Just standing in . . . the somersaults stopped instantly.

'I might faint,' I whispered. I could feel myself going hot and then cold. The pain in my eye paled into insignificance. 'I can't believe I've entrusted Sapphire's dinner party to a bad-tempered social worker.'

'Who says I'm bad-tempered?' He looked affronted. 'I'm very easy going. Well, unless someone annoys me and then I can't help speaking my mind.'

The inside of my mouth had gone so dry I could barely get my words out. I went back into the kitchen and started pacing back and forth.

'At the risk of annoying you, you're not a chef so who cooked dinner? It takes real skill to cook Asian food properly. I thought I was phoning professional caterers this morning to come to my rescue, but this . . . this is a disaster.'

He leaned on the doorframe and folded his arms, casually. 'I *have* come to your rescue. Although I'm not sure whether to be flattered or insulted that the first thing you did when I came through the door was to ask me to get naked.'

'Sorry.' I swallowed the lump in my throat. 'I'm on edge. This is such a big booking for Brightside Holidays, I'm trying to help Theo put this place on the map and—'

'I'll stop you there, calm down,' he said, striding across the kitchen. He placed his hands on my arms and breathed in through his nose and blew out through his mouth, nodding at me to do the same. 'Deep breaths. That's it. I am not a stripper, and you're right, I'm not a chef. But—'

I whimpered at that but he guided me gently towards the front door. A dark blue van with Deliciously Devon painted in silver in large letters down the side of it was parked in the courtyard.

'When you rang this morning I did try to fob you off but you were getting upset and I felt duty bound to help.'

'Thank you,' I said on an out-breath. 'What a kind thing to do.'

I could have kissed him. Although I still hadn't seen any sign of the food.

He rubbed the back of his neck shyly. 'No problem. Anyway, I like a challenge so I used my initiative and – feast your eyes on this!'

He opened up the back of the van with a flourish to reveal six cardboard boxes printed with the logo of a Thai restaurant.

'A takeaway?' My jaw dropped; my fancy dinner party was courtesy of the Siam Palace takeaway. 'You ordered in?'

He gave me a lopsided smile, which pushed a dimple into his cheek. 'Okay, I bent the rules a bit. But it is the best takeaway in Devon. All authentic, all homemade by a lady from Chang Mai. Had to drive nearly forty miles for this.' He pointed to the heated pads underneath the boxes. 'But don't worry, it'll be piping hot.'

I felt myself calming down. Catherine had said Sapphire loved this sort of food and if the aroma was anything to go by it was going to be delicious. Everything would be fine. Better than fine. It would be a huge success.

'You,' I said, throwing my arms round his neck, 'are a hero.'

'All in a day's work.' Jude laughed softly in my ear. 'Cash most welcome.'

There was a cough from behind us and I turned to see Theo watching us, a concerned frown on his face.

'Deliciously Devon has arrived!' I said brightly.

'So I see,' said Theo with a thin smile. 'Just in time, the ladies are asking if dinner is nearly ready.'

'It is,' said Jude, picking up two boxes at once. I picked up a third. 'All we need to do is transfer it from the takeaway cartons.'

Theo's face folded into a frown. 'Takeaway?'

'Stand aside.' I winked at him as we walked past to go inside. 'Hot stuff coming through.'

Two hours later, the girls were getting ready to go back to Penguin's Pad to play some after-dinner games Catherine had planned. No male nudity whatsoever. I needn't have worried. About anything. Theo and Jude were clearing up while I made up some pots of coffee for them to take over. I'd been on the go all day and felt exhausted. But happy. Very happy. Tonight couldn't have gone any better if I'd brought in the royal caterers to the Queen. Sapphire had loved the decorations, the food had been declared delicious and *so* authentic, and the conversation had been lively and full of fun.

Sapphire wrapped me in a hug as she stood to leave.

'Thank you so much for tonight. I can scarcely move,' she groaned, patting her tiny taut stomach. 'Your caterer is amazing and so knowledgeable about Thai food.'

'I'll pass it on,' I said, somehow managing to keep my face straight. What she hadn't seen was Jude whipping his take-away menu out of his jacket pocket every now and then to remind himself what all the dishes were called. I was proud of both men; he and Theo had done a sterling job and had been really good sports amidst all the teasing and banter you'd expect from an excitable group of girls who, by Catherine's reckoning, were now on bottle of champagne number thirty-five.

'You've made a good impression on our guests,' I said when I handed Jude an envelope full of cash to cover his hastily scribbled invoice. 'When is Angie coming back? Just in case next time you can't rely on the takeaway.'

'End of June, so try not to call until then, I can't take the pressure.' He grinned, reaching a hand instinctively to where the thin silver scar traced a line above his ear. His hazel eyes were framed by strong brows and crinkled at the corners when he smiled. He bristled with energy. Shorter and stockier than Theo but in a good way. In a solid muscly good way. 'But in the meantime we could catch up over coffee one day, or a drink at The Sea Urchin?'

I was taken aback. Eliza had implied that he kept himself to himself, that he preferred his dog to people. Having said that, I'd found him nothing but charming tonight and I'd really like a chance to get to know him better.

'Sure,' I said with a shy smile.

'I know Deliciously Devon didn't quite supply what you were hoping for tonight but . . .'

Oh, I don't know.

'But there might be more opportunity for us to work together as Brightside Holidays grows?'

So he wanted to talk business . . . My smile slipped a bit.

'I'd like that,' I managed to say brightly.

He picked up the box containing the food warmers he'd borrowed from the Siam Palace and I followed him outside.

'I'd like to find out more about the lifeboat house too. You seemed really upset that it's for sale?'

Jude's brow furrowed instantly as he slid the box into

the back of the van. 'Yeah, I am. Long story, but I don't want to see it sold. It's such a great place, full of possibility.' He stopped suddenly as if a thought had occurred to him. 'How are you fixed to come and see it now – just you and me?'

He smiled at me in the darkness and a cool breeze fluttered over my bare skin still hot from an evening of hostessing. The sky was clear, a pale moon sat regally amongst the stars, in the distance I could hear the gentle roar of the waves and the air was fragrant with wild garlic, bluebells and the ever-present aroma of the sea. A walk on the beach with Jude would be lovely.

'Why not?' I felt my insides ping. 'Come back in while I fetch a jacket.'

Theo was in the hallway waiting for us.

'Nina,' he said abruptly, 'I need to talk to you about something as soon as the ladies have gone.'

'But I was about to go out with Jude.'

'It can't really keep,' he added. 'It's about Kate.'

'Sure,' I said, swallowing my disappointment. 'I'll be right there.'

'No worries. We'll do it another time,' Jude murmured. He picked up his dinner jacket from the chair in the hall and shrugged his arms into it. 'I'll be off.'

The girls appeared *en masse* from the kitchen ready to go back to the cottages.

'Do you have to go?' Ruby sidled up to him and stroked his arm. 'Catherine wants us to play boring games. We need a man to liven things up.'

'I don't think so,' Jude laughed shyly.

I stifled a smile. For some reason I didn't like to dwell on, I didn't want him to join them.

'Oh, I insist!' Sapphire called from the doorway, beaming. 'It's been such a fun evening.'

'And the fun is only just beginning,' said Catherine mischievously.

'Kidnap him!' yelled Belinda, one of the *Maidens of Mayfair* cast. And then a gang of women descended on him and Jude, with a silly grin on his face, disappeared into a sea of blonde hair, false eyelashes and rather a lot of bosom.

'This is refreshing,' I said, pulling the collar up on my jacket; the breeze down on the beach was much sharper than at Driftwood Lodge. 'After the heat of that kitchen.'

Theo and I were padding across the soft sand. It was after eleven o'clock and unsurprisingly it was deserted. The cove was in darkness, just the reflection of the moon on the water and the occasional flash of light from ships far away on the horizon. I was intrigued to find out what Theo wanted to tell me. It must be serious; he'd been very adamant about talking to me immediately. I was a willing listener, but a part of me couldn't help wondering what might have happened if it had been Jude on the beach with me instead.

Theo shook out a rug he'd brought in a rucksack and set it down on a dry part of the beach in the shelter of the rocks. I sat down obediently and pulled my knees up to my chest.

He drew a bottle of wine and two plastic cups from his rucksack and poured us both a drink. I wished he'd brought a flask of tea instead. Or some strong caffeine to keep me awake.

'So what did you want to talk about?' I said with a yawn.

He sipped his wine and looked out to sea.

'Since the call came from London about this hen weekend we've hardly had a chance to think. I thought it would be nice to share a moment.'

'It is,' I agreed. Although right now I was thinking about what Jude was getting up to with eleven women and Catherine's games.

'I think they've enjoyed it,' he said, settling back against the rock. 'You were wrong, you see, about your London friends wanting posh restaurants and shops. That quiet one, Virginia, said she'd never been anywhere so quaint.'

'Theo,' I said softly, 'I thought you wanted to talk about Kate?'

He knocked his wine back and wiped his mouth with the back of his hand. 'I do. I think she's trying to tell me something.'

I sat forward, all ears. 'Has she been in touch?'

He shook his head and cast his eyes down. 'Not at all. Which is my point. The last email I had from her was that one about Bruce Nutley's booking. At the time she said some nice things. That she was pleased I was making a go of the business and finally thinking about the future. But I've emailed her several times since, keeping her updated, asking her opinion, and she's ignored them all. Reading between the lines, I think what she meant before was that she was glad I was managing without her because perhaps she has no intention of coming back.'

'That's quite a leap.' I blinked at him. 'She's miles away, Theo. Give her a chance.'

'I've given her several chances. I even sent her a message this afternoon letting her know that Brightside Holidays has gone live on the Coastal Cottages website. Still nothing. I mean, that was her ultimate dream. And I've done it. *We've* done it. You and me.'

'But the time difference, access to the internet . . . there could be a perfectly reasonable explanation for her silence. Perhaps she's ill?'

He looked up at me, almost hopeful for a second, and then shrugged.

'Time to face facts, Nina. She obviously no longer cares about me or our marriage. Which made me think: perhaps she was right to leave me, perhaps without Ivy, our family can never be fixed.'

I could see how much it hurt him to utter these words. Maybe this was a self-preservation thing; preparing himself for the worst. Just in case. But I didn't think the worst would happen, he was simply over-reacting.

I covered his hand with mine. 'Don't say that. Look how far you've come in these last few weeks. You've been on fire since the hen party arrived. And when Kate comes back you'll be able to pour that same energy into your marriage.'

Theo's curls riffled in the wind and he laughed softly to himself.

'At first all this hard work *was* to impress Kate, to win her back. I took on board her ultimatum and together you and I have smashed it. But I realized today that I'm not doing it for her any more. I'm doing it because *I* want it. I want a life here.'

'That's good!' I clonked my plastic cup against his. 'That's really good news.'

'I think so.' Theo smiled shyly. 'And if Kate doesn't want me, then there are plenty more fish in the sea.'

That was an unexpected plot twist. I'd given up my time – willingly, admittedly – to rise to the challenge of Kate's ultimatum. With the sole purpose of reuniting two people who loved each other. Not to groom Theo ready for the dating scene. I wasn't sure quite what to say.

He topped up both of our wines, although mine was barely touched. 'You love it down here too, don't you?'

Behind him, the lights from the village twinkled on the clifftops; above us, the moon reigned over a velvet sky sparkling with stars and at our feet gentle waves lapped at the shore. No TV location manager could have done a better job of creating a romantic scene.

He reached towards me and brushed a stray hair from my cheek and my heart thumped.

'I love it.' My voice came out as a squeak.

'Perhaps you could stay?' he murmured. 'For ever.'

A seagull squealed from the rocks behind us and the harsh noise startled us both. I leapt to my feet. 'We ought to be getting back.'

He jumped to his feet. 'You're right. Of course, let's go.'

'Please don't give up on your marriage,' I said, as we repacked his rucksack. 'I came here to help you win Kate back. That's still our goal, isn't it?'

He nodded but didn't meet my eye. 'But what happens if she's removed the goalposts altogether?'

'Then you build your own,' I said softly. 'For you.'

My heart squeezed for him as we trudged back to Driftwood Lodge and I sent up a silent message to the heavens hoping that Kate would get in touch with him soon.

That night, sleep didn't come easily. My head was full of Sapphire and Ruby's differing quests for fame, mistaking Jude for the stripper and then Theo and his revelations on the beach. My body, on the other hand, was so exhausted that I could barely be bothered to get undressed and when I did I couldn't find my nightshirt and ended up crawling under the covers naked.

The hen party across the courtyard had turned rowdy and I put my earphones in and listened to some music and must have fallen asleep. At three, I was woken up by a screech of laughter from the cottages and when I looked out lights shone through the downstairs window of Penguin's Pad and the party was still in full swing. Jude's van was still there too. There was something about Jude that intrigued me; he was attractive, of course, with an infectious laugh that made me laugh too. But it was more than that, and the thought that I'd like to get to know him better sent me to sleep with a smile on my face. And a lovely dream it was too.

An annoying choking, ratchety noise woke me up. It sounded like a poorly engine. I lay there for a few seconds willing it to stop, and despite keeping my eyes shut tight I could feel the sunlight streaming through the gap in the curtains.

The engine noise stopped and there was a loud metallic slamming sound.

'You have got to be joking!' yelled a voice.

I got up, wrapping the duvet around me, and stood looking out of the window. Across the courtyard, at the upstairs window of Kittiwake's Cabin I caught a quick flash of pink skin and blonde hair before the curtain was quickly drawn. And immediately below my window was Jude.

What was he doing here so early?

My breath caught in my throat as the penny dropped: he hadn't been home. He was still in last night's clothes, his white shirt streaked with oil, and was trying to open the bonnet of his van. He fiddled with the catch for a moment and flung it up and then he dived under it out of view.

Who had I just seen at the window across the courtyard? Had he spent the night with one of our guests? I racked my brains trying to remember who was staying where. Not Sapphire, thank goodness, she was in Penguin's Pad. Not Virginia, she had brown hair? Catherine or Ruby? I shuddered. How could he? I mean, he was a free man and all that, but surely there was some sort of caterer's code: thou shall not sleep with the one you feed or something.

I gripped the duvet tightly under my armpits before opening the window, making sure it was covering my assets; he'd seen them once already and didn't need a second viewing.

'Quite the party animal, aren't you?' I called. Did that sound casually amused, or a bit waspish? Possibly the latter. 'I didn't expect our caterer to still be here for breakfast.'

He reappeared from underneath the bonnet and frowned. 'Yep. Van won't start. Thank goodness football practice is cancelled this morning, or I'd be in even worse trouble.'

A football player; that explained the trim physique and the lovely toned bum . . . I gave myself a shake and leaned my elbows on the window sill.

'Who will you be in trouble with?' I said, arching an eyebrow. 'Angie?'

222

'Far worse than that.' He wiped his hands on his trousers. 'I need to get back for Mabel, a neighbour let her out last night and first thing this morning, but she'll be bouncing off the walls ready for a walk.'

'Oh, poor Mabel.' My concern for his lovely dog instantly took priority over my interest in his nocturnal activities. 'What do you need, petrol, or oil or something?'

Jude's lips twitched. 'Something. Flat battery.'

'Must have been all that partying,' I said, unable to resist it.

My bedroom door creaked open to the side of me and before I had a chance to flip the duvet round my naked bottom, Theo entered carrying a tray.

'I've brought you some cheeks . . . *tea*. I mean tea.' He froze, staring at my exposed posterior.

'Theo!' I yelped. 'You should have knocked.'

In my panic to cover my bum, the duvet slipped to the floor. I scrabbled to pick it up, conscious that due to the low windows I'd just given Jude a 360-degree view of myself, but in my haste, I trod on the end of the duvet and stumbled forward crashing straight into Theo and his tray. The mug of tea went everywhere, including a few splashes on my bare skin and a slice of toast dropped to the floor.

I squealed at the heat from the hot liquid.

'I've burned you, I'm so sorry.' Theo flung the tray on my bed, grabbed hold of a paper napkin and started dabbing me.

I pushed him away. 'Please, get off me!'

'Nina!' a familiar female voice gasped from below the window. 'And *Theo*!'

I grabbed the duvet from the floor and spun round to see who it was. Outside, still astride her bicycle, was Molly, here earlier than arranged, to collect the laundry. She was staring up at me, her brown eyes wide with shock. Jude, on the other hand, was leaning against his van helpless with laughter.

'If you were a gentleman, you'd look away!' I fumed at Jude who covered his mouth with his hand and tried to look serious.

'Nothing I haven't seen before,' he said with a twinkle in his eye.

Molly looked from me to Jude and back again with a gasp.

'What's going on?' she asked, looking bewildered. 'Why are you entertaining someone else's husband in your bedroom? Naked?'

'I'm asking myself the same question,' I said with a nervous laugh. 'But it's not how it looks.'

'Although it does look ravishing,' said Theo under his breath. He joined me at the window and I leapt away from him. 'Morning, Molly. All just a misunderstanding. I was hoping to surprise her in bed.'

I glared at him.

'Sorry. With *breakfast* in bed,' he stammered.

Molly harrumphed and Jude buried his face in his hands to stifle his snorts. My stomach had dropped to somewhere near my knees and I looked to Jude for help.

'In their defence,' said Jude, clearing his throat, 'Theo was in the kitchen a moment ago, so I don't think—'

'Save your excuses for Kate. All of you,' Molly's voice trembled as she wheeled her bike around to face in the direction she'd just come from and put her foot on the pedal. '*I've* heard them all before.'

'I wasn't lying when I said there was nothing going on between Theo and me, honestly,' I said, leaning my head as far as I could out of the window in one last-ditch attempt to rescue the situation. 'Come on, we're friends, aren't we?'

Theo, the idiot, squeezed in next to me so that we were shoulder to shoulder, which didn't help one bit.

Molly looked up, her eyes brimming with tears, and shook her head. 'You are a terrible actress, Nina, and an even more terrible friend. I am *so* disappointed in you.'

I felt like crying too as I watched her cycle off. She

couldn't have said anything more hurtful. It was all so unfortunate and unfair.

Beside me Theo swore under his breath.

'Molly wouldn't tell Kate, would she?' he muttered.

I sucked in breath and lifted my shoulders. 'She thinks all men are knobs and you've just proved her right.'

'But I didn't do anything!' he protested.

There was a coughing noise outside and we both looked out of the window.

'Sorry to *butt* in,' called Jude, attempting to hide his mirth, 'but have you got any jump leads I can borrow?'

Ten minutes later, Theo had gone out to help Jude and I was dressed and downstairs in the kitchen with a new mug of tea, wondering what on earth we were going to do about Molly. Mittens, who was growing bigger and bolder by the day, was playing a game of chase with a champagne cork on the kitchen floor while I was checking on the sausages that Theo had shoved into the Aga for breakfast when the phone rang. I went through to the hall to pick it up but the answerphone beat me to it.

Good morning, dear heart. This is Maxine Pearce, I've decided to take you up on your offer and book into one of your cottages for a week while the place is still a backwater with no phone calls to distract me. Any of them will do. The dates are . . .

My heart pinged with excitement. I reached for the phone to interrupt her message and speak to her myself but the kitten distracted me with a meow. He had followed me into the hall and was now eyeing up the big wide world through the open front door. Theo's engine revved into life. I left the phone and I ran to scoop up his little furry body and shut the door before he met a sticky end under the van's wheels. Maxine was still talking: *Not a holiday strictly speaking; I've a pile of scripts to read as tall as the Shard and I can't hear myself think around here. And thinking is something I really need to do. Bye, bye, bye.*

I tried to grab the phone before she rang off but I was too late; the line was dead. But no sooner had I replaced it in its cradle than the phone rang again. I smiled to myself as I lifted it to my ear, thinking that Maxine had forgotten to tell me some detail or other.

'Brightside Holidays,' I said playfully. 'Lady of the house speaking.'

There was a beat of silence.

'This is Kate Fletcher,' said a low voice, humming with anger.

The blood rushed from my head to my feet; bad news certainly travelled fast.

'Kate! I'm so sorry, I was expecting someone else. That was just a joke.' I was hugely thankful that this wasn't a video call; my face was burning. 'A bad joke.'

'A joke,' she said flatly. 'Not unlike my marriage.'

'Don't say that,' I pleaded. 'When you've seen how much we've – Theo – has done—'

'So I've seen. The Coastal Cottages website has made it very clear just what the two of you have been up to.'

'Does it look good? I tried to make the cottages look cosy.'

'Oh, you look cosy all right. You and Theo look *very cosy* in your profile picture. *Mr and Mrs Fletcher.*' Her voice had gone scarily loud.

'What profile picture?' I repeated.

She gave a hollow laugh. 'Every holiday property on the website has a write-up about the owners. And a photograph. Brightside Holidays has a picture of you and Theo looking every inch the welcoming hosts.'

My heart rate suddenly trebled and I had a flashback to the moment Nigel had taken a picture of us. I had no idea that was what it had been for.

'Kate, I—'

'Put my husband on the line.'

At that moment the front door opened and eleven slightly bedraggled women filed in in search of food.

'Need Diet Coke,' demanded a green-faced Ruby.

I put Mittens into Sapphire's hands, pointed Catherine in the direction of the sausages and the soft drinks and ran outside to find Theo.

'Kate's on the phone for you,' I said, feeling as sick as Ruby looked. 'I don't think she's very happy.'

When he staggered back outside a few minutes later he looked like he'd gone ten rounds with a boxer and lost.

'What did she say?' I said, jumping out of Jude's van, where I'd been trying the key in the ignition for him.

'She wants a divorce,' he said in a dull voice. 'Seeing you and me together on the Coastal Cottages website was the final straw.'

Jude rubbed the back of his neck awkwardly, not knowing where to put himself.

'No way,' I said grimly. 'Not on my watch. Not after all this.'

'Afraid so.' Theo raked a hand through his hair wearily. 'She's convinced we're having an affair and that's even before Molly gets to her. It's my fault for not confessing that you were here.'

'Let me talk to her. She's got it all wrong.' I stepped towards the house but Theo barred my way and caught hold of my hand.

Jude got into his van discreetly out of earshot.

'Maybe a divorce is the right thing,' he swallowed. 'Maybe it is time to go our separate ways.'

'Don't give up now!' I cried. 'When I first arrived here you were desperate to win her back. What's happened to change that?'

'Me. I've changed.' He blew out a breath, glanced at Jude and lowered his voice. 'Nina, what I was trying to say last night—'

'No!' I clapped my hands over my ears. 'Stop.'

All that talk last night about plenty more fish in the sea

227

and then asking me to stay in Devon . . . I had an awful feeling that his next words would be ones I didn't want to hear. Over the last few days he'd been making little comments, standing too close, touching me . . . That was not what I wanted, it was not why I was here, and deep down I couldn't believe it was what he wanted either.

Suddenly it was all too much for me and tears sprang to my eyes. Molly had accused me of being a terrible actress and a terrible friend. It seemed as if Theo was ready to call time on his marriage and Kate was asking to do the same. Instead of getting them back together I'd driven a wedge between them. I'd failed. I'd failed at everything and it was all my fault.

At that moment Jude's engine roared to life and he jumped out and dropped the bonnet ready to go.

'Thanks, mate,' he shouted to Theo, raising a hand.

'Jude, hold on,' I cried, flinging open the passenger door. 'Please can I have a lift?'

Theo grabbed hold of the door to stop me shutting it. 'Don't go, I need you.'

'I'm sorry,' I said, peeling his fingers from the door. 'I can't be here right now.'

'Sure.' Jude put the van into reverse. 'Where are you heading?'

I shook my head, swallowing the lump in my throat as the van bumped down the drive, putting more and more distance between Driftwood Lodge and me, the figure of Theo getting smaller and smaller in the wing mirror.

You are a terrible actress and an even more terrible friend. My life was a mess.

'For once in my life,' I said with a sob, 'I have no idea what to do next.'

PART THREE

The Frenemies

Chapter 21

Jude steered his blue Deliciously Devon van away from the coast road and headed inland. Getting home to let Mabel out was his priority, so presumably that was his destination. Right now, I didn't mind where I went; *my* priority was putting some space between me and Theo. Other than answering Jude's queries about whether I was warm enough, I hadn't said much.

I glanced now and then at his profile, catching a flash of his hazel eyes, watching as he drummed his thumbs on the steering wheel. We made eye contact once or twice and although he smiled at me we were content to lose ourselves in our own thoughts.

My thoughts weren't comfortable ones.

What a fiasco. This was on a par with my storyline leak to *Entertainer's News*. All I'd tried to do was help Theo launch Brightside Holidays in preparation for Kate's return. And now she was demanding a divorce and he was just accepting it. On top of that he seemed to have developed feelings for me.

Not quite the happy ending for them I'd hoped for, to say the least.

I felt awful about it. I'd been a thorn in their side ever since their wedding day when I'd rashly declared my feelings for Theo. But that had been a silly crush; having grown up without a male role model, when Theo had come along as a friend of Archie's, so sensible and kind, I'd fallen head over heels. He'd done nothing to encourage me other than listen to me pour out my dreams of becoming an actress.

Since coming to Devon three weeks ago, he and I had become good friends and I'd done the same for him: listened to him talk about Ivy and Kate and his simple faded dreams of being a family.

I kept going over and over it in my head. Had I led him on in some way? But other than do my utmost to make a success of the holiday cottage business to help him get back into his wife's good books, I truly didn't think I had. And deep down I didn't really believe Theo wanted another woman other than Kate. He'd said something to Archie on my very first day in Brightside Cove about his libido . . . this soldier hasn't been in active service for months, or something. Perhaps Theo's soldier was simply ready for action again and I was a convenient target . . . I shuddered. No need to go any further with that image.

Why couldn't Kate have read all the joyful emails from Theo, bursting with good news about the business he was building for the two of them, instead of looking at the Coastal Cottages website and spotting the photo of the two of us? But it was a misunderstanding and like all good romances, there was still hope, still a chance that everything would work out in the end. Maybe I could help, email her perhaps, set the record straight? No that was no good; she'd probably delete it without reading . . .

The van swerved to the right and I shook myself out of my reverie. Jude had pulled into a layby. Had I asked him to drop me off? I'd been in such a daze since leaving Driftwood Lodge that I might have said anything.

'So,' he turned off the engine, 'can I tempt you?'

That woke me up.

He'd taken off his jacket and his white shirt strained pleasingly across his broad chest. He'd pushed up his sleeves and my eye was drawn to the taut muscles in his forearms and a smear of engine oil on his tanned skin.

He really was very attractive.

After an extremely dry period on the man front in London, Devon was turning out to be incredibly good for my ego; last week, Danny had offered to go Dutch on a plate of mussels, this morning Theo had caught me naked and pronounced me to be 'ravishing' and now *this*. Third time lucky. Of the three, Jude was definitely the most appealing.

Could he tempt me?

Yes, I thought, conscious of a sudden pull in my stomach. Yes, he could.

I'd taken so long to reply that Jude started to laugh. That rich warm laugh that had caught my attention the first time I'd heard it.

'It's just breakfast.' He nodded ahead of us. There was a mobile café parked at the far end of the layby. 'I thought we could grab something to eat now before I pick up Mabel. Plus, there's nothing in at home.'

Just breakfast. Of course it was. This was a man who'd been up partying with eleven gorgeous women all night. What was I thinking? I almost laughed out loud. Breakfast sounded great. Not as great as whatever I thought had just been about to happen, but still great.

I was starving and a chalk board propped up outside was advertising bacon and brie melts. I reached down towards my feet for my purse in my handbag but it wasn't there. I'd left Driftwood Lodge with just the clothes I stood up in: no phone or money, nothing.

'Oh, not for me, thanks,' I said, doing a 'I couldn't possibly eat a thing' face.

My stomach gave a loud rumble.

He grinned. 'My treat.'

He hopped out of the van with my order and came back a few minutes later with coffees, my bacon and brie and a sausage sandwich for himself.

'To make up for the one Theo promised me after I helped get breakfast ready for the ladies,' said Jude, squeezing two sachets of ketchup under the bread.

'*You* helped?'

'Yep. In exchange for kipping on his sofa last night.'

I was confused. 'But I thought I saw . . .'

'You thought I'd come from the guest cottages this morning, didn't you?' He grinned and took a big bite of his sandwich. 'I'd only popped back to fetch my jacket.'

'Oh, I'm so glad!' The words blurted out of me before I could stop them. 'I mean, I thought . . . I was worried.'

'Worried?' He looked amused.

'You know, impropriety. With guests.'

Sort of. I felt my face heat up and bit into my breakfast to hide my expression.

He hadn't spent the night with anyone. What a relief. I didn't want him to be a man who took advantage of women who'd had too much to drink because . . . because I just didn't. Was he single? I wondered. Eliza had said that he didn't give his heart away easily, so I'd assumed he was. But what about Angie, was she a business partner like Jude said, or the other sort of partner?

He grimaced. 'It was me you should have been worried about. Ruby is wild. She was very keen to play strip poker. That's how I lost my jacket. Even the game of truth or dare got a bit close to the bone at times.' He shuddered. 'I was grateful to get out with my trousers on. I managed to escape the party just after three but then the van wouldn't start. It's Angie's van and it has always been temperamental. I gave up in the end because it was making such a noise right under your bedroom window. Luckily Theo heard me and offered me his sofa for the night.'

'Good.' I had a big silly grin on my face. 'That's all right then.'

A blob of ketchup landed on his chin and I reached across and wiped it away with my fingertip.

'You should use your mirror more often,' I said cheekily. 'That was the first thing you ever said to me.'

I held up my finger to show him the sauce.

He took hold of my hand and sucked the ketchup from the tip of my finger. I bit back a gasp at the intimacy of the gesture.

Single. Definitely. Hopefully.

I lowered my sandwich down to the bag on my lap, still looking at him. He did the same and for a second time hovered between us and I could hear my heart thudding with anticipation. And then we kissed.

One exciting fierce kiss. Which came out of nowhere and any thoughts I had about whether he was single or not evaporated into thin air.

It was shocking: the feel of his stubble on my skin, his lips against mine, the smell of him, the taste . . .

We broke apart, our breathing heavy, and stared at each other. The amber flecks in his eyes looked like fire, his pupils dark and intense.

'I guess I could say something about using your brakes,' he said huskily. 'Like the first words you said to me, but I'm not sure I want to stop.'

He remembered, my stomach flipped.

'Nina Penhaligon,' he murmured, a smile playing on his lips, 'this is not usually the way I behave on a first breakfast. But I'm glad I did, that was amazing.'

'Ditto.' The way he was looking at me heated me up from inside and then something struck me . . . I hadn't realized he knew my surname. 'Please don't mention this to anyone, will you? I'd rather not be in any more gossip columns for a while.'

'I'm the soul of discretion.' He mimed zipping his lips. 'Eliza said you were an actress but I only know your name because Sapphire told me about you last night,' he explained. 'I don't watch much TV. I've never kissed anyone famous before; I feel . . . honoured.'

Jude looked so bashful that I couldn't resist teasing him.

'We learn to kiss like that in drama school,' I said lightly. 'All in a day's work.'

'Oh.' He looked deflated. 'Not for me, it isn't.'

'I'm kidding,' I said with a soft laugh. 'A screen kiss is more like . . .'

I leaned across cupping his face in my hands, hardly believing what I was doing. But why not? I could treat this as an experience to add depth to my craft just like Maxine had recommended. How had she put it? Oh yes, *feast on life*. And Jude was delicious. Deliciously Devon, in fact . . .

There was a sharp blast on a car horn behind us and we both jumped.

'Just as we were getting to the good bit,' Jude murmured.

'Saved by the horn,' I agreed.

Jude flashed me a look of amusement. 'Fancy a walk on the beach?'

After fleeing from Driftwood Lodge, I had nowhere else to be. 'I'd like that very much.'

He looked pleased. 'Let's go and collect Mabel.'

'Would you mind waiting here? I'll only be five minutes, I promise,' Jude said, rubbing a hand through his dark hair. Whatever product he used to tame his hair had worn off now and it was springing up from his forehead in thick waves.

'I'm timing you,' I said, turning on the van's radio.

He laughed and ran up the driveway, disappearing indoors.

Jude's house was a surprise. I'd envisaged him living somewhere quirky like a little studio with views of the sea. But this was a modest 1950s semi in a quiet avenue. Edging the lawn was a narrow border of lavender and pots of purple pansies lined the steps leading to the front door. There were net curtains at every window and a vase of yellow silk flowers adorned the window sill in the wide bay window to the right of the door. The place was neat and homely and reminded me that I still didn't have a clue who Angie was. And that perhaps before I resumed my demonstration of the perfect screen kiss, I ought to find out.

True to his word, Jude reappeared a few minutes later. Mabel bounded out ahead of him and I opened the van to let her in.

She yelped with delight, pinned me to my seat and tried to lick my face.

'Thanks for the wash, Mabel,' I said, trying to escape her hot tongue, 'but I'm all good.'

'She celebrates my homecoming like that every time.' Jude started the engine and snapped on his seat belt. 'Whether I've been gone two minutes or two hours. Daft dog.'

'Don't listen, Mabel.' I pressed my hands over her floppy ears. 'You're not daft; I think you're very clever.'

'I'll take that as a compliment.'

His hair, still damp from the shower, was all glossy and he smelled lovely and his eyes lit up when he smiled.

You should, I thought.

The drive to the beach at Brightside Cove only took ten minutes and as soon as Mabel caught a glimpse of the sea on the horizon she turned to rubber and started to bounce off every surface. Jude pulled up behind the lifeboat house next to another car, opened his door and Mabel flew down the slipway and down on to the sand barking with glee.

'There's someone in there,' said Jude as we walked past the other car, a battered VW Polo.

The driver's seat was fully reclined and a young man was fast asleep with a newspaper on his lap. Empty burger cartons and takeaway coffee cups littered the passenger seat.

'A surfer, probably,' I said. The tide was coming in but the beach was still wide and golden. There was a light breeze and the fresh smell of the sea filled me with joy. 'He might have driven up last night ready for a Sunday spent riding the waves.'

'I hope not, for his sake,' he said, shielding his eyes with his hand and scanning the beach.

'Oh?' Not that I was an expert, but the sea looked perfectly surf-able to me. 'Why's that?'

'He's forgotten his surfboard.'

I glanced back at the car: no roof rack. 'Ah.'

Jude rubbed his chin as if trying to conceal a smile.

It was still early and apart from a runner at the far end of the cove, we had the beach to ourselves. We walked down the slipway and on to the sand, following Mabel's paw prints to the edge of the shore. Jude pulled a tennis ball out of his pocket and threw it into the sea for her. She leapt into the waves and came back with it seconds later with a big doggy smile. She dropped it at my feet and when I went to pick it up she shook herself.

'Oh, right in my eyes!' I yelped, as the salt water stung my eyes.

'Mabel!' Jude chided, quickly throwing the ball back into the sea. Mabel chased after it. 'No manners, that dog.'

He offered me a tissue and I wiped my face.

'Your eyes.' He tipped my chin up and stepped closer. 'They're what? Grey, no, blue, or maybe green . . . they're constantly changing, like the colour of the sea. Like magic.'

The magic of the sea.

My head spun. That was the memory that I hadn't quite been able to catch hold of when I was talking to Big Dave the other day. The beach, the warm safe hand over mine, skimming stones, and laughing, always laughing . . . I remembered it all so clearly now.

'What have I said?' Jude's smile faltered.

I shook my head, lost in the memory.

A piece of sea glass sparkling in the sunlight caught my eye and I bent to pick it up. It was triangular with a notch at the top, a rough heart-shape. I turned it over in my hands, recalling the man who had once owned the whole of my heart. And then broke it.

'It's nothing. It's . . . You're the second person to say that to me, that's all.'

'And the first?' he asked softly.

I took a deep breath and held the piece of sea glass out to Jude.

'My dad,' I said finally.

Chapter 22

'My dad once said that my eyes held the magic of the sea.' I glanced up at Jude.

He took the sea glass from me and studied it before slipping it in his pocket.

'And I thought I was being original.'

I smiled as Jude threw the ball again for Mabel and I altered my gaze to look at the waves, rolling in, one on top of another, and I was transported back to another time, and to a place I'd almost forgotten . . .

We'd been on a beach, just me, Dad and Archie. It must have been shortly before he disappeared from our lives for ever. When I'd asked what Dad meant by the magic of the sea, he'd pointed to all the different colours in the water: the pale green of the shallows at our feet, then out to where the waves swirled grey against the rocks and then again far, far out on the horizon where an indigo sea merged into a turquoise sky. I'd felt so special, my small hand wrapped in his. I, Nina Penhaligon, had the magic of the sea in her eyes, and because Daddy loved the sea, he must love me very much too.

'You're close to your father?' Jude asked after a while.

'I was once, but he's forgotten all about us, probably wouldn't even remember the colour of my eyes now. He left us when I was small. I'm over it now.' I flapped a hand, dismissing the absolute heartbreak of my childhood with a casual flick of my wrist; I didn't want to spoil our walk with talk of my past. 'So tell me about you, your family. You aren't from here originally, Danny said, but your accent is local.'

He frowned slightly as if unconvinced by my flippant reference to my father.

'Come on,' I said, 'let's walk and you can talk.'

He took my hand and tucked it through his arm and while Mabel leapt and danced around us we set off again towards the harbour, weaving as we walked to keep our feet out of the surf.

'Okay, but you've been warned; it's not a happy tale. My dad didn't leave me. But I spent every waking hour wishing he would. He was violent and erratic and earned a living selling drugs, although we never seemed to have much money. We lived on an estate so rough that the postman refused to deliver to us.'

'That's awful. Why didn't your parents move?'

'My parents,' he said drily, 'were part of the problem. There were people on the estate who petitioned to get our sort evicted. We had messages posted through our door all the time. Not by the postman, obviously.'

'What sort of messages?'

'Well.' He took a sharp breath. 'On my ninth birthday, I heard the letter box clatter and ran downstairs amazed that someone had remembered me. Only to find that someone had shovelled dog mess through the flap and a note that read, "Scum out." I knew it was aimed at my dad, but all the same, I was devastated.'

The thought of a nine-year-old boy daring to hope that he might have a birthday present only to have those hopes so brutally dashed made my heart ache for him.

'Oh Jude, and on your birthday. My mum might have been a cold fish towards my brother Archie and me, but we always got presents. No parties because she didn't like letting strangers in to the house, but even so, compared to your upbringing, mine was idyllic. What did your mum think about it?'

'Huh. She idolized my old man, wouldn't hear a word against him.'

Unlike my mum, who wouldn't even mention my father's name. The word Dad was strictly taboo after he left. Most confusing for Archie and me when we were little. I was still confused now.

'Other people's relationships are a mystery to me,' I said, frowning. 'You never really know what goes on between two people behind closed doors: what makes it work; what causes it to break.'

The hairs on my spine stood up as I thought about Mum and Dad, who couldn't have been suited for them to fall out so catastrophically, and then Theo and Kate, who I still believed did have a chance.

I'd have to be getting back to Driftwood Lodge soon; I couldn't leave things as they were, I needed to do something to salvage the situation between them before anyone did anything silly. But not yet, not while Jude was sharing such an intimate part of himself. I pressed closer to him as we ambled along, a subtle sign that I understood and cared.

'Mum chose Dad over me every time. Whenever he beat me, she'd say I had it coming.' He shook his head sadly.

'Did your dad do that?' I flicked my eyes to the silvery scar above his ear.

'Yeah. I was showing Mum a painting I'd done at school. Dad said I was no Van Gogh but maybe cutting my ear off would help. He grabbed the tip of my ear and pretended to slice it with his knife. I fought him off and the knife slipped and cut me. It poured with blood. They laughed about it for the rest of the night.'

My eyes pricked with tears. 'How can someone be so unspeakably cruel to a child?'

'It happens,' he said dully. 'I'm afraid to say I've seen all sorts of cases of neglect and abuse.'

How brave he was to pursue a career in social work after the childhood he'd endured.

'Did social services intervene?'

'Not before I ran away when I was twelve. I thought the longer I stayed, the more likely it was that I'd end up like my father. I wanted to forget my dad, get all traces of him out of my system.'

Whereas I'd spent my whole life wondering why my dad had forgotten me.

I looked at him. The man who'd stepped in to help out at my dinner last night even though he clearly couldn't cook, who'd stayed to clear up, who'd humoured the hen party girls, helped cook breakfast, not to mention kissed me so amazingly this morning . . . No, he'd never end up like his dad. Besides, Mabel loved him and dogs were very astute at picking out good humans.

'I'm sure you were never in danger of ending up like him,' I said fiercely.

His face softened. 'Thanks. Never saw them again. I later found out that they hadn't even bothered reporting my absence. I escaped to Devon. I'd heard other kids at school talking about their holidays by the seaside and it always sounded so perfect: the buckets and spades, the paddling, fish-and-chip suppers and ice creams on the beach.'

We stopped and Jude turned to face the sea. The tide was getting higher and the boats in the harbour were beginning to shift on the sand. Soon they would be afloat, ready for the sailors who appeared in the little harbour car park at the weekend, ready for the healing power of the salty air and the roll of the sea. In the distance, Big Dave was throwing lobster cages on to his boat and behind his shack I could just about make out Eliza washing the windows of the Mermaid Gift and Gallery.

It *was* perfect.

Jude had done the right thing, as had I, I thought, and Big Dave, and Theo and Kate: we'd all been on the run from something when we'd first arrived in Devon, all been drawn to the restorative powers of Brightside Cove.

He turned to me and smiled and my heart melted. He'd endured so much and yet here he was to tell the tale – and still smiling.

'You were just a child; how did you survive?'

'A café owner in Exeter noticed me stealing food from his bins and sleeping rough and reported me to social services. And so began the next adventure.' He shrugged as if it was nothing.

'You must have been terrified,' I said, my voice thick with emotion. And how unloved and alone too. For all Mum's faults – and there were a few – at least Archie and I knew we were safe and would always have a roof over our heads.

'When home is a scary place, you have a skewed sense of risk. The big wide world seemed a safer bet than home.'

Jude blotted a tear from my face with his thumb which I hadn't even realised I'd shed. It was all I could do not to throw my arms around him and weep for the lost little boy he had been.

He whistled for the dog and when she came charging towards us, we both bent down to fuss her. I took Jude's hand and squeezed it. 'And what was the next adventure?'

'Shall we head back and I'll tell you the rest?'

We turned back towards the van and I listened as he described how he'd been taken into care, put into a children's home, which he'd hated so much that he kept trying to escape, terrified that he'd be sent back home. He'd fallen in with a gang, copied their dialect to fit in and started to go off the rails: getting involved with vandalism, dabbling in arson, the odd bit of shoplifting. Hating himself for becoming like his father, but not having the maturity to escape. And then, finally, when he was fifteen, his luck changed and he was introduced to Angie, a woman whose own children had already flown the nest.

'Officially Angie was my foster mum.' He grinned. 'But she did more than mother me, she saved me, persuaded me to go back to school and study for a career. She's still the most important woman in my life.'

Mabel barked loudly and bounced up at Jude.

'Yes, you're important too,' he said, ruffling the fur around her ears, and we both laughed.

He gave me a boyish grin and my heart stalled; he was lovely and I wondered why there was no other important woman in his life.

'You're incredible,' I said simply. 'And your story is an inspiration.'

Jude shrugged. 'I wouldn't go quite that far, I'm no angel. But now I'm a social worker with a decent job, I like to think I can be a role model to some of the kids I come across in my work, not to mention do my bit to support people who can't stand up for themselves.'

Danny had said Jude was never happier than when he had a campaign to fight. That made sense now.

'And Deliciously Devon is Angie's business?'

He nodded. 'Mainly buffets for weddings and anniversaries, that sort of thing. Although at the moment, it's on hold.' He gave a rueful smile. 'Angie's daughter Sophie has just had triplets and is suffering from post-natal depression. Angie is staying with her until she can cope by herself, so I'm answering enquiries and taking bookings for later in the summer.'

Mabel, having run and swum continuously for the last twenty minutes, was now panting at Jude's side, her pink tongue lolling. She stopped suddenly, ears pricked and gave a low warning woof.

'She's seen something,' he said.

Mabel broke into a run, flying across the sand towards the lifeboat house, barking loudly.

245

'It's that guy who was asleep in the car,' I said, recognizing him.

'Oh yeah, the surfer who forgot his board.' Jude grinned.

In the distance we could just make out that the man was standing on the slipway, alternately looking up at the building and then down at something in his hands.

'He seems more interested in the lifeboat house than the sea,' I pointed out.

'You might be right.' Jude swore under his breath and held a hand out to me. 'Come on, I've got to say something.'

We hurried over but Mabel had already stopped barking. Instead, she was rolling on her back and letting him tickle her tummy.

'Look at that,' he tutted. 'Such a flirt. She's supposed to be on my side.'

'Which is what?' I said breathlessly, tugging his arm to make him stop. 'You never got the chance to tell me last night. Why are you against the lifeboat house being auctioned off?'

He planted his feet in the sand and ran a hand through his hair angrily.

'Although I wasn't born here I feel like I belong. Brightside Cove is a special place and it's our duty to keep it that way for future generations.'

'I get that,' I said. 'But there's a new lifeboat station around the other side of the headland. This one is derelict. Surely it's best to let someone breathe new life into it?'

Theo had shown me the new lifeboat station on one of our walks. It was a state-of-the-art glass building with a visitors' centre and a café. This pretty little lifeboat house at the edge of Brightside Cove was far more charming, but its days of being useful to the community were long gone.

'Agreed,' Jude said grimly. 'It's the *someone* I've got a problem with. And that'll be whoever's got the biggest wallet.'

I looked back to where the young man was now throwing sticks for Mabel. His car was a beaten-up old VW with a dent in the door. He didn't strike me as a man with a big wallet.

'That's good, isn't it?' I said, still not really sure why he was getting so het up. 'Anyone who wants to invest in Brightside Cove gets the thumbs-up from me.'

His eyes shifted from me to the man. 'But then we'll get another boutique or bistro or beachside apartment block. I've been hoping the council would do something with this place for years, instead of letting it crumble away. But I wanted them to repair it, not get rid of it.'

'So what's your plan,' I asked, 'other than setting your dog on any prospective buyer?'

His mouth attempted a smile. 'Recently I offered to start a campaign to buy it from the council, so *we* can be the ones to renovate and restore it, keep it in the hands of the village. And I thought they were considering my proposal. But . . .' He nodded towards the building. 'It seems not.'

'And auctioning it means that a buyer will be found quickly,' I finished for him, finally understanding his disappointment. 'I'm sorry.'

He shrugged hopelessly. 'It's all about money. They're only interested in budgets and cost-cutting exercises and releasing capital to fund new housing that most of us can't afford. They want cash, and time isn't on my side.'

'But I'm on your side. If I can help, just shout.'

'Really?' His eyes lit up.

I nodded. There was something compelling about Jude: his sincerity, his passion, his dogged determination to fight the system, not to mention the fact that he was devastatingly handsome.

'Thanks. With a bit of money spent on it, it could be a great space for lots of different groups to use: youth clubs, dancing, sport, even . . .'

'Dog training? I said, nodding at Mabel, who'd abandoned stick-chasing and was now humping the man's leg. I didn't even know female dogs did that. I could hear my mother's voice in my head: 'Disgusting behaviour; look away, children.'

'Excuse me?' yelled the young man. 'Can you sort your dog out, she's not my type.'

We covered the last few yards towards the slipway and, much to the man's relief, Mabel released his leg and bounded up to Jude.

'And what type are *you*?' Jude bristled.

'A journalist.' He thrust his card at us. Robin Barker, News Thirst Media Agency.

'And you're . . .' He clicked his fingers three times. 'Nina Penhaligon, the actress who chucked ice on Cecily Carmichael.'

I cringed. How long would it be before I was remembered for something I did on screen rather than off?

He scrabbled in his pocket for his phone. 'Can I take a picture?'

'Sure,' I said flatly, knowing he'd take it with or without my consent. I raked my fingers through my hair in a vague attempt at looking groomed, but a gust of wind from behind reversed my efforts. Robin glanced at the pictures and shrugged.

'Never mind, I'm actually looking for the Mermaids of Mayfair. Don't suppose you know where I can find them? The pic in the *Daily News* must have been taken from about here.'

'You mean *Maidens* of Mayfair.'

'Nope.' He handed me a newspaper. The photo Ruby had posted on Facebook took up half the page with the headline: *Mermaids of Mayfair: Sexy Sapphire Spencer and her fellow maidens swap skin for scales at mystery seaside location.*

No mention of Sapphire's sister, Ruby; she'd be livid about that.

'Took me ages to work out where they were. The lifeboat house gave it away in the end: I zoomed in on the auctioneer's sign, googled the auction site, found the location and drove through the night.'

'Why are you here?' Jude folded his arms across his chest.

'For an exclusive. I'm on a month's trial with News Thirst. Come on, guys, I need a story. This could be my big break. I was at the *Derbyshire Bugle* before that, covering village shows, although I did once interview actress Lucinda Miller in a swimsuit.' He winked at Jude who stared blankly back, none the wiser.

'There's been an embargo until now on Sapphire Spencer's wedding,' Robin continued, 'but now *My Dream Day* has pulled out, there'll be a scrabble to be the first newspaper to print proper details. I want it to be my byline.'

'A wedding isn't news. I can give you a better story,' Jude scoffed.

'Really?' Robin's eyes widened. He looked over his shoulder and took a step closer to Jude. 'I'm all ears.'

'Look behind you,' Jude said in a low voice. 'The Brightside Cove lifeboat house. The council is throwing away our heritage. Selling out to tourism. What about the people who live here twelve months a year? What about the legacy of our fishing communities? We must save it from falling into the wrong hands and you, Mr Barker, could be our champion.'

Robin looked quite taken with the idea of being a champion but then he scratched his head. 'The thing is, I need a story with national interest.'

'Oh, I see.' Jude nodded irritably. 'And a group of posh girls having a party ticks that box, does it?'

'Sorry, mate, in my world,' said Robin, scratching his head sheepishly, 'yes.'

Jude made a growling noise. 'Then your world is full of—'

'They're getting ready to depart as we speak,' I said, interrupting Jude before steam started billowing from his ears.

Robin blinked. 'How do you know?'

'Look up there.' I gestured up to the clifftops where two white limousines were gliding towards Driftwood Lodge. The girls would be frantically packing by now. I'd have loved to say goodbye myself; we'd had such a great weekend.

'Arrgghh, I'm too late!' Robin thrust his hands into his bed-head hair. 'Disaster.'

'You're telling me,' I muttered under my breath. 'I should be there saying goodbye. Not down here skulking in the shadows, waiting until the coast is clear.'

Jude smirked. 'That's more like it.'

I stared at him. 'You think I should have stayed at Driftwood Lodge instead of running off?'

His eyes sparkled. 'And miss the hours we've spent together this morning? No way. But from the little I know of you, you seem feisty enough to fight your corner.'

I felt a glow of pride at his confidence in me. 'I guess I panicked and . . . Well, let's just say I'm not Theo's wife's favourite person. I thought it might be easier if I simply removed myself from the situation.'

'And now you've changed your mind?' Jude asked.

I took a deep breath. 'It's time to sort things out once and for all.'

Maybe I couldn't save Theo and Kate's marriage, maybe too much water had gone under the bridge for them ever to get back to where they were, but I would not stand by and be the reason for a divorce.

'Robin, all is not lost, we've still got a chance,' I said to the young journalist who was looking at his mobile phone dismally.

He looked up in surprise. 'We?'

I nodded. Now that Sapphire's exclusive deal with the bridal magazine was off, I might as well try to get some publicity from having celebrity guests. A piece in a national newspaper would increase bookings tenfold. 'They'll be ages getting their things together. Well, most of them.' Catherine would probably be standing by the front door, bag packed and tapping her toe. 'I can't promise Sapphire will speak to you, mind you,' I warned.

'You're a lifesaver.' Robin punched the air and ran to his car. 'Come on.'

I lingered for a moment, not wanting to leave Jude. 'Thank you for everything, for last night and today. I owe you one.'

'Nina?' He caught hold of my fingers. 'Did you mean it about helping me fight for the lifeboat house?'

I stared into those hazel eyes and felt a stirring in the pit of my stomach. Eliza was right: Jude was fiery, but his heart was in the right place and he seemed to be motivated by purely selfless reasons.

'I did.' I reached up and pressed a swift kiss to his cheek. 'And did *you* mean it when you said that kiss we had was amazing?'

He flashed me a lopsided smile. 'Do you need to ask?'

'It's the actress in me; I'm terribly needy.'

'Then yes, it was,' he murmured. 'But, Nina, I must tell you—'

Robin tooted the car horn.

'And it's another cliffhanger ending,' I said, pulling away reluctantly.

'We'll have to wait for the next episode.'

There was unfinished business between Jude Trevone and me, and I couldn't wait to see what would come next.

Chapter 23

We bumped up the drive towards Driftwood Lodge and Robin parked next to the two white limos in the courtyard.

'So, which cottage is the blushing bride in?'

He pulled the keys from the ignition and prepared to get out.

'Might be better if you wait here,' I said, unclipping my seat belt. 'I'll go and butter her up first, talk her into it.'

I got out of the car and looked around. It was chaotic here this morning. All the doors and windows of the cottages were wide open and the hen party girls were racing around like headless chickens scooping up phone chargers from the kitchen and single shoes from the garden and, oddly, a pair of skinny jeans from the roof of Kittiwake's Cabin. One of the chauffeurs was pacing around with his mobile phone at arm's length trying to get a signal and the other was polishing his chrome hub caps.

I couldn't see Theo, which I was glad about. A few minutes to sort out Robin and gather my thoughts wouldn't go amiss. Just then a flash of red hair caught my eye. Molly was here! My heart pitched; she was another person with whom I had to set the record straight.

She was running from the cottages to the main house, her ponytail flying behind her and her arms trailing bed-linen and towels across the gravel. She stopped abruptly when she saw me.

'Nina! You're back!'

I steeled myself for whatever mood she was in as she marched briskly towards me; I still hadn't quite got the measure of Molly, so far she had loved and loathed me in equal measure. She came to a halt in front of me.

'Please.' I held my palms up. 'I've come to see Sapphire; I don't want another argument.'

'Nor me.' She exhaled, her brown eyes just visible over her armload of laundry. 'I'm sorry I jumped to conclusions about you and Theo. *Again*. My mouth runs away with me sometimes, as does my imagination. In my defence, I just really need to see their marriage work. It gives me hope that one day I might manage a serious relationship again. But I am very sorry that I called you a terrible actress and it's me who's the terrible friend. Please accept my apology.'

'Apology accepted.' I let out a sigh of relief, glad that was out of the way. 'But you do know Kate's asked for a divorce,' I added. 'Because of a picture of Theo and me on the Coastal Cottages website.'

She shuddered. 'Yep. She's supposed to be Skyping me tomorrow; I'll talk to her about it then.'

I wondered why Kate hadn't been in touch with Theo that way? If they'd been in contact with each other more regularly this whole misunderstanding could have been avoided. 'Or maybe I should speak to her myself?'

'Brave woman.' Molly sucked in air, but smiled. 'I think that would be awesome.'

'I'm glad you came back to help after all,' I said.

'Theo called in a flap.' Molly grinned. 'New guests are arriving in the morning and without you here, he knew he'd never manage.'

I racked my brains. 'But we don't have any bookings tomorrow.'

'There's one new one,' Molly filled me in. 'Some guy from London, Theo said, Carl. He sounds like he could be a handful, requesting that all ceilings should be hoovered for cobwebs and the curtains removed from his bedroom window because he likes to wake with the dawn.'

I tutted. 'Who does he think we are – The Savoy?'

Molly grinned. 'And your friend Maxine has brought her booking forward; she'll be arriving tomorrow too.'

'Gosh, no wonder Theo's panicking,' I said. I couldn't wait to see Maxine; I wanted to ask her advice about finding a new agent and get all the gossip from the *Victory Road* set.

'Who's he, by the way?' She jerked her head towards Robin's car.

'A journalist wanting to speak to Sapphire. I'd better go and find her.'

Molly blew her hair out of her eyes. 'Strip the beds while you're there, will you? And tell those girls to hurry up and clear off!'

As predicted, in Penguin's Pad, Catherine was ready to leave. She was doing a thorough check for forgotten items inside every cupboard and under every chair while the others rushed round her. All except Sapphire who was nowhere to be seen.

'She's been in her room for ages.' Catherine frowned, picking up the famous itinerary from the kitchen table. 'Making important phone calls. We should have left eighteen minutes ago. If she's much longer, we'll have to miss our scheduled stop at Bristol services.'

I patted her shoulder sympathetically.

'There's a reporter from London outside hoping for an exclusive interview with her,' I said. 'I guess the answer will be no, but I promised I'd ask.'

'A reporter? Here?'

Catherine and I turned to see Sapphire running down the stairs. Her eyes were red, there were tear stains on her cheeks and she was still in her pyjamas.

I nodded. 'From the News Thirst Media Agency, but

don't worry, I can send him away if you don't want to talk to him.'

'Oh, Sapph.' Catherine scanned Sapphire's face. 'You've been crying, is the wedding off?'

Sapphire giggled and threaded an arm around her friend's waist. 'No, you silly goose, but something exciting has happened.' She turned to me, her eyes shining. 'I need five minutes to get dressed. But tell him yes, he can have his interview.' She ran back upstairs. 'Actually, make that ten minutes.'

Catherine flung the itinerary in the air. 'I give up.'

'Sorry for keeping you waiting, everyone!' said Sapphire, twenty minutes later, appearing from Penguin's Pad with Robin after giving him a very quick interview.

'Right, people. Go, go, go,' yelled Catherine. She held one of the limo doors open and flapped her arm frantically to usher the girls in.

'Have you got what you came for, Robin?' I asked, swallowing a smile.

The poor boy looked completely star struck, he was bright red and wearing a goofy smile. 'They're never going to believe this at the office.'

'But you recorded it all?' I said anxiously.

He took his Dictaphone out of his pocket and held it up. 'Oh yeah, although I'll never forget a word.'

He stumbled off to his car punch drunk and disappeared down the drive in a cloud of dust.

'Thank you for a wonderful hen weekend.' Sapphire kissed my cheeks. 'But most of all thank you for helping me with a decision I'd been struggling with for a while.'

I blinked at her uncertainly. 'What did I say?'

The driver approached us and took her suitcase.

'You said that if working in the lab was where my heart lay, I should rethink. So I did,' she shrugged casually. 'I realize that *Maidens of Mayfair* is never going to let me mention my ant research project. So if I want to make a name for myself in the field of cleptobiosis, that's where I need to focus my efforts. I've pulled out of the next series of *Maidens of Mayfair* and I'm going to start lobbying companies for funding. Robin is going to get the story printed.'

I hugged her warmly. 'If anyone can make a name for herself studying theft in ants, it's you.'

'And guess what?' Ruby said, poking her head out of the car. 'They offered me the chance to replace Sapphire.'

'Brilliant,' I cried, genuinely pleased for her, 'just what you wanted.'

'I turned them down.' Ruby flicked her hair over her shoulder. 'I haven't got time for that any more. I'm going to work on my singing career; I'll probably win *The X Factor* next year,' she added before slamming the door.

Sapphire shook her head fondly as she climbed into the other limo beside an apoplectic Catherine. 'She'll have changed her mind before we hit the motorway.'

'Drive!' I heard Catherine yell as soon as the door closed.

Theo poked his head over the gate from the back garden and Molly appeared at the window of Kittiwake's Cabin and we all waved as both limos turned around and glided away.

If it were possible for a house to sigh, I think Driftwood Lodge would have done it just then.

For a moment I stood while the air settled around us and the sounds of Brightside Cove made themselves heard again. The wind carried children's laughter from the beach along with the ever-present roar of the sea. And closer to home, from the patch of grass in front of the kitchen window, came the sound of the chickens chatting to each other in their comical *took-took-took* language. I looked back at the house with its thatched roof and tiny windows and crooked cream walls and smiled.

'Peace at last,' I said out loud. 'But not, I fear, for long.'

And I went inside to make coffee.

*

Just as I switched on the kettle, I heard the sound of tyres on the gravel and crossed to the window. I smiled to myself, assuming one of the girls had left something behind. But it wasn't the hen party, it was Archie.

I ran outside and flung my arms around my brother's neck. 'What a surprise,' I said, winking at him.

He looked tired. There were dark circles under his eyes and a ghostly pallor to his skin.

'Everything okay? You're not ill, are you?'

'I'm fine.' He seemed to give himself a shake. 'The usual cut and thrust of business, but you know me, I thrive on a bit of pressure.'

'Hmm,' I said, unconvinced. 'I'm just making coffee, come in.'

He looked around the courtyard, craning his neck to see in the garden. 'Is Molly around?'

I grinned at him. 'She is. I'll make us all a drink and give her a shout.'

'Great.' He smoothed the non-existent creases from his shirt. 'Does my hair look all right?'

'You look fine. Tired, but fine.'

He made a dismissive noise to tell me to stop fussing. I poured mugs of coffee for us all, glancing at him sideways from time to time. Perhaps he was simply nervous. Who could blame him? Molly wasn't the easiest girl to try to impress.

Archie had phoned me after seeing Molly in her mermaid outfit last week and asked whether I thought he stood any chance with her. I wasn't sure if any man stood a chance with her. But my brother hadn't become successful in business by not taking risks. So I'd told him if he happened to be in the area this morning, he might bump into her collecting the laundry. And here he was.

And here she was, right on cue, blowing her long red hair out of her eyes, arms full of more laundry.

'The beds are done. Give me caffeine. I need a hit before

257

I bundle as much of that washing on the back of my bike as I can manage and cycle home,' Molly said as she came in and then noticed Archie. 'Oh, you're here.'

'Yes,' he said, with false jollity. 'I am. How nice to see you again. You look well.'

'I am roasting,' said Molly, sniffing her armpit and pulling a face. She gulped her coffee and put the mug back down on the kitchen table. 'Thanks for that. I'll go and tell Theo his is ready too.'

Archie coughed to get my attention and jerked his head towards the door.

'I'll go and tell him,' I said swiftly.

'Lovely weather,' Archie blurted out in a thinly disguised attempt to keep her chatting.

I stuck my head out of the front door and yelled at the top of my lungs, 'Theo! Coffee's ready!'

'I should think they just about heard that on Jersey,' Molly winced, uncovering her ears when I came back inside.

'I use a diaphragmatic breathing technique for voice projection,' I said. 'Very useful for theatre acting.'

'What do you prefer: theatre,' Molly asked, pinching a biscuit from the plate on the table and snapping it in half, 'or telly?'

Archie sent me go-away signals with his eyes. I took the hint and poured Molly a top-up.

'I'll mull that one over while I empty the washing machine,' I said, pretending to rack my brains, 'and leave you to chat over your coffee.'

I stuck my thumb up discreetly at Archie as I passed him on my way through to the utility room.

'I left the Triumph TR6 at home today, I'm in my Range Rover Vogue instead,' I heard him say. 'Not as much fun, but a more forgiving ride.'

I groaned inwardly. Showing off to Molly would never win her round. I opened the washing-machine drum and pulled out the wet towels. Quietly. So I could eavesdrop.

'Really,' she said flatly. 'Sounds like Tess, my ex's new girlfriend.'

There was a pause.

'Yeah, bought it new,' Archie tried again. 'It's got all the extras: Xenon headlights, which are really clear, surround sound, all-terrain response—'

'Yeah?' Her voice was loaded with sarcasm. 'Today *I'm* on my bike. Got it from the charity shop. It's got dynamo head-lights. Not terribly bright but I have been known to dazzle the odd rabbit, and as I can hear in every direction, I guess you could say I've got surround sound too. Also, *I* respond to all terrains by cycling round the potholes.'

I willed Archie to come back with a killer response.

'Um.'

There was a pause while he tried to think of a different tack. 'I'm only telling you because—'

'You're a knob?' Molly said innocently. 'Like the rest of them.'

I started forward to defend my brother but then faltered. Having your sister fight your battles for you was only one step up from your mum interfering.

'No, I'm . . . Oh, for heaven's sake.' I could hear the frustration in his voice. 'Look, I'm not very good at talking to women, at chatting them up, I mean. I can spot a business opportunity a mile off: give me a balance sheet and I under-stand it straight away, ask me for ten ideas to generate sales and I can do it in a flash. But put me in front of a beautiful woman and I go to pieces. I thought you might like to go for a drive with me, or perhaps I could even take you for a driv-ing lesson. Clearly I was wrong. My apologies.'

Yay, go Archie! I crept to the utility-room door and spied on them through the crack.

'You just called me beautiful,' she said accusingly.

'You are.' He shrugged. 'Your smile is like sunshine. Not that I get to see it very often.'

Molly shuffled her feet and fiddled with her hair.

'Sorry about that.' She was cradling her mug and seemed very intent on whatever was at the bottom of it. She cleared her throat. 'And you remembered that I can't drive. That was kind of you.'

'I thought I could impress you with my car,' said Archie in a resigned voice. 'I haven't got anything else to work with.'

The breath caught in my throat. How could she resist that? How?

Molly exhaled, plonked her mug down roughly and straightened up.

'Look,' she said in a more conciliatory tone, 'I'm not impressed by fancy cars. I'm a single mum with a shitload of washing to do before Ellis gets back from his dad's. Nina said you've got your own laundrette?'

'We-ll, it's more of a commercial laundry, hotel linen, workwear, large res—'

'Whatever,' Molly cut in. 'Do you know where the powder goes?'

'Um, yes?'

'And is your car boot empty?'

'Yes?' Archie blinked at her, confused.

'What would really impress me is some practical help. Interested?'

'Er . . . okay.' He scratched his head.

'Great.' She shooed him towards the door. 'Let's go.'

I leapt out from my hiding place and grinned at him as together they piled three cottages' worth of bedlinen into the back of the Range Rover.

'Wow,' Archie murmured, stooping to kiss me goodbye. 'What a woman.'

After I waved them off, there was the sound of someone clearing their throat behind me.

'Alone at last,' said Theo.

My heart skittered when I looked around. He was walking towards me pushing a wheelbarrow overflowing with empty bottles. A few hours ago we'd both stood in this same spot when he delivered the news that his wife was asking for a divorce because of me. I felt like I'd lived a dozen lifetimes since then: the drive with Jude, the kiss, our walk on the beach; meeting the journalist and seeing off the hen party. But now it came flooding back: the look Theo had given me when I'd denied that there was anything for Kate to be suspicious about. A look that implied that he'd possibly begun to think of me as more than just a friend.

'Theo, we need to talk.'

He set the wheelbarrow down and raked a hand through his curls. 'Can I have coffee first?'

'Sure.'

I gestured towards the kitchen and passed him his mug. 'Lukewarm now, I'm afraid.'

'Not at all!' He gulped it down as he followed me outside to the washing line. 'It's great. You make great coffee. It's one of the things I like about you.'

I silenced him with a stern look and picked up a wet towel. 'When Archie and I arrived here to look at that sports car, you said Kate had given you an ultimatum to get your act together. What you wanted was to win her back. That's why I'm here, aren't I?'

He passed me two pegs. 'Correct.'

'So what was all that about last night and this morning? Why are you giving up on her and not fighting her demands for a divorce?'

'I'm no good on my own.' He sighed. 'I like having you here, and when Kate stopped replying to my emails, I lost hope.'

'But did she stop replying?' I countered. 'Or did she simply not receive them?'

Theo ran a finger round the neck of his T-shirt. 'I wasn't to know she was on a yoga retreat in the rainforest.'

'For goodness' sake!'

We fell silent for a moment and I moved down the line,

steadily pegging up the towels with his help. I reached back down to the laundry basket and he placed his hand on mine.

'I miss Kate,' he said softly. 'I don't want to get a divorce.'

I breathed a sigh of relief. 'Tell me about her; tell me what you miss.'

He smiled wistfully. 'I miss her warm skin next to mine when I wake up. Kate is always warm. I miss her smell. She smells of flowers and shampoo and sunshine. I love—' He started to laugh. 'I can't believe I'm saying this but I love the way she carries her wet teabag on a spoon to the bin and leaves a trail of drips *every single time*. And I love her little night-time routine. She gets into bed, checks her alarm, rubs oil into her cuticles and then, before turning out the light, she . . .' His voice dropped to a whisper. 'She kisses Ivy's picture and says, "Sweet dreams, angel." I do that now.'

'Oh Theo.' I sniffed, pulling a tissue from my pocket. 'That's the loveliest thing I've ever heard.'

He picked up the empty laundry basket from the grass.

'I don't want to lose her. I want to say all the things I should have said when Ivy died. I never stopped loving her, Nina. I just couldn't find the words to tell her.'

I nodded. It was all I could do right now; the lump in my throat made speaking impossible. There was a special love story here and I was determined to make sure it had its own perfect happy ending.

Chapter 24

By lunchtime the following day we were almost ready. I put the final pillowcase on the double bed in Kittiwake's Cabin and smoothed the duvet before leaving the room. The plan was to put our male guest in here. Maxine would go next door in Beaver's Barn. Theo had been rather distracted when the man had phoned to make the booking, but as far as we knew he was Carl Michael from London and he was travelling alone.

I went into Beaver's Barn next, remembering the last time we'd had two single bookings at Brightside Holidays: Bruce and Penelope, who'd arrived in separate cars and yet gone home as a couple. A match made in Devon, Theo had called it. Who knew – perhaps Cupid would strike again. Maxine had never mentioned a significant other; in fact, other than the fact that she'd had a disapproving mother like mine, I realized I didn't know much about her personal life at all.

Everywhere looked immaculate again; it was as if the Maidens of Mayfair had never been. Only Penguin's Pad on the end was unmade for now, which was fine because it would remain empty unless we had another surprise booking.

Mr Michael's travel arrangements had been vague but Maxine would be here at lunchtime. I was looking forward to seeing her and showing her round Brightside Cove. It was odd that she'd changed her booking; her time was always so pressured, the filming schedule for *Victory Road* so regimented that having a week off unexpectedly was unheard of. But perhaps the lure of a mobile-phone-signal-free zone coupled with her teetering reading pile was too strong to resist.

I'd just got time to nip down to the Mermaid Gift and Gallery for some more of Eliza's lovely soaps; Maxine would appreciate that.

When I pushed open the door of Eliza's shop she was behind the counter talking to someone on the phone.

'And how will you get me on and off the sofa in the mermaid tail,' she said, 'because if I have to hop, it ruins the magic?'

I selected some handmade sea kelp soap and some matching shower crème and took them to the till.

'Got you.' She nodded. 'And I can bring my tropical tail if Holly Willoughby fancies trying . . . No? Okay, fair enough.

'See you in two days, then,' she said down the line. 'At the studios.'

She put down the phone, ran round to my side of the counter and squealed with excitement.

'I can't believe it! I'm going to be a mermaid on *This Morning*! On the sofa with those two famous presenters. Well, not sofa exactly,' she corrected herself, twirling a lock of pink hair around a plump finger. 'They're going to recline me on some fake rocks.'

'I'm thrilled for you,' I said, hugging her. 'Sapphire and her friends loved their mermaid photo shoot and I'm sure I'd have appreciated mine if I hadn't been dropped headfirst in the sea and given Jude a flash of my boobs.'

'Never mind, beauty,' she winked, 'Jude appreciated it. Didn't I see you on the beach with him yesterday morning?'

'I don't know,' I replied innocently. 'Did you?'

My heart pinged at the mention of his name. His story had really touched me and as for him describing my eyes as the colour of the sea, that had brought back long-forgotten happy memories too. I wished I had more memories of my dad to draw on. I had a sudden urge to call up Archie and quiz him on everything he could remember about him; there was bound to be something he could tell me that I didn't already know. Getting him to open up about it was another matter; even mentioning Dad's name was usually enough to make Archie's hackles rise and he always changed the subject.

I snapped back into the moment to realize that Eliza was watching me.

'You have got it bad,' Eliza laughed, clicking her fingers in front of my face to wake me up. 'You didn't hear a word I said.'

'Sorry, miles away,' I said, not wanting to explain.

'I was saying that since that photo of your hen party girls in their mermaid tails was in the press yesterday, the phone hasn't stopped ringing. I've taken new bookings for the mermaid school, done an interview on the radio and now this – national TV in two days' time! I'm going to go up tomorrow to do a bit of sightseeing.'

She popped my purchases in a bag while I counted out the right money. 'I'll be more famous than you before long.'

'You're welcome to my share of fame,' I said, remembering the lesson I learned from Big Dave about staying true to your passion. 'From now on, I'll be focusing on my acting.'

Victory Road was on TV tonight and it was the episode with the bomb explosion where I end up in a coma. The episode with the worst kept secret in the history of cliffhanger endings. From tomorrow my life in *Victory Road* was literally hanging in the balance. After tonight Nurse Elsie probably wouldn't speak again. I just hoped this wasn't a metaphor for my acting career . . .

'Who is going to look after the shop while you're away?'

She pulled a face. 'I forgot about that in all the excitement.'

'I can do it.'

'I don't know,' she said, looking worried. 'It can get very hectic in here.'

I bit back a chuckle; I think I'd only ever seen one person in here ever. In fact, it had crossed my mind that she must barely scrape a living. That would change, of course, now that the world had seemingly gone mermaid-mad.

'You'd be doing me a favour, really,' I assured her. 'I'll have nothing to do.'

Once the guests had arrived later and we'd handed them their keys, the rest of the week yawned emptily ahead. A holiday cottage business was mostly about laundry and making beds, and I needed more than that. Acting might not be rocket science but the filming schedules were gruelling; learning my lines was challenging; even the daily commute to the studios was tiring. Here, I fell out of bed and I was immediately at work. A few hours at the Mermaid Gift and Gallery would do me just fine.

'Then I accept,' she beamed and added a couple of scented candles to the bag. 'Have this on the house. I can't thank you enough, you know. Everyone in Brightside Cove laughed at my mermaid school until you came along and gave me a boost. Well, everyone except my mum, and mums are bound to be on your side, aren't they?'

'Hmm.' Mine hadn't always been.

'And Danny's had a stroke of luck too because of you,' she continued. 'A media company in Plymouth found out that he took the Mermaids of Mayfair picture that's been in all the papers and they offered him a job.'

'That's great,' I said with a grin, 'perhaps he'll take me out for dinner and offer to pick up the *whole* bill, what do you reckon?'

But she was miles away.

'This is really happening.' Her round cheeks flushed. 'Eliza Tyler, professional mermaid on TV! I'll be a bag of nerves.'

'You'll be great; just be yourself,' I said, hugging her goodbye. 'Unless you can be a mermaid.'

'Then always be a mermaid,' we said in unison, laughing.

The Brightside Cove Mermaid School off to London: the capital wouldn't know what had hit it . . .

Five minutes later, I was marching back to Driftwood Lodge lost in my thoughts. I paused, leaning on the wall at the top of the beach steps. The sound of the waves, the faint tinkling of masts in the harbour, the cawing of birds circling overhead . . . I breathed deeply and absorbed the moment.

The sound of footsteps interrupted me and I turned to see Jude approaching. He was more smartly dressed than usual and had a laptop bag slung over his shoulder.

'Hey.' I smiled as he joined me.

'I haven't stopped thinking about yesterday,' said Jude, looking ahead.

My heart tingled. Me too: our kiss in his van, the walk on the beach . . . 'It was a very pleasant morning.'

'I reckon with your help I can get the council to listen to my proposal to keep the lifeboat house in local hands.'

'Right,' I said, disappointed that it didn't look as if he was interested in more kissing. 'Tell me more.'

'My problem is,' he shuffled his feet, 'that when I believe in something, I get frustrated when people don't see things my way.'

'It's passion,' I said with a smile. 'Danny said you aren't happy unless you're fighting some cause or other.'

'He remembers me when I first arrived here as a mixed-up teenager at war with the world. I was jealous of him. He was the smooth-talking charmer who always knew what to say to everyone: teachers, girls . . . especially girls.' He grinned. 'I guess neither of us has changed.'

'I don't know,' I countered, remembering his comment about my eyes yesterday. 'You charmed me.'

He laughed softly. 'Good, because I'm hoping you'll agree to be the face of the "Save the Lifeboat House" campaign. What with you being an actress.'

I was flattered but unconvinced. 'I'm only famous for my mistakes. I doubt I'd lend any weight to your campaign.'

'I don't need your fame. I need you to *act* like you care, even if deep down you're not bothered who buys the boat house. And you'll be a better public speaker than me.'

His hazel eyes searched mine hopefully.

'I think there's a compliment in there somewhere,' I said, raising an eyebrow, 'just give me a minute to find it.'

'Sorry. I'm not saying you *don't* care,' he said hastily. 'But probably not much. You're not a local, you're just passing through.'

'Still looking for the compliment.'

'You see my problem?' he groaned. 'My mouth gets me into trouble all the time.'

I looked at his mouth. He had very kissable lips. They could probably get me into trouble too, given half a chance.

I glanced at my watch. 'We're expecting guests, so I need to get back, but walk with me and tell me your thoughts.'

We set off together, shoulder to shoulder on the narrow coastal path.

'See that row of cottages?' Jude pointed past the harbour to the row of pastel-coloured cottages.

'I can see them from my bedroom window at Driftwood Lodge,' I said. 'It's my favourite view in the whole village.'

'I had a view of your bedroom window on Sunday morning.' He glanced sideways at me. 'That wasn't bad either.'

'You were saying, about the cottages?' I asked primly, marching ahead.

And as we walked, his laptop bag occasionally bumping against my hip, he told me how the last cottage that came up for sale was snapped up by an American couple who had paid over the odds for it and had only visited twice. The same for the rest of the cottages: all second homes. The only one lived in as a permanent home these days was the yellow one, from where he'd just come. It was inhabited by an elderly couple, his clients, Nora and Ned, who were valiantly hanging on to their independence but having to accept a bit of council help now and again.

The whole row had been built for fishermen and their families. The families who had lived and worked here were the lifeblood of the community.

'With the exception of Big Dave, fishing in Brightside Cove is just a hobby now. Such a shame,' said Jude. 'I want us to build businesses for ourselves, facilities for our young people, our families and the elderly. Services that benefit *us*, not tourists. Because otherwise in ten years' time what will we be? Not a community, that's for sure. The kids will cause trouble through boredom, just like I did, and then as soon as they're old enough they'll leave and never come back. I've got another client, Mrs Thompson, wondering what to do with her huge farm because her grown-up children can't be tempted home.'

His passion and enthusiasm was so heartfelt. How could the council refuse him? I was won over already.

'And the lifeboat house? How do you think that will help?'

His eyes glittered. 'Brightside Cove doesn't have a village hall any more since the chapel and its outbuildings were sold off by the church for residential development. We need a place for kids to hang out, somewhere for the elderly to have a hot lunch once a month, the mums and little ones from the council estate a few miles away to get together, have coffee, play on the sand. Zumba classes, drama club . . .' He lifted his palms up to the sky. 'The possibilities are endless.'

'And expensive,' I put in, 'the building is very quirky and lovely but it will take money to make it fit for the sort of activities you're talking about.'

'It's not that bad.' Jude looked affronted. 'It's got running water. Well, one tap.'

I looked at him, amused. 'Whoop-e-do.'

'Minor detail.' He laughed. 'The main thing is to not let it fall into the wrong hands. It belongs to Brightside Cove and I want it to stay that way. I need to get support. And quickly. It's not long until the auction so I need to get in there quick and persuade the council to lease it to us cheaply before a load of cash-rich investors get wind of it.'

'How are you planning on doing that?'

A flicker of doubt appeared for a second before he grinned. 'Still working on that. But I've told Nora and Ned and they're right behind me. And now you. So that's three supporters.'

'Word of mouth is great,' I agreed, 'but we need to come up with a quicker way of spreading the message. I'll give it some thought.'

His smile lit up his face and my insides tweaked with longing for a repeat performance of yesterday. I edged my feet closer so that we were almost touching.

'So you'll definitely help?' he asked.

I nodded, lifting my eyes to his.

'And be the face of the campaign?'

There was something so honest and true about Jude. And I liked the way he was taking action about this. How could I not want to help him? We'd reached the gate at the bottom of the drive leading to Driftwood Lodge.

'Happily.'

'Thank you. You're a pal.' Jude grabbed my face, kissed my cheek roughly and ran off down the road yelling something about petitions and posters.

A pal, hey? I thought with a sigh. Well, it was a start.

My thoughts were cut short by the slow approach of a car. It was a taxi. I stood to the side to let it pass, waving madly when I recognized Maxine's profile through the tinted glass of the front passenger window. I ran to meet her as the car came to a halt in the courtyard.

'Maxine!' I yelled, opening her door. 'Welcome!'

She thrust a briefcase at me and scowled as she climbed out of the car.

'You could have warned me,' she hissed, pushing her long grey curls hair from her eyes.

'What about?'

'Him.' She jerked her head to the other side of the car.

A big jowly man in his sixties with a thatch of white hair under a trilby hat and a bristly moustache unfolded himself from the back seat and flicked his eyes over me from head to toe.

'I'm Carmichael, Campion Carmichael,' he said archly. 'And you must be Miss Penhaligon?'

My mouth went dry. What the hell was Cecily's father doing in Brightside Cove?

Chapter 25

So much for Eliza taking Brightside Cove to London; it seemed London had come to Brightside Cove.

'Mr Carmichael, this is a surprise.' I scurried to his side of the car to try to shake his hand.

'It shouldn't be,' he said sourly, ignoring my outstretched hand.

'It bloody well was to me,' Maxine said, unloading her luggage from the boot of the taxi. She gave me a look that implied I had some explaining to do.

As did she. I vaguely remembered her mentioning some shared history, but I was curious to know what he could have done to invoke such animosity from the usually unflappable director.

Sorry, I mouthed with a grimace.

The booking had been written down as a 'Mr Carl Michael'. Mr *Carmichael*. It was an easy mistake to make and Theo would have been distracted taking the call yesterday morning after Kate had phoned and I'd done a runner. It would have been panic stations at Driftwood Lodge.

Still, I was here now. And so was Mr Carmichael. Although goodness only knew why. Perhaps Cecily wanted to wreak revenge . . . I gave myself a little shake; I didn't want to think about why just yet. First I had duties to perform. No one was going to say that at Brightside Holidays we gave anything less than the warmest of welcomes. No matter who turned up unexpectedly. No matter how much my heart was hammering with nerves.

'The cottages are ready for you both,' I said breezily, 'and I'm sure you'll find everything to your satisfaction.'

'I'll be the judge of that,' said Mr Carmichael.

'Getting the last word as usual, Campion?' Maxine flicked her hands over the creases in her black wrap dress.

There was a small kerfuffle while both guests insisted on paying for the taxi and asking for receipts and tipping the driver, giving me a moment to catch my breath.

The taxi drove off, leaving the three of us staring at each other in awkward silence. Maxine looked like she'd cheerfully commit murder; I hoped I wasn't to be the victim. I looked around for Theo to come and help with the bags, his van was here but there was no sign of him. He'd muttered something about a gardening project earlier, so perhaps he was round the back of the house where he couldn't hear cars arriving.

'You haven't brought an easel with you, Mr Carmichael,' I observed. In fact, judging by the size of his tiny bag, he couldn't have brought more than a change of clothes and a toothbrush.

'Give the girl a banana,' Mr Carmichael said with a sniff, picking up his bag. 'I've brought a camera.'

'I see.' I nodded gravely. I didn't see at all; I thought he was an artist, not a photographer.

'Campion paints landscapes from photographs,' Maxine explained, struggling to loop her various bags over her shoulders. 'He finds a flat emotionless image easier to cope with.'

'You remember?' Mr Carmichael cocked an eyebrow, making no effort to help with her luggage.

'Oh, I remember all right.' She fixed him with an icy look. 'I remember everything.'

This exchange was loaded with subtext; unfortunately, I didn't understand a word of it.

'Well, if you'd like any tips on exploring the area, do ask,' I said cheerily.

Another awkward silence. The two of them were still giving each other daggers. I cleared my throat.

'If you'd like to follow me,' I said, including both of them in my warmest smile, 'I'll show you to your cottages.'

I wrestled one of Maxine's bags from her and led them across the courtyard.

'I understood there to be afternoon tea served on arrival?' said Mr Carmichael, stalking ahead with his long legs and almost baggage-free arms. 'I'm ready for cake. I hope it's freshly baked.'

'Of course,' I said, mentally sifting through the remains of the cakes from the weekend. 'I'll bring you a selection on a tray to Kittiwake's Cabin. That's the middle one of the three, Campion.'

'*Mr Carmichael*,' he corrected me.

'Middle?' Maxine almost screeched. 'So we'll be neighbours? Oh no.' She stopped dead in her tracks, dropping her case again. 'Nina, this is the limit. No. I'm sorry, we need to be at opposite ends.'

Mr Carmichael sighed dramatically and scooped up her case. 'I can assure you I shan't be paying you any unwanted attention during my stay. What do think I'm going to do, attempt nocturnal break-ins to try and seduce you? I gave up that sort of thing in the Seventies. And so, if I remember correctly,' he added snidely, 'did you.'

Maxine roared with frustration and stomped off towards the cottages. 'This was meant to be a relaxing break!'

Mr Carmichael laughed mirthlessly. 'Always was easily rattled.'

I dashed after Maxine and caught her arm. To my horror her eyes sparkled with tears of frustration.

'It will be relaxing, Maxine,' I promised. 'I'll make Penguin's Pad up for you, it won't take long. Take a seat at the patio table for a moment. I'll put him at the opposite end of the row.'

I didn't know what his game was, why he was here or what must have happened in the past to set Maxine so against him. But whatever it was, I was on her side.

'So you'll be in here,' I said, waving him up the path of Beaver's Barn.

He narrowed his eyes. 'Have you hoovered the ceiling?'

'Not still scared of spiders?' Maxine sniggered across the wall from the terrace at Penguin's Pad.

'All done,' I confirmed. I pushed open the door and handed him the key, swapping it for Maxine's case. 'And it won't take me a moment to remove the bedroom curtains.'

Mr Carmichael stepped over the threshold and peered inside. 'I'd like afternoon tea immediately.'

I nodded. 'Tea or—'

The door slammed in my face.

'Tea, then.'

I exhaled with relief and looked across the cottage gardens to Maxine.

'I feel like I've been run over by a truck,' she said, shaking her head.

I crossed to Penguin's Pad and tentatively held out my arms. To my relief she stepped into them for a hug.

'I take it you and he aren't the best of friends?'

She pursed her lips. 'Coffee for me, please.'

Message received and understood. I patted her arm gently. 'Coming right up.'

Later on, I went to join Theo who was digging down at the bottom of the garden.

'There you are,' I called as I got closer. 'I've brought you some tea.'

'Wait there!' He abandoned his spade and jogged to meet

me. 'Don't look!' He spun me around so that the tea slopped over the edge of the mug.

'Okay,' I laughed, holding the dripping mug at arm's length. 'I'm off to Molly's in a minute. But I wanted to update you on our guests.'

He sipped his tea while I told him that I'd remade Penguin's Pad with the clean linen from Kittiwake's Cabin and that Mr Campion *Carmichael*, the renowned landscape artist, was in residence in Beaver's Barn and not Mr Michael as he'd thought.

'Another artist,' he said, nodding happily. 'Word must be spreading about how good the light is here for painting.'

'Possibly, but this is too much of a coincidence.'

I reminded him of the incident with Cecily Carmichael that had brought me to Devon in the first place and wondered aloud for the first time whether her father had come to exact some sort of revenge.

Theo stiffened. 'He'll have me to answer to if he tries anything.'

I assured him that wouldn't be necessary and that I'd be capable of fighting my own battles.

'The other odd thing is the connection between the two of them,' I said with a frown, wiping a smear of mud from Theo's forehead. 'I'm dying to know what the story is behind Maxine and Mr Carmichael.'

'Some stories can be painful to tell,' he said knowingly. 'A good friend will be ready to listen but will never insist.'

'You mean like you telling me about Ivy?'

He nodded. 'While Kate was here I felt a constant pressure to get over losing our baby. But I didn't want to get over Ivy. I wanted her in my every waking thought. I wanted to wallow.'

'And now?' I asked, looking at him: his eyes bright, his face, knees and boots covered in mud, his nose sunburned from being outdoors all day.

'She's still here.' Theo tapped his head and then his heart. 'And in here. But I'm ready for a new chapter and I want Kate to be in it.'

'Glad to hear it. And on that note,' I said, pressing a swift kiss to the cleanest bit of his cheek, 'I'm off to give my side of the story to your wife. Wish me luck!'

Further north, just along the coast from Brightside Cove, was a village that seemed to consist of about a thousand mobile homes clinging to the cliffs, a short parade of non-descript shops and a housing estate where Molly lived with her son. I checked the address Theo had given me and turned his van into Molly's road.

Her Skype call with Kate was due in an hour. She'd invited me round early for cake.

'Come in!' Molly threw back the door to let me enter. She looked like she was dressed for yoga in a vest top and stretchy pants.

'Thanks. I smell chocolate cake,' I said, sniffing the air.

'Go through to the kitchen,' she said, nodding towards the back of the house. 'And you'll see why.'

I walked through the sparsely decorated living room ahead of her. There was a grey two-seater sofa and an arm-chair facing a tiny television. Cupboards and shelves had been built into the alcove along with two rows of books: one of well-thumbed crime novels and another of children's picture books. There was a crate of toys in the corner but no pictures, no mirrors, and apart from a vase of red tulips on the window sill and red scatter cushions adding a pop of colour, very neutral.

'Boring, isn't it?' said Molly, following my gaze. 'You can say it. I couldn't face taking on a mortgage when we split up so we're renting. And the landlord is a bit pernickety when it comes to touching his precious walls. I'll make it more homely eventually.'

'It's already a home,' I argued. 'Don't put yourself down.'

'My ex's flat is like a show home. Mind you, they are architects . . .' Her voice faded into a sigh.

'You should be proud of what you've achieved on your own,' I said. 'Besides, I have never felt strongly enough about a place to call it home. So you're one up on me already.'

'Not even Brightside Cove?' She pulled a surprised face. 'How could you not fall in love with it here?'

I grinned. 'Admittedly, it's growing on me.'

Molly reached for the kitchen door and cocked an eyebrow. '*It* or him?'

My stomach flipped. 'I thought we'd established that Theo and I were just—'

'You were spotted on the beach,' she continued, her brown eyes glinting mischievously, 'with Jude Trevone. You've succeeded where half of them have failed. He's a tough nut to crack that one, and believe me, many have tried. All the football mums are jealous; it's all over WhatsApp.'

'Football mums?' I said.

She pressed a hand to my face and pretended to flinch with the heat of it. 'He coaches the kids most Sunday mornings. Including . . .'

She pushed open the door to the kitchen. 'My own budding David Beckham. Ellis, say hello to Nina.'

Kneeling up to the worktop on a stool, in a red plastic Disney apron with Lightning McQueen on the front, was a little boy with glasses and a cloud of shoulder-length curls as red as his mum's. He looked up from arranging chocolate buttons on top of a cake. His face was mostly covered in chocolate buttercream. He was possibly the cutest child I'd ever seen.

'Hello. Cooking is for boys too,' he said solemnly.

'Of course it is,' I agreed.

Molly looked like a proud mother hen. 'I want him to be at home in the kitchen. Not like some men I could mention,' she added in a low voice.

'Daddy's girlfriend doesn't like cooking either,' Ellis piped up perceptively.

She winced at being so transparent. 'I'll make us a drink and perhaps Ellis will let us have some cake too.'

'Milk goes best with chocolate cake,' he said in a voice that brooked no argument. He picked up a pot of chocolate sprinkles and shook it liberally over the top of the cake, filling in the gaps between buttons.

'Ice-cold milk and chocolate cake, yum,' I agreed, patting my tummy.

Ellis pressed the sprinkles into the icing with both hands. 'Finished.'

Molly replaced the kettle, her lips twitching. 'Milk it is.'

The kitchen was a long thin room. At the far end was an industrial-sized washing machine and in front of it, a huge steam contraption set up on an ironing board. There was a mounded basket of laundry waiting to be ironed and a neat pile of folded bedlinen ready to be collected. The door to the garden was open and in front of it stood a clothes horse hung with pillowcases.

Ellis insisted on being the one to cut us all wedges of cake as he was the chef. He took his through to the living room with his milk. We cleared a space at the worktop and settled on to stools. Molly set up her laptop ready for Kate's Skype call while I started to eat.

'Great cake,' I said, after just one mouthful. 'I don't know about David Beckham, but Ellis can certainly give Gordon Ramsay a run for his money.'

'He's multi-talented. Gets it from me.'

'Naturally.' I sipped my milk. Ellis had been right about that too; it was the perfect combo.

Our cake took up our attention for the next couple of minutes or so until finally I collected the last few crumbs with my fingertip.

'So. Archie. What do you think? He likes you,' I said.

'He's been pretty clear about that,' she said wryly. 'But I can't make him out.'

'He's lovely,' I said defensively.

'He's pretty obsessed with money.' She wrinkled her nose. 'How much his car cost, how much his house cost, the profit he's going to make by selling his sports car . . . He judges his own happiness by his bank balance. I haven't got a bean, but I look at that little boy in there and I feel as rich as Croesus. Money doesn't impress me. I want a man who'll listen to me, who understands what I need, who'll spend time with me and Ellis. A kind man.' She gave herself a shake. 'What am I even saying? I don't want a man full stop. Moving on. Over to you. Jude Trevone: discuss.'

She folded her arms.

'Wait.' I held her gaze. 'Archie *wasn't* kind?'

Archie was the kindest, most generous man I knew. Either she wasn't giving him a chance or he'd been too nervous to show himself in his best light.

'Not exactly.' She huffed and puffed, clearly struggling to find the right words. 'When he brought me home to help out with the laundry yesterday he tried to take over.' She shrugged. 'I didn't like it.'

'Oh, Archie.' I chuckled softly, shaking my head in despair. 'It's not that he wants to take over, although I can totally see that that's how it looks, it's that he wants to make things right.'

'I don't need a man to make things right,' she said crossly.

'Maybe not, but it's all he knows.' I looked out into the garden. It was only small: a washing line zigzagged several times across the width of it but beyond that I could see a football goal and an assortment of balls, a sandpit and a swing. It was Ellis's place to play, to be a child. A privilege Archie had had taken away from him.

'Taking control of women?' she scoffed. 'He needs to get a grip.'

'You don't understand,' I began. 'It goes way back.'

I eyed her for a moment, considering how much to tell her. Molly was a lovely girl: feisty, hard-working, fiercely independent. She'd be good for Archie and he was clearly keen on her, and if a nudge from me could help things on their way . . . But on the other hand, whereas I kept alive a secret hope that one day our father would come looking for us, Archie didn't feel the same way and it was that resentment that had fuelled his determination to be a successful businessman. I wasn't sure how happy he'd be that I'd showed her his Achilles heel.

Molly, sensing that I was wrestling with something, reached out to touch my arm. 'Hey, we can change the subject if you like?'

'It's fine, I'm in the mood to tell someone,' I admitted. Jude had stirred up memories of my dad yesterday, and he'd been on my mind on and off ever since. 'Archie became the man of the house when he was eight years old. Or at least *in his eyes* he did. The day Dad disappeared from the scene, our fortunes changed considerably. Archie changed overnight too. It was as if he'd decided that his childhood had ended and he took on the role of protector and provider.'

'At eight?' Molly glanced automatically towards the living room. Ellis had the TV on and we could hear his gurgling laughter above the chatter of the cartoon he was watching.

I swallowed as the heartache of that time came back to me. 'And I was only five, just a bit older than Ellis.'

'I'm sorry.' She squeezed my hand. 'Do you want to talk about it?'

And so I talked. I told her about the day we'd come home from school to find Mum sitting at the kitchen table, eyes unblinking, lips pursed. There was a man outside fixing a for-sale sign into the ground. She was holding a piece of paper by its edges as if she couldn't bear to touch it.

'We've had a letter from your father,' she said crisply. She paused, pulling her lips into a grim line. Archie and I exchanged worried looks; Mum was moody at the best of times. 'He's moved away, a long way away. We might not see him again for some time.'

She had a buttoned-up expression, as if she was full to

bursting with emotions but didn't dare let them out. I had leaned against my brother, needing his solid presence for reassurance.

'But he still loves us, doesn't he?' I'd asked.

'Not enough, clearly.' She dipped her head and her eyes blazed and for a moment I thought she was going to erupt with fury. 'He's chosen to live a different life.'

'Is that why we're selling the house?' Archie asked.

'We can't afford this house any longer,' Mum confirmed. 'And we need a fresh start. Somewhere smaller and cheaper.' Adding under her breath, 'With no wagging tongues.'

Leaving our home had doubled our sadness. Our new house was only twenty miles away but it might as well have been on another planet. It was small and identical to its neighbours and its walls were so thin that I could hear Mum muttering angrily in her sleep. But the money from the sale of the house meant that she didn't have to go out to work, which was good because I don't think she really liked other people.

She never married again. She rarely smiled again either.

'I feel so sorry for you all,' said Molly, shaking her head. 'I moan like hell about Steve, but at least I know where he is.'

'And at least he hasn't forgotten about Ellis, even if he doesn't get to see him much. My heart broke in two when Dad left.' I stared into the bottom of my glass, remembering his laugh, his jokes and the stories he used to make up at bedtime. 'He was the chocolate sprinkles in my life. Dad made things special, made *me* feel special. When he vanished the fun seeped out from our home. Mum systematically rubbed out every trace of him. We even stopped seeing our gran, Dad's mum . . .' I paused, trying to recall the face of the old lady who had Dad's kind eyes. Tricky when Mum had destroyed every photograph documenting her marriage.

'Have you ever tried to find him?' Molly slipped from her

stool, scooped up crumbs, switched the kettle on and stacked our plates in the sink.

I let out a breath. 'Almost impossible. I know nothing about him. Mum shut me down every time I tried to bring up the subject and she passed away when I was nineteen, so it's too late to ask now. I've googled Graeme Penhaligon a hundred times but nothing has ever come up. Our parents were older when they got together. He'd be in his seventies now, assuming he's still alive. I would have tried harder to get in touch but Archie has always been so adamant that he wanted nothing to do with him.'

'Your mum sounds like she took it hard,' Molly said, spooning coffee into mugs.

I smiled ruefully. 'She certainly kept her maternal instincts on a tight leash. Looking back, I wonder if she only had children because it was something she felt she ought to do. She was nearly forty when she had Archie. We each had our own ways of getting her attention. For me it was putting on shows, acting and reciting silly poems. Archie wanted to help financially from day one. He did everything to help the family budget from snipping out discount coupons from the newspaper, to sweeping leaves, delivering newspapers, wheeling and dealing in the playground. And all of it went to Mum, he didn't spend anything on himself. To this day he's still looking out for me; he's set me up a fund for my old age because I haven't got round to it.'

She set two mugs on the worktop, offered me milk and settled back on her stool. 'Okay, you win; the man's a saint.'

'So you'll give him a second chance?'

Before she could answer the laptop screen lit up in front of us. An army of butterflies began to march in my stomach.

Kate was on the line.

Chapter 26

Molly nudged me out of the way so fast that I almost flew off my stool.

'Stand clear of the screen and I'll announce your presence,' she muttered without moving her lips, 'as soon as it's safe.'

I nodded and scooted to the side where I could still see Kate on the screen.

She looked pretty much the same as the last time I saw her on her wedding day, only with a better tan. She was bursting with wholesome goodness: glossy chestnut-brown hair tied back off her face, dark-rimmed glasses that magnified her eyes and her trademark bright lipstick. A few more crinkles around the eyes, a line or two across her forehead, but then five tough years had gone by since I'd last seen her.

She was in an internet café by the look of it: other people were on laptops behind her, there was some sort of tinny trumpet music in the background, and she had a tall frothy iced drink in front of her.

'Look at you, all tan-tastic!' said Molly brightly. 'How are you doing, love?'

'Oh Mols, I asked Theo for a divorce!' Kate's face loomed close to the screen. 'It was a knee-jerk reaction; exactly what my therapist said not to do. I'm supposed to pause, take a breath, think it through. And THEN speak.'

'I'd have done the same,' Molly admitted. 'Steve has just

bought Ellis twenty of the latest Disney DVDs because he's Disney mad at the moment. I went crazy. Again. Said he should entertain Ellis himself, not park him in front of the telly.'

Another peal of laughter reached the kitchen from the living room. I raised my eyebrows.

'That's the CBeebies bedtime story,' she said haughtily. 'Totally different.'

'What?' said Kate, looking confused. 'Who are you talking to?'

Molly froze. 'Nina,' she blurted out.

'Molly Asher!' Kate choked on her drink. 'You . . . you Judas!'

She reached towards her laptop as if she was going to close it.

'No wait,' Molly yelped. She dragged me in front of the screen so Kate could see me. 'Pause, remember, like the therapist said, and breathe!'

Kate blew out a whistly breath, her eyes not leaving mine for a second. 'I'm pausing,' she said through gritted teeth.

'Good girl,' said Molly with relief. She nodded to me. 'Over to you.'

This was it. This was my chance. I almost cocked up their wedding day with my stupid crush on Theo, now was my opportunity to make amends and reunite two people who had simply lost their way through no fault of their own.

I reminded myself of Kate's ultimatum to Theo: get his life back on track and set up Brightside Holidays or else. There was no way 'or else' was going to happen, not while I had anything to do with it.

'Kate,' I began tentatively, 'Theo says he misses you.'

'Yeah right,' she scoffed. 'That's why the profile picture on the Coastal Cottages website shows you two gazing at each other.'

'That was taken out of context, but I can see why you think that,' I said quickly.

285

'And what was the context?' Kate demanded. 'Or shouldn't I ask?'

'When Nigel Rees arrived to do his inspection there were two naked artists in the garden using their body parts to paint.'

Beside me, Molly snorted.

'Yes, very funny,' I said wryly, 'except it was when we were trying to make a good impression for Coastal Cottages. We thought we'd blown our chances. Luckily, Nigel from the booking agency has a good sense of humour. Theo and I hugged with relief when he said the cottages had passed muster just as Nigel took the picture.'

'And Theo has sent them a new one, Kate,' Molly put in. 'One of you and him when you first moved in. If you look at the website again, you'll see.'

Kate grunted and sipped her drink. 'Still not exactly the picture of a tortured man missing his wife, is it?'

I soldiered on. 'He says he misses your warmth in the morning. You're always toasty, apparently.'

'Even warmer in Brazil,' she said, fanning her face, trying hard not to look pleased. 'What else does he say about me?'

'He misses the smell of your skin; he says you smell of flowers and sunshine.'

Beside me, Molly made a tiny 'aww' noise. I had Kate's attention now.

'Go on.'

'He misses the way you drip a teabag all the way to the bin.'

Kate shook her head fondly, a smile twitching at the corners of her lips. 'He always used to tell me off about that.'

'He misses your night-time routine.'

Her eyes widened. 'What did he say about that?'

My heart thumped; from the expectant look on Kate's face, I knew I had to get this right.

'You check your alarm.'

'Yes?' She nodded.

'You rub oil into every cuticle.'

'Correct.' Her face crumpled. 'I do.'

'And then you kiss Ivy's photograph and say—'

'Sweet dreams, angel.' Kate pressed a hand to her mouth as tears sprang to her eyes.

I felt my own voice catch. 'And now he says that too, every night.'

'Oh Kate,' said Molly, swallowing hard. 'You poor lambs.'

From the other room, Ellis shouted for his mum and Molly squeezed my arm as she went through to see to him. I sat down on the stool and pulled the laptop closer.

'Does he really say that?' Kate whispered.

I nodded. 'Kate, he hasn't done the things you think he has, but he *has* done the things you asked him to.'

She rummaged around in her bag, found a tissue and blew her nose.

'The cottages are gorgeous,' I continued, 'we've got some bookings and Theo has even started on the garden.'

'Does he really miss me?' she sobbed, wiping her eyes.

'Yes. He misses both of you. And he loves you.'

She smiled through her tears.

'I thought he'd given up on me, on life, it was as if he was in a coma. The house was getting on top of us – we should never have moved there. We got in a mess with money and nothing I tried could bring him out of it. It had always been his dream to travel one day, so as a last resort I suggested we just take off. My parents thought it was a brilliant idea and offered to pay. But at the last minute he refused to leave Brightside Cove and he refused to speak to me about Ivy . . . I was at my wits' end.'

'He has spoken to me about her.' I nibbled my lip, wishing I could reach out and hold her hand. She looked so alone and forlorn, God knows how many thousands of miles away. 'What the two of you have been through would test any marriage.'

'How did you do it?' She gazed at me. 'How did you succeed where I failed?'

I shrugged. 'I didn't. It was just timing. He loves you, Kate, and when he realized he might lose you if he didn't start living again he knew what he had to do.'

Okay, so that wasn't entirely honest. In my opinion Theo simply dealt with his grief differently to Kate. Whereas she wanted action, he wanted time. She needed to talk; he wanted to think. Nobody was in the wrong, it was just hopelessly sad.

'So what do I do?'

'Tell him you're calling off the d-i-v-o-r-c-e for starters.' Molly bounced back into the room with Ellis trailing behind her. He'd changed into his pyjamas and had a well-loved teddy tucked under his chin. 'Because take it from one who knows, that's no picnic.'

She poured him some more milk and he wandered out of the room and up the stairs.

'And that you definitely want to give it another shot?' I suggested.

Kate took a deep breath. 'I don't want Ivy forgotten, Nina. She was part of our lives. I was a mum. I want to be able to speak about her.'

My heart ached for her.

'You'll always be Ivy's mum,' I promised. Just as I will always be a daughter, even though my parents have gone, I thought to myself. 'You and Theo are her parents, her family.'

'Family,' Kate repeated softly.

'Just a thought,' I said cautiously, 'but perhaps you and Theo could Skype each other like this? I think he'd love to speak to you regularly.'

Kate frowned. 'I had thought it was better to have a complete break from each other, but maybe you're right.'

'So do you finally accept that Nina's defo not after your man, then?' Molly grinned hopefully at her friend.

Kate's eyes softened. 'Okay. And I can't tell you how much having this chat has meant to me. I really wish I could give you both a hug.'

'Me too.' I held my fingers up to the screen. Thousands of miles away, Kate did the same.

'I really must go,' she said, brushing a stray tear from her cheek. 'My internet time is about to run out and I need to email Mum. Bye-bye, both of you.'

'Ooh, before you go,' Molly said with a gasp, 'guess who Nina's got a crush on?'

I opened my mouth to protest, but Molly clapped a hand over my mouth. 'Jude Trevone!'

Kate frowned. 'Isn't he the one you fancied—'

'Bye-bye!' Molly said in a shrill voice cutting her off. 'Damn, I'd forgotten I'd told her that.'

I stared at her, arms folded while she powered down her laptop.

'If you're keen on Jude, just say, because I'm not going to tread on anyone's toes.'

Molly met my eye and gave me a sheepish smile. 'You can keep Jude on one condition.'

'What's that?'

'You give me Archie's number.'

'You're giving him another chance!' I flung my arms round her. 'You won't regret it.'

'I hope not, for your sake,' she joked.

At least I hoped she was joking.

It was dark when I swept back up the drive and parked outside the kitchen window of Driftwood Lodge. I had a huge smile on my face; Theo was going to be thrilled. All was not lost as far as he and Kate were concerned, they just needed to find their way back together again. He loved her, she loved him, and I was more sure than ever that love would bring them home. I darted inside, desperate to tell him all the things she'd said, but there was no Theo, only Mittens was there to greet me. I scooped up the kitten, pressing my lips to his soft fur and went outside. A lantern was lit up the end of the garden.

'Theo?' I walked towards the light. 'Is that you?'

'Yep,' he replied, sounding out of breath. 'How was Kate, what did she say?'

'That she loves you,' I beamed. 'That unless we do something else monumentally stupid there'll be no divorce.'

'Yes!' I caught the flash of his white teeth as he jumped up from his knees and prepared to hug me.

'Watch the kitten!' I laughed, leaping away. 'There was one thing, though,' I said, my voice more serious.

'Okay.' Theo shuffled his feet nervously. 'Tell me.'

'Kate wants to be able to talk to you about Ivy, she doesn't want to forget about her.'

'I'm on it.' His face spread into a slow smile. 'Because I want that too.'

And then he picked up the lantern so that it illuminated the patch of garden he'd been working on.

'Oh Theo,' I said, swallowing the lump in my throat, when I saw what he'd created. 'You've nailed it, my friend. You have totally nailed it.'

I was flagging a bit after another long day, but I couldn't go to bed without solving something that had bothered me all afternoon: the mysterious case of Maxine and Campion. I deposited Mittens back in the kitchen, pulled a cold bottle of wine from the fridge and set off for Penguin's Pad.

The light was on in the open-plan living room and through the window I spotted Maxine sitting hunched over the coffee table, a stack of papers in front of her. I knocked and held the bottle up as she opened the door.

'Wine?' I said, raising my eyebrows hopefully. 'A peace offering.'

'You can relax; I've calmed down now.' Maxine rubbed her eyes and stepped aside to let me into her cosy cottage. The little wood stove was lit, as were Eliza's scented candles and a vase of twisted willow and greenery added a homely touch. 'But yes to the wine. I've been reading non-stop since I arrived, I haven't even stepped out of the door yet.'

'Oh, you must! If you fancy a guided tour while you're here, just shout.'

'Thanks, I'll see how I get on.'

I found glasses and the corkscrew while Maxine tipped some cashew nuts into a bowl and we arranged ourselves near the heat of the fire.

I set my glass down on the coffee table and tried to see what she'd been reading.

'A script,' said Maxine, following my gaze. 'Get them all the time, but someone thinks I'm going to find this one irresistible. It's about a vicar locking horns with the greedy lord of the manor. Quite promising, actually, although I'm not sure about the planned location, which is supposed to be on a tiny island. I don't think there'd be enough scope for the action, or all the different characters needed to make a decent series out of it.'

'Is there a small part for me?' I asked, only half joking. I tried to read the title of it, but Maxine grabbed the pile and shoved it under the table.

'Hey, nosy.' She slurped her wine. 'And shouldn't you be aiming higher than that?'

I stretched my legs out, relishing the warmth of the fire.

'I know my limits. I'm not lead actress material. It's fine,' I added brightly, catching her baffled expression. 'I'm just being realistic. There are plenty of great roles for me to go after. I'm not saying I'm not a good actress, just that the main parts go to the beautiful girls, the ones with swishy blonde hair, long legs and cheekbones sharp enough to slice cheese on.'

'Is that so? Someone had better let Julie Walters, Emma Thompson and Meryl Streep know, then, because they obviously didn't get the memo,' she said crossly. 'Honestly. Who fed you that rot? Sebastian?'

'Amongst others.' I stared into the flames, remembering

my mum's comment when I announced that I was going to be an actress. About being the chubby and cheerful best friend. It hadn't stopped me, of course; if anything her lack of faith in me had made me more determined than ever. I wasn't so chubby these days, either. 'Sebastian told me more than once that I lacked a certain star quality, unlike Cecily Carmichael.'

Maxine frowned and wagged a finger at me. 'Your performance in *Victory Road* has got star quality by the bucket load. And after tonight's episode, when you're crushed inside that house in the bombing raid, you'll be bombarded with messages from viewers, you wait.'

'Thank you,' I said meekly, making a mental note to log on to the WiFi and check everything tonight.

'And as for Cecily,' she said ominously, 'watch this space.'

Which was the perfect opening for me to probe into her earlier mood.

'Talking of that particular family, I had no idea her father was coming, I promise.' I topped up her glass. 'Theo took the booking and got the name wrong. And I still haven't got a clue why he's here; do you think he knew you were coming?'

'Not unless he's a bloody good actor,' she said, taking another big gulp of her wine. 'He was as shocked as I was when we both got off the train and headed towards the taxi rank.'

I shuddered. 'In that case, he must be here because of me. When Cecily and I had that very public row, she said her father would be furious. Perhaps he's here for revenge.'

Maxine winced. 'I hate to be the bearer of bad news, dear heart, but I wouldn't put it past him.'

My heart sank. I'd rather hoped that that incident was behind me now. 'You obviously have history, so I'll take your word for it.'

'Campion is an ex-boyfriend.' She took a handful of nuts and tipped them into her mouth. 'It didn't end well.'

'Ah, enough said.' I tapped my nose, expecting that to be her last word on the matter. Maxine never, ever revealed details about herself. It was her thing. She was a mistress of compartmentalization. At work she was intensely private and totally work-centric.

'The only ex-boyfriend, as it turned out,' she said under her breath.

'You don't have to tell me anything,' I said, secretly hoping she'd tell me everything.

'Of course I don't. But I shall, nonetheless.' She got up, shoved some more wood inside the stove and sat back down. 'Because it's time, Nina. It's time.'

Her gaze fell on the fire and she let out a heartfelt sigh.

'Campion and I got together forty years ago. Before you were even born,' she said with a wry smile. 'Ridiculous, looking back. We were never suited, right from the beginning. Two strong-willed, ambitious young creatures; we were constantly at loggerheads. And that brought its own electricity, as you can imagine,' she said knowingly over the top of her glasses. 'We met at Elstree Studios; he was a junior set designer. I was a runner on the set of *Star Wars*, can you believe? What a golden age that was to make films: there was no computer technology back then.'

I settled back in my seat, loving this story already.

'I threw myself into my job with gusto. My father had recently died and work was a form of therapy for me. But Campion wasn't so content. He had his own vision, couldn't take direction and he had continual battles with his boss, insisting that his ideas were better than everyone else's. I was amused by him, I suppose, and impressed by his tenacity. I'd come from a very submissive family where everyone quietly got on with what was expected of them and didn't question it.'

My eyebrows flew up; Maxine and submissive weren't two words I'd ever heard in a sentence before.

'Yes, well, I've come a long way since then,' she said with

293

a chuckle, catching my expression. 'He was too possessive right from the off, which never sat well with me, so I began to ease myself out of the relationship. And then bam – I fell in love with someone else. Hopelessly, breathlessly in love.'

Her eyes had softened but then she seemed to give herself a shake and resumed in her normal brisk tone.

'I realized that what I had with Campion was nothing more than friendship. So I finished with him. Now let me tell you, Campion is not a man who likes to lose. He started stalking me, following me home, ringing me late at night and at work, when our paths crossed, I could feel his eyes tracking my every move.'

I rolled my eyes. 'As if that was going to win you back.'

'Then someone from Elstree left to go to the BBC Studios in White City and offered me a job as her assistant. It was a step up the ladder and a chance to get away from Campion. I grabbed it with both hands. Campion didn't take my promotion well. And having happiness on the work and love-life front helped me cope with my mother who was still drowning in the grief of losing Dad.

'It was while I was working out my notice that Campion stalked me one last time and found me in a dark smoke-filled club in Soho with my new love. It was late and we'd been drinking and I leaned in for a kiss and—'

There was a loud rap at the door and both of us started. Just as she was getting to the good bit . . .

'Please open up, Maxine; I'd like a word.'

We stared at each other, frozen to the spot.

'I could pretend I'd already gone to bed,' she hissed.

Campion's jowly face appeared at the window, his hands cupping around his eyes. 'There you are. Chop chop.'

'Damn it. Might as well get it over with,' she said, setting her glass down.

I sprang up. 'I'll let him in and leave you two to talk.'

'You'll do no such thing. Sit back down.'

I did as I was told and she stomped over to the door.

'Fancy a nightcap?' Campion held out a bottle of brandy and waggled it at her.

'I thought you said you wouldn't be bothering me at night.' She blocked his way, arms folded.

'I think we've got unfinished business, don't you?' he said gruffly.

'You can't hurt me now, you snake, so why don't you slither back under your rock and bugger off.'

The hairs on the back of my neck prickled; I leapt up to join her at the door to see Mr Carmichael lower himself precariously to his knees. His expression flickered when he spotted me but he carried on nonetheless.

'Let me apologize. I've always loved you.'

'Oh, please.'

'I know, I know, hard to believe, given my behaviour. But I did, *I do*, even after I understood why you broke it off between us. I never got over you really,' he said with a sniff. 'I married eventually, had Cecily. Didn't last, of course – the marriage, that is; Cecily is still alive and kicking, as you know.' He shot me a sour look. 'I've admired you from afar. Too proud to get in touch. Should have apologized years ago.'

'You should,' she agreed, nodding. 'But you didn't. Get up, you old fool, and come in.'

I coughed discreetly. 'I should probably go.'

She jerked her head back to the living room.

'Sit. I've started so I'll finish.'

I resumed my position in the armchair. Mr Carmichael stared at me resentfully from the far end of the little sofa while Maxine fetched him a glass.

'Always fancied a little bolthole by the sea,' he said, looking round. 'Somewhere to come and paint surrounded by cliffs and clouds.'

'I was halfway through telling Nina how you tried to ruin my life,' she said, ignoring his comment. She sat as far away

295

from him on the sofa as possible. She looked at me, chin tilted. 'In case you hadn't guessed, Nina, my new love was a woman, Joy.'

I had to fight my own jaw to stop it from gaping open. Up until now I don't think she'd even told me when her birthday was let alone anything as personal as this.

'I hadn't guessed and I'm honoured that you've confided in me.' I reached for her hand and squeezed it. Maxine being gay was of no consequence to me. But the tremor in her voice told me just what it had cost to make such an admission about her private life.

'Campion said I had to finish with Joy immediately or he'd make sure everyone knew about me.'

Mr Carmichael poured himself a large brandy.

'I thought if I couldn't have you, nobody should,' he said gruffly. 'I was humiliated and I lashed out. I'm not proud of my actions.'

'I should think not,' I said indignantly.

'Different times then, of course; lesbians weren't the done thing at the BBC,' he said. 'Now if you're gay you're welcomed with open arms. Diversity they call it.'

Maxine shot him a venomous look.

'It wasn't the BBC I was worried about, you baboon. It was my mother. She had very traditional views about men and women and marriage. It would have broken her heart to know I was gay. Especially coming so soon after my dad's death. I couldn't do it to her.'

'The Maxine I know wouldn't have given in to being bullied,' I said.

She regarded me for a moment, acknowledging my compliment with a sad smile.

'But I did and it broke Joy's heart.' Her eyes were definitely brimming with tears now. 'I had been her first girlfriend. She was so confused by my desertion that she suffered a breakdown. And I have regretted being a coward every day of my life. I never heard from her again. I turned my back on who I was and who I loved to save face, and I've had to live with that for my whole life.'

'I hope you've lived to regret it too?' I said to Mr Carmichael.

'I was a young, selfish fool.' His face sagged and for a moment he looked like a vulnerable old man. But then his expression lifted and he looked at Maxine, full of hope. 'But now here we are, four decades on.'

'I'm still gay, before you go any further, it wasn't just a phase,' she retorted. 'Once Mum died I fell in love again with Paul, short for Pauline. I keep my private life to myself, but if you were thinking of threatening me again, forget it. I'm at the top of my game professionally. I know who I am and I'm proud of it.'

'Hear, hear,' I said, raising my glass.

'And I'm a grumpy, self-centred, conceited fool,' Carmichael grunted. 'But do you think we can be friends?'

Maxine scowled at him. 'Let's start with frenemies and take it from there.'

He held out his glass, she chinked hers against it and both of them drank.

I let out a breath of relief.

'I'm going to wish you both goodnight. Unless . . .'

They both looked at me expectantly.

'Nothing.' I swallowed hard. 'Goodnight.'

I let myself out and crossed the courtyard back to Drift-wood Lodge.

Unless anyone has anything else to confess, I was about to add, but it was late enough and although Campion Carmichael still hadn't revealed exactly what had brought him to Bright-side Cove I had had enough surprises for one day.

Chapter 27

Next morning, I set off for the Mermaid Gift and Gallery. Eliza had left the keys to the shop under a plant pot and after buying a takeaway coffee from The Sea Urchin next door and a packet of Jammy Dodgers from Jethro, I'd settled myself in for the morning behind the counter. By lunchtime, I'd reached the conclusion that a career in retail was not for me. After four hours cooped up I had cabin fever.

So far, I'd sold some nautical bunting, an abstract drift-wood sculpture and a canvas of Brightside Cove. In between customers, I'd watched last night's episode of *Victory Road* on Theo's laptop.

I stared out of the shop window towards Big Dave's Lob-ster Shack and then let my eyes focus on my reflection in the glass instead. *There she is, Nina Penhaligon, minding a shop for a friend. Later on she'll go back to the holiday cottages she's helping to run and look through cake recipes . . .*

What was I doing here; I mean, actually doing? Theo didn't really need me, not any more. Kate would be back soon and I'd definitely have to be off then. But off where, exactly? Trudy had filled my room with students, my role in *Victory Road* was all but over, I had no agent, nothing in the pipeline . . .

I dropped my head into my hands and groaned.

The bell at the door dinged and Campion Carmichael swept in in his mac and trilby.

'Lamenting the end of your TV career, are you?' he said, casting an arrogant eye around Eliza's dear little shop. 'I heard you'd been dropped from *Victory Road*.'

I arranged my features in a bewildered smile. 'You heard wrong, I'm afraid,' I said with more confidence than I felt. 'How's Cecily getting on with the filming of *Mary Queen of Scots*?'

'It's a challenge for her,' he said vaguely, heading for the canvases on the back wall. 'But that's the sort of thing my family thrives on. When we want something badly enough we generally get it.'

Urgh, this man gave me the creeps; I couldn't abide the type who railroaded everyone else to get their own way. He peered at a small watercolour of the cove, took it from the wall and turned it over.

'Very popular those are,' I said. I had no idea if that was true, but the sneering look on his face made me want to defend them.

'No accounting for taste,' he said and turned away.

'Can I interest you in a ship-in-a-bottle, or a shell mosaic, or was it me you're looking for? Cecily did warn me that I might hear from you after our incident. Not that I didn't try to apologize at the time.'

'Don't flatter yourself that I'd travel to the ends of the country to see you,' he scoffed. 'I'm here on business. And anyway, as much as I abhor social media, Cecily hasn't done too badly after your little spat. A bit of wounded pride, nothing more, and we all have to deal with that from time to time.'

'Yes, how are your knees from all that grovelling last night?' I said innocently.

He ignored me and pulled a piece of paper from his pocket. 'Do you know where this is?'

He was holding up the Mermaids of Mayfair article from the *Daily News* that Robin the journalist had shown me on Sunday. He stabbed a finger at the picture of the hen party girls lined up in their mermaid tails in front of the slipway and behind it, the lifeboat house.

Alarm bells began to sound in my head.

'The section of beach just past the harbour is very nice. Great view over the sea wall, if you mean the beach generally?'

'I mean the lifeboat house. *Specifically.*'

'Right.' My mouth had gone dry. 'Turn left out of the shop and keep walking as far as the path allows. You can't miss it.'

'Thank you.' He turned abruptly and marched to the door.

'Why do you want to know where that is?' I called, fighting a rising tide of panic.

'Because that's why I'm here,' he said with a smirk.

I gave an involuntary shiver; I didn't have a clue what Campion Carmichael was up to but something told me that Jude was not going to be very happy about this development. Not one bit.

I locked the shop door and stuck Eliza's 'back soon' notice on it. I needed some fresh air, some lunch and some insight into what Campion Carmichael was really doing in Brightside Cove. I stopped off at Jethro's for some bread rolls and bought a couple of dressed crabs from Big Dave.

Ten minutes later I'd raced home and made lunch: brown crabmeat mixed with mayonnaise and lemon juice and topped with a layer of the white meat – as per Big Dave's instructions. Theo was sitting outside with a calculator and a stack of invoices with Mittens on his knee. His cat allergy had subsided a little because of the medication. He still sneezed about ten times in a row now and again, but his eyes were back to their normal colour and as long as he kept the bundle of fur away from his face, things weren't too bad.

I left them both licking their lips at the prospect of sharing a crab lunch and took the other two rolls over to Penguin's Pad.

Maxine's eyes looked tired when she opened the door to me.

'Have you even smelled the sea yet?' I said, hand on hip. 'All work and no play—'

'Gives me bags under my eyes, yes I know,' she replied irritably. 'It is a reading week, though, I'm not here to play.'

'Come on, you've got time for a picnic on the beach,' I said, holding up the bread rolls.

She glanced back at the heap of reading material on the coffee table and sighed. 'Sounds like heaven.'

She wouldn't change out of her heels, but I did manage to persuade her to put on a thick jacket and we were soon on our way. It took us no time to walk along the coastal path and then drop down to the bench outside Big Dave's Lobster Shack. I pulled bottles of water out of my bag and handed her a sandwich.

'Oof.' Maxine sat down heavily and wiped a sheen of perspiration from her brow. 'I'm so unfit.'

She swigged her water and tried to catch her breath. I'd got used to striding up and down the coastal paths and could run up the steps from the beach now without panting. And after sitting in the shop all morning it felt good to use my muscles.

'I'll take you exploring tomorrow and force you to get some exercise.' I stretched my calf muscles out before taking a seat next to her. 'If you're allowed to have some time off, that is?'

'I've got two weeks of filming schedules for *Victory Road* to approve, at least a month's worth of emails to reply to and four scripts to skim read. So not really,' she said, pulling a face.

'Remember what you told me to do,' I chided: 'drink in experiences, feast on life, and all that. I'm sure it must apply just as much to directors as actors.'

'Too clever by half you are,' she grumbled, picking up a juicy piece of crab from her lap and popping it in her mouth.

The sun was hiding behind a veil of thin cloud today, casting a muted palette over the usually vibrant bay, and a sea breeze was rattling masts and churning water into a sea of frothy meringues and making our eyes water. Every so often a wave sent a fine mist in our direction as it broke on the rocks. But even with the softer colours Brightside Cove still looked picture-postcard perfect.

'They're quaint.' She wafted her roll in the direction of the pastel cottages.

'They're fishermen's cottages,' I said. 'That elderly chap down there is the last of the fishermen.'

Jude's clients, Nora and Ned, were in their usual positions in deckchairs: him glued to his binoculars, her with her knitting on her lap.

'It would have been quite a sight back in the day, the men mending nets in the harbour, the women waving them off on their quest for a good catch and then watching the sky and the sea anxiously waiting for their safe return.'

'What a romantic image.' Maxine bit into her crab roll. 'It is a bit like a film set. I bet it hasn't changed for a hundred years.'

'The village stores and pub have hardly changed since then, but the clientele has.'

'Tourists?'

'Some but mostly walkers, day trippers and second-home owners.'

I breathed in the air, closed my eyes and tilted my face to the sky.

'You love it here, don't you?'

I grinned at her. 'If only there was a TV studio tucked away in the hills, I'd never go back to London again.'

'I wouldn't last long here; all these cobbles would ruin my shoes. And I'm more of a round-the-pool woman, nothing worse than sunbathing with sand blowing in all my crevices.' She chuckled. 'What's that chapel-shaped building near the rocks?'

'Funny you should ask,' I said. 'You're not the only person interested in that today.'

I told her about the lifeboat house and how important it was to the community and Jude's plans to save it from being developed.

'And worryingly, it's also the reason Campion's here.'

'What would he want with that?' she pondered aloud, her focus sharpening on the little boat house.

'No idea,' I shrugged, 'but whatever his reason, it was important enough for him to make a last-minute booking and hotfoot it to Devon.'

'I'll invite him in for another nightcap later and see if I can wheedle it out of him.' She stifled a yawn. 'That is, if I can stay awake until then.'

'That would be brilliant.'

I needed to let Jude know as soon as possible. Firstly because of the impact it might have on his plans, secondly because . . . well, any excuse to talk to him, really.

I collected up the wrappers from our lunch and popped them in the bin at the side of Big Dave's shack. 'And you?' I asked. 'Why was your booking suddenly brought forward?'

'At the risk of getting sand in my shoes,' she said, 'let's walk and talk on the beach.'

I followed her down the slipway to the beach. And for a couple of minutes, the only sound was the push and pull of the tide on the shingle along the harbour.

'The ratings were good last night for your cliffhanger episode,' she said finally.

'Phew! So you don't think my leak did any damage?'

She shook her head. 'Viewing figures are up again. Which is why . . .' She glanced over her shoulder before continuing. 'Well, I'm leaving the show. Leave on a high, eh? Isn't that what they say?'

I gaped at her. The thought of *Victory Road* without Maxine at the helm was unimaginable.

'But *Victory Road* is your baby!'

'And I'm proud of it; the show has been far more successful than any of us imagined. I'm riding the crest of a wave on to something even bigger. Whoops, literally!'

We both laughed as an ambitious wave rolled up the beach and we had to scamper out of its reach. Or rather, I scampered; she tottered on her ridiculous heels.

'Where are you going?' I asked.

'I've been offered an opportunity to join a brand-new TV production company, SparkTV. I'd be able to hand-pick my own team, and they've already taken TV rights out on some really juicy novels. Hence the huge reading pile. It's a big jump and a lot of location work, so I'll have to get used to being out of London, but I'm excited for the future. I've come a long way from being that runner at Elstree Studios in the Seventies.'

'Congratulations!' I hugged her, hoping I had as much drive and ambition when I was her age.

'Always push yourself, Nina,' she said, as if reading my mind. 'Acknowledge your limits but never stop challenging them.'

I nibbled my lip. 'I need to sort my life out. Being away from London has helped clear my head. Now I feel ready to take on something new.' I raked a hand through my wind-knotted hair. 'I need to start calling agents, update my résumé. I might not get another role as good as Nurse Elsie, but I need to act in something.'

'Oh, get a grip!' she huffed. 'With that attitude you'll be back to playing corpses on *Silent Witness*.'

My insides quivered at the thought. 'Don't say that. Holding my stomach in for hours on end was murder.'

I'd never forget that part. I'd told Archie that I was in the show, but omitted to tell him that I'd be nude for the whole scene. He'd been so proud that he'd invited his mates round to watch me and had been horrified at the first glimpse of his sister's privates. He'd spent the entire time in front of the screen trying to cover me from the lads' prying eyes.

'Well, honestly,' she said, lobbing pebbles into the waves. 'Yesterday you said you didn't think you had star quality. What a load of baloney. What do you think makes a great actor? Hmm?'

I thought carefully, wanting to get it right. 'Imagination, empathy, creativity, not being afraid of hard work?'

'Exactly!' she boomed. 'Even what you've told me over lunch shows me that you have all these things.'

Talk about a boost to the ego.

'Day made,' I said with a grin. 'I guess if no one has ever told you you're good, then . . .'

'Then tell yourself.' She rounded on me sternly, her dark eyes blinking behind her glasses. 'Have you ever heard Meryl Streep speak about how she was turned down for the female lead in *King Kong*?'

I nodded. 'Didn't the Italian director call her ugly?'

'Exactly! I mean, how bloody dare he? But did she let that knockback ruin her confidence? No. Did that make her think she wasn't worthy of major roles? It did not. She went on to be one of the most respected actresses in the world. I love her,' she finished with a heartfelt sigh.

We reached the bottom of the steps that led up to Driftwood Lodge.

'From now on my mantra will be: *Be more Meryl*,' I promised with a smile.

'Excellent. Now I'm going back to put the finishing touches to the cast list for my island vicarage drama,' she said and raised an eyebrow expectantly.

'Right. Oh,' I said, realizing she was waiting for me to comment. 'Do you think there might be a part in it for me?'

She patted my cheek. 'That's more like it.'

I felt a wave of admiration for her as I watched her trot up the steps towards her cottage.

And it was only when I got back to the Mermaid Gift and Gallery that I realized something: she hadn't actually answered the question.

Chapter 28

The wind blew fiercely that night. I lay awake in bed listening to the thick thatch creaking above my head, the garden gate rattling against the latch and the distant crashing of waves on the rocks. I felt as restless as the sea. I'd been content just pootling along in Brightside Cove. Theo was good company now that he'd decided to grasp the future with both hands and I was enjoying running the cottages with him, seeing to the guests' requests and assisting with marketing plans. But now that Maxine was here, acting as a reminder of my other life, I felt as if I should be focusing on my own future and I couldn't stop wondering about that new drama and whether she would let me audition for it.

It was time for me to take some action. And I would, I told myself, just as soon as I'd fulfilled my promise to Jude to help him take action of his own.

Be more Meryl, I chanted softly, pulling the duvet up to my chin. *Be more Meryl*.

I must have drifted off at some point because I woke up at five o'clock from a vivid dream. Meryl Streep and I, dressed as mermaids, had emerged from the lifeboat house holding golden Oscars to a round of spontaneous applause from a grinning audience. All except Campion Carmichael, who stood at the back of the crowd booing us both and shouting that we weren't wanted until Jude threw him in the sea and everyone cheered.

Ah well, a girl can dream . . .

At five thirty I got up and made coffee. I'd come up with a plan and there was no time to waste lying in bed. The wind was still blustery but the clouds had cleared and the skies were streaked in a palette of silvery lavender, pink and powder blue as the sun prepared to make its appearance over the headland.

I showered and dressed and managed to wait until six o'clock to call Jude. Unfortunately, I only had the number of Deliciously Devon so it took me several attempts to get him to answer the phone.

'Morning! Fancy walking Mabel on the beach before breakfast?'

'Nina?' His voice was still thick with sleep.

'Correct,' I said, pleased that he'd recognized me. 'Come on, I'm bursting with ideas and you need to hear them.'

He chuckled softly. 'Can't you tell me over the phone?'

I imagined him stretching his muscles, rubbing a hand through the bouncy bit at the front of his hair, blinking those lovely eyes awake. I bet he was all toasty and warm. Perhaps I should offer to go round and take him breakfast in bed.

'Well, I could—'

'I'm kidding. Give me twenty minutes,' he said, sounding more awake. 'Meet you at the slipway.'

Jude was waiting in his van behind the lifeboat house when I got there.

'I know you said *before* breakfast,' he said, 'but an army can't march on an empty stomach.'

He handed me a polystyrene takeaway cup with a tiny plume of steam escaping from a hole in the lid and then produced a paper bag from his pocket containing two warm almond croissants.

I bit into one immediately. It was delicious: sweet and flaky. Mabel sat at my feet and gazed at me imploringly.

'Almost as good as breakfast in bed,' I said, breaking off a tiny piece for her.

Jude caught my eye and then smiled into his coffee. 'Almost.'

Heat flooded my face. 'No idea why I said that.'

He brushed a crumb from my chin, Mabel snapped it up and we both laughed.

As it turned out the beach was a no-go zone due to the high tide and big waves. Instead, Jude steered me towards the steep path that led up and over the headland. We were both bundled up in our windproof jackets and boots, and we needed to be: the breeze swirled around our faces and we had to press close to each other to prevent our words getting swept away. They weren't the ideal conditions to hold a conversation but I gathered he'd been in touch with the council, begging them to hear his proposals, and I managed to convey that Eliza needed somewhere for her mermaids to get changed near the beach, which was another use for it to add to the list.

After about ten minutes of shouting to each other, I was beginning to regret choosing an outdoor venue for this conversation. We rounded a bend to find a bench set a short way down the cliff, sheltered by rocks and thorny bushes. I pointed to it and Jude nodded. Mabel loved the wind, she danced and jumped in and out of the rocks, snapping at swirling leaves, ears flying and tail swishing left and right, but we were both glad to be out of it.

'I've been thinking,' I said once we were sitting down, 'we need to attract the biggest audience possible to save the lifeboat house. We need to tug at heart strings, ramp up the drama, capture the imagination.'

'Sounds like one of your TV shows.' He nodded. 'How do we do that?'

I smiled. I liked the way he said *shows* as if I was never off the telly. I also liked how cosy we were; sitting here sheltered from the weather, cocooned from the world, our own private escape. I turned my body towards him so that our knees were touching.

'Firstly, to use your army analogy, we have to mobilize the troops. All the groups you think would benefit from saving the boat house – get them involved.'

He nodded. 'Easily done. I can run up some leaflets. Get a couple of lads to post them through doors.'

'Good idea,' I agreed. 'We can put them in the pub, and Jethro and Eliza's shops. Molly can WhatsApp the football mums. I can use Twitter to target some groups: the local history society, the big new lifeboat station, sailing groups, sea fishing clubs . . . And I can put a call in to the local radio if there is one?'

'Yes, Devon Sounds. And then what?'

'We get them all to come to a public meeting at the lifeboat house. The bigger the crowd, the better the impact. And we invite the council too. We get them to hear your proposal right there where it matters, and we show them how important this is to Brightside Cove.'

'I like it.' Jude's eyes glimmered. 'At the moment they think I'm a bit of a crackpot who just wants to hold back the tide of progress. This would prove I'm not on my own.'

You're not on your own, I wanted to say. I wanted to take his hands and bat my eyelashes at him and hope he got the message that I'd quite like us to be more than pals. But although he was at ease with me, friendly and relaxed, the flirty edge to his body language wasn't there today and I couldn't help but feel a pang of disappointment.

'We need to move fast, though,' he continued. 'Do you think Friday is too soon?'

I laughed, pleased he liked my idea. 'It doesn't give us much time but Eliza is going to be on national TV later this morning, we can text her now and get her to give our campaign a mention.'

'Whoa. Definitely not,' Jude said at once. 'That's what I want to avoid. We have to do this ourselves, as a community.'

'But surely, the bigger the audience—'

'The more interest we attract from outsiders,' he finished off. 'And we don't want that. The ideal scenario would be that the lifeboat house attracts zero bids at auction. But that's never going to happen; it's one of Brightside Cove's most prized possessions. But we can try to keep the auction on the low. Which means no unwanted attention to the area. Can you imagine if we get people from London down here waving fistfuls of notes at the South Devon council? They'd probably cancel the auction and hand over the keys immediately.'

People like Campion Carmichael.

I swallowed down a wave of fear. 'Then we might already have a problem.'

Jude's brow furrowed. 'Oh?'

I told him what I knew about Mr Carmichael, which wasn't a lot other than he'd said he was down here on business and he'd been on a mission to find the lifeboat house.

'This is exactly what I was worried about when I saw that piece in the paper,' he groaned. 'An artist, you say?'

'Of landscapes,' I said weakly.

'So what would he want a derelict boat house for?' he said, puzzled.

I cleared my throat. 'I don't know. I have history with his daughter. I thought at first it might be something to do with that, but he denied it.'

'Whatever he's here for, we need to keep him out of this public meeting,' Jude muttered. 'He mustn't know what we're up to.'

'Leave that with me,' I said, anxious to redeem myself. I'd think of something . . .

It was time to be heading back ready to open Eliza's shop

at nine. I stood up and looked towards the cove. Its beauty took my breath away. 'Look at that view.'

'You should see it from out there.' Jude nodded towards the sea. 'The curve of the bay, the boat house at one end, the cottages at the other, the fields rising from the cliffs and the boats in the harbour just smudges of colour as they bob on the waves.'

The thought of someone spoiling it brought a lump to my throat.

My throat tightened. 'Jude, I'm so sorry about Mr Carmichael. I brought the Maidens of Mayfair here. Without them there'd have been no photograph of the boat house in the national press. I feel responsible.'

'Hey.' He leaned against me. 'Do not blame yourself. You weren't to know.'

'But what if the council won't listen?'

'Then we will fight them on the beaches,' said Jude, deadpan.

I snorted. 'Was that your Winston Churchill impression?'

He pretended to puff on a cigar. 'Never give in, never, never, never.'

'And also,' I said, grinning, 'never give up your day job.'

He took my hand and we retraced our steps back down the cliff, entertaining each other with funny voices. Brightside Cove was very lucky to have a man like Jude on its side. If I had to make a list of things I'd miss when I went back to London, Jude Trevone might very well be at the top.

'Hey, beauty!'

It was late in the afternoon when the taxi dropped Eliza off outside the shop door. She pushed her way in, weighed down with bags, her dungarees hanging off her shoulder as usual.

'It's Brightside Cove's newest celebrity mermaid!' I jumped up from behind the counter. 'Welcome home.'

I'd only had one customer this afternoon: a tourist who'd

wanted stamps, which we didn't sell, but he'd already tried Jethro who'd shouted at him and told him to "go home" and then he wouldn't need to send a postcard at all, would he? On the plus side, Jude and I had managed over email to get leaflets and posters designed and printed, I'd discovered at least ten community groups who said they'd attend our public meeting and I'd given a radio interview to Devon Sounds about playing a nurse in a Second World War drama and how important it was to remember local history, and by the way, I was spearheading a campaign to save the lifeboat house if anyone was free to attend our event on Friday . . .

'Oh home,' Eliza sighed, trailing a hand over a display of hand-painted stones. 'London is just brilliant, but loud. How do you stand all that noise?' She clamped her hands to the side of her face, doing a mean impression of Edvard Munch's *The Scream*. 'The cars and sirens, music blaring out of every shop. People yacking and yelling at each other all the time.'

She paused for a second to kiss my cheek.

'I'm sure you gave as good as you got,' I said with a grin. 'Sit and tell me everything.'

I made her a cup of herbal tea while she peeled off her shoes, rubbed her swollen feet and told me all about the hotel, which had mood lighting depending on whether she wanted to feel energized or relaxed. She chose somewhere in the middle – aqua, which made her feel like she was underwater.

'Obviously,' I said, handing her a mug.

'The whole experience was immense,' she said, inhaling the steam from the tea. 'It was so brilliant to get the positive message out there that we should celebrate our body diversity, and that being a mermaid is about feeling free and confident. But the crazy bit was afterwards. Five people called into the show begging me to open a mermaid school in their seaside towns. And then this researcher woman asked me if I'd consider going on *Dragons' Den*. I said why would I do that, and she looked at me like I'd got a screw loose and explained that I was sitting on a goldmine and that with the right investment I could go national. But enough about me. What have you been up to?'

I gawped at her. 'Eliza, that's incredible. You must be blown away.'

She blinked rapidly. 'It's all going so fast. I'm out of my depth.'

'You're a mermaid, remember,' I said firmly. 'You can swim to the surface any time you like.'

'You're good.' She grinned and then her face fell. 'But what do I tell them? And more to the point, do I even want all this?'

'Only you can answer that one,' I said. 'All I'll say is: always be you. Be true to yourself. Listen to what your heart tells you and you won't go wrong.'

'Wow, is that actually your advice or did you get it from a script?'

'Busted.' I grinned. 'The matron at *Victory Road* had said something along those lines to a hospital porter who'd been thinking of becoming a priest. I thought it was quite apt.'

I gave her a hug and listened as she told me about the price of a vodka and Coke in London. I loved giving advice; it was so much easier to solve other people's problems than my own.

Eliza sent me home soon after that and I found Theo in the garage, sorting the contents into various indistinguishable piles.

'Chuck, sell, keep,' he said, pointing to the piles in turn. 'I'm having a clear-out.'

I had a sudden flashback to when Mum had her first stroke. It had only been a mild one, but she'd seen it as a sign to start packing up her things, that her days for this world were numbered. By the time Archie and I had had the chance to visit her, she'd been through the house like a dose of salts. The few remnants of our childhood had stood waiting for us in cardboard boxes, the attic was empty and she'd sent most of her own things to the charity shop. I'd been heartbroken at the time; I'd always thought that one day I'd have the chance to search the whole house for photographs of my dad, but it seemed I'd left it too late.

'Don't be too ruthless,' I said with a shiver, 'don't get rid of anything you might regret.'

'That's true.' Theo paled. 'Some of this is Kate's. I've only just escaped one divorce threat; I don't want to face another.'

He rummaged through the 'chuck' pile and drew out a glittery disco ball and a small denim jacket, setting them on top of the 'keep' pile.

'Wise move. What's the plan, anyway?'

'I reckon I can divide this space into two, put in mezzanine floors and create two studio apartments,' said Theo, polishing a brass door knocker in the shape of a fox's head on his T-shirt. He set it carefully back in its box and on top of the pile for selling. 'What do you think?'

A glow of pride spread through me.

'I think you're on fire, that's what I think. You're really throwing yourself into this holiday venture, aren't you?' I said, smiling at his bashful expression.

'I want to build a business that's big enough to support a family,' he said gruffly. 'Given time.'

'Kate will love that.'

We grinned at each other for a moment, swallowing our respective lumps.

They'd agreed to speak to each other nightly now and Theo was walking round in a permanent state of bliss, a dreamy faraway look on his face. It warmed my heart to see it, even if it was difficult to get him to concentrate on anything for more than five minutes. When I'd left for the shop this morning, he'd covered the living room with dustsheets, saying that he was going to try sweeping the chimney and when I'd come back for lunch he'd abandoned that job and he was up a ladder, checking that the thatched roof hadn't been damaged by the wind. But on the basis that we'd all thought only a week ago that he was suicidal, I wasn't complaining. This new energetic Theo was a big improvement on the wet lettuce I'd found when I first arrived.

He gave himself a shake and started throwing old paintbrushes into a black bin bag.

'Oh, talking of families, Archie called. He wanted to know whether we had a spare cottage. I said Kittiwake's Cabin was empty so he's arriving tonight for a few days.'

I stared at him. 'For a holiday?'

Theo shrugged. 'Didn't ask. I explained that you were in the spare room, and that the living room was out of action waiting for a proper chimney sweep, otherwise he could have stayed in the house, but he said he preferred having his own space.'

I was amazed. Archie rarely took a day off at the weekend, let alone during the week. Perhaps Molly had got in touch. For him to pay more than a fleeting visit to Brightside Cove he must be even keener on her than I thought. Love certainly was in the air today; maybe a second match made in Devon could be on the cards?

'Have you seen or heard anything from our guests?' I asked.

'The guy asked about the art scene.'

My senses switched to high alert. 'And what did you say?'

He scratched his head. 'Told him about the annual art festival in Shapford, the one Pen-Pen and Brucey-darling went to.' We shared a smile at the memory of our naked artists. 'I should have given him all that claptrap about the light down here being unique, but I didn't think about it until afterwards.'

'Good, and if he asks again, don't mention it,' I said. 'In fact, tell him art isn't popular in these parts.'

He looked at me like I'd gone mad. 'Okay, whatever you

say. Flowers must be popular, though; you've had some delivered today.'

I sprinted off to investigate.

Theo had left the bouquet propped up in the sink in water. They were exquisite: a hand-tied bunch of pale-pink roses, pink-tipped lilies and fuchsia gerberas, tied with curls of white ribbon. My pulse was racing as I ripped the little envelope away from the cellophane and I tried to make myself calm down. They were probably just from Sapphire to say thank you for her hen party. My eyes skipped over the words, not believing what I was seeing.

No. This couldn't be real.

I released the card from my fingers, flinging it as if it had stung me. I gasped for air, my heart hammering in disbelief. After a few seconds I picked it up again with shaking hands and tried to focus on the typed words.

Congratulations on that amazing cliffhanger episode of *Victory Road*. Your dad would be so proud. T x

Who was T? Was this the same person who'd been sending me flowers anonymously back in London? And how did he or she know my dad?

Chapter 29

Later that evening, Archie was waving his mobile phone fruitlessly in wide arcs around the kitchen in Kitti-wake's Cabin. 'I'd forgotten just how back of beyond this place is.'

'You'll get used to it. Now, sit and eat it all,' I ordered, setting a big fry-up on the table. 'And this.' I placed a plate of bread and butter at his elbow.

He grinned. 'I don't know why you're treating me like an invalid, but I'm not complaining.'

'I'm doing it because you look like death warmed up, you're too thin and you're willingly taking a holiday, i.e. you're not your normal self.'

'Gee thanks.' He squeezed ketchup on to the plate with a loud splat.

'Also, you're all the family I've got. If you snuff it, who's going to worry about me?' I poured us both a glass of water and smiled sweetly at him.

'Jude?' He cocked an eyebrow. 'Molly told me you two were canoodling down in the cove.'

'Is nothing sacred?' I flushed. 'We're just pals, he even said so himself. But while we're on the subject of Molly, is she why you're here?'

'Um. Not really.' He stabbed both eggs with his fork and stared as the yellow yolk mixed with the ketchup. A cold panic gripped me suddenly. He must be ill. The doctor had

317

warned him only a month ago to ease up a bit. And there was I making jokes about snuffing it.

I sat down in the chair opposite and rested my hand on his arm.

'If something's wrong, you would tell me, wouldn't you?'

He set his knife and fork down and sighed. 'Do you remember my first big break outside of the uni business?'

I nodded. 'The big hotel on the front? How could I forget our celebratory Japanese dinner?'

We shared a smile; while he'd still been at uni he'd won a contract that had taken his small laundry venture to the next level, doubling his turnover. He'd advertised for new staff, looked for bigger premises and never looked back. He'd been so proud that he'd invited Mum and me out for dinner. Mum didn't come – she said it was sinful to be self-congratulatory. And besides she didn't like the seaside. A small piece of me never forgave her for that.

'Over ten years I've been doing business with them, giving them a top-class service too. Last week they asked to renegotiate our terms, because someone else has offered them lower prices. This week three more of my biggest customers have done the same.'

'Do you know who this other firm is?'

He smiled wanly. 'Yes, and I can't compete. They're national; they can afford to undercut me long enough for me to go bust.'

'Where's the loyalty from your customers?' I said, outraged on his behalf. 'Surely they'll stick by you in return for the service you've given them over the years.'

'Money is too tight for niceties these days.'

'So what can you do?'

'Make a plan of attack.' He heaved another sigh. 'That's why I'm here; I thought a few days away from the office looking at the lovely views of Brightside Cove would help clear my head.'

My heart dipped. 'And I thought you'd come to spend time with Molly.'

'I hope to do that too.' He grinned. 'She's the lovely view. I fully intend to be her not-so-secret admirer, whether she likes it or not.'

'Oh, that reminds me. I thought I'd got a secret admirer. But now I'm not so sure.'

I pulled the little florist's card from my jeans pocket and I held it between my fingers, adrenalin whooshing through my veins. Normally I told Archie everything; we had no secrets from each other. But where Dad was concerned, Archie was a closed book. He must remember more about him than I did, but he never shared those memories with me.

'I've been sent some flowers.' I handed the card over and held my breath.

'"Congratulations on that amazing cliffhanger episode" . . .' Archie's frown deepened as he got to the end of the message. He looked up at me. '"Your dad would be so proud"?'

'How weird is that?' I said with a catch in my throat. 'Who do you think could have sent them?'

He shook his head. 'Have you ever had anything like this before?'

'I've been getting anonymous flowers for a while. Never a mention of Dad on them, though.'

'Ignore it.' He handed back the card. 'Probably just a crank.'

I swallowed back my disappointment. 'But what if it isn't?'

He pursed his lips. 'Still ignore it.'

'I tell you what I think,' I said, my stomach fizzing with hope. 'I think Dad's out there and I think someone wants me to come looking for him.'

'Well,' Archie pushed his chair back, 'good luck with that.'

I stared at him. 'Don't you want to know where he is? Aren't you at all curious?'

He ran a hand over his stubble. 'He chose a different life, Nina. One that didn't include us. Why should I care about someone who doesn't care about me?'

'How do you know that?' I said, pouncing on him. 'All sorts of things happen between couples when they split up. For all we know it was Mum's fault. She moved us away from where he could find us.'

'We only moved twenty miles,' he said patiently. 'We weren't exactly impossible to track down.'

'Maybe there was a reason for it. I'll never forget a story in the newspapers when I was about fifteen about a singer being reunited with her father who had disappeared from her life when she was a baby. He saw her on the TV and contacted her.'

'I hope she told him where to go?'

'No, he became part of her life. I think that's been in the back of my mind since I was little. I've always had this crazy idea that he'd spot my name one day and get in touch.'

'Is that why you became an actress?' His face softened and he reached for my hand. 'That is so you.'

'Yes. No. That's over-simplifying it. I'd have become an actress anyway. But that story sowed the seed of an idea in my head and I've kept it alive ever since. And maybe it's worked? Maybe whoever sent the flowers could be trying to put us back in touch with him?'

'Not *us*,' Archie said, raising his palms. 'Some humans do bad things to each other every single day. And it's natural to hold on to the belief that our own parents aren't like that. But sometimes they are. Sometimes we're better off without them. As far as I'm concerned, I've done okay without Dad's help.'

I thought of Jude and how badly his parents had treated him. Archie was right; some children were better off without their parents. But our dad had shown us nothing but kindness right up until he left.

'You and me against the world?' he murmured, drawing me into a hug.

I nodded yes, but deep down I felt like I was on my own. My few precious memories of Dad were happy ones; I didn't believe that my childhood had been better for not having him in it. These flowers had given me fresh hope. And I didn't know how I was going to prove I was right, but I was going to give it a shot.

Archie and I didn't see much of each other the next day. He did some work and then went out in the afternoon while I drummed up support for our public meeting. Even though we hadn't had much time, Jude and I were hoping that we'd have a good turnout.

Then on Friday the day dawned crisp and clear and the sun sparkled on a flat turquoise sea. Perfect conditions to save our lifeboat house, I thought, after I'd flung back the bedroom curtains and plucked my dressing gown from the floor.

Our lifeboat house.

I was interrupted from my thoughts by the crunch of footsteps across the gravel. It was Maxine strutting towards Driftwood Lodge, head to toe in black as usual. With her frizz of dark grey hair, knee-high boots and long cardigan flapping behind her, she looked like a blackbird out to catch an early worm.

I knocked on the window and waved and then ran down to let her in, scooping up Mittens from the bottom of the stairs as I did so.

'Who knew chickens made so much noise?' she grumbled, following me into the kitchen.

I grinned. 'I quite like waking up to the sound of them chatting and the waves in the background whispering on the shore.'

Mittens padded straight to his litter tray and began scratching round for a suitable spot.

'You really have fitted into life here,' Maxine marvelled, getting in my way as I attempted to slide the kettle to the hotplate. 'Does that offer of a guided tour still stand? I'd like to get some fresh air today.'

I winced, feeling guilty. 'No can do, I'm being the face of – don't laugh – the Save the Brightside Cove Lifeboat House campaign.' I handed her a leaflet from the pile on the kitchen table. 'Petitions, protests, the lot. You're welcome to join us if you like?'

'So you're happy to lead a protest, but you don't think you have the star quality to be a leading lady.' She tutted under her breath. 'Madness.'

'When you put it like that . . .' I said, pulling a face. I crossed to the doorway and yelled up the stairs, 'Theo, do you want tea?'

'He can't hear you,' she said. 'He's at the bottom of the garden with a watering can.'

I chuckled to myself as I poured hot water into mugs; the man was a machine these days, always pottering about doing jobs.

'We'll do the tour another time,' she said, heaping sugar into her mug. 'I just fancied some company, that was all. But I won't join you; I'll ask that lobster man if he'll take me out on his boat. It would be good research for that drama I was telling you about. In fact, about that—'

'Ooh, if you wanted some company, could you do me a massive favour?' I held out the biscuit barrel and hoped my hazelnut and cranberry granola bars might win her over.

'Will I like doing it?' She selected a big nutty one and snapped a piece off with her teeth.

'No,' I said honestly, 'but please do it anyway.'

I explained that I needed her to keep Campion away for a while and she agreed, admitting that she hadn't had the opportunity to grill him about his intentions with the boat house yet and this would give her the perfect opportunity. So while we finished our tea, I called Big Dave from the landline, to ask if he could accommodate Maxine plus a guest on his boat today. He was happy to oblige, even more so when he found out Maxine worked in TV. I had a feeling she'd have heard all about his fifteen minutes of fame by the time they were out of the harbour, even though he didn't like to talk about it. A few minutes later she crossed back over the courtyard to issue a probably less than gracious invitation to Campion and I busied myself clearing up after Mittens and forking some kitten food into his bowl.

Today was going to be a good day, I thought, turning on the radio and busting a few moves to the latest Beyoncé single, a very good day indeed. So enthusiastic was my dancing that it took me a while to realize that I wasn't alone.

'Ahem. Hello.'

I whirled round to see a small tanned person hovering in the doorway, hand raised in a shy wave. Glossy hair screwed up in a bun, red lipstick, massive backpack . . .

'Kate!' I squealed.

I launched myself at her and wrapped her in a hug.

'But how—' I spluttered. 'When did you . . . Why didn't you say?'

Her eyes glittered with tears. 'Suddenly I didn't want to be three thousand miles away, trying to find myself. I wanted to be home, with Theo, where I belong. So here I am.'

I nodded, swallowing the lump in my throat. I was so glad to see her. And I knew someone else would be too. I helped her off with the backpack and led her outside to the garden gate.

'He's at the bottom of the garden.'

'Thank you,' she whispered, her breath catching in her throat. And then she squeezed my hand and went through the gate to her husband.

As if sensing her presence, he looked up from the garden

he'd been working on: Ivy's remembrance garden, with the selection of plants to ensure flowers all year round, the three types of ivy that wove in and around every shrub, the tiny pond surrounded by little flower fairy statues. And the crowning glory – a wooden seat for two carved with the words:

Ivy, you were in our lives for such a little while but you'll be in our hearts for ever. Love always, Mummy and Daddy xxxx

And then they were in each other's arms, crying for their daughter and for each other. For the love they had lost and the even greater love that entwined their hearts like fronds of ivy that would forever bind them together.

I tiptoed away, crying happy tears that two lovely people had finally found their way back home. To each other.

Chapter 30

By a quarter to noon, the area of beach around the lifeboat house was heaving with people. Jude and I had decided to address the crowd from directly outside the double doors so that if anyone took pictures they would have the lifeboat house in it behind us. At this rate the people down at the bottom would have their feet in the sea, the slipway was packed!

'I had no idea we'd get such a response,' I marvelled, raising a hand to wave to Raquel from the pub.

'Oh ye of little faith,' Jude replied with a wink.

We grinned at each other. He might seem outwardly cocky today but it wasn't me who'd been on the phone at five this morning, panicking that no one would come and the only audience would be the ever loyal Mabel, who right now was fast asleep in his van with the window open. I hadn't minded; nothing wrong with showing a bit of vulnerability now and again. In fact, I thought more of him because of it. Although quite how much more I could think of him, I wasn't sure. He was so lovely. And kind. Look at him now, shaking hands with that old lady, I thought with a girlie sigh.

'Hello, glad you could come,' he said to the old dear, who was wearing a mac, wellingtons and plastic rain hood.

'Wouldn't have missed it for all the tea in China,' she said staunchly. 'My dad was on the lifeboats. I spent hours on this beach as a girl waiting for him to come back safe.'

Jude and I exchanged a look. She was exactly the reason we were doing this. Then she reached for my hand, her skin papery and dry.

'Don't marry him,' she leaned in and whispered loudly to me. Her breath smelt of peppermint. 'He's not good enough for you. I can tell by his eyes: too narrow.'

'I'll bear that in mind,' I said, hiding my giggle as I patted her hand. 'Thanks for the advice.'

'If you survive the bombing that is.' She winked conspiratorially. 'Or was that story-leak a decoy?'

The penny dropped: she was talking about my love interest in *Victory Road*, not Jude.

'You mean Nurse Elsie and Constable Hardy! You'll have to stay tuned to find out,' I said, ridiculously pleased a) to be recognized and b) that she hadn't meant I shouldn't marry Jude.

'Oh, I will,' she promised and then leaned even closer and cocked her head towards Jude. 'Mind you, this one's quite a catch if the acting job falls through.'

'I'll bear that in mind too.' I shot Jude a look and was tickled to see that he was blushing a bit.

And therein lies the rub, I thought sadly. It was an *either-or* situation: either Jude and Brightside Cove or acting and London.

'Recruiting you was a smart move on my part,' he murmured close to my ear. 'She was quite star-struck.'

'*All of this* was a smart move on your part.' I turned to face him. 'Whatever happens, you should be proud of what you've started.'

We grinned at each other for a second – a mutual appreciation society – until a car horn distracted us. A camper van had just pulled up and disgorged a group of scruffy-haired surfers in board shorts and hoodies.

'I didn't even know there were this many people in Brightside Cove,' I said, watching the crowd spill on to the sand and some set up camp on the rocks to the left of us.

'There aren't,' Jude replied with a chuckle. 'That lot wearing walking boots are the local history society. The women on the rocks with the notepads and wine are over from Brixham on a writing retreat. There's the University of the Third Age brigade, the WI, the drama club from Thymeford, some of my colleagues from social services. Plus, I've seen fishermen, ex-coastguards, those surfers as well as all the village residents.'

Theo and Kate weren't coming. They'd apologized for not supporting us but understandably said that they had so much to catch up on that they were going to take advantage of the house being empty for a couple of hours. There'd been some squeals from the bathroom when I'd left. Say no more.

'And the media is here.' I pointed out the intern from Devon Sounds, a blonde-haired, generously built girl who was flitting excitedly from group to group recording soundbites to broadcast later on. She was wearing huge headphones and shoving a big furry outdoor microphone in people's faces. There was a photographer from the newspaper too, taking down names and snapping away at groups of people.

'We could actually do this, you know.' He laughed, his eyes shining with determination. 'When the council sees how much support we've got, how can they continue with the auction?'

'Exactly, they'd be fools,' I said with as much vigour as I could muster. As long as Campion Carmichael hadn't got there first . . .

'Oh, there's my brother Archie!' I waved to him. He waved back but he didn't join us. He seemed to be looking out for someone.

Jude was called away to pose for selfies in the middle of an exuberant group of women who I could only imagine were the football mums. I stood alone, running over my speech in my head. *Welcome . . . good cause . . . heart of the community . . . irreplaceable part of history.* I muttered the words under my breath, conscious of the rise in my pulse rate at my impending moment in the spotlight. Between us we had managed to gather an audience and it was my job to get the message across. I wanted to do Jude proud.

An elderly couple, a man in a wheelchair with a lady pushing him, hesitated at the top of the slipway, clearly unsure as to how to get down. I held my breath for a second: the little old lady was only slight, one false move and the pair of them would end up in the sea. I started towards them just as Jude spotted them too and we ran up the slope together to help.

'This is Nora and Ned,' he said, introducing us as he came to a halt and applied Ned's brakes.

'From the pretty cottages!' I said, shaking hands with them both. 'My favourite view in Brightside Cove.'

'View's not bad from here, either, eh Jude, lad,' Ned sparked, grinning up at me. He was tucked under a multi-coloured crocheted blanket and seemed to only have one leg.

Nora rolled her eyes. 'Doesn't get out much, you'll be glad to hear.'

'Haven't been in there for years,' said Ned, jerking his head towards the boat house. He had an unlit pipe poking out of his mouth, a weather-beaten face and a rascally grin. 'Brings back memories, eh, Nor?'

Nora fiddled with a small St Christopher medallion around her neck. 'Out in all weathers, he was. He might be a nuisance these days, but at least I know where he is.'

'Ned is one of the only original fishermen left in the village,' Jude explained.

'Did you go out on the lifeboats too?' I asked, fascinated.

'Oh yes, we was all volunteers back in the day. Saw some terrible accidents in my time. Mind you, not as terrible as losing the boat house would be. And look.' He delved under his blanket and brought out a large iron key. 'I can let us in if it rains. That's where me and Nora used to do our courting.'

He caught my eye and winked.

'I thought I was a widow on more than one occasion,'

said Nora fondly, smoothing a wispy strand of white hair down on her husband's head.

'I'd have been in there like a shot.'

Jethro had joined us and snaked an arm round Nora's waist.

'Oi, get round the front where I can see your hands,' Ned grunted.

The three old people erupted into laughter.

I was flabbergasted by this exchange. I'd never seen Jethro so cheerful; he was like a different person.

Jude crouched lower to speak to Ned. 'Are you sure about saying a few words?'

'Sure?' Nora chuckled. 'He's been writing his speech for two days, you'd think he was accepting an Oscar.'

'I'll say a few if you like,' Jethro said darkly. 'Bugger off, tourists. There's three.'

That was the Jethro we knew and loved.

'Grumpy old sod,' Ned chortled.

'Don't call us, Jethro,' Jude grinned, 'we'll call you.'

I glanced up at the sky; rain seemed unlikely, thank goodness. There was a thin layer of cloud, but the sky was white rather than grey. The air was completely still and the sea was as flat as a mill pond.

Ned caught my eye. 'Looks calm, don't it? Don't be fooled.' He tapped his nose. 'I can smell a storm brewing.'

Let's just hope the storm he was referring to would be in the sky and not with the council, I mused, glancing at my watch.

'It's nearly noon,' said Jude. He glanced up to the road nervously. 'And still no sign of the woman from the council.'

'Don't panic,' I soothed, 'the council will never miss a PR opportunity; they'll be here.'

'Hmm, I might just phone and check.'

He wandered off again just as Molly arrived with Ellis strapped into his child seat on the back of her bicycle. Archie gave her a chaste kiss on the cheek and shook hands solemnly with Ellis. I waved and the three of them walked down to meet me, Ellis between them swinging a yellow bucket and spade.

'This feels good.' Archie tipped his head back and filled his lungs with fresh Devon air. 'I already feel better. I love being on the beach.'

'Ditto,' I agreed, watching Ellis fling himself to the ground and begin to dig with a vengeance. 'There's something about being so close to the sea. I feel mellow and at home.' Far more than I did in London, I realized.

'Must be in your blood,' said Molly, looking from Archie to me. 'With a Cornish name like Penhaligon, you must have the sea in your veins?'

'We don't really know much about Dad's side of the family,' I said, shooting a sideways glance at Archie.

He scratched his nose. 'Granny Bev lived in Cornwall. So Dad probably was Cornish.'

Bev. I'd even forgotten her name. My heart thudded. What else did he know about our family that he hadn't told me?

'Where exactly was that?' I probed while he was in the rare mood for sharing.

He shrugged. 'I can't remember; I can't have been more than six or seven the last time we went. The beach we used to visit was always crowded, busier than here.'

'Not difficult,' Molly put in.

I felt a tug of frustration; why had he never mentioned this before? But then I supposed he'd answered the other night; he didn't want to remember Dad.

'There was a steep walk down to the beach, as I recall,' he said, frowning as he combed through his memories. 'I think we went once before you were born and then again afterwards. You'd have been three or four.'

I swallowed. No wonder my memory of it was so patchy. Happy but vague. 'I do remember something about it. Dad was great fun, wasn't he?'

'Oh look.' Archie dropped to the sand and picked up a small shell. He handed it to Ellis who looked less than impressed, understandably. I rolled my eyes at my brother's pathetic attempt to change the subject.

Ellis dropped it into his bucket politely. 'Thank you. Mummy,' he said, tugging on her sleeve, 'can I collect some shells?'

He looked adorable today in a Batman outfit: a grey and black jumpsuit with a gold printed belt and a big bat on his chest. A tiny cape fluttered behind him as he bounced on the spot excitedly. It had clearly been bought with growing room in mind; it had been folded several times at the ankle and cuff and the crotch hung down almost to his knees.

'Yes I know,' she said, catching my eye. 'Not exactly the ideal outfit for the beach, but I couldn't be bothered to argue. He starts school in September and will have to wear a uniform every day. He might as well enjoy his freedom while it lasts. Only thing is if he needs a wee – *which he will* – the whole lot will have to come off.'

She bent down and pulled the Velcro tightly across the front of his trainers. 'And no getting wet,' she shouted after him feebly as he headed straight for the shoreline. 'Fat chance,' she added softly.

'I remember collecting shells on that holiday,' I began again, challenging Archie with my stare, 'and skimming stones. Do you?'

Archie stood, hands on hips, watching Ellis race straight into the sea and out again. He snorted softly. 'You were rubbish. Dad spent ages trying to show you how to flick your wrist.'

He picked up a flat stone and tossed it in a skimming motion across the sand.

'I can skim stones.' Ellis was back panting and only a bit wet.

'How many bounces can you do?' Archie grinned at him. 'Shall we see if you can beat me?'

'YES,' said Ellis with a roar of delight.

331

'Is that okay with you, Mummy?' Archie gave Molly his best winning smile.

Molly nodded. 'You might want to take those posh shoes off, though.'

'Good point.' Archie slipped off his brogues and stuck his socks inside them, handing them to me.

Ellis immediately did the same, abandoning his socks straight on to the damp sand.

'Can I show you my best rock pool?' he said eagerly. He slipped his small hand into Archie's trustingly and they trundled off to the water's edge.

'Sure.'

'And later, can me and Mummy dig a hole and bury you so just your nose sticks out?'

'Er . . . maybe not today. I don't think we'll have enough time.'

'My daddy is very busy. He's building houses so he can't play with me today. Are you too busy to play with me?'

We couldn't hear Archie's reply but we did hear Ellis's answering laugh. We exchanged looks.

'If Archie thinks the way to my heart is through Ellis,' Molly muttered, not taking her eyes off them for a second, 'he's smarter than he looks.'

'Hey, it's the Siren Sisters!' Eliza whooped. She dropped her bag and threw her arms round us both. 'Can you two come and shield me to give me some privacy round the back of the boat house? I thought I should be a mermaid for this and I need to get changed. Damn, I should have brought three outfits.'

Molly and I looked at each other. Yeah, damn.

'Privacy,' Molly scoffed.

'With this crowd?' I added.

'Good point.' Eliza cringed, focusing on the heaving mass of people. 'Well, we'll have to do something. Being a mermaid might be about body confidence, but I don't want to overshadow today's meeting.'

'Your bum's not *that* big,' Molly sniggered.

Eliza whacked her with her shell bra.

'Hold on, I've got an idea,' I said.

I ran and begged the key off Ned and beckoned the girls to follow me.

'Poo!' the three of us chorused when I pushed open the door.

Inside it smelled of fish and damp wood. There was a lot of bird poo on the concrete floor and the remains of a bird's nest wedged high up in the roof. It was mostly empty except for a small wooden rowing boat in need of a new coat of varnish. There were coils of old rope in the corner, shelves of various sizes along both long walls and a set of metal steps which led up to a mezzanine level. The row of slatted windows either side let in a muted light and the roof with its sets of wooden beams gave an ecclesiastical feeling to the building.

'Never been in here before,' said Eliza. 'You're right; it would be a fab place for my ladies to change in. We could put mirrors over here and a little curtain like in a clothes shop.'

'Does Jude realize how much work it will take, I wonder,' Molly mused.

I left them chatting and walked to the staircase. At about chest height on one of the steps was a glossy A4 folder with *Mernick's, The South West's Premier Auctioneers* embossed in gold across the front. That was the company in charge of auctioning the boat house. Whoever had been here must have left this by accident. I flicked through the pages and out fell a business card: *Campion Carmichael, Artist.*

My stomach quivered with nerves. It looked as if Campion had wasted no time in arranging a viewing of the boat house, which meant he really must be interested in it. Thank goodness Maxine was keeping him occupied today; the less information he had about our plans the better.

I shoved the card in my pocket just as one of the big

double doors at the front of the boat house opened a crack and Jude's head appeared.

'Katrina Berry from the council is here; I think we should get started. Oh sorry, Eliza.'

Eliza squealed. 'Nearly ready.'

Jude quickly averted his eyes as she wriggled the pink and orange tail up over her bikini bottoms, straightened her clamshell bra and hastily wedged on a shell and ribbon headdress. She bunny-hopped forward, sending her boobs jiggling and grabbed on to Molly for support. Jude didn't know where to look. Again.

'Could take me a while,' she laughed.

'I can offer you a fireman's lift,' he said doubtfully.

'I've got a better idea,' I said with a giggle, pointing at the little wooden boat.

It was a brilliant way to start our public meeting: we launched the boat with Eliza in it through the doors and a short way down the slipway. The assembled crowd instantly stopped chatting and began to cheer and clap at the brightly coloured mermaid with pink hair waving demurely as she reclined in the boat.

'Right,' Jude nudged me forward. 'You're on.'

I stepped forward, took a deep breath and smiled. Everyone fell silent.

'A warm welcome to everyone, the people of Brightside Cove, the communities who will benefit from this beautiful building in decades to come, the ladies and gentlemen of the press and especially Katrina Berry who joins us from South Devon council . . .'

Jude led the crowd in another enthusiastic round of applause at her name.

And then I gave my speech about the way in which the building had nobly served its community in the past and the many ways we hoped it would do so in the future and that with everyone's support and some strategic, long-term thinking on the part of the council, we could achieve wonders.

The crowd cheered and whistled and then collectively took a sharp intake of breath as Ned pushed himself up on to his one leg. Jude and Nora were by his side instantly supporting him.

'I'd like to say my piece, if I may. The lifeboat house is falling apart. It's old and decrepit and has seen better days. Not unlike meself.' His voice was hesitant and wheezy.

In the distance I saw Archie near the rocks with Ellis. Ellis was running around naked and poor Archie was trying to catch him and persuade him to put his Batman suit back on. I nudged Molly and we both stifled a giggle.

Ned gave a phlegmy cough and tried again. 'You might think it would be nice to see it all smartened up, perhaps with a shop in it, or some fancy flats, instead of looking at its scruffy woodwork and the great gaping holes in the roof.'

Jude shot me a look of concern which I echoed: where was Ned going with this, exactly?

'But once our boat house has slipped from our hands, it's gone for ever.' His eyes misted over and Nora clutched his arm. 'This is a piece of our history, it represents the life that I lived, and my dad, and my grandfather before him. In its day it was as important to our community as the police station or the church. If we let it go to developers, we're saying we don't care about our heritage. It's already disappearing. Look around us, what signs are there that Brightside Cove was once a thriving fishing community? The quayside has all but been taken over by a car park and the only working fisherman is not even a Devonian. There might never be enough fish in these waters for it to support us again, but the lifeboat house should stay to serve its community as it has for the last hundred years.' He sought Katrina Berry from the council out in the crowd and doffed his cap. 'My dear girl, over to you, do the right thing. That's it.'

He dropped back into his chair. He looked exhausted, his chest rising and failing with the effort.

The crowd erupted with applause. Jude stepped forward and cleared his throat.

'Go Jude!' yelled one of the football mums. Someone else wolf-whistled.

He gave the group a lopsided smile and held a hand up to calm them down.

Honestly. It was like his own private fan club. I realized I was sucking my cheeks in peevishly and released them immediately. Out of the corner of my eye in the distance, I noticed two figures walking briskly along the path on the headland towards us.

'All we're asking for is a chance, Mrs Berry.' He found the young woman from the council, whose cheeks were still flushed from being singled out by Ned. He beckoned her forward and she walked up to us as if pulled by a magnetic force. She was in a smart skirt, sensible heels and held her briefcase in front of her like a shield. Jude clasped his hands together. 'A chance. Please.'

'It's *Miss*,' she said coyly. 'I'm not married.'

I just about managed not to tut. Not another one. Jude fixed her with his hazel eyes. 'Can we show you our proposal, please? Before the auction? Just hear us out, that's all we ask. You've seen from the turnout how deeply we care about this.' He lowered his voice, focusing all his attention on her. 'I beg you.'

Miss Berry almost swooned. The crowd was motionless, everyone waiting to hear her response. She flipped open her diary and flapped through the pages.

'Very well,' she said in a breathy voice. 'I do have one space for another meeting, take it or leave it. I'll see you a week today at the council chamber, but I want to see proper, costed proposals, not an airy-fairy list of ideas.'

Jude looked at me, seeking approval. I thought my heart would burst at the smile on his face when I nodded.

'Yes! We'll take it.' Jude raised both arms in the air in triumph.

The sound of whistling, whooping and hollering would have given even the crowd at an England home game a run for its money. Eliza squealed and kicked her tail in the air, and Molly and I hugged each other.

'Thank you, *Miss* Berry,' Jude continued. 'And thanks everyone for your support, that wraps things up for today, make sure you've signed the petition and I'll keep you updated on our progress.'

'And three cheers for Jude Trevone,' cried Nora in a shaky voice, raising her fist. 'Hip, hip!'

'HOORAY!' yelled the crowd in response. Including me.

Jude flapped his hands up as if to say it was nothing. But I could see how thrilled he was with their reaction. People started to move away except Miss Berry who leaned forward as if expecting him to shake her hand, but he didn't, he turned to me and took my hands.

'Thank you, Nina.' His eyes bore into mine and pathetically my knees went weak. 'I couldn't have organized any of this without you.'

'My pleasure,' I cooed, pursing my lips as I said it, hoping that he'd get the hint that kissing me right about now would be a good idea. 'And actually you totally could have done this without me.'

'OWOWOW!'

Everyone looked round to see where the caterwauling was coming from.

Striding towards us up the beach was Archie carrying Ellis in his arms. Archie looked very pale, Ellis's face was pink and blood was pouring from his foot.

Molly nearly tripped over herself in her haste to get to them through the departing crowd. 'What's up, kiddo?'

I raced beside her. Eliza got to her feet, or rather fin, but stayed in the boat.

'I'm so sorry,' said Archie in a shaky voice. 'My fault entirely. He stood on something sharp in a rock pool.'

He looked at me and pulled a wretched face. Poor Archie, and he was trying so hard to impress Molly.

'My foot hurts, Mummy; you can see the meat and bones.'

'Oh don't.' Archie shuddered. I stifled a smile despite myself; Archie and blood did not go well together. I remember Mum leaving a leg of lamb in the kitchen to defrost once and blood had seeped over the plate, on to the worktop and dripped a puddle on the floor. Archie had come home from school, taken one look at the bone sticking out of the lamb surrounded by blood and thrown up.

Molly pulled a tissue out of her pocket and dabbed Ellis's foot. 'That will need stitches. Damn. This is when I really regret not having passed my driving test.'

'I'll drive you,' Archie offered in the next breath. 'No problem, the least I can do.'

Molly bit her lip. 'But we'll drip blood all over your nice car.'

'What car is it?' Ellis asked in a small voice.

'A clean one,' said Molly dully.

'Come on.' Archie marched up the slipway.

'Here!' Eliza pulled a towel from her bag and chucked it to Molly as they passed on their way to Archie's Range Rover. 'Put his foot on that to protect the upholstery.'

Archie shot her a look of eternal gratitude and Eliza winked back.

'First law of mermaid club: always be prepared for damp patches.'

She peered round at her own wet backside. 'Talking of which, I think this boat is leaking. Can someone help me out?'

I got one side of her and Jude the other, and together we heaved her out so we were all standing on the slipway.

'Stick her on my lap if you like,' Ned offered with a throaty chuckle. 'I'll give you a ride.'

'You see, Nora,' said Jethro quick as a flash, 'you wouldn't get that sort of comment from me.'

'I think we can manage, thank you,' I said breathlessly, casting a wistful eye on the distance from here back to the boat house.

'Nina, dear heart?'

I froze. No one else called me dear heart, except . . . it couldn't be. I spun round as best I could with Eliza's arm draped over my shoulders to find Maxine and Mr Carmichael on the slipway.

Maxine was looking decidedly green around the gills, and Mr Carmichael's head was spinning round like a CCTV camera trying to absorb all the action going on around him.

'Are you all right?' I gasped. Which was probably a stupid question given the colour of her face.

'Seasick,' she spluttered.

She sank down on to the front edge of the rowing boat, causing it to pitch and she fell into it. Mr Carmichael hauled her out and sat her down, wiping his hands on his waterproof trousers.

'Boats,' she wailed. 'Never again.'

'That fisherman drove over every wave on purpose,' Mr Carmichael spat disgustedly. 'He could see Maxine was suffering.'

Ned pushed himself up in his chair. 'You can't avoid the waves, you blithering idiot,' he blustered, going red in the face.

'Now, now,' said Nora, patting his shoulder.

'Bloody tourists,' Jethro put in.

'Where have you come from?' I asked.

'Big Dave set us down on the other side of the headland,' said Maxine wearily. 'We've walked across from there.'

Katrina Berry coughed loudly. 'I've got to get to another meeting. See you next week.'

Jude adjusted Eliza's weight and managed to shake Katrina's hand and thank her again. And then his eyes found mine.

'One week today,' he said softly. 'You will still be in Brightside Cove then, won't you?'

I nodded. 'Just try stopping me.'

'What precisely is going on?' Mr Carmichael fumed. 'Why are all these people here and the boat house doors open?'

'I'm so sorry, Nina,' Maxine murmured, dropping her head into her hands.

Someone came over and handed her a glass of water. At least I think it was water, it might have been one of the writers from Brixham with a glass of wine. Whatever it was, she gulped at it.

'It's okay.' I peeled myself away from Eliza and went to Maxine's side and gave her a hug.

'I'm waiting for an answer,' said Mr Carmichael imperiously.

Jude pulled himself up to his full height. 'We at Brightside Cove are planning on keeping the boat house for our own purposes.'

Mr Carmichael gave a hollow laugh. 'Shame, because I've got other plans.'

'Oh yes?' Jude's voice had taken on a low menacing tone and goose pimples pinged up all over my scalp. 'Care to share them?' He extended an arm to the remaining people on the slipway. 'I'm sure we'd love to hear, wouldn't we, folks?'

'Don't be preposterous, why would I do that?' Mr Carmichael scoffed.

'Whatever they are, we don't want them.' Jethro sniffed.

Jude shrugged. 'Well, may the best man win,' he said, coolly.

'Don't be absurd,' Mr Carmichael spat at him. 'The best *offer* will win.'

'That settles it, then.' Jude gave him an icy smile. 'You lose. My team is unbeatable.'

He was including me in that. A glow spread over me and I gripped Maxine's clammy hand in mine.

'Unbeatable?' Mr Carmichael threw his head back and laughed. 'A one-legged man, a mermaid and an out-of-work actress. Very quirky, I'm sure, but at the end of the day money talks.'

I shivered a bit at that; it was the sort of thing Archie would say.

'Why, you . . .' Jude squared up to Mr Carmichael, letting go of Eliza, who dropped with a thud back into the boat. The bow of the boat see-sawed up and caught Mr Carmichael's backside. He was flung forwards, almost falling into Ned's lap. Nora took aim and kicked him in the nuts. Jethro punched the air and Ned cackled with delight. Eliza and I were nearly wetting ourselves with the effort of keeping in our laughter and even Maxine made a noise halfway between a groan and a belly laugh.

'Arrgghh.' Mr Carmichael was doubled up, writhing in pain on his knees in front of Nora. 'The truth hurts, eh?' he wheezed.

'It's not the truth.' Maxine staggered to her feet, pulling me with her. 'You're looking at a hero, an astute business-woman and . . .' Her lips twitched into a smile. 'Nina isn't an out-of-work actress.'

'Aren't I?' I stared at her.

Mr Carmichael put a hand out to steady himself and Jude helped him up.

'I'm offering Nina Penhaligon the lead role in my new drama, *The Holy Coast*,' Maxine said firmly.

'Me?' My heart thumped. 'But . . . I thought . . . isn't the lead role a vicar?'

She nodded. 'A lady vicar. A kind and cheerful girl, everyone's best friend.'

'Yay!' Eliza clapped her hands. 'Well done, beauty!'

I swallowed. That was incredible. Me. Nina Penhaligon. The starring role.

'We've got our first meeting on location in the Scottish Highlands. We'll be travelling up a week today. We'll be doing press shots too. I shall be spending the next forty-eight hours finalizing details.'

'Oh no.' My eyes met Jude's. 'That clashes with our presentation to the council. Maxine, I'm sorry but I can't come.'

'Nonsense, dear heart,' she scoffed. 'You do realize what this will mean for you? How important for the rest of the cast it is to meet their leading lady? No, I'm sorry you have to be there.'

'But I've made a promise,' I said weakly, feeling as queasy as Maxine still looked.

'Listen to Maxine,' said Jude resignedly. 'Of course you have to be there. I insist. You deserve this. Congratulations.'

He smiled. A kind understanding smile. Which tore my heart. Maxine was still looking at me, puzzled at my hesitation. I hadn't even given her an answer, but I couldn't take my eyes off Jude. Surely he would see what this would mean to us – if there even was an us. This last week I'd thought there might be something there, a spark, a connection, but maybe I'd imagined it.

He swung Eliza out of the boat as if she weighed no more than a feather and carried her off to the boat house to change. I watched him walk away, willing him to turn around and beg me to stay. But of course he didn't. The lump in my throat was threatening to choke me completely. I should be delirious with happiness, jumping for joy. But . . .

No more boat house campaign, no more Driftwood Lodge, no more Jude. Instead a part in a new drama. *The* part in a new Maxine Pearce drama – that was what I'd always dreamed of, wasn't it . . . ?

PART FOUR

The Leading Lady

Chapter 31

It was Saturday, the morning after our public meeting on the beach, and Driftwood Lodge had taken on that by now familiar chaotic atmosphere that was changeover day.

Campion Carmichael's taxi had been booked to take him to the train station. He'd been in the house a few minutes ago to use the landline, yelling down the phone to some poor individual about something being ridiculous and appalling and he'd better see some action or else. Good riddance, I thought, leaning on the old stone wall and letting the steam from my tea warm my face.

I still hadn't got to the bottom of why he wanted our lifeboat house. *The* lifeboat house, I reminded myself. Not mine. I'd be leaving Brightside Cove soon . . .

Anyway, back to the job in hand. A party of seven would-be mermaids, courtesy of Eliza's new booming business, was arriving just after lunch; they would be staying in Penguin's Pad and Kittiwake's Cabin. It was only for a night, but the beds would all need changing and the cottages cleaning and I was here on my own at the moment.

Theo and Kate had disappeared at dawn to visit her parents in Birmingham to impart the good news that Team Fletcher was very much game-on and to show them the plans that Theo had drawn up to convert the garages into two studios. Meanwhile, a chimneysweep was blasting approximately one hundred years' worth of soot out of

Driftwood Lodge's chimneys after Theo had admitted defeat and abandoned the job. Archie had gone to fetch Molly, who was on laundry duty for today's changeovers, and I was attempting to tidy up.

The place was a mess and so was I, although most of my mess was internal and revolved around my career, my love life (ha), the new clues I'd picked up about the possible whereabouts of my father, and what to do about my promise to help Jude save the lifeboat house. Other than that my life was totally simple, not a care in the world . . .

The phone in the hall rang, breaking into my thoughts.

'Brightside Holidays, Nina speaking.'

'Hi, this is Sebastian.'

It was so unexpected that for a moment I was speechless.

'Sebastian Nichols, the agent?'

'Hello.' I collected myself rapidly. 'I hadn't forgotten.'

I also hadn't forgotten our last conversation. The one where I'd slammed the phone down shortly after informing him that he'd be the last person I'd turn to if I needed advice or something along those lines, which was kind of a shame, because I could really do with picking his brains now.

'Sooo,' he said. 'I thought it was time for a catch-up.'

He started blabbing on about what an incredible coincidence it was that Maxine and Campion were staying at Driftwood Lodge and how he'd like to be a fly on the wall, quizzing me as to how that had transpired. He obviously had no idea about their fling years ago and I began to wonder where this was leading. At that moment, the chimneysweep's assistant opened the living-room door and a cyclone of soot swirled out into the hall.

'Sorry, Miss,' he yelped, slamming it again.

'So you're well?' Sebastian asked.

'I'm knee deep in soot, actually,' I replied, looking at the floor miserably.

Damn. The hall had been one of the only remaining clear areas. The kitchen was heaped with washing-up which I'd promised to do last night so that Kate and Theo could have an early night. As it turned out I'd stayed up late in Archie's cottage listening to how brave Ellis had been when he'd had three stitches to mend his cut foot and what an amazing woman Molly was and how Archie was only now beginning to realize how much he'd missed out on due to being such a workaholic.

'Soot? Is that a euphemism?' Sebastian asked hesitantly.

'If only. What can I do for you?'

'I owe you an apology. Several, actually.'

'I'm listening.' I tucked the phone under my chin and picked my way across the layer of soot to the kitchen.

'I watched the last few episodes of *Victory Road*, the ones where the storyline about you and the policeman were being developed. You created magic in those scenes, Nina. True magic. You shone. I made a big mistake not fighting for you to keep the part in *Mary Queen of Scots*. So I apologize for that and I apologize for begging the casting director to squeeze Cecily Carmichael into the casting session at the last minute. The thing is, I was dazzled, caught in her spotlight, and I made a severe error of judgement.'

Magic. He said I created magic.

I tackled the debris on the kitchen table while he waffled on about how he'd been desperate to secure Cecily on his books and she'd been desperate to appear in a period drama so he'd hooked her up with the casting director, Oscar, on the premise that she'd join Sebastian Nichols Talent if she was successful. It turned out Oscar owed her father a favour, so that was how she got the job.

So Cecily didn't have star quality after all, she simply had an influential father. Lucky her. On balance I think I'd rather not have a father than one like Campion. Not that I was bothered any more. The whole *Mary Queen of Scots* thing was water under the bridge now. I was glad I hadn't got the part, I thought, looking out to see two ducks splashing in a corner of the courtyard happily. I'd have missed all this. I'd never have come here, helped Theo get back together with

Kate, set the holiday cottage business up, met Eliza, Molly or . . . Jude. I jolted myself out of my reverie, catching the tail end of Sebastian's monologue.

'. . . my inferiority complex, I suppose,' he concluded miserably.

'Your *what*?' I spluttered, just about managing not to laugh. Sebastian had to be one of the most self-assured men I'd ever met.

There was an awkward silence down the line.

'I created a persona for myself when I came to London. I come from Blackpool. My mum and dad run a newsagent's shop. The only press contacts they have is the man who drops the newspapers off at six a.m. I've had to fight every step of the way to get where I have in the entertainment industry. When Cecily entered my orbit, I saw it as a way of climbing up another rung on the ladder of who-knows-who.'

'But I'm sure you said . . . I thought . . . ?'

'You thought I was a posh boy with a public-school background?' He sighed heavily. 'It's an illusion. It's probably my own insecurities but I was convinced that no one would want an agent who'd spent their Saturdays delivering newspapers instead of competing in some sort of posh sports event at public school. So I pretended. It's all rather tiring after a while. Sometimes all I want to do is escape back up north and have fish and chips on the pier and a pint of bitter at the Pump and Truncheon with my dad. I don't even know why I'm telling you this. The entertainment industry thrives under a thick veneer of glamour; I've completely blown mine now.'

And I never had one, I thought, scraping food into the bin and loading plates into the dishwasher.

'You deserve an Oscar,' I said. 'I'd never have guessed. And I'm much more impressed by what you've achieved now I know the truth. I think a trip to your parents sounds wonderful and I bet they couldn't be more proud of their son. And as for being a newspaper boy, I once read an article that said having a paper round as a child is one of the most valued jobs on anyone's CV.'

'Really?' he said, sounding brighter.

'Definitely. It takes discipline, dedication and commitment to do a crap job like that.'

'Thanks for saying that.' He paused. 'Anyway, back to Cecily. She's been dropped from *Mary Queen of Scots*. Officially they've written her out of it. But we all know the truth: she's been axed. Too many mistakes, too many retakes, too many demands and – confidentially – too little talent.'

'Oh poor thing,' I said. Despite our history, I did feel for her; she must be gutted.

'And her father has been on the phone this morning, demanding explanations, telling me to insist Cecily is put back in the show. Or else.'

That explained the conversation I'd overheard in the garden earlier. It must have been Sebastian on the other end of the line. I'd assumed Mr Carmichael was on the phone to the auctioneers complaining about the council's decision to hear our proposal. But he wasn't. Phew.

'Oh that's good!' I exclaimed.

'Hardly,' Sebastian said, confused. 'Of course, I'll make the right noises, but I don't hold out much hope. Cecily is more suited to reality TV than drama. I hate to ask, but if you get any chance to point this out to him, I'd be very grateful.'

I made a harrumphing sound. 'I'm the last person he'd listen to.'

I briefly told him about the lifeboat house incident, which had ended with Campion being kicked in the privates by an old lady, laughed at by a mermaid and insulted by the world's grumpiest shopkeeper.

'No wonder he's in such a foul mood,' he said miserably. 'Oh well, worth a try. Anyway, enough about my problems, as well as apologizing, I called to congratulate you. Is it true you've been offered a starring role in a new drama with Maxine Pearce?'

'Gosh, word does travel fast. She only offered me the part yesterday.'

'Congratulations. I heard the rumour this morning. You must be thrilled. I know actors who'd give a kidney to work with her. I don't suppose—' He cleared his throat shiftily. 'Might she have a role for Cecily?'

'No,' I said firmly.

'No, quite right.' He sighed. 'I'll have to ease her into panto or something. But back to you: a vicar in the highlands, eh?'

I bit my lip. It was a fantastic opportunity. Everyone said so. Which was why I hadn't dare voice my fears before now.

'I know,' I said quietly. 'Twenty weeks of filming in Scotland. That's a long time to be away from home.'

I was being ridiculous, I knew; I wasn't even sure where home was. Trudy and I had had a long chat in bed last night via Facebook about my room in her flat. She'd fallen hotly in lust with Matt from Harrods' carpet department and was already talking about moving him into my room and peeling off his underlay with her teeth.

'So?' He gave a dry laugh. 'You don't have a husband, or kids, or even a cat, unless I've missed something?'

He was right; I had nothing, no one, nowhere. I swallowed. 'I'm being silly, it's just a big step up from Nurse Elsie, that's all.'

'It's called your big break,' he said kindly. 'Which you deserve. Maxine really wants you. Apparently she has even made script changes to accommodate you. It said on the SparkTV website she's been working on revisions to the script while she's been in Devon.'

This was news to me. 'So it's not all set in stone, then?'

'I guess not. For example, your character, Charlie Mackenzie, was originally born and bred in Scotland. Maxine tweaked it to accommodate your English accent. So you're of Scottish descent but brought up in England.'

'That's a relief.' I could just about keep up a Scottish

accent for a sentence or two but I doubted I could manage an entire series. 'What else do you know?'

'Nothing. But I will say this: get the best deal possible for yourself. It has to be right for you. She has tailored this part *for you*. Take advantage of that before you sign on the dotted line, and if you want me to look over your contract, as a favour, for old times' sake, I will. You're going to be a star, Nina, and I'm very proud.'

I ended the call on a high after that, his words ringing in my ears. If I was going to be a star, perhaps 'T', the mystery flowers sender, would be in touch again soon?

By eleven o'clock, Campion Carmichael had gone. Nobody had been sad to see him go, although we'd all like to have heard more about his plans for the boat house. Maxine had tried to wheedle it out of him, breaking off from her work briefly to watch him leave. The two of them had formed a truce of sorts and although she said they'd never be more than nodding acquaintances, she admitted to feeling glad she'd been able to lay old ghosts to rest. She'd disappeared back inside then with a flap of her cardigan and a request not to be disturbed.

Molly and Archie had been and gone with the laundry. The cottages were sparkling again and ready for the guests who'd be here in an hour or so. Maxine had graciously moved from our largest cottage, Penguin's Pad, to Beaver's Barn to give them more room and Archie had put his things in the back of his car, secretly hoping to wangle a night at Molly's.

'No chance,' Molly had murmured to me when she spotted his holdall tucked behind the driver's seat of the Range Rover. 'Ellis is at home tonight. Archie is my first dabble since Steve, I can do without an audience.'

'I'll make up the sofa for him,' I'd whispered back, thrilled that Archie had got as far as being dubbed a dabble by the feisty Molly.

The chimneysweeps had done a sterling job of cleaning

up their mess and Driftwood Lodge was peaceful and soot-free once again. I baked some scones for the guests' afternoon tea and called at Maxine's new home, Beaver's Barn, to deliver some. She was on the phone doing some sort of complicated three-way conference call, which was a shame; I was at a loose end. I really wanted company and if I was being honest, the person whose company I really craved was Jude's. Would it look really desperate if I hung around on the beach for a while in the hope of bumping into him? What the hell, I thought, I'm an actress, I could feign surprise if required.

I kept my fingers crossed as I headed down to the beach along the zigzag path that cut through the gorse and I was rewarded with the sight of Mabel cavorting in the waves. I skirted the rocks, looking for Jude, and headed to the water's edge and within seconds Mabel had homed in on me as a potential playmate and dropped a plastic bottle at my feet.

I ruffled her ears before throwing the bottle into the air and laughed as her eager paws kicked up wet sand at me.

'Nina!'

I felt my heart twang; jogging towards me was Jude.

'Hey! This is a nice surprise,' I said. See: fantastic actress.

'Look what fell into my possession!' He held up a large metal object and came to a panting halt in front of me, his eyes shining with mischief.

'Ned gave you the key to the boat shed?'

'Yep, shall we?'

We fell into step and headed across the sand. Ned had given Jude the key yesterday so he could take some photos of the interior to get some trade estimates on the cost of renovations.

'On the strict understanding that I don't do anything he wouldn't do once those doors are shut,' Jude waggled his eyebrows. 'Which judging by the colour Nora's cheeks turned, doesn't rule much out.'

A tiny bolt of lust shot through me. 'Naughty man,' I murmured vaguely.

Mabel flew past us, showering us with salt water, and leapt into the sea to catch the bottle that one of a group of surfers had thrown for her.

'She's having a whale of a time,' I laughed.

'We're lucky here,' Jude said. 'She can run free on this beach all year round; most of the others insist on dogs being on leads from May to September.'

'I suppose if tourism expanded in Brightside Cove then that rule might come in here too?'

'I guess. Shame, though.' He paused and cast his eyes across the bay. 'This beach is probably my favourite place in the world and it's certainly Mabel's.'

I grinned at him. 'Mine too.'

It was true. Whatever came next in my life, I felt like Brightside Cove would always hold a special place in my heart. The wide blue sky, the moody sea, the golden sand, the scenery, but mostly the people and specifically this person. As if in agreement, Mabel flopped down on the slipway beside us with a contented sigh. She rested her chin on her paws and gazed adoringly at Jude as he unlocked the double doors at the front of the boat house. He turned to look out at the water. 'It would be awful if our lives had to change to accommodate people who only stay for a short time and then leave.'

There was an undertone in his voice that made me look up at him. His hazel eyes shifted from the horizon to me.

'Not all visitors are bad news, though, surely?' I said, fluttering my eyelashes shamelessly.

'Not all.' He smiled and tucked a strand of my hair behind my ear in a tender gesture. 'Some of them are very good news. But your Mr Carmichael isn't one of them.'

'He's not *mine*,' I said quickly. Although I did feel responsible for inflicting him on Brightside Cove.

Jude stepped aside to let me in. The fishy smell wasn't as bad today. Or perhaps I'd just got acclimatized to it. Jude propped both doors open and then went to the far end of the boat house and opened the other set too. The space instantly flooded with light and a fresh breeze whistled through it, ruffling Mabel's fur.

I sat at the bottom of the metal steps while Jude took his phone out and began to take pictures.

'Imagine waking up to that,' he marvelled, staring at the view of the slipway and the retreating tide.

'Imagine,' I purred, dragging my eyes away from his neat bum in his jeans.

He turned to examine the louvre windows along each side. 'We could replace all these panels with glass, change the double doors to triple-glazed sliding doors and—'

'Move in?' I suggested with a glint in my eye. 'It would make a lovely—' I interrupted myself with a gasp. *'Bolt hole!* That was how Mr Carmichael described it. He said he'd like a bolt hole by the sea. I bet that's what he's planning.'

'Excellent,' Jude said smugly. 'He'd never get planning permission so close to the water. He'd certainly never get insurance.'

'Ah, then that can't be it,' I said, deflated. 'He's too smart to buy something that he couldn't use.'

'So what is he up to?'

The glossy brochure I'd spotted yesterday on the steps was still there, which gave me an idea. I picked it up and turned it over to read the phone number on the back.

'Only one way to find out,' I said, already tapping in the number.

He cocked one eyebrow dubiously but nonetheless squashed on the step beside me to listen in. The heat of his body against mine did nothing to quell my already racing heart.

'It's ringing,' I whispered, 'wish me luck.'

'Good luck,' he murmured, giving me such a wide smile that a dimple appeared in his cheek.

We looked at each other, listening to the ringing tone and my eyes roamed his handsome face, from his long amber lashes to the stubble on his strong chin, to the faint scar on his head, a reminder to me of Jude's rocky start in life. I could feel his breath on my cheek and smell his heavenly scent, and I thought how much I'd like to kiss him and feel his arms around me.

'Good afternoon, Mernick's, how may I direct your call?' announced a perky voice.

'Oh hello.' I snapped out of my daydream and put on a breathy high-pitched voice. 'So sorry to bother you but my father wanted to ask a question regarding planning permission for the Brightside Cove lifeboat house?'

'Please hold the line while I connect you.'

'Mernick,' growled a deep voice.

Mr Mernick sounded like he started his day by gargling with fish hooks. Jude's eyes widened and I felt a prickle of perspiration on my top lip.

'Hi there, my father, Campion Carmichael, asked me to call with a query.'

'Ah, yes?' The voice on the other end brightened considerably. 'Fire away.'

'It's about planning requirements, oh,' I said with a tinkly laugh, 'I've forgotten what he said to ask exactly, silly me, but do you think he'll have any problems?'

'For an art gallery? Shouldn't think so. The council are practically falling over themselves to get shot of the place, they'll be snapping your father's hand off.'

Jude and I stared at each other. So that was what Mr Carmichael was up to. Of course, it made total sense. And, I thought for one disloyal millisecond, it would be a beautiful space for selling art.

'Hello? Are you still there?'

'Yes, thank you so much, he'll be so relieved to hear that.'

'Excellent, excellent, do send him my regards, er, I didn't catch your name, dear?'

'Oh, got to go, Mr Mernick, call coming through from my father, I'll remember you to him.'

I stabbed the end call button and smiled at Jude, who smiled grimly back.

'An art gallery? None of the local people who turned up yesterday will see any benefit from that.'

He stood and closed the doors at the back of the shed; he looked totally downcast.

'Hey,' I said, feeling the weight of his disappointment as if it was my own. 'At least we know what we're up against. Knowledge is power, and all that.'

'But if Mernick's right and the council is as keen as he says they are to get rid of the boat house, I don't see how we can win.'

He slung an arm casually around my shoulders as he led me to the doors and I went all tingly at the touch of his skin. The two of us walked out and I waited while Jude pulled both doors closed and turned the big old key in the lock. Mabel jumped to her feet and pushed her wet nose into my hand.

Until that moment I'd been wrangling with what to do about next Friday: fly to Scotland with Maxine or stay and help Jude. Now my decision was easy, he and I were in this together.

'Of course we can win,' I insisted. 'They haven't heard our proposal yet. We'll blow their socks off.'

His eyes searched mine. 'But you won't be here. Your boss wants you in Scotland.'

'I *will* be here,' I blurted out.

He passed a hand over his hair and puffed out his cheeks.

'I'm touched, truly, but I can't allow you to jeopardize your career for this.'

I tilted my chin up. 'I don't remember asking for your permission.'

His lips tweaked into a smile and I stepped closer and pulled him in for a hug.

I was going to be in so much trouble with Maxine. But as his arms went around me and I felt his warm hands on my spine, frankly, I didn't give a damn.

Chapter 32

The following afternoon, after our overnight guests had been and gone, I wandered down to the village to see Eliza. It was Sunday and the Mermaid Gift and Gallery in theory should have been closed, but she'd asked me to give her a hand with something and so, intrigued and feeling like a gooseberry after Archie had gone out with Molly leaving me with Kate and Theo, who were back from Birmingham, I was happy to oblige.

There were big SALE banners plastered across the shop windows, and inside more red and white signs fluttered from the ceiling. The seascape pictures had been taken off the back wall and sat in piles here and there. Several rotating stands housing everything from postcards to personalized pens (no Ninas, as usual, I'd checked) were pushed into the corner by the counter and Eliza was on her knees stripping animals made from shells, beads and rather too much glue from a shelf and stacking them carefully in a box.

'Can I interest you in a shell cat? Or maybe a mouse?' She held one up after the other. 'Seventy-five per cent off?'

'Um.' I pulled an unconvinced face.

'Exactly.' She sat back on her heels. 'Which is why I'm having a mammoth revamp.'

She handed me a box, pointed me in the direction of a display of cork coasters and placemats illustrated with sea birds of Britain, and told me to get packing.

'So what's the plan?' I grimaced at a particularly mean-looking cormorant on a placemat and shoved it in the box.

'I'm doing what I should have done years ago.'

'You're not closing down?' I said, aghast. I looked around at the little shop and all its treasures. That would be awful. But then if Campion Carmichael opened a gallery . . .

'Over my dead body,' I muttered aloud inadvertently. He wasn't opening a gallery. Full stop.

Eliza giggled. 'No need to panic! The Tylers have run a gift shop here for decades, course I'm not closing down.'

She got up and put the kettle on.

'I inherited this shop from Mum and apart from a name change and adding a few new lines, it's still the cute little gift shop it's always been. Now it's finally dawned on me that I can run it my way. I can't remember the last time I sold one of these shell animals. But the nautical bunting and the candles and the driftwood sculptures are really popular. So I'm taking the 80:20 rule and applying it to my business.'

I looked blankly at her.

'Twenty per cent of my products generate eighty per cent of my profit.' She shrugged. 'So I ditch the non-profitable stuff and make some more room.'

'Cor,' I said, impressed. 'One encounter with a researcher from *Dragons' Den* and you know all the jargon. You'll be wearing power suits and heels next.'

Eliza clanked mugs and let out such a long and heartfelt sigh that her shoulders dropped a full ten inches. 'Don't say the DD words. Not today. Let's just concentrate on what's in these four walls, it's much less scary.'

'Okay.'

I looked around the shop at the chaos that Eliza had created since I was last in here. In the space of a week, Eliza had entertained Sapphire and her hens, been plastered on the pages of a newspaper, featured on morning telly and had received business offers from around the country. No wonder she was scared.

'It's all moving a bit fast, isn't it?' I sidled up to her.

'It's mental.' Eliza's turquoise eyes blinked at me. 'Since the whole *Mermaids of Mayfair* stuff, my feet haven't touched the ground.'

'Sounds ideal,' I said, nudging her, to cheer her up. 'For a mermaid.'

'Ha. Very good.' She handed me a cup of green liquid that smelled vaguely of wee. 'Kelp tea, also ideal for a mermaid.'

I sipped it and almost spat it out. 'Intriguing flavour. Chewing gum?'

I offered her one from a battered pack in my pocket but she declined. The chewing gum reminded me of Freddie Major, my on-screen boyfriend, and his habitually eggy breath; I'd always offered him some before a scene together. He'd rarely accepted, worse luck. Jude, by comparison, tasted delicious: of the sea and the salty air and sexy man . . . A tremor of electricity shot through me. I had to stop doing this, thinking these thoughts. Besides, I'd given Jude the perfect opportunity to kiss me in the boat house yesterday and he hadn't taken it. Just a hug. *Pals*, it seemed, was the extent of his interest in me.

'Nina, your eyes have gone all glassy.' Eliza snapped her fingers to wake me up.

'Sorry. I am now all ears.'

We perched on a couple of packing boxes, cradling our mugs.

'As I was saying, my mermaid business is booming,' she continued, 'I've got offers to open mermaid schools at ten different locations around the coast, a top TV show is trying to throw money at me to go "big". And I've got more radio and magazine interview requests than I can shake my tail at. And all because Brightside Cove has got the first mermaid school of its kind in the UK.'

'You'll be living the dream.' I smiled proudly at her. 'But I'm sensing a *but*.'

She nodded. 'I'm *already* living the dream. Or I thought I was. I thought I'd got everything I wanted right here, that Brightside Cove was where I belonged. Managing this shop, running the mermaid school, it's enough, isn't it? Or do I want more? I don't know.'

'Sometimes people just hit on a brilliant idea and it goes stratospheric. I think that's what has happened with you and your mermaid school. When the world seems scary and dark, people are drawn to things that take them away from reality for a while. Being a mermaid for a day is a crazy and fun idea and exactly what we need right now. Basically, Eliza,' I concluded with a grin, 'you've got the power to cheer up the entire country.'

'I don't want power,' she said, horrified. 'I don't want a mermaid empire; I don't even want loads of money.'

My heart ached for her; she'd been bamboozled by opportunities and couldn't see the wood for the trees, or should that be the coral for the reef?

'Don't panic.' I took a postcard from the rack and picked up a dusty 'Zachariah' personalized pen. 'Here. Make a list of what you *do* want. Forget reality.'

'And then what?' She looked at me, eyes hopeful.

'Then we make it happen,' I said boldly.

'Great,' she breathed, eyes dancing. 'Drink your tea.'

Ten minutes and eight postcards later she was done.

'That was so liberating.' She handed me her efforts and got to her feet. 'More kelp tea?'

'I've had enough, thank you.' *For life*, I added under my breath.

'So,' I said once I'd read through Eliza's wish list, which was actually very sensible and included an indoor studio for her mermaid photo shoots in case of bad weather and employing a Saturday person to free up her time. 'No *Dragons' Den*?'

She bit her lip. 'Do you think I'm boring?'

'You have pink hair and dress as a mermaid. So no.'

'Success for me is having happy customers. Here in Brightside Cove.' She shrugged. 'I enjoyed my moment on TV, but I'm going to leave being famous to you. I'm going to miss you, though, when you go.'

'Loads of time until then,' I said briskly, mentally blocking out the thought. 'Now I'd better go, I promised Kate I'd get her some stock cubes from Jethro for tonight's dinner.'

The last time I'd seen Jethro, he'd been cackling with glee at Campion Carmichael's misfortune on the beach after his old friend Nora had given him a piece of her mind with her right foot and he'd tumbled into the boat. Today he was back to his normal gloomy self, slumped in his deckchair behind the counter.

"'T'aint right at my age,' he grumbled from underneath the peak of his Yankees baseball cap. 'Working on a Sunday. Working at all, come to that.'

'Couldn't you have the afternoon off?' I said, walking up and down the aisles until I found the small dried foods display. Kate had asked for beef stock but she'd have to make do with turkey – probably left over from Christmas. I rubbed the dust off the box to check the date but it had worn away. Christmas in this millennium hopefully.

'Nah, there's always some idiot who needs . . .' He paused to eye up what was in my hand. 'Oxo or something. And if I wasn't open, then what?'

Do without? Drive elsewhere? I thought.

'What *would* make you happy, Jethro?'

'Eighty pence, please.'

I rummaged for the change. 'I mean it, if you only had a month left to live what would you do?'

He harrumphed. 'Easy. Empty the till. Burn the shop. Go on holiday.'

My lips twitched. 'And be a tourist? Heaven forbid.'

'Well.' He scowled at me, dropping my coins into the till and slamming it shut. "'T'aint fair.'

It suddenly crossed my mind that maybe Jethro didn't so much hate the tourists, but hated not being able to take a holiday himself. The shop was open seven days a week. Didn't he ever get a day off?

'Have you never fancied travelling?' I said gently.

He nodded, his rheumy old eyes softening. 'Travelled the world in the army as a steward, I did. Ceylon, Egypt, Italy, even got as far as Vietnam. Best years of my life. Then when I got back here I found the girl I'd been too shy to ask to the dance before I joined up had got married to a fisherman.'

'Nora?'

'Nora,' he echoed wistfully. 'When I realized there was nothing here for me, I was about to set off travelling again. But then Dad got ill. His dying wish was for me to carry on the family business. Never been anywhere since. I've had to sit in this shop watching other people come and go on their holidays, and I've had to see Nora every day too. But Ned's a good man; if she'd had to marry someone other than me, I was glad it was him.'

My heart melted for him. No wonder he was such an old misery guts.

'How long ago did your dad make that wish, Jethro?'

He scratched his head, dislodging his cap and sucked in air. 'Sixty years?'

'Then you've done him proud.' I pulled a small reporter's notepad out of a rack near the till and handed over the one pound fifty to pay for it. 'And I think it might be time to make a few wishes of your own come true. Here, go wild. Make a list of what would make you happy.'

I left him writing a list, just as Eliza had done, and hummed cheerfully to myself on the way back to Driftwood Lodge. That was two people's lives I'd sorted out today, now all I needed to do was to work out how to save the lifeboat house and convince Maxine to let me stay in Brightside Cove long enough to do it . . .

*

Archie's Range Rover was back in the courtyard, presumably having brought Molly with him, as we'd all been invited to dinner by Theo and Kate. I took a detour to Beaver's Barn, and through the window I could see Maxine hunched over the table, working as usual. She'd barely moved in six days.

I knocked on her door and she opened it irritably. 'Yes?'

There was a pair of glasses nestled in her hair and she looked pale and tired. I felt a pang of concern for the long hours she'd been keeping. Most of our previous guests had left here with a bit of colour in their cheeks, a lightness to their step and far fewer wrinkles on their foreheads than they arrived with. If anything, Maxine looked more haggard than when she'd arrived.

'Hi,' I said brightly. 'We wondered if you'd like to join us for Sunday dinner. We're having Yorkshire puddings and roast potatoes and Theo is rigging a laptop up to the TV so we can all look at the pictures from Kate's travels after we've eaten.'

She shuddered. 'Someone else's holiday photographs. Ugh. Is there anything more mind-numbing in the world?'

'I'll take that as a no, then.'

'I'll have the food, though; stick some on a plate and I'll reheat it later. Thank you.' She began to close the door and then hesitated. 'I have to say,' she said, gazing at me steadily, 'I am underwhelmed by your reaction to the news about *The Holy Coast*. I've handed you the biggest part of your career and you've barely batted an eye. I expected you to be beating down my door wanting details. You haven't even asked to see the script. Have I made a mistake by casting you as my leading lady?'

I withered under her scrutiny. She looked so stern and disappointed. As well she might; I was disappointed with myself, to be honest. I had lots to say to her, I just didn't quite have the words in the right order yet.

'You haven't made a mistake, Maxine. It just came as a

shock, that's all, and my plate has had an awful lot on it lately. And I have called by but you've always been on the phone.'

She waved away my excuses with an impatient hand. 'Just don't let me down.'

'I wouldn't.' I shook my head. 'I'm . . . I'm trying not to let anyone down. That's part of the problem.'

She opened the door again fully and leaned against the frame. 'If it's *Victory Road* you're worried about, you can relax,' she said more gently. 'Had an update from the writers. They're definitely killing you off. Nurse Marjorie and Constable Hardy will be canoodling inside your cubicle on the ward when Nurse Elsie flatlines. They might need you for one more scene and that will be that. You'll be free. Perfect timing, I think you'll agree?'

'Absolutely,' I said with a big smile. I pushed aside the small niggle of sadness at not being part of the cast any more; onwards and upwards, and all that. And as Maxine said, she had handed me a much bigger part to take its place. 'It's your last day here tomorrow, so I thought we could—'

She interrupted me with a shimmy of her frizzy hair as she shook her head. 'No it's not. I've booked a few extra days with Theo. Getting so much done here I've decided to stay.'

'Great! Perhaps we can do lunch at The Sea Urchin before you go, and fit in that guided tour I mentioned?'

'All right, but no more boats.'

'Deal.'

Phew. I scampered back to Driftwood Lodge clutching my turkey stock cubes, pleased to have got that out of the way. I had some extra time to come up with a plan, I just hoped it would be enough.

Chapter 33

Kate met me at the door, a bottle of wine in one hand and three glasses in the other. She was wearing one of Theo's shirts, which came down to her knees, leggings and slippers and she was ... glowing, there was no other word for it. Cheeks flushed, eyes bright and a ready laugh, like a child on Christmas morning.

'Goody!' she beamed, pressing red lips to my cheek. 'Now the party can get started.'

'Sorry I've been ages, I ended up doing a life coaching session with Jethro.'

'Good grief, you are honoured,' she said, amused. 'I'm normally sent out with a flea in my ear for asking how he is.'

'He finds it hard to open up,' I said diplomatically.

'Well, he's a man, isn't he?' She rolled her eyes. 'Anyway, no need to apologize. We had a nap this afternoon and Theo is a bit behind with the potatoes. We probably needed the rest.'

'Probably,' I agreed, although privately I thought the noises coming from their bedroom as I'd left hadn't sounded particularly sleep-related. 'And dinner smells delicious.'

'It's the least we can do after all the work you and Molly have done,' she insisted, pushing the door shut with her foot. 'We're very lucky to have you.'

There were absolutely no hard feelings on Kate's part that I had secretly spent a month in her home with her husband.

She was just delighted that he was back on his feet and ready to face the future again. With her.

Absence had definitely worked miracles in their case. I was thrilled for them, although it did make my presence here redundant. I supposed really I should go, perhaps move into Archie's house until we began shooting *The Holy Coast*, or go and clear out my room at Trudy's flat. But something was holding me back, keeping me here. There was something about this place that made my heart soar and I didn't want to leave until I absolutely had to. Something and possibly some*one*.

There was a woof from the kitchen followed by men's laughter and I shot Kate an amused look; I recognized that bark.

'Jude's here with Mabel,' she admitted. 'Theo invited him to even up the numbers. You don't mind, do you?'

'No,' I said, willing my cheeks not to colour. 'The more the merrier.'

'Thought not,' she said with a smirk. 'Come on, we girls are in here.'

She popped the stock cubes into the kitchen and ushered me into the living room while I tried to rake fingers through my wind-tousled hair and wondered whether it would be really obvious if I went upstairs, changed out of my jeans and put on some make-up.

This room was my favourite in the house. I loved the double aspect with views out to the field at the back and across to the cottages at the front. The soft leather sofas were so comfy you could easily sink into them and doze in front of the open fire, which was lit this evening and gave a lovely woody aroma to the room. Mittens was curled up asleep on the back of the sofa, probably hoping not to be spotted by Mabel, and Molly was kneeling at the coffee table poring over sheets of paper. A laptop was propped up next to her with wires trailing to the television, ready for our slideshow later.

'Hi!' Molly looked up from the table. 'Look at these. Brightside Holidays is going large.'

Another one with a loved-up glow to her cheeks. She looked like a different woman: pretty and carefree in a denim miniskirt, high-heeled boots and a clingy T-shirt which showed off her trim figure perfectly.

I accepted a glass of wine from Kate and knelt down beside Molly. The large sheets of paper were plans to convert the garage and one of the outbuildings into accommodation.

'These look amazing!' I said, impressed.

'Theo drew them roughly to show my parents,' Kate blushed prettily. She kicked off her slippers and tucked her feet underneath her on the sofa. 'His way of proving to them that he means business.'

I scanned the pages quickly. With these new units, they'd have six properties to rent out. Theo had been concerned that having only three wouldn't give them enough income. This would make a huge difference. 'And were they impressed?'

'Very. In fact,' Kate's voice caught in her throat and she swallowed, 'Dad said he was proud of him. And that he understood what a difficult time he'd had after Ivy died. All a bit emotional, actually.'

She paused to shove a tissue under her glasses and I squeezed her knee.

'Mum even had a few ideas of her own.' Kate sniffed and blinked her tears away. 'She suggested that we install outside facilities and make room for a small caravan site on the field at the back.'

'Don't your parents have a caravan?' Molly asked.

Kate grinned. 'Yes, we realized straight away that she had an ulterior motive. But Mum and Dad went off into the kitchen for an unsubtle whisper and came back with the proposal that they invest in our business in return for first dibs on a pitch for their caravan.'

'So that would mean you won't have to borrow money for the building work,' I said.

Kate nodded.

'I'd snap their hands off,' Molly said, getting off her knees to peer out of the living-room window at the field. 'I reckon you could get around five or six caravans out there.'

'I suppose so,' said Kate, 'and it would mean that we could get started straight away, rather than wait until we've saved up some money. I just don't want Theo feeling as if he's failed because we can't afford to pay for it ourselves. You know what men are like.'

'Arrogant, pig-headed, cheating knobs ... Sorry, old habits.' Molly looked sheepish. 'Present men excepted, obviously.'

'And you said your dad is proud of Theo; this is their way of showing it, showing their support,' I added, feeling a curious ache in my throat. 'It's a lovely thing to do.'

That was all I ever wanted really: for my dad – and my mum – to be proud of me. I was still at university when Mum died, although I knew she wasn't impressed with my intended choice of career. But Dad ... I couldn't help wondering whether he'd ever seen me on television and, if so, was he proud?

I looked at the flowers that had been sent to me with the mysterious message on the window sill next to Molly. I'd left the card tucked into the top of them, meaning to do something about it. I crossed the room, plucked a couple of faded rose petals off and reread it.

Congratulations on that amazing cliffhanger episode of *Victory Road*. Your dad would be so proud. T x

Would be. Which I took to mean that he hadn't seen it. Perhaps 'T' was his second wife? If so, perhaps I had half-siblings? With the lifeboat house campaign and then being offered this new role, not to mention Archie's reluctance to get involved, I hadn't had the chance to try to track down the sender.

'Another admirer?' Molly said, looking over my shoulder.

'Sort of.' I passed her the card.

'Ooh. This is exciting. Does Archie know?'

I nodded. 'He thinks I should ignore it.'

'As if,' Molly scoffed. 'Mind you, it's not a lot to go on. Do you have any idea who "T" could be?'

'No,' I said with a sigh. 'I wish now I'd checked through all the papers when we'd cleared Mum's house after she died. There wasn't a lot because she'd already had a sort-out. But Archie was in such a rush to get the house on the market so that he could get back to work that there simply wasn't time.'

Kate pushed between us and topped up our glasses. 'He told Theo that he's trying to protect you. He's worried you'll get hurt if you investigate who these flowers are from.'

'For goodness' sake, I'm a big girl now,' I said crossly.

'I think it's sweet that he cares,' said Molly.

'Anyway, talking of admirers, what's the latest?' Kate said in a low voice. She nudged Molly and they both grinned at me. 'Any snogging behind the boat shed?'

'If you mean with Jude, there's nothing to report,' I said, which was mostly the truth.

I wedged the card back into the flowers to deal with later and sank down on the sofa. 'He's made it perfectly plain that he's not bothered one way or another about my imminent departure from Brightside Cove.'

'Don't be fooled,' Kate said wisely, 'as I keep saying, men are masters at keeping their feelings well hidden.'

'And you've got further than any of the other women who've tried to lure him,' Molly put in.

'I haven't tried to lure him!' I protested. Our first kiss in his van had been a joint effort. And that had been our only proper one. Other than that I'd only managed to get the odd hug and peck on the cheek from him.

369

'Molly just means that he's not known as a womanizer,' Kate said with a giggle.

He certainly wasn't. Even when I'd blatantly posed for a kiss outside the boat shed yesterday, all I'd managed to extract from him was a hug before he pulled away and whistled to Mabel.

'None of my business either way,' I said breezily, 'I'll be leaving soon, so there's no point Jude and I starting something we can't finish. It will be much neater that way; no loose ends.'

Say it fast, Nina, and it doesn't seem so bad . . .

'Ahem.' Jude was at the door, a blank expression on his face. 'Theo said to say that dinner is ready.'

Three women with rosy faces trotted meekly into the kitchen in his wake.

Dinner had been delicious and now Molly, Archie, Jude and I were back in the living room slumped on sofas and waiting to make room for the cheeseboard.

Theo was busy dimming the lights and lighting scented candles, while Kate was pouring port into a decanter and rooting out matching crystal glasses from the cupboard. Archie and Molly were thigh to thigh with hands entwined, while I was sitting in the middle of one sofa with Jude beside me. Mabel had her head pressed in between us and now and then our hands touched as we both reached to stroke her ears, sending a pulse of electricity up my arm.

This, I thought, feeling mellow with wine and gazing sleepily into the flames of the fire, was the perfect way to spend a Sunday evening. There was a tray of coffee on the table but I was too comfortable to reach for it. Besides, the sensation of Jude's body against mine kept me exactly where I was.

'She's in heaven,' said Jude, echoing my thoughts, albeit about his beloved pooch.

'So who's ready to see some photos of my travels?' Kate said, taking a big slurp of port.

'By *some*, she means about a thousand,' Theo teased.

'Oi, you.' She smacked his leg as he took the empty space beside me. She picked up the TV remote and selected the correct channel and settled at his feet. A picture appeared on the screen of a sea of penguins dotted over a barren landscape pitted with small holes, most of which had penguins nesting in them.

'Oh, Punta Arenas in Chile!' she gasped. 'Look at the baby penguins!'

'And look at you, Kate!' said Molly. 'You look so cute in your little ski jacket and woolly hat.'

'And so . . . on your own,' Theo added wistfully.

'This was such an amazing experience. Flippin' cold, but amazing,' Kate replied.

'It looks it.' Theo's eyes were glued to the screen as it filled time and time again with selfies of Kate pointing excitedly at baby penguins.

'Aww, baby.' Kate tilted her head back so that he could kiss her. 'I won't go anywhere without you from now on, I promise. I don't even mind if I never leave here again.'

'I'll drink to that,' said Molly, lifting her glass. 'In fact, none of us should leave.'

'I haven't even got a passport,' said Jude, sipping his wine. 'So I'm not going anywhere. I made it to Brightside Cove and liked what I saw, so I stayed.'

My eyes met his and he gently reached for my hand and squeezed it. He smiled at me and in that split second I could see we were on the same wavelength. I knew how he felt because I felt the same, except I couldn't stay, could I?

'I'll be leaving before too long,' I said, with more positivity than I felt. 'I'm sure Theo and Kate will be glad to have the house back to themselves.'

'And I've got to go soon,' said Archie, pulling a face. 'I've got people at work clamouring for answers. I made the mistake of checking my emails when I went to the loo.'

'La la la la la.' Molly put fingers in her ears. 'Not listening.'

'But I'll be back,' he said earnestly, 'that's a promise.'

Archie had offered to drive Molly home and was the only one not drinking. Molly had confided to me that if he played his cards right, he wouldn't be coming back to Driftwood Lodge tonight. He was a great kisser, she'd said, and had a lovely pert bum. At which point I'd reminded her that there were only so many images of my brother I could deal with and thankfully she'd shut up.

'And I bet Nina will be back.' Theo grinned, glancing at Jude's hand over mine.

I smiled but said nothing. Goodness only knew when that would be.

Kate tapped the table to get our attention. 'Look, everyone, this was that yoga week I did in Argentina.'

We all obediently looked at the screen and then simultaneously cocked our heads to the left to work out what we were seeing.

'Good grief,' said Theo on behalf of all of us, his eyes out on stalks. 'That's what I call flexible.'

'Whoops, sorry,' Kate giggled, reaching for the remote to click forward. 'Clothes optional for that session. I was in over my head a bit there.'

'Literally,' Molly said, still gawping.

'Christ,' said Archie, shuddering, 'I've only just recovered from seeing my own sister naked on TV in *Silent Witness*.'

'Nina!' Jude's eyes glinted with mirth. 'I didn't realize you were that sort of actress.'

I could feel him shaking with laughter beside me.

'It was for the BBC,' I protested. 'All above board.'

'I'm glad you're not going to be back to London for this new show, Neen,' said Archie, helping himself to coffee.

No, I thought miserably, just the opposite end of the British Isles.

'You look like a washed-out, watercolour version of yourself when you're there,' he added, pouring a splash of milk into his cup.

'Gee thanks,' I said, amused. 'And what do I look like here?'

He thought about that for a moment. 'A big pollock.'

Molly snorted. 'You can't describe your sister like that.'

Archie's eyebrows leapt up, feigning innocence. 'I meant that she's bright and bold here, that's all. Alive.'

'A backhanded compliment but I'll take it,' I said.

'What about me?' Molly asked. 'What sort of painting am I?'

'Something Pre-Raphaelite: all gorgeous and goddess-like.'

'Great,' I laughed. 'She gets gorgeous goddess and I get Pollock, which we all know you only chose because of what it rhymes with.'

Everyone laughed.

'I think you look beautiful,' Jude murmured. The candle-light caught the flecks of amber in his eyes and my stomach swooped.

'Thank you,' I replied softly. 'You're not so bad yourself.'

'Another toast.' Kate was looking a bit witch-like now, with port-stained lips. She raised a glass precariously. 'Congratulations to Nina. And to your big part!'

We all raised our glasses obediently.

'Do you feel like you've made it, Nina, like this is definitely your living?' said Molly.

I shook my head. 'Ask me again in a year; perhaps I'll feel more secure.'

'You could be in Hollywood by then.' She beamed proudly. 'What do you reckon, Jude?'

'I hope so,' he said quietly.

My heart lurched. 'You can't wait to get rid of me, can you?' I said. My voice sounded more shrill than I'd intended.

'That came out wrong.' He scratched Mabel's head, avoiding my eye. 'I just meant—'

Theo cleared his throat deliberately to get our attention. Kate's eyes had closed, her head tucked into his neck, her mouth open and snoring lightly.

'I think perhaps we'll save the rest of the pictures for another day,' Theo whispered. 'Our intrepid explorer appears to have left for the Land of Nod.'

'No!' Kate's eyes popped open with a start. 'No, not yet, there's just one more I have to show you; I took it especially for you, Archie. And you, Nina,' she said.

'Go on then,' Theo said, laughing softly. He put the TV remote back in her hand.

'It's right near the end.' She slipped off his knee and crawled over to the laptop. 'Are you ready, you two? I found this in Recife, in Brazil. Wait till you see this. Ta dah!'

For a split second, nobody spoke. I gasped and I heard Archie swear under his breath.

A picture had been taken from the street at night-time. It was of some sort of restaurant or bar: a long white flat-roofed place, open on two of its sides and with white canvas awnings stretching out above the pavements, lit with hundreds of tiny lights. Under the awnings were clusters of tables and chairs, many of them packed with customers. Lots of men but plenty of glamorous women in extravagant dresses. But the most eye-catching feature was the name that ran along the length of one side: 'Penhaligon's'.

'What are the chances of that!' Jude grinned at me. 'You Penhaligons get everywhere.'

'And you said it was a Cornish name, Molly!' I said. My pulse was thundering at my temples.

'It's more Cornish than Brazilian, that's for sure.'

'I heard about this club from a couple of men I met and thought, Ooh, I must take a picture to show Archie,' Kate beamed.

'A couple of men, eh?' Theo commented archly.

'No need to be jealous, darling,' she laughed, 'when I say couple, I *mean* couple.'

374

Archie jumped up, phone in hand. His face was pale and his skin looked clammy. 'I'm so sorry, folks, I'm going to have to go.'

'What? Where?' said Molly.

'Home. Exeter. Can't be helped.' He pressed a hurried kiss to her cheek and darted to the door.

'But I thought you were giving me a lift home,' she argued.

Archie hesitated. 'I'm sorry, Molly.' He took a twenty-pound note out of his wallet and held it out to her. 'I'll pay for a taxi.'

She glared at him. 'I do not want your money.'

He sighed and left it on the table. 'I really am sorry, but something has come up. Bye.'

Molly looked heartbroken. I was furious with him; he was behaving like the old Archie, throwing money at a problem to make it go away. I dashed after him and managed to grab his sleeve as he yanked open the front door. 'Archie, what is it?'

'Nothing. It's fine,' he said, looking anything but fine.

I cocked an eyebrow. 'You're a terrible actor. Is it something to do with that picture?'

'No, no, honestly.' He put a hand on my arm. 'I just had an emergency email; nothing I can't handle. Just a work thing, I really have to get back.'

I leaned on the doorframe, watching as his Range Rover sped away and wondering why he'd lied to me. Over my shoulder the screen still showed the picture of Penhaligon's in Brazil. Something had caused him to run, that much was obvious. And I didn't care that he didn't want to talk about it, one way or another, I was going to winkle it out of him.

Chapter 34

Well, that was a night to remember, I thought next morning as I staggered downstairs for coffee. I was aching in places I'd never ached before and I'd hardly got a wink of sleep. I spooned coffee into two cups, added boiling water and milk and carried them back upstairs to my room.

The party had broken up after Archie left. Kate was only half awake anyway and Theo almost had to carry her up to bed. Despite some massive and toe-curlingly embarrassing hints from Molly that Jude should stay and keep me company, he and Mabel set off on the long walk home to Thymeford. And after I'd uncurled my toes, Molly and I had cleared up. She was understandably frustrated that Archie had left so abruptly. My brother's behaviour had been very odd, but I knew him well enough to know that he must have had his reasons for leaving. Molly, on the other hand, wasn't so easily pacified.

In the end I persuaded her to stay the night and share my double bed. Ellis was at his dad's because it was a bank holiday weekend and so Molly didn't have to be home until lunchtime. She cheered up once we'd taken mugs of hot chocolate and marshmallows up to bed with us. She borrowed some of my pyjamas and we sat up sipping our drinks and telling each other funny stories from our teenage years until eventually we settled down to sleep. Correction – she slept; I spent most of the night dodging her long limbs. My back ached from clinging to the edge of the bed and I felt like I was covered in bruises.

I looked at her now, stretching said lethal weapons above her head and brushing her red hair from her face.

'Morning, sleeping beauty.' I set her mug down at her side of the bed and rubbed my shin. For the first time, I actually had some sympathy with her ex-husband; it had been like sleeping with a starfish.

'I've been thinking,' were her first words. 'How *are* you and Jude actually going to save the lifeboat house?'

I drew back the curtains, folded my arms and swept my gaze from the right – where I could just make out Nora pegging out washing in the garden of the little yellow cottage – to the left across the cove where the pointed roof of the lifeboat house was just visible. Just looking at this view made my heart fill up.

'I don't know, Molly,' I said pensively. 'I think we're going to have to try to make the lady from the council fall in love with it as much as us.'

Her question came back to me later that morning after she'd left with Theo, who'd offered to drop her home. How *were* we going to prevent the boat house from being auctioned off? It was all very well talking about it, but we only had four days; we needed action. I called Jude who answered on the first ring, laughing that he'd been in the process of dialling my number to see if I was free for lunch.

We met at The Sea Urchin at one. The first day of May had arrived and with it not only an ice-cream van at the top of the steps down to the beach, but also the first properly warm day of the year. We ordered ciabattas at the busy bar and took our drinks on to the terrace where a thick glass screen protected us from the worst of the sea breeze. There was a big dish of water for dogs, and Mabel stopped to lap at it gratefully.

Jude had already developed a bit of a tan: his cheeks were

bronzed, which added to his healthy rugged good looks. He could give any of the leading men I'd ever met on set a run for their money, I thought approvingly as he gallantly pulled out a chair for me.

'My plan is to follow Maxine up to Scotland a day later,' I explained once our food had arrived and we'd managed to persuade Mabel to take her paws off the table. 'That way I can still come with you to see the council.'

Jude looked unsure. 'She seemed adamant that you'd have to leave before then.'

'Yes, well,' I said, not meeting his eye, 'I can be adamant too. Anyway, leave that with me. The main thing is to work out what we are going to say that will convince Katrina Berry to let the boat house stay in the hands of Brightside Cove.'

He pulled a folded sheet of paper out of his jacket pocket and laid it on the table. 'A bit rough, but these are my initial thoughts.'

'A twenty-year lease from the council to a charity set up as Brightside Cove Community?' I cut into my ciabatta: steak and Devon blue cheese with rocket. Mabel, who had been banished to a respectful distance edged a bit closer, licking her lips. 'Sounds good for us, but not very profitable for the council.'

'It was your brother's idea.' Jude looked around for a waiter and while he was distracted I slipped a piece of steak under the table to the dog.

'Can I have some mayonnaise please?' he said to Raquel the landlady when she came over, adding to me, 'I saw that.'

Mabel whined comically and lay down between us, tucking her nose under her paws as if to say, 'Busted.' We both laughed.

'Hey, who's the actress here?' I patted Mabel on the head and smiled at Jude. 'It's that pleading look; I find it impossible to deny her anything.'

'I'm the same,' he admitted. 'Dark brown eyes like melted chocolate – irresistible.'

He held my gaze and I caught myself feeling jealous of a dog.

'As I was saying,' he said, plunging a skinny fry into a pile of mayonnaise, 'Archie thinks that the council might see the long-term benefits of keeping the boat house themselves as their own asset if we can persuade them that we'll earn enough via bookings to pay them an annual rent.'

'Would they earn more in the long run from renting it to us than selling it?'

Jude sucked in through his teeth. 'Hard to know what it will fetch at auction. But an ex lifeboat station not dissimilar to ours was sold a couple of years ago for a hundred thousand pounds.'

I pulled a face. 'Gosh, for a tiny building, that's an awful lot of money.'

He nodded gravely. 'As any property tycoon will tell you, the three most important factors with property are location, location, location.'

We swivelled in our chairs to scan the length of the cove to where the little boat house reigned over the bay at the far end.

'And that location takes some beating,' I said.

'Agreed.' He leaned forward conspiratorially. 'But if anyone asks, it's draughty, prone to flooding and hard to access, got it?'

'Got it.' I tapped the side of my nose. 'So if we could offer to pay an annual rent of, say, five thousand pounds, in twenty years they'd have their hundred thousand and still own the building?'

'That's the idea.'

I gave him a dubious look. 'I know which I'd prefer: a bird in the hand, and all that . . .'

'It's risky,' Jude agreed. 'But it's all we've got. Archie suggested crowdfunding to raise the whole amount. He even offered to stick in the first ten thousand, but much as I appreciate the gesture, we don't have time to raise that sort of money.'

My heart squeezed for my brother, what a generous thing to do, especially at a time when his own profits were suffering from being undercut by a competitor. 'Good old Archie.'

'He's got a good head for business,' Jude agreed. 'He knows money talks.'

'Not sure Molly would say the same,' I said wryly, remembering the look of disgust on her face last night when Archie tried to give her cash for a taxi.

Jude laughed, swallowing the last mouthful of his chicken ciabatta. 'She's a feisty one, Molly. You should hear her on the side-lines cheering Ellis on at football training.'

'I can imagine.' I grinned and then thought of how happy Archie had been in her company these last few days. I sighed. 'And she and Archie were getting along so well too.'

There was a small blob of mayonnaise on his chin and I had a sudden flashback to the breakfast we'd shared in his van and me wiping ketchup from exactly the same place. It was the moment that prompted our first kiss.

I picked up my napkin. 'Come here, messy boy,' I said, wiping away the mayo.

He caught my hand, his eyes flashing with an emotion I couldn't quite read; I felt a warm squirming feeling in my stomach.

'Nina, I think, I hope, that you and I were getting on well too. The thing is . . .' He paused, casting his eyes down as if gathering strength.

Were. Past tense. My ears pricked up at the change in his tone.

'Yes?' I held my breath.

He looked at me again and this time there was no mistaking the emotion in his gaze: a mix of sadness and regret. 'I like you. I like you a lot.'

'But I'm leaving Brightside Cove, yes I know,' I blurted out impatiently. 'I thought that at first, too. But I'm here now. Can't we just enjoy each other's company and see where it leads? After all, I won't be filming in Scotland for ever and anyway we can visit each other and—'

'It's five hundred miles away,' he said softly. 'Not exactly a weekend jaunt.'

He'd looked it up. I felt a swoop of hope; that had to mean something.

'That's nothing,' I joked, 'even the Proclaimers would walk that far. Remember the song? I would walk—'

'Nina,' he said, quietly interrupting my terrible rendition of the song, 'it's not about the distance.'

'Oh. Right.' I gulped. That must mean it was about me. He liked me enough to be pals, but nothing more. I thought I'd never hated a word more. *Pals.*

He raked a hand through his hair self-consciously.

'It's about me. You know what my childhood was like, my parents, my particularly loving father. And the thing is . . .' He raised his head up and looked at the sky, swallowing hard. 'I am them. They are part of me. It's DNA, plain and simple. I might no longer live with them, but I can't forget where I come from. I can't get away from the truth. And the fact is I'm not good enough for you. I can't allow myself to get close to you, because I daren't. You know the saying: an apple doesn't fall far from the tree? Well what if, deep down, I'm rotten to the core? I thought I should tell you because . . .' He swallowed. 'Sometimes, I get the feeling you want more from me and I want you to understand why I can't give it.'

For a moment I was speechless. Of all the scenarios I'd envisaged, this one hadn't even occurred to me. I stared at him incredulously. Did he really think that about himself?

'My father didn't hang around long enough for me to find out what characteristics he and I might share,' I said softly, 'but I don't let that worry me, I am me, I am who I choose to be. And so are you. And Jude, I have to tell you the person you chose to be is easily the most selfless, kind-hearted and intrinsically *good* man I have ever met.'

He gave a laugh of surprise. 'Is that really how you see me?'

'Yes! And it would be a privilege for any woman to be loved by you. Put your fears aside my friend and be proud of who you are.'

'You know, sometimes I do feel proud.' He shook his head bashfully. 'I think I turned out well, all things considered. I just . . . A *privilege*, you said?' He was laughing now.

I eyed him cheekily. 'You can compliment me now, if you like?'

He cupped a hand to my face. 'Easy: you're beautiful, sparkly, slightly crazy . . .' He sighed. 'But when this new TV show takes off with you as the lead actress, you'll be properly famous. You'll be recognized wherever you go. I'm no match for that. I'm just an ordinary guy.'

I shrugged. 'And I'm an ordinary girl. Landing a role like this is my dream, but I'll still be me.'

I thought about what Big Dave had said. How he'd had his head turned by fame. I was determined not to be like that. In fact, I was confident that I wouldn't be. Even my brush with fame a month ago had had me running to escape the media glare.

His eyes burned with such an intensity that I felt my face heat up and then he gave me that lopsided smile, the one that made my insides flip and we leaned towards each other and kissed, a slow and tender kiss, our lips, our hearts and our bodies connecting for a few sweet seconds until we felt the presence of a third person hovering nearby.

Whoever it was, Mabel approved because she jumped to her feet, tail wagging enthusiastically. We broke apart to see Archie shifting nervously from foot to foot.

'Archie, where did you spring from?' I said a bit sharply, to cover my embarrassment.

He grinned.

'Thanks for the warm greeting. Sorry, mate,' said Archie, resting a brotherly hand on Jude's shoulder. 'Looks like I couldn't have picked a worse time to interrupt.'

'Not at all,' Jude countered, pulling Mabel off Archie's leg. 'Pull up a chair, come and join us, we've been talking about plans for the boat house.'

'Is that what you were doing? I see.' Archie gave me another look and I let out a guilty laugh.

'Oh, stop,' I protested. 'Sit down and have a drink with us.'

Archie held his palms up.

'I'd better not.' His skin was so pale in comparison to Jude's and his eyes had dark circles underneath. He was wearing the same clothes he'd been in yesterday, crumpled now as if he'd slept in them, if in fact he'd been to bed at all. My mouth went dry.

'Is something wrong?'

'Possibly.' My brother stared at me and rubbed a weary hand over his eyes, the same sea green as mine. 'I don't know. I don't know what to think any more.'

Jude got to his feet. 'Sit,' he said, pressing Archie into his chair. 'Come on, Mabel.'

Mabel was at his side instantly. 'I'll order you both coffees and then leave you to it for a while. If I can do anything, let me know.'

He smiled at me, squeezing my shoulder softly as he went. Archie sank into Jude's chair and rested his face in his hands. 'Coffee would be good, but then,' he lifted his eyes up to me, 'can we get out of here and find somewhere private, to talk?'

My stomach clenched with fear. 'Sure.'

I glanced at the bar, willing the coffees to come quickly. Whatever Archie had to tell me, I needed to know as soon as possible, the suspense was killing me.

Twenty minutes later Archie was striding along, with me scampering at his elbow trying to keep up. We went down the slipway by Big Dave's Lobster Shack, skirted the harbour where the boats were marooned in less than a metre of sea water and by the time we'd hit the wide sandy beach I was out of breath.

'Okay,' I tugged his arm. 'Enough. I can't keep this pace up and have any chance of speech. Archie, slow down.'

He stopped abruptly, pushing his hair off his face. 'Nina, I'm sorry.'

'It's okay,' I said breathlessly, 'it's just my legs aren't as long as yours.'

He sighed, a smile playing at his lips. 'Not about that. About something that happened a long time ago.'

A rush of goosebumps covered my skin suddenly. 'Go on.'

He took a deep breath. 'Before Mum died, her speech was slurred, can you remember?'

I nodded. 'The penultimate stroke affected her speech and mobility in her right side; of course I remember.'

'I went to see her just before she died and she tried to tell me something. She was trying really hard to communicate with me, making a *Gr* sound. She kept saying it over and over again. I'd bought her some grapes and thought that was what she wanted, but she pushed them away. Then she produced a photograph from that little bedside cupboard she had in her room. And said the word again. It sounded like "grame". It didn't make any sense at the time, but now I think she might have been trying to say *Graeme.*'

'Dad's name? What was in the photo? Why didn't I see this, where is it now?'

Archie's face was pale. 'You've got to understand, Nina, I could never forgive Dad the way that you seemed to do. In your eyes, he could do no wrong. All I could think at the time was that no decent man – no father – would abandon his children and never ever get in touch again.'

'And now?' I said hoarsely.

'Now I think that he may have tried.'

He took a photograph from his pocket.

I went ice cold. It was a photograph of a white flat-roofed building, open with white canvas awnings on two sides, tables and chairs on the pavement, glamorous clientele smiling over cocktail glasses. This picture had been taken in full sunshine but apart from that the only difference from Kate's photo was the name. It wasn't called Penhaligon's but The Paradise Club.

My knees felt in danger of giving way. I looked at him, confused, my poor brain trying to make sense of what I was seeing. 'This is freaky; I don't understand. What does this mean?'

'Turn it over. It gets even more freaky.'

Written in biro in shaky letters were just a few words: *Diane, tell them I'm losing my mind.*

Diane, Mum's name. My fingers traced the indentations made by the pen.

'At the time, there was nothing about the message to make me think it had come from Dad. And of course, being called The Paradise Club, the name didn't mean anything to me either.'

'I get that. So do you think Dad is in Brazil at this restaurant or bar or whatever it is?'

Archie held his hands up. 'Right now, I have no idea. But the thing is, I knew about this photograph. That's why I want to apologize. Okay, I didn't know it was from Dad, had no idea this place was in Brazil or what the message signified, but I knew it was important to Mum and somewhere deep inside I had my suspicions that only Dad would have written a message like that. I should have told you. But I was busy, I'm always busy, and then shortly after that she died. And if I'm honest, I didn't want him coming back into our lives, possibly only to disappear again. We were doing okay. You and me against the world, Neen.'

I nodded weakly, unable to drag my eyes from the words on the back of the picture. *Tell them.* Did that mean us? I had to know more.

'Archie, I don't blame you at all. I love you. You are in fact the world's best brother, but two things: firstly, you have got to stop protecting me, and secondly, I want you to help me to find Dad.'

He nodded. 'I had a feeling you were going to say that.'

'Come on.' I was already marching back across the sand to the zigzag steps up the cliff.

'Where are we going?'

'We're going to Google Penhaligon's and then we're going to phone up and see if we can locate Dad.'

'Whoa, whoa, whoa.' Archie caught my arm. 'Slow down. He's been gone nearly twenty-five years. There's no rush, we need to think about this properly, if he is in Brazil he could be married, with kids.'

My heart fizzed with joy. 'We could have an entire Brazilian family, just think!'

'Exactly, so we need to tread carefully. The new family might get a bit of shock if Dad hasn't told them about us.'

'Good point,' I conceded. 'But that doesn't stop a bit of Google research. Last one up the steps buys the ice creams.'

Chapter 35

I paid for the ice creams, although technically Archie cheated by hanging on to the back of my jacket and then sprinting past me on the top step. We ate them as we headed back to Driftwood Lodge. There was a van parked next to his Range Rover and I recognized it as Vic the builder's, and through the gates behind the cottages I could see him talking to Kate and Theo outside the garage.

'Gosh, they're not wasting any time with these plans, are they?' I said, nibbling my chocolate flake, which I'd left until last. 'Goodness knows how Kate persuaded Vic to come out on a bank holiday.'

'It could have been Theo,' Archie argued. He eyed up my chocolate, having already demolished his own. 'At uni, he used to go from random idea to reality before the rest of us had even woken up. It's great to see him back to his old self.'

'I think he was paralysed by guilt,' I said, watching Theo slide his arm around Kate's waist and kiss her hair as Vic wafted his arms in front of the old wooden garage doors, presumably explaining how to replace them with a feature more aesthetically pleasing. 'Kate too. They both felt so guilty when Ivy died, even though there was nothing they could have done to prevent it.'

I shuddered, remembering that first day on the beach when Theo had confided in me about the pain of losing his daughter.

'And I was useless,' Archie admitted gruffly. 'Didn't know what to say to them. So I did what I always do when things get emotional: I buried my head in the sand and pretended not to notice what was going on.'

That was Archie to a 't'. He'd tackle a business problem head on, but anything personal and he'd shy away from it, had done ever since I could remember. Was that what he was doing with Molly? I wondered. I filed that one away to ask another time; today I wanted to focus on my own family. I looped my arm through his and drew him towards the house.

'You helped in the end,' I said fondly. 'Besides, I think this was something they had to work out for themselves. They had to find a way to live with what happened to their little family. For a while it pushed them apart but they made it eventually.'

Archie frowned. 'Do you think that's what happened with Mum and Dad? Something so fundamental that neither of them could face each other again afterwards?'

Mittens flew out of the house as I opened the door and I scooped him up. He was such a loving little thing and instantly bumped his head against my jaw, purring like a tiny motor.

'I don't know. I've racked my brains over the years, trying to recall if anything had happened in the run-up to Dad disappearing, but I was only little and I can't remember anything.'

'Me neither,' he said thoughtfully. 'So whatever happened, they managed to keep it hidden from both of us. It would have to be pretty major, though, for Dad to completely sever all ties with his family.'

'I know,' I said absently, 'because if they loved each other shouldn't they have found a way to work things out for the sake of their marriage, like Theo and Kate did?'

Archie gave a half-smile. 'Remember what Mum always used to say when she was in a bad mood: love is blind—'

'And marriage restores the sight.' We both finished off her mantra together.

'Good old Mum, never one for romance, was she?' Archie said with a rueful smile. 'Told it like it was.'

'Hmm,' I said, remembering how crotchety she could be. 'But did she, I wonder? Or was she keeping secrets?'

Archie opened up the laptop on the kitchen table and pressed on the power button. 'Let's find out.'

'Can it really be this simple?' I murmured, watching him type in his password. 'One photograph taken on a friend's holiday and suddenly the mystery of our family gets unravelled. Doesn't it all seem a bit . . . I don't know, convenient?'

'Perhaps it's fate, and you've been getting those flowers and then . . .' He cleared his throat. 'Right, let's google this place.'

'It was in Brazil somewhere, shall I go and ask Kate the name of the town?'

'It was Recife,' Archie said without looking up.

My eyes narrowed. 'How do you remember that? Have you already googled it?'

'No!' He laughed at my suspicious face. 'I haven't had time. When I said last night I had a work emergency I was telling the truth. An email came through informing me that another customer has terminated their contract with me.'

'Oh Archie, I'm sorry.'

'But there's something else. I wasn't going to mention it, but . . . hold on, I'll read it.' He pulled his phone from his back pocket and scrolled through his messages. 'Regret to inform, blah, blah, blah . . . Here it is, listen to this: "I took you on when you first started in business as a favour to your father who was a friend of mine in college. And you have never let me down, but due to our restructuring, blah, blah, blah" . . .'

My scalp prickled; Dad had secretly helped Archie from a distance.

'So Dad knew about your company?' I whispered.

'Knew and put some contacts my way to help me along.' He rubbed his neck sheepishly. 'And if the anonymous flowers are from him too, that means he's been keeping up with both of us from afar.'

We were quiet for a moment and I felt my eyes well up with tears. All the time I'd been thinking about Dad, assuming he'd forgotten about us. Perhaps he hadn't after all?

'Let's get on with it,' said Archie, reading my thoughts.

'I'm sorry,' I said suddenly, 'about the problems you're having with this competitor, you've worked so hard and achieved so much, it seems unfair.'

'Funny thing is,' he said slowly, 'I wonder what I *have* achieved. I've got money in the bank, a nice house, a good pension fund, but so what? When I was on the beach playing with Ellis last week in those rock pools, I had such a great time. I thought what a fool his dad was not to spend time with his boy because he was too busy working. What a hypocrite I am – me, the man too busy working even to have a family of my own. My balance sheet looks great – or it did – but my work–life balance is appalling. I've put making money before making memories.'

'Not ill, are you?' I pressed a hand to his forehead teasingly. 'Seriously, though, I agree, you do work too hard and forget to play hard. But do you know what you're going to do about it?'

He inhaled a long breath and looked at me. 'Actually, I do. But for now, let's try to track down Graeme Penhaligon, shall we?'

I squeezed his hand. 'Okay.'

He returned his fingers to the keyboard and typed into Google: *Penhaligon's Recife Brazil* and then shot me a look before hitting enter.

A website came up for Recife's premier gay cabaret club boasting Broadway nights every Thursday, the world-class Paradise Girls dance troupe on a Friday and Carnival night on Saturdays.

'A gay club? That can't be the same place,' murmured Archie, scrolling down.

'Wait.' I stilled his hand with mine. 'I think it might be. Click on "images".'

The screen filled with pictures. It was definitely the right place: the name, the white flat roof, the tables and chairs . . . There was no mistaking it. And the glamorous women I'd seen in the photographs were there too, except . . .

'The Paradise Girls seem a bit . . . um,' Archie began tentatively.

'Manly?'

We looked at each other, communicating our unspoken thoughts. A gay club frequented by transvestites. Called Penhaligon's.

'If this really is something to do with Dad,' Archie's eyes were like saucers, 'no wonder Mum never spoke his name again. Can you imagine what she thought about her husband's new life?'

'Disgusted, probably,' I said with a nervous giggle. 'Remember Hairy Sue?'

Archie snorted. 'How could I forget?'

There'd been a transvestite who worked at our supermarket. A lovely lady: I remember her hands being a bit on the large side but she always had lovely nails. Her badge declared her name to be Sue, and Mum would often exchange a few words with her while our shopping was being whizzed along the conveyor belt. Until one day when Sue must have been in a hurry to get ready for work and hadn't shaved her chest. Mum took one look at the tuft of black hair peeking out of Sue's overalls, let out a yelp and ran from the shop muttering words like abomination, pervert and freak of nature. We went straight home, minus our shopping, and Mum never set foot in there again.

'I don't think sexual diversity ever really entered Mum's world.' I grinned.

Unless . . .

Archie's eyes widened. 'Oh God. Are you thinking what I'm thinking?'

We both hunched over the screen. 'Type in "Graeme Penhaligon drag artist",' I urged.

He blew out a breath. 'Okay, but I can't see it somehow. Mum once said he was an accountant.'

I stared at him. 'I didn't know that.'

He waved his hand. 'It was at careers evening at school. The teacher asked what professions were in the family. I said there were none and Mum jumped in and said that her husband had been a well-respected accountant.'

'Oh, Archie.' I looked at him affectionately. 'She was probably lying to save face.'

'Either that or accountants in Brazil like feathers,' he said drily, nodding his head at the screen.

His latest Google search had mostly thrown up the same results as last time. The name Graeme didn't appear at all, but there was one picture taken at Penhaligon's of a man dressed in a white suit who looked so much like Archie that we both blinked at it.

'It has to be Dad. He looks . . .' I swallowed the lump in my throat. 'He looks happy, doesn't he?'

My eyes blurred with tears as they tried to focus on the picture. It was the first image I'd seen of my father for nearly twenty-five years.

And next to him was a drag artist in a sequined strappy dress and an elaborate headdress made of peacock feathers and more sequins. They had arms around each other, glasses decorated with cocktail umbrellas and slices of fruit in their hands.

My heart was in my mouth. My dad, the man who'd read me bedtime stories, cuddled me when I tripped and told me my eyes held the magic of the sea . . .

'This wasn't quite what I was expecting,' said Archie faintly, 'to find my missing father with his arms round a tranny.'

'Weird,' I agreed, puffing out my cheeks. 'I had this vision of discovering Dad living in a cottage by the sea somewhere, digging the garden, an apple-cheeked wife at his side.'

'So now what?' Archie sighed.

I had so many questions: was Dad a transvestite, or gay, and if so why had he married Mum and had children? I wanted to know why, even though he'd apparently chosen a new life, he couldn't have kept in touch with the old. But most of all, I wanted to know if he was still alive.

'Go back to the website,' I said.

Archie clicked on the Penhaligon's home page.

'There's a phone number,' I said. 'Why don't we ring and ask to speak to Graeme? At least we'll know whether we're barking up the right tree or not.'

He frowned. 'I still think we need to be cautious. There's an email address, why don't we start there?'

This seemed like a sensible suggestion, so while Archie composed a suitably calm and collected email, I put the kettle on the Aga hotplate and then rejected the idea of tea and poured us both a glass of wine.

'Medicinal,' I said, setting it in front of him.

'Okay, send.' Archie hit the button. 'Now we wait.'

We both sat back and sipped our wine. I felt drained. What a day. That kiss with Jude on the terrace at The Sea Urchin felt like a lifetime ago. A smile crept over my face as I remembered his expression when I told him how I felt about him. I felt proud of myself, actually, proud for opening up to him and now proud for being brave about contacting the man who abandoned us all those years ago.

'Archie,' I said suddenly, 'what you said to me earlier about Ellis and his dad? You should say that to Molly; let her know how you feel.'

He raked a hand through his hair. 'I don't know, Neen. She's a lovely girl but I seem to rub her up the wrong way. Trouble is, I don't really know what she wants.'

I smiled at him. 'You're in luck. Because I do.'

Bless him. He leaned forward, listening so intently to the things Molly had told Eliza and me that day we first met when we were trying on the mermaid costumes. About earning enough to pay the bills, learning to drive and taking Ellis on holiday. I told him about Ellis loving Disney and about making chocolate cakes and playing football. And after I'd finished a slow smile spread across his face.

'Consider it done.' His eyes sparked with intent.

'Hey, don't tell me, tell Molly,' I said, chinking my glass against his. 'But remember, don't splash the cash. Big turn-off. She's fiercely independent.'

Archie shook his head, laughing at himself. 'All these years I've been doing it wrong. Could have saved myself a fortune . . . Oh, I've had an email back from Brazil already.'

We both leaned over to read the screen.

'Due to the public holiday, Penhaligon's has taken this opportunity to have a mini break and close for two days,' he read. 'We reopen on Wednesday and will reply to your message then. Best wishes, Tim Pen . . .' Archie's voice fizzled out to nothing.

'Tim Penhaligon?' I finished, reading over his shoulder. 'Who on earth is that? Archie, my flowers were from someone whose name starts with T!'

'Vic is so good,' said Kate brightly, marching into the kitchen. She picked up the kettle, shook it then added some more water. 'He's off to the lifeboat house now to give Jude an estimate for work there too.' She stared at us. 'What's the matter with you two? You look like you've seen a ghost.'

'Not a ghost,' Archie stuttered. 'Perhaps a skeleton in the closet.'

'And whoever it is,' I said, trying to quell my nervous excitement, 'is most definitely alive.'

A little while later I crossed the courtyard to Beaver's Barn. I'd been summoned by Maxine. She was leaving tomorrow after all, because her executive producer on *The Holy Coast* had requested a meeting in London before heading up to Scotland on Friday, and so she had finally agreed to do a bit of last-minute exploring with me now. The afternoon was still warm and as the tide was low, I planned to drag her for a long walk across the beach and finish up on the terrace at the pub for a cream tea.

'I'm missing Paul now,' she confided as we headed down the drive. She clomped inelegantly along the potholes in her heeled boots, despite my advice to borrow my trainers. 'She would love it here.'

'You should have brought her.'

'She's lecturing in Australia at the moment, but even so I wouldn't have brought her. I needed this week on my own to work, to think and read. I knew I had to make the decision whether to stay on *Victory Road* or head into uncharted waters. I'm glad I came. The peace and quiet is every bit as wonderful as you promised.'

'Except for bumping into Campion?'

'Oh, I'm glad he came too. I have no reason to hide who I am any more. I'm far more confident than I was when I first met him. I was fooling myself for a long time as a young woman. Growing up, I had a picture of Cliff Richard pinned above my bed, not the butchest of men, I grant you, but even then I secretly preferred Tammy Wynette. Somehow I knew it wouldn't be the done thing to pin a poster of her up in Cliff's place.'

It was hard to imagine Maxine Pearce ever lacking confidence, but I kept quiet. I just felt terribly sorry for her that she'd felt as if she'd had to hide her true self from the outside world for so long.

'Well, I wish Campion hadn't come.' I sighed. 'He wants to turn the boat house into an art gallery.'

'Oh, that would be lovely! Sorry,' she said, catching my mutinous expression. 'I mean, that would be awful. What a lovely building, though, it should be made the most of.'

'Which is why we want to keep it for the community to use.'

Maxine winced. 'I hate to say this, but that man does have a habit of getting what he wants.'

'I don't suppose you could have a word with him for us? Ask him to open an art gallery somewhere else?'

She harrumphed. 'Sorry, dear heart, but then I'd be beholden to him; he'd most certainly want something in return. Look what happened to Oscar Johnson, he repaid a favour by letting Cecily take that plum role in *Mary Queen of Scots*. And what a disaster that turned out to be.'

'Is there a part in *The Holy Coast* she could have? A small one?'

Maxine didn't even dignify that with a reply. She simply raised her eyebrows.

'Fair enough,' I said. 'Just investigating all avenues.'

'So,' she said, changing the subject, 'while I've had my head hanging over the desk burning the midnight oil, what have you been doing other than the laundry?'

'Last night I shared my bed with a starfish, at lunchtime I think I might have told a man that I'm falling in love with him and this afternoon I discovered that my father is running a gay club in Brazil.'

'Crikey,' said Maxine, looking impressed. 'Sod the cream tea, this calls for gin.'

'Careful!' I said as she sprang mountain-goat-like over a slimy piece of seaweed.

'Ooh!' she yelped as she lost her footing.

I grabbed her arm but she was too heavy for me. Her heels caught the edge of a wet rock and she landed with a thump on her back.

'Ouch. Oh seriously, ouch. My back and my ankle.'

I dropped to my knees beside her and she gripped my hand. Her face had gone a greeny colour.

'I'll get help,' I promised.

My phone, of course, didn't work, but at the far side of the harbour I could see Big Dave tossing lobster cages from his boat to the quayside. I jumped up and waved my arms.

'My rape alarm,' muttered Maxine. 'In my pocket. It's ancient but it should still work.'

I found the small device and pulled out the pin. The noise was deafening.

Big Dave looked around for a second and then saw me waving my arms and began running down the slipway.

I replaced the pin to stop the awful high-pitched alarm and knelt back down. 'Help is on its way.'

'Good. But I still need gin.' Maxine's eyes were squeezed tight and tears of pain were leaking from them.

'So do I,' I said, pressing a hand to my racing heart. 'At least a double.'

Chapter 36

'Right, that's great,' I said into the phone the following morning. 'Four adults in four single beds with two dogs for a week in September. It's in the diary for you.'

I put the phone down in the hall and flicked through the pages of the months ahead. That was the first booking for September and there were only one or two vacancies left during the school holidays now.

Word was spreading about Brightside Holidays: the Coastal Cottages website was helping to generate interest and Kate and Theo's own website had its fair share of enquiries too, although it had to be said, most of the people who got in touch mentioned the *Maidens of Mayfair* and asked for the cottage that Sapphire Spencer had stayed in.

I'd kept an eye on Sapphire's Facebook page. It was only four more sleeps until her wedding and yet hardly a thing had been posted about it publicly. I felt proud of her for keeping her and her fiancé's plans away from the public eye. It made it more special, more personal, and I was sure they'd look back in the future with satisfaction at the choice they'd made.

The news section on the *Maidens of Mayfair* website had announced that Sapphire was leaving the show after marrying scientist Brad on Saturday and that she would be taking up a research position at a Canadian zoo. And the article even had a link to her JustGiving page in lieu of wedding gifts to raise money for her ant project. I'd smiled to myself when I'd seen it; so she had managed to raise some awareness of that clepto thing she'd been obsessed with. Good for her. No mention of who would be taking her place in the show, though, so I guessed her sister Ruby had stuck to her guns and was concentrating on her singing career. God help Simon Cowell . . .

'No offence, but you look a bit mental sitting there grinning to yourself.' Molly's voice made me jump and I swivelled round to look at the front door, still grinning.

In London you'd never keep the door open, but here it was propped wide with a cast-iron door stop whenever the weather was good enough. I loved it. Fresh air billowing in, carrying with it the smell of the sea and the faint scent of bluebells from the hedgerows. Heavenly.

'Better happy than sad, though,' she added, walking through to the kitchen and dumping a basket of clean bed-linen on the table. She pulled off her cycle helmet and her hair tumbled round her shoulders. 'I wasn't sure how you'd be feeling after yesterday.'

'It was an epic day,' I replied cautiously, wondering how much Archie had told her.

'Are you putting the kettle on or what?'

'You look happy too,' I said, obeying orders and clinking mugs and spoons. I waited, hoping that Archie was the source of the flush to her cheeks.

'I am. I've just been offered a job!' She scooped her hair up into a ponytail and secured it with a band from around her wrist.

'By whom?'

'Jethro.' She pulled a face. 'Can you believe it? He's going on a cruise.'

I felt a twinge of pride. So the grumpy old git had actually done it. 'He mentioned that he'd always fancied it.'

'Just for a couple of weeks, but you never know,' she continued, 'if he's happy with what I do, it might lead to more hours.'

'Gosh, just think, with your influence he might get rid of some of those antique tins of new potatoes and actually put in some decent veg. And a deli counter, imagine! Our self-catering guests would love it.'

'Well, baby steps, Nina. If I can persuade him to stock proper coffee instead of that dreadful cheap instant, I'll consider myself a success.'

'Well, I'm glad for you. For both of you.'

'My new role is nothing like you with your fancypants-one-step-away-from-Hollywood acting role, but hey, beggars can't be choosers.'

I glanced sharply at her. 'You're not that strapped for cash, are you?' And if she was, I knew Archie would want to be straight in there, trying to help her out.

'I can afford the basics; it's the little extras I need help with.'

I told her about all the new holiday bookings and the regular laundry that would inevitably come her way, which cheered her up.

'Good, because Jethro doesn't need me for another month or so and I'm still trying to save for a holiday for Ellis and me. I reckon I need five hundred pounds.'

'How much have you got saved?'

'Eighty.' She wrinkled her nose. 'Might get us a day trip to Legoland, but that's about it.'

My heart squeezed for her. She was such a determinedly positive person and a great mum, she deserved a bit of luck in her life.

'In that case, I hope Jethro gets the travelling bug and goes away more often,' I said.

'By the way, he said he saw you last night jumping the queue in A&E at the hospital. He said he'd jumped through hoops to get an appointment about his bad leg and you and your friend just waltzed in. I said no wonder his leg hurt if that was what he'd been up to.'

I snorted. 'And by waltzed in, he actually means arriving on a stretcher by ambulance.'

'Yes, he did admit that eventually.'

Poor Maxine. She was feeling very sorry for herself. She'd almost passed out with pain yesterday as two paramedics plus Big Dave had helped her on to the stretcher and into the ambulance. She was lucky: no broken bones, just an ankle sprain, a tender coccyx and a bruised ego that she was nursing today in Beaver's Barn having crawled up to bed on all fours last night.

Her main concern throughout the whole incident was that she absolutely had to be on the train back to London today. She was quite vocal about this until the doctor, peering down at her as she lay flat on her back, had said simply, 'Then get up and leave and stop wasting everyone's time.'

She'd gone quiet after that.

'What's wrong with Jethro's leg?' I asked Molly now, getting another mug out for Maxine and setting it on a tray with a plateful of biscuits – shop bought, say what you like about Jethro's vegetable assortment, but his biscuit shelf wasn't bad.

'Apparently the doctor had told him to do some exercise to get himself fit for this cruise and he'd overdone his "physical jerks". Don't ask,' she said darkly, catching my quizzical look. 'Anyway, he's pulled the muscles in his inner thighs. The nurse gave him some ibuprofen gel and a worksheet of gentle stretches and told him to give his exercise routine a second chance.'

We giggled for a moment or two at the thought of Jethro doing star jumps behind the counter of the shop. Then I got up to re-boil the kettle to make a cafetière of coffee for the patient.

'And talking of second chances,' I said softly, 'how did it go with Archie?'

Molly sighed, took a biscuit from the plate I'd set out for

Maxine and nibbled into it. 'I'm not a high-maintenance woman. I just want someone who'll put their money where their mouth is ... No, scratch that. That's precisely what Archie does do. I want someone I can rely on, not just me but Ellis too. And when a man says he'll show up, he has to deliver on that promise.'

I nodded, sympathizing with her totally. 'But did he tell you about that club in Brazil, the one in Kate's photos? That was part of the reason he dashed off the other night.'

She placed her hand over mine. 'He did. He told me all about finding the photo amongst your mum's things and everything. I hope you don't mind?'

Hope bubbled in my chest as I protested that I didn't mind in the least. For Archie to open up to someone, he had to really like them a lot. I'd love for him to fall in love and live happily ever after, have a focus to his life other than his business.

'So what's next for the two of you?' I said, pouring water on to the coffee grounds.

'The three of us,' she said shyly. 'We've made a date for Friday. He's taking me and Ellis for pizza and ice cream. But this is it; if he bails on me again then ...' She laid her biscuit on the kitchen table very deliberately, raised her hand and karate-chopped it.

'Crumbs,' I muttered.

'Do you want the good news or the bad news?' Jude said later that day.

It was early evening and I'd gone down to meet him on the beach after work. He was sitting on a rock at the bottom of the slipway watching Mabel galloping along the sand playing with two golden retrievers and a noisy Jack Russell and he stood up to greet me, kissing my cheek.

'Good, definitely,' I grumbled. 'I've been looking after the patient from hell all day. Maxine has not taken to the notion of bed rest at all well.'

402

'I heard she was still here.' Jude chuckled. 'I passed the pub on the way down to the beach and Raquel said Maxine had phoned up and placed an order for lunch and was most disgruntled when Raquel told her that no she could not have a chicken Caesar salad delivered to her cottage and that Deliveroo, whatever that is, was not available in this part of Devon.'

We both laughed. He gestured towards the water and rested his hand lightly on my waist. We began to walk along the shoreline and with each step I felt my shoulders relax a bit more, my smile come back and my heart skip. I stole a sideways glance at him; I loved this, just him and me and Mabel, of course.

I hadn't felt like this about anyone before. I'd been so career-focused, telling myself that work had to come first, that there was no room in my life for love. I shook my head at myself. I was just as bad as Archie really, when it came down to it. But no more, from now on I was going to give my love life equal billing to my career.

I filled my lungs with sea air purposefully and smiled up at him. 'I made her an egg salad in the end and even then she checked twice to make sure I'd boiled the eggs for seven minutes. Fastidious to the last is Maxine, but then that's what makes her so good at her job directing TV shows.'

Jude's face fell briefly but he rallied. 'So do you want to hear the good news . . . ?'

'Oh yes, sorry. I got carried away with the view for a second.' I eyed him cheekily and he grinned back.

'Vic the builder can do the work on the boat house. He says the basics to put some plumbing into it – a loo, kitchen sink, that sort of thing – will be simple enough. We could have it up and running as a rough and ready venue in a few weeks.'

'Great!' I beamed, but I could already sense by the look of defeat on his face that the bad news was going to far outweigh the good. 'And the bad?'

'The cost.' He puffed his cheeks out. 'The builder might be willing, but the bank balance is weak. Just to do the initial work will be five thousand quid, and that's before we think about changing the big doors either end, which were designed for boats to slip in and out of. He reckons we'll need at least another ten for that.'

'So actually we need fifteen thousand pounds just to make it look more of a meeting place and less of a shed,' I mused. 'Quite an ambitious target.'

'Impossible, more like.' He gave a harsh laugh. 'If we can pull this off, I'll strip off, run down the beach and go skinny dipping.'

'More good news.'

He laughed, properly this time. 'Seriously, though, short of a miracle, I really can't see that happening, can you?'

I turned to face him, pressing an impulsive kiss to his cheek. 'I'm not giving up now. We've still got a few days. And besides, seeing as my next role is playing a vicar, perhaps I can conjure up a bit of divine intervention?'

I supposed the easiest thing to do would be to ask Archie for a loan. But I wouldn't do that. Firstly, I didn't think Jude would accept it, and secondly, given Archie's confession that things were difficult at the moment for his business, it wasn't fair on him either. No, I thought, stomping back along the coastal path half an hour later, this time I wouldn't go running to my big brother for help, I'd try to figure something out on my own.

I called into the fish and chip shop on my way home for Maxine's order – plaice and chips with plenty of salt and no vinegar – and then jogged back so that it would still be warm enough for her ladyship.

'I need a favour, dear heart.' Maxine sat forward so that I could adjust the cushion behind her back. Her injured ankle was propped up on the coffee table, tightly bandaged, with an ice pack from the first-aid box tucked over it. The other foot was still wearing its high-heeled shoe. 'My meeting really does need to go ahead as planned tomorrow.'

I paused from handing her her dinner on a tray. 'You're not seriously thinking of travelling to London?'

'Of course not.' She settled her dinner on her lap. 'I can't see me negotiating the platform at Paddington with crutches and a suitcase, can you? No, I've arranged for Richard, the executive producer, to come here instead. He sounded rather pleased about it, actually, and says he's looking forward to meeting you.'

'Likewise.' I felt a flutter of nerves; this was beginning to get real. 'Will he stay overnight? Shall I make up next door for him?'

She looked at me blankly. 'Hadn't thought of that, but good idea.'

'Can I have a read of the script tonight?'

She beamed. 'Pour us some wine and we'll read episode one together.'

The next morning, a taxi pulled up just after nine o'clock. Richard Kildare from SparkTV must have left London at dawn. I showed him first to Kittiwake's Cabin to drop off his overnight bag, and then took him round to see Maxine. He was a rugged, outdoorsy man in his forties, with crinkly eyes, neatly trimmed beard, warm smile and a jolly Dublin accent. He'd brought a bag of freshly baked croissants with him from the bakery outside the station and I left them to their meeting with a promise to show Richard where the local shop was later so he could rustle them up something to eat.

Driftwood Lodge was empty. Archie had gone straight back to Exeter on Monday after calling in to see Molly and I hadn't heard from him since. Kate and Theo had gone into town to see the council's planning officer about the alterations they wanted to make to the garage, which left Mittens and me. He snoozed in a patch of sunshine on the kitchen floor while I immersed myself in the script for the next episode of *The Holy Coast*.

Two hours later, a polite knock at the door dragged me

from the story. I blinked up at Richard, completely spellbound.

'I am hooked on this drama. I'm rooting for Charlie Mackenzie right from the start,' I said, wide-eyed. 'The hints at her backstory are so compelling and her little parish is seething with tension and secrets. It's brilliant. Are you sure I'm the right actress for this?'

Richard grinned, delighted. 'You couldn't be more "Charlie" if you tried. Look, I'm sorry for disturbing you. Especially as you're enjoying it so much. Could you point me in the direction of the shop now? Maxine is out of coffee.'

I pulled a face. 'We can't have that.'

He looked over his shoulder to check we were alone. 'She is very demanding,' he admitted with a wry smile.

I grabbed my jacket and insisted on going with him. I was getting a stiff neck from reading for so long and I figured getting to know my new producer would be time well spent.

'Not a bad day at the office,' said Richard, exhaling appreciatively as we reached the top of the beach steps. 'I've never been to Devon before, I had no idea it had beaches and coves like this.'

'Glorious, isn't it?' I agreed proudly.

'Heavenly. And I'm sure it's a few degrees warmer here than Scotland, where I was last week.'

We paused for a moment and I pointed out the landmarks on view while he took out his phone to take pictures to send his wife. The tide was in so there was no point trying to reach Jethro's shop via the beach so we carried on along the clifftop path towards the village and I questioned him about his career.

'Probably way before your time,' he said, sauntering along in no particular hurry. 'But I started out as a junior writer on *Ballykissangel*. Remember that show?'

'Yes.' I smiled, my eyes lighting up. 'My mum loved it. Right up until the episode when the nice priest kissed that barmaid. Then it was banned from our house. Filth, she called it.'

Richard roared with laughter. 'I'd left the show by then, tell your mother it wasn't my fault.'

'Actually, my mum died.'

'Oh. Sorry.'

There was a dip in the conversation and I could have kicked myself for making him feel awkward.

'Anyway, it was a great programme,' I said smoothly. 'I used to watch it in my pyjamas before going to bed on a Sunday night.'

'Now I feel really old.' He grinned. 'So are you ready to blaze a trail as our female vicar?'

'Absolutely, unless . . .' I grinned back at him. 'Will I have to kiss any barmaids?'

'Not as far as I know.' Richard laughed again. 'But I've only read up until the end of series one, so anything could happen.'

'Did you visit the location while you were up in Scotland?'

He wrinkled his brow. 'Spot of contention there. Not a word, mind you.'

'My lips are sealed,' I promised.

'We'd been hoping to use a part of the Scottish coast where our locations manager had found a small hamlet with just a few cottages and a deserted chapel but we've had a problem getting the right permits. We've got a large stone barn lined up for all the interior shots, but it's the outdoors stuff that's causing us nightmares. That's where I was last week. So at the moment the exact location is undetermined.' He shrugged and smiled. 'Nothing new there, we've got until September to finalize the details so it'll be grand.'

'So does that mean Friday's meeting in Scotland is being postponed?' I said, trying not to sound too hopeful.

'As the main members of the cast and crew had the date in their diaries, it's still going ahead on Friday but it will be in London instead – that'll be easier for you, won't it?'

I swallowed. Friday was the day of our meeting with the council. Now what was I going to do?

'Yes,' I said weakly. 'Much easier.' *Help . . .*

The bell dinged flatly as usual over the door at Jethro's but the man himself leapt out of his deckchair with extraordinary vigour and only a slight limp to indicate the previously pulled muscles.

'Nina!' He rubbed his hands together and scurried round the counter. 'Did you hear? I'm going travelling. Don't know why I didn't think of it before. I went and had a word with my old dad, told him what I was thinking, and you were right, he said it was time I did summat for meself.'

'But your dad is . . . dead, I thought?' I said tentatively.

'Well, yes, obviously.' He rolled his eyes at Richard as if I was the village idiot. 'But it's all up here, isn't it?' He tapped the side of his head.

Richard smirked to himself, while adding pasta, bacon and cream, some coffee and wine to his basket.

'Who's this, then?' Jethro looked down his nose at the newcomer. 'Another tourist?'

'Now, now.' I tutted. 'I thought you were a reformed character as far as tourists go. And no, Richard is the executive producer in the new programme I'm going to be in. We were just discussing locations.'

'And saying what a lovely part of the world Brightside Cove is,' Richard added.

''Bout time we got a look-in,' said Jethro, totting up Richard's bill with a stub of pencil and a scrap of paper. 'Pig sick I was when those *Doc Martin* people chose Cornwall over Devon. Still love that show, mind.'

Richard and I grinned at each other. Jethro obviously thought we were filming *The Holy Coast* here.

And then my stomach flipped. Why didn't we? Oh, good Lord! The answer to our prayers. I looked up at the skies and smiled. This could be the miracle Jude was hoping for . . .

Chapter 37

Richard was happy to stroll back to Driftwood Lodge on his own, so I called in to see Eliza. My idea was still only partly formed, and if anyone was going to be non-judgemental about what was potentially a mad-cap scheme, it would be the woman whose CV listed her profession as mermaid. Danny was there too, his camera hanging around his neck. The back of the shop was clear now and a large sheet of white paper had been erected, which draped on the floor creating a backdrop with a series of white boxes of varying sizes sitting on top of it. He noticed me before Eliza did and opened his arms wide, cocking his head to one side.

'I knew it. You find me irresistible. Okay, I surrender, I *will* take you out for a drink.'

I shook my head and grinned. 'You're *irrepressible,* Danny. Big difference.'

'Hey, beauty!' Eliza's head popped up from behind the counter. There was a cobweb in her hair and dust smudges on her chin. 'Ignore him. Seen this?'

She tapped a glass frame behind her with a photograph of her and the *This Morning* crew from last week in it. She was in her mermaid outfit perched on a rock in the centre looking like a princess with the others around her.

'No regrets, then?' I said, remembering how torn she'd been at the weekend trying to decide whether to expand her business or stick with what she knew and loved.

409

'None whatsoever.' She held both palms up. 'I turned all the offers down. Well, apart from agreeing that a company in Norfolk could use my logo for a fee. Which I'm using to buy three mermen's tails and six children's outfits. But apart from that, no.'

'*I* have regrets,' Danny said with a cheeky wink, 'I told her to get that blonde weathergirl's number and she forgot.'

'Totally slipped my mind.' Eliza widened her eyes innocently. 'Anyway, I owe you one for that idea of writing down what I really want out of life. I'm happy now, *really* happy. Brightside Cove is where I want to be. I can be myself here.' She pulled a face. 'Probably sounds really boring to you.'

'Not at all.' I hesitated. I wanted to talk to her about my idea, but ideally not in front of Danny. 'Have you got a minute?'

'Right, Eliza, what's next?' Danny tapped the toe of his trainer impatiently on the floor.

'Give me two ticks,' she said to me and then pushed a large cardboard box to Danny's makeshift photo booth, giving him instructions on how she wanted him to photograph the contents.

'We're putting all the old stock on eBay in job lots,' Eliza explained a couple of minutes later as we headed out into the fresh air. 'It might not sell in Brightside Cove but someone will buy my pottery paperweights etched with fish.'

'Of course they will. There's a lid for every pot,' I said. I frowned: who'd said that? It must have been someone deep in my past; I hadn't heard that expression for years.

'So what's new with you?'

I looped my arm through hers and we ambled towards the quayside to sit on the bench overlooking the boats while I told her what was on my mind. She listened intently, not interrupting once when I told her a bit about *The Holy Coast* and the problems they were having with the location and the major flaw we'd hit in the plans to lease the boat house from the council.

'Gosh, you have got a lot to think about,' she said sympathetically.

We sat down side by side and she took two chocolates out of her pocket and handed me one.

Mine was in a tiny paper case, had fluted sides and was embossed with fine gold lettering that I couldn't quite read.

'This looks too good to eat, where did you get it?' I raised an eyebrow. 'Not Jethro's, I'm guessing.'

She laughed and shook her head.

'There were four of them originally. They're from that fabulous hotel I stayed in in London, the one with the mood lighting? I thought I couldn't love the place any more than I did, but when I came back from dinner I found these on my pillow, I thought I'd died and gone to heaven. It was a real wrench to drag myself away the next morning.'

I bit into the chocolate, enjoying the sensation of the truffle centre melting on my tongue, while formulating my thoughts.

'It's probably totally unfeasible, but if Maxine and Richard could be persuaded to film here instead of Scotland,' I said finally, 'it would solve everyone's problems. We'd all benefit: all the businesses, the holiday cottages, the council would earn money, tourism would increase and we'd be able to raise the money to keep the lifeboat house locally owned.'

'I don't know much about making television programmes,' Eliza said, 'but if the characters and the story stay the same and the location suits the tone of the show well enough, I can't see why not. But doesn't a vicar need a church?'

I turned to her, my eyes shining. 'Look at the lifeboat house. The shape of it, the pitch of the roof . . . Imagine if we replaced that little stone statue on the apex with a cross.'

Eliza squinted across the bay into the distance and nodded. 'Now you mention it, it does look like a little chapel. In that case, go for it.'

She licked the last piece of chocolate off her fingers and scrunched up the gold wrapper.

I sighed. 'Am I being totally crazy, do you think?'

'If Brightside Cove can have the UK's first mermaid school, I don't see why we can't play host to a TV series too.' She twirled a strand of pink hair around a pudgy finger. 'It's like you told me. Make a wish list of the things you most want to happen. Forget practical and sensible. Pour out your heart's desires.'

A million images flickered through my head: the sunrise over the headland, the gentle swell of the sea at high tide, running along the sand throwing sticks for Mabel with Jude, walking hand in hand with Jude, laughing with Jude . . .

I gave myself a shake. If I was serious about this, my motivation had to come from a stronger place than simply the promise of a new relationship.

'I want to help Jude save the lifeboat house from being turned into an art gallery. Especially after seeing all the support from local people.'

'That is sweet of you,' she said. She stretched her legs out in front of her and crossed her ankles. She was wearing flip-flops and each of her toenails was painted a different shade of blue or green. 'I must admit, I'd never given the place much thought until Jude started banging on about it, but now I understand why he feels so strongly about it.'

'Me too. Also I want . . . I'd like to make Brightside Cove my home.'

'Yay!' She threw her arms around me. 'Siren Sisters rule. Because of Jude?'

'No,' I protested. 'Not because of him. I love being by the sea. I've never felt as drawn to a place as I do here. It is probably totally impractical given my job, but . . .' I shrugged helplessly.

'Unless you get your wish,' she reminded me. 'But is Jude perhaps a tiny part of the reason you love it here?'

I took a deep breath.

'Jude is . . .' I paused, trying to find the right words to describe how I felt about him. 'He's like the chocolate on your pillow. Just when I thought I couldn't love a place more . . .'

Eliza grinned at me. 'Got you. Then to answer your question: no, what you're proposing isn't crazy. It's compulsory.'

'Thanks for the chat,' I said, getting to my feet. 'I'm all fired up about it now. I can't wait to pitch my idea to Maxine and Richard. By the way, I thought Danny had a new job with that media company?'

She rolled her eyes affectionately. 'Got fired for chatting up the boss's girlfriend.'

I laughed. 'He doesn't change, does he?'

'That's what I said!' she agreed. 'He said he shouldn't have to change for other people. He says he's an optimist and he likes himself just as he is.'

I gave Eliza a kiss and said goodbye. I quite admired Danny for his eternal hope. I might have to employ a similar tactic myself if I was to get what was on my own wish list.

Right, first things first, I thought as I strode home. Actually, what was the first thing? By the time I got back to Driftwood Lodge I'd tied myself in knots deciding what to do next.

Should I go straight over to Beaver's Barn and blurt out my plans to Maxine and Richard? Or talk to Jude first? It was a tough one. If there was a flat no to my proposal from them, then there would be no need to get Jude's hopes up, but if it was a yes, then I'd need his input from the start.

I chewed my lip. Of course, there was also the real possibility that he'd be totally opposed to using the boat house for anything other than the good of the community.

I plunged my energies into baking a sticky-toffee tray bake while I decided what to do. And when it emerged from the oven glossy and golden an hour later, I'd made up my mind. I dialled Jude's number and held my breath.

He answered immediately. 'Jude Trevone?'

413

'I have three questions for you,' I said without any preamble.

'Okay,' he chuckled.

'Would you like the boat house to earn its keep right from day one?'

'Of course.'

I ploughed on. 'Are you prepared to share it with people other than Brightside Covers?'

'Not if it was with people like Campion Carmichael.'

'It won't be. I'll take that as a yes. Thirdly, do you know anyone with a big empty barn we can borrow semi-permanently?'

He answered without hesitation. 'Yes. Mrs Thompson at Top Valley Farm – the lady farmer I told you about.'

'Brilliant.' I beamed down the phone. So far so good. 'Finally, do you like sticky-toffee cake warm from the oven?'

'That's four questions.'

'Yes or no, Trevone?'

'Yes, you crazy woman, I love sticky-toffee cake.'

'In that case, one more question,' I grinned. 'What time can I expect you?'

There was a box of Christmas decorations on the kitchen table the next morning and everywhere smelled of cinnamon and vanilla.

I rubbed my eyes, mystified, and staggered sleepily to the kettle; I knew I'd slept in later than planned, after a long night spent planning and plotting with Jude but even so . . .

'Jingle bells, jingle bells,' Kate sang merrily. She looked up from piping a white icing outline around a star-shaped biscuit. 'Grab that reel of ribbon, you can start tying loops on the first batch of cookies.'

'Talking of loops,' I said with a yawn. 'I'm feeling decidedly out of it. Why is it Christmas all of a sudden?'

'Our Christmas advertising campaign starts today,' she said. 'Penguin's Pad will be a winter wonderland by tonight, with any luck, ready for a photo shoot tomorrow. We're offering a special Brightside Holidays Christmas package to include the tree fully decorated, a turkey and all the trimmings and a case of wine.'

Theo walked past the window dragging an enormous fir tree and waved in at us.

'Even he's getting into the Christmas spirit.' She sighed contentedly. 'The last two years have been awful but I'm determined to make this one special.'

I swallowed a lump in my throat: Christmas in Brightside Cove. 'That sounds perfect.'

'Why don't you join us this year, you and Archie?' She wrapped an arm round my shoulders and pressed a rosy cheek to mine. 'You have an open invitation, if your filming commitments allow, of course.'

'Thank you, I'll definitely bear that in mind.' I smiled serenely.

If my plan worked out as I hoped, my filming commitments wouldn't interfere with Christmas at Brightside Cove one jot.

'Oh, that reminds me,' she said, wiping her hands on her apron and picking up the little notepad we normally kept by the phone. 'Your brother called and left a message. He said he'll be here at about eleven thirty. Something about an email from Tim. He's arranged for you all to have a chat over Skype at lunchtime.'

'Oh, thanks.' My voice came out in a whisper and my heart leapt into overdrive. It was really happening. Today was the day we'd find out who Tim was and hopefully get to speak to Dad for the first time in nearly twenty-five years too. Unbelievable. I gulped at my coffee to moisten my dry mouth.

I couldn't wait to find out what secrets Mum and Dad had been keeping for all these years and why . . .

Theo and Kate were in Penguin's Pad decorating their Christmas tree when Archie arrived. He set his laptop up on the kitchen table while I raced up and down the stairs in a flap like a teenager getting ready for her first date: changing my outfit three times, doing my hair, putting make-up on and taking it off again in case I looked like I was trying too hard. But by noon we were ready for our Skype call with Tim Penhaligon. Whoever that was.

Right on time, Archie's laptop began to make a ringing sound and Penhaligon's flashed up on the screen.

Archie clicked to answer the call and a man with short blonde hair appeared onscreen. He had a deeply tanned face, sculpted eyebrows and wore a pink open-necked shirt. He had a pair of sunglasses perched on top of his head just behind a neat little quiff. He looked to be in his mid-sixties and clearly looked after his appearance. Behind him was a row of optics and above that a shelf of cocktail glasses.

'Och, look at you two.' The man clapped his hand over his mouth and shook his head. His voice was warm and bubbly, his accent broad Scottish. 'Hello, darlings, I'm Tim and no need to tell me who you are, I've seen you on screen, Nina, and Archie, you're the image of Graeme.'

My pulse began to thrum in my ears; so we had found the right Penhaligon. Archie and I exchanged looks and instinctively reached for each other's hands across the table.

'Hi, Tim.' I swallowed hard. 'Thanks for calling. We were trying to get in touch with our father?'

Tears sprang out of Tim's eyes and he made no attempt to brush them away.

'I've been both hoping for and dreading the day you found us. I'm so sorry but your dad—' His voice cracked and he shook his head. 'He's no longer with us.'

Chapter 38

'He passed away?' I gasped. Tim nodded, reaching into his pocket for a tissue.

So Dad was dead. I had found the man I'd loved and who I was convinced loved me, but we were too late.

I thought my heart would break. I was devastated, but even as the sorrow began to gather like a hard ball at the back of my throat, I realized that this was what I'd suspected ever since I'd received those flowers: *Your Dad would be so proud. T x*

Archie lowered his head to his hands and swore under his breath. I put my arm round his shoulders.

'Tell us, Tim,' he said huskily. 'Help us understand what went wrong for our family.'

Tim nodded, took a sip from a glass and blotted under his eyes with a tissue as if being careful not to smear his make-up . . . I put my face up to the screen. I couldn't be sure but he did seem to have overly prominent eyelashes.

'Shall we start with a tour of Penhaligon's?' said Tim, reaching towards whatever device he was calling from. He turned it round so we could see a raised stage hidden behind long gold curtains, white wooden tables and chairs, and a long white and glass bar which ran along the length of the place. Two women walked past dressed in long white marabou-trimmed gowns and waved at the screen. 'We're still closed at the moment but the boys and girls start arriving about now for morning rehearsals. This was your father's empire, his pride and joy. It wasn't called Penhaligon's when we first bought it. It was called The Paradise Club then. I changed the name after Graeme died as a lasting memory.'

He turned the phone back to himself. 'I changed my name too. Penhaligon has a much nicer ring to it than O'Boyle.'

'I like it too,' I said. 'We weren't sure whether we'd be meeting a new family member today.'

'Out here, far away from home, we were each other's family, I suppose,' said Tim wistfully.

'I'd like to hear about Dad,' Archie said, his voice thick with emotion. 'Like how he ended up in Brazil and why he never got in touch.'

But I understood exactly what Tim was doing: he was introducing us to Dad's life, easing us into it gently. Whatever Dad had been doing since leaving us twenty-four years ago, it was worlds away from his life as a father and a husband in Manchester.

'Tim,' I said, resting a hand on Archie's arm, 'I think we're ready. To know the truth about Dad.'

Although I think I knew what was coming. Tim had clearly loved Dad and I guessed Dad had loved him back.

'Okay, if you're sure.' He blew out his cheeks. He picked up his glass and settled himself in a corner against high white upholstered cushions. 'But if it's okay with you, I'll start at the beginning?'

We both nodded.

'So, even as a boy Graeme felt like an outsider in his village in Cornwall,' he began.

Tim paused now and then as he told us about Dad's family life, how he'd loved his mum but never felt comfortable in his own skin and didn't feel at ease with people. His mother tried to get him to settle down and marry but Graeme didn't find it easy to talk to girls. He'd got so frustrated with her pushiness and interference that when he was offered a job selling catering equipment in Manchester, he left without a backwards glance. His mother had felt so abandoned that they'd rowed and she wouldn't speak to him for years. He'd felt less judged and less obtrusive in a big city. He was good at his job and got promoted several times, and eventually made it up with his mother, but he'd always lived alone, wondering if he'd ever meet someone and fall in love like his friends had. By then he'd begun to suspect that he might be gay, but he hadn't known what to do about it, how to investigate the feelings he was having.

Tim stopped, his eyes worriedly scanning our faces for a reaction. 'This is probably a shock, are you both okay?'

I was holding everything in, determined to keep it together until he got to the end of his story. Archie's face was as unyielding as granite, I had no idea what he was thinking.

'Okay?' Archie murmured to me.

I nodded. 'You?'

'Yeah, it's starting to make sense,' he said gruffly.

'Poor Dad,' I said to Tim, who was patiently watching us. 'So where did he meet Mum?'

'At a fortieth birthday party of a colleague's sister. He was over forty himself by then, a confirmed bachelor, as they say. Diane was quite tipsy.'

My eyebrows shot up. 'She never drank at all! Said it didn't agree with her.'

Tim nodded. 'Graeme thinks someone might have spiked the drinks, he'd only had a couple but felt quite woozy himself. She confessed to him that she was nearly forty and still a virgin and would he show her what all the fuss was about.'

'Good grief,' Archie spluttered.

'Which I think was your father's reaction,' said Tim. 'Given that he was pretty much in the same boat.'

A drunken encounter at a party. Two lonely people on the

periphery of the action, who'd somehow not been given a copy of the rules. It should have been the start of their love story, but it already felt like a tragedy waiting to happen. Archie held my hand while Tim told us that Mum had got pregnant on the night of the party. There was no doubt in her mind that they would have to get married but Dad had been mired in guilt, knowing that he'd be living a lie, but at the same time wanting to do the right thing by her. Archie was born and then three years later, I came along, by which time Dad had almost managed to convince himself that he was living the life he should be.

'Graeme's mother was delighted,' said Tim, 'I don't think she ever really got on with Diane, but she loved you two with all her heart.'

'We visited her in Cornwall,' Archie said. 'We had family holidays with her.'

'Without Mum,' I added.

Tim smoothed his hair back. 'The cracks began to show soon after you were born, Nina. Graeme had a nervous breakdown from the strain of keeping up appearances and he lost his job. Your mum refused to face up to the problems they were having and they grew further and further apart. Then one day she stumbled across a gay magazine that Graeme had hidden in his desk.'

'Oh, poor Dad.' Archie squeezed his eyes shut. 'I can imagine how that went down.'

He'd been discovered with something similar when he was sixteen, Mum had threatened to throw him out and yelled at him for being depraved and perverted.

'After that it all came out,' Tim continued. 'Graeme said he couldn't deny it to himself or her any longer. He wanted to live as a gay man. Although he never wanted his mother Bev to find out because he was worried it would kill her.'

My heart thumped at that. It was so similar to what had happened to Maxine a decade earlier. How sad that people's attitudes to others were so negative. I resolved that I'd be bringing my children up to accept others for who they were and to love unconditionally.

'Diane told him he had to choose between being gay and having contact with his children.' Tim smiled sadly. 'As if your sexuality is a choice. When he refused, she threatened to tell his mother. She made the decision for him in the end and packed his cases while he was out looking for work. She told him that he was sick and that she didn't want her children knowing what sort of man their father was.'

I felt tears prick at my eyes. Mum had had her faults but I'd always thought that deep down she wasn't a bad person. I knew how much this would have hurt and humiliated her, how she would have done anything to prevent the reason for their break-up becoming public knowledge.

I remembered that day so clearly when we'd come home from school to find Dad gone and a 'for sale' sign up outside. We'd left the area as soon as we could. It answered a lot of questions about her extreme views on sex and sexuality. For the first time probably in my life I felt sorry for her.

My poor unloved Mum. And as for my poor conflicted Dad; what an impossible situation. My heart broke for him.

Archie pulled a packet of tissues from his pocket, passed me one and dabbed his own face.

'But things got happier for Dad?' I asked Tim hopefully.

'Initially no. He was beaten up more than once just for being himself. Back then, there wasn't the acceptance or protection that there is now. Part of him wanted to reach out to you both, he missed you so much, but the other part wanted to protect you from the dangers of his new lifestyle.

'But then he moved to Brazil and found happiness here. He and I met in 1995 when I came to work here as a drag artiste, my stage name is Tammie La Tango. He was the manager then. We bought it together from the original owners in 2005, the year before Nina turned eighteen. We celebrated our civil partnership shortly afterwards, a month after Elton John and David Furnish. They did it on the first day it came into force. Show-offs.' He made a moue with his lips. 'We weren't perhaps the most obvious couple, he was a salesman before running the club, and me a drag artiste. But Graeme said his mum used to say that there was a lid for every pot and I was his. Our party was fabulous.'

His gaze drifted then, lost in memories. And I smiled a secret smile to myself. I'd remembered Granny Bev's saying all these years later. It gave me a warm glow, knowing we had ties even though we hadn't seen each other for so long.

'Why mention my eighteenth?' I asked suddenly.

Tim hesitated and pressed his lips together as if choosing his words carefully before he spoke.

'Your parents came to an agreement of sorts when they split. Diane was supposed to tell you about Graeme being gay when Nina came of age so that you could decide for yourselves whether you wanted to get in touch.'

He hadn't forgotten us at all; he was simply honouring their agreement. This was possibly the best news of my entire life.

'But Mum didn't tell us,' I gasped. 'Oh, that would have changed everything.'

'She had a stroke that year,' Archie explained. 'She was paralysed down one side and lost much of her speech. She died a few months later.'

'Your father's health was deteriorating too. Dementia. To begin with he'd joke about losing his mind, but eventually it became clear that it was more serious than that.'

Archie's eyes met mine: so that explained the message on the back of the photograph.

'I wanted him to get in touch with you without Diane's blessing but he wouldn't.' Tim sighed. 'We managed to track you down, though; Archie, you'd just started your business in Exeter.'

'And Dad helped me land a big contract.'

'You know about that?' Tim looked surprised.

Archie nodded. 'I'd never have had the success I've had without that leg-up.' His eyes misted over. 'I wish I'd been able to thank him.'

'And Nina, he knew you were at uni in Bournemouth studying drama; he said he'd always known you had star quality. Right from when you used to recite nursery rhymes to him when you were tiny.'

'He said that?' I whispered.

'Oh yes,' Tim replied with a teary smile. 'He was so proud when you moved to London. He even saw you on TV a couple of times. *Silent Witness*, was it?'

I stifled a groan. Was there anyone who hadn't seen my body naked and covered in grey body paint? Archie chuckled under his breath.

'He used to scour the internet looking for you in the credits of television shows. And then one day I read a press release saying you'd got an agent.'

'And he sent me flowers?' I said excitedly.

Tim wrinkled his nose. 'By then he was quite confused. Some days he barely recognized me. I sent the flowers on his behalf. I wanted you to know that he loved you, that he was proud . . .' His voice faltered. 'I managed to get him a place in an English-speaking care home. I made sure they put *Victory Road* on for him religiously and I sent you flowers from time to time to congratulate you on your achievements.'

'Why anonymously? I would have loved to have known who they were from.' I stood up to switch the lights on. The sun had disappeared behind the clouds and the kitchen had gone a bit gloomy.

'Yes, I wondered that,' Archie said. 'We could have come to visit Dad before he died.'

'I know, I know.' Tim sighed. 'Believe me, I deliberated long and hard over it, but in the end I couldn't bring myself to interfere. You aren't my children; it wasn't my place to contact you. It was only once he died that I felt it was okay to come clean. But I do regret not doing so earlier. Graeme passed away peacefully last autumn. He had people in his life who loved him, but he didn't have his children with him, just a photograph of the three of you skimming stones on a beach.' He stopped to dry his tears again. 'He was a wonderful man. I miss him so much.'

'Thank you, Tim,' I said, wishing I could reach through the screen and give him a hug. 'Thank you for loving him and giving him a happy life.'

'And thank you, darling.' Tim sniffed. 'I know you'd prefer to hear it from him, but he loved you with all his heart. He really did.'

Ten minutes later, after the Skype call had ended, Archie and I sat in silence, letting all of that new information sink in.

'I'm glad for him,' said Archie finally. 'I'm glad Dad had the courage to let go of the life that was making him unhappy and celebrate the man he truly was. Even if that meant we had to lose him.'

'That's a lovely thing to say,' I said, leaning my head against his. 'And I can't believe Dad said I had star quality even though I was so small.'

'Everyone could see that, Neen.' His eyes shone with pride and I felt emotion well up in me.

'He was proud of us,' I said gruffly.

'Yep.'

'Thank heavens for Tim, that he left this world being loved,' I said softly.

'That's all that matters really, isn't it?' Archie said. 'Being important to someone else, being there for them?'

I nodded. 'Strip everything else away and the most precious thing we have is love.'

We went quiet for a moment and then Archie's eyes lit up.

'Hey, I've just had a thought: does this mean we get free holidays to Brazil?'

I laughed. 'And more to the point does this mean Tammie La Tango is our stepdad?'

An email message flashed up on Archie's computer screen and interrupted our childish giggling. He fell quiet as he scanned it, his shoulders hunched.

'Right. Enough is enough,' he said grimly. He dropped the lid down on his laptop and sprang to his feet, hurriedly pressing a swift kiss to my cheek and striding to the door. 'I'm going and I won't be back until I've got all this crap with work sorted out.'

I frowned at him. 'What do you mean? You're not dashing off to Exeter again?'

He smiled. 'I mean, I'm going to be the man I really want to be. Just like Dad.'

I opened my mouth to argue but Archie was off. His car was still spinning out of the drive when I remembered: he was supposed to be taking Molly and Ellis out for pizza tomorrow; I hoped he'd be back in time. My stomach flipped; if he let her down again she'd never give him another chance, and really, who could blame her?

The next few hours passed by in a blur, Tim had given me so much to think about. I was sad knowing that I'd never get to see my dad again, but content that he'd led a happy life for the last twenty-odd years, and most of all I was heartened to know that he'd kept an eye on me from afar and had been proud of me. That meant more to me than anything. I was so wrapped up in my thoughts that I didn't even notice when Jude arrived late for our meeting with Maxine and Richard. After a hectic few hours last night, we'd come up with a proposal and had asked them to hear it from us this afternoon. How much more stressful could one day be?

'Sorry,' he said, jumping out of his van with a sheaf of papers under his arm. 'Got held up on the phone and then . . .' He looked down at his trousers, which were dripping wet from the shin down. 'I got a bit wet by accident. I won't make a very good impression with your bosses looking like something the tide has washed up, will I?'

I laughed; he looked like a naughty boy. 'How old are you? Follow me; we've just about got time to dry your clothes before we're due to meet them.'

I led him through to the utility room and he stripped off his jeans and I put them in the tumble dryer. I studied his naked bottom half surreptitiously. His legs were just as nice as I'd imagined. Lean, tanned and muscly, but not too stocky. I wasn't keen on bodybuilder types, I liked my men more natural and healthy looking, Jude definitely looked that. Very healthy.

'You're giving me a complex, staring like that.' He grinned.

'Don't worry,' I said briskly, feigning nonchalance, 'in my profession I see half-naked men all the time. My eyes don't even register them.'

'Really?' he smirked. 'I think your cheeks have registered me: they've gone pink.'

I cleared my throat and marched out of view.

'Shall we run through what we're going to say in the living room?' I called over my shoulder. 'And you still haven't explained why you're wet.'

As we sat beside each other on the sofa, Jude just in his boxer shorts, it took all my powers of concentration to study the papers he'd spread out on the table.

'I'm wet because,' he smirked boyishly at me, 'I may have done something naughty.'

'Come on, spill the beans,' I laughed, thinking how easily I could be persuaded to do something naughty too.

'I spoke to Katrina at the council to run your idea by her.'

'First-name terms now, is it?' I said pointedly. 'Good work.'

Jude grinned. 'It turns out she's secretly in favour of our campaign to keep the boat house. She and her boyfriend are keen surfers and she thinks the beach needs a facility like

426

we're proposing and that people will be prepared to pay to use it.'

'Brilliant! Did she give you any insider info on other interested parties?'

'She told me that there has been a serious enquiry from a group of old university friends who fancy clubbing together to buy the boat house for get-togethers and big birthdays.'

I pulled a face. 'They actually sound like quite a nice bunch.'

Jude handed me some estate agent's details from his pile of papers. 'Katrina has sent them this instead, it's about ten miles away, on the road to Plymouth. An ex-fishing shed. It's cheaper and needs less work.'

I exhaled. 'Fingers crossed they go for it. So, back to your wet jeans. Have you been for a paddle?'

'Sort of.' He laughed that gloriously warm laugh that had attracted me to him in the first place. 'Katrina let slip that Mr Carmichael is sending a surveyor down this afternoon to do a feasibility report on the boathouse. So I . . .' He rubbed a hand through the springy waves at the front of his head. 'I opened up and soaked the internal walls with seawater.'

I laughed. 'So that the surveyor would assume that the water level comes up higher than it really does? That is genius!'

'I'm already feeling underhand about it.' He scratched his chin. 'I know I said may the best man win, but I'm not sure where cheating fits into that.'

'Well, don't give it a moment's thought,' I reassured him. 'Mr Carmichael's the sort of man who'd stop at nothing to get what he wants. I think he may have met his match in you. I'm proud of you.'

'Ditto.' Jude's face coloured and we grinned at each other shyly for a moment until the timer went off on the tumble dryer and he put his jeans back on. 'Now, would you like to see pictures of the barn you asked for?'

For the next ten minutes we worked out who was going

to say what in order to persuade Richard and Maxine that Brightside Cove would be a much better location than Scotland to film *The Holy Coast*, and I tried not to keep thinking that his legs looked much better without his jeans on. And then we gathered our ammunition and paid them a visit.

'We've got the countryside, the coastline, facilities for indoor filming and, most importantly, a coastal building that can easily be mocked-up to look like a church,' Jude concluded half an hour later. 'Maxine, you even thought it was a chapel when you first arrived.'

Maxine inclined her head; she wasn't giving much away.

She had her foot propped up and a cushion wedged into the small of her back. I was used to her steely glare but Jude had been a bit daunted by her to begin with and had let me do most of the talking. But eventually his passion for the cause had overtaken his nerves. He'd done really well, raising points that I'd not even known about such as the new mobile phone mast that Mrs Thompson had just had erected on her farm that would be giving Brightside Cove a decent signal by tomorrow and also the drama school in Thymeford, which would be able to provide child actors if required.

'It's stunning, it's secluded and it's self-contained,' I added. 'That's why we think that Brightside Cove offers everything that you'll need to make award-winning drama.'

'Award-winning?' Richard sipped his coffee, his eyes smiling at me over his mug. 'Now that would be good, eh, Maxine?'

I detected an ally and felt a wave of hope. I did like him; he'd be great to work for.

'So what do you think?' I wriggled forward on my chair at the kitchen table in Beaver's Barn, my eyes locked on his.

Maxine and Richard looked at each other. I watched their shoulders, eyebrows and lips closely trying to interpret their body language. I held my breath, not daring to look at

Jude but sensing his tension. Eventually Maxine cleared her throat.

'It is funny that you should suggest a change of location. You must have read our minds; we had another report from the locations manager last night with a couple of new places to consider.' She gave me a sympathetic smile. 'But—' She broke off, looking at Richard.

'The setting is key to this whole show,' Richard said in his soft Dublin accent. 'I have to be honest with you, we were thinking about moving further up the coast in Scotland rather than coming south.'

I gulped. Not further north, please. Five hundred miles away from here was already four hundred and ninety-nine too many.

'But time is not on our side.' Maxine frowned and flicked through the photographs Jude had printed out of the interior of the boat house. 'And I'm all for making life simple.'

'I'm with you there.' Richard gave a half laugh. He pulled the photograph of Mrs Thompson's barn towards him. 'And this looks bigger than any we've looked at so far. We'd easily get four interiors built into it.'

'The lifeboat house would need some alteration to make it suitable; new windows to replace the louvre slats and doors, of course,' Jude said, biting his lip.

'We've got estimates for the initial work and it can be done in the next few weeks,' I said. 'So there'd be no delays to the filming schedule.'

Maxine had told me that they hoped to shoot series one in the autumn. If they didn't sort the location out soon, that schedule was looking highly unlikely.

'And don't forget, Maxine,' Richard put in, 'the original novel was set on the Norfolk coast. It was our writers who suggested we set it around a remote Scottish community. That would imply that the story is transferable, i.e. not deeply rooted in Scottish culture.'

Maxine nodded slowly. 'And you know that was always the aspect of the storyline that I felt was the weakest: the island location. It seems an awful lot of conflict and too many weird characters for one small place.'

Oh, I don't know, I thought, this village was tiny and contained all sorts of unusual folk. I suppressed a smile, and when I looked up Jude was doing the same.

'Okay, cards on the table.' Richard rocked back in his chair and folded his arms. 'I like the concept. I felt this place was special the moment I got out of the taxi. It's got a time-lessness, an authenticity and a natural beauty that reminds me of some of my favourite places in Southern Ireland. So at first glance, I'd be happy to pursue Brightside Cove as an option. Maxine?'

I just about resisted punching the air and looked at my boss, mentor and friend expectantly. Her face as usual gave nothing away.

She pushed her reading glasses up into her frizz of charcoal hair and fixed her eyes on me.

'What about the not insignificant fact that Campion is planning on buying the boathouse? If that happens, what then?'

Jude and I exchanged uncomfortable looks. There was no denying that that was a possibility.

He spread his hands out on the table. 'Nina and I are meeting the council tomorrow. We'll know the outcome of that pretty quickly. However, I have it on good authority from the council that they would look favourably on our proposal if we could guarantee a regular income from lettings for the first two years. *The Holy Coast* would more than do that for us.'

Maxine hobbled to her feet, grabbing the table for support and my heart sank: our time was up. Had we done enough to convince her?

'Nina, dear heart, email me all these pictures.' She waved her hand over the printed photographs on the table.

'Richard and I will have another talk and send them up to our locations manager straight away.'

'So you'll seriously think about it?' I said, hardly daring to breathe.

She and Richard exchanged looks and a tiny nod passed between them. 'You've done your homework, both of you,' she said, her face softening. 'You've thought of everything, from accommodation to catering, transport to extra cast members.'

'You'll have my wife's vote,' said Richard with a grin. 'She's already been on the website this morning to book a cottage for the summer. Jude, did you say there's a field at the back that's going to have caravans?'

The two men went outside to examine the caravan site we'd proposed would be suitable for accommodation for the crew, leaving me with Maxine.

'Thanks for listening,' I said, giving her a quick hug. 'This means the world to me. I feel like all my life I've been searching for a place where I fitted in. Nowhere has ever felt so important to me.'

'Nowhere or no one?' she said, cocking an eyebrow.

I smiled. 'He is cute, isn't he?'

'Not my type, but I can see he's good for you.'

'Uh-huh,' I corrected her. 'Don't worry, my mind is on the job. My career still comes first.'

She frowned. 'Always make room for love, dear heart.'

'Plenty of time for that when I'm famous,' I replied flippantly. 'When I'm the star of a successful show set in Devon.'

'If – *if* – we set *The Holy Coast* here, the decision will be based on what's right for all concerned.'

'Absolutely. But you won't find a better location.'

Maxine shook her head, amused. 'You're like a different girl, Nina. You seem so much more confident in your own skin.'

I felt a glow of pride: a compliment from Maxine was like

a double-yolked egg from one of the Driftwood Lodge hens – a rare and precious thing.

'I used to doubt my own judgement; I didn't believe in myself enough to go with my gut instinct. I never felt good enough. When my dad left home, I thought it must be because I wasn't special enough for him to love me. And I think that feeling has followed me all through my life.'

The words came from nowhere and with them the prick of tears.

'Oh, dear heart.' Maxine rubbed away a stray teardrop with her thumb. 'I'm sure that wasn't true.'

I gave her a watery smile. 'It wasn't. We spoke to Dad's partner Tim this morning.'

Her eyes lit up with a mixture of curiosity and kindness.

'I'll tell you the full story sometime but I think you'd have liked my dad. And it turns out he followed my career from a distance and was proud of me, he even watched *Victory Road*! I've learned from him how important it is to be brave and bold. It's time for me to start standing up for what I believe in and what I want for my own life.'

I held her gaze.

'And that's why I'd really like you to choose Brightside Cove for our location.'

She quirked an eyebrow. 'You might have mentioned that. Anything else on your wish list?'

I opened my mouth and then hesitated, wondering if I was asking too much. Oh what the hell: *be more Meryl* . . .

'Actually, there is one other thing . . .'

Chapter 39

It was Friday lunchtime and Jude and I were on the outside terrace at The Sea Urchin.

'Cheers.' He tapped his glass against mine. 'We did it. Whatever happens now at least we know we've done our best.'

'Yes, cheers,' I said with a nervous smile. 'And congratulations.'

The last twenty-four hours, ever since mine and Archie's call to Tim, had been exhilarating and exciting and filled with last-minute adrenalin. Yesterday evening, Richard had called into Driftwood Lodge to tell us that Brightside Cove was now definitely in the running and the locations manager, Phil Turner, was very keen. He had driven down at the crack of dawn this morning to check out the place for himself, and Jude had given him a whistle-stop tour of all our facilities before Phil had given us the seal of approval, jumped back in the car and headed off to London, taking Maxine and Richard with him. My final cheeky request to Maxine had been to reschedule the press briefing meeting so that I could be here for the council meeting and due to the fact that the location of her new show was depending on it, she'd agreed.

I'd waved them off – quite tearfully, actually, I was going to really miss Maxine. She'd rolled her eyes when she'd noticed my wobbly bottom lip, and reminded me briskly that I'd be seeing her again next week to film my final scene for *Victory Road*. And she'd made me promise to tell her any news as soon as we got it from the council.

So at eleven, Jude and I had made our pitch to Katrina Berry at South Devon Council. At the crux of our plan to revitalize the lifeboat house for the community of Brightside Cove and its future generations was our formal request from SparkTV to convert it from dilapidated shed to nineteenth-century chapel to appear in the new TV drama, *The Holy Coast*. Katrina had been as enthusiastic and receptive as we could have hoped for, asking all sorts of questions about the TV show and even suggesting a couple of deserted beauty spots that would be perfect for some of the outdoor scenes.

Afterwards, Jude had driven me back towards Driftwood Lodge but just before the turning to the drive had asked whether I'd join him for a drink and a debrief instead. So here we were.

I took a sip and let the Prosecco bubbles burst on my tongue before setting my glass down on the table.

'Councils are notoriously slow-moving with decisions, but I hope Katrina keeps her promise and comes back to us by the end of the day,' I said, holding up my crossed fingers. 'Phil's paying a flying visit to somewhere near Inverness tomorrow; we don't want him to like it more than here.'

'And the waiting is the worst part,' Jude agreed. 'My stomach's in knots.'

I felt a tremor of nerves. I hoped he was right. But a part of me couldn't help thinking that if the decision didn't go in our favour then the anxiety of waiting would pale into insignificance. Because not only would Jude have lost something he felt so strongly about, but my time in Brightside Cove would be finite. And suddenly I couldn't bear it. I lifted my glass again for something to do, but I couldn't drink: the lump in my throat was too large.

'Angie is coming back,' said Jude. 'She'll be over the moon

if Deliciously Devon gets the contract to supply catering to the cast and crew.'

'Does that mean her daughter is coping a little better with her babies?' I said, relieved that we'd changed the subject.

Jude nodded. 'Correct. But also she has some big bookings coming up that she didn't want to turn down. Summer is always a busier time for outside catering.'

'And she didn't trust you to do the cooking?' I said with mock affront. 'How rude.'

He grinned. 'She has never trusted me to do the cooking, as you know. But I'm exceptionally good at taking the lids off takeaway dishes. Anyway, I've got a big workload next week, so even if I was a talented chef, I wouldn't be able to help out.'

'Aren't you supposed to be at work today?' Come to think of it, he seemed to have been around an awful lot this week.

He shook his head. 'I've got lots of annual leave owing to me; I thought I'd take as much time off as I could at the moment. Make the most of . . .' He paused and gulped his beer.

'Because of the boat house campaign?' I nudged.

'Partly.'

I waited, expecting more, but he set his glass down and started jiggling his legs, his heels bouncing up and down. I watched him, recognizing the gesture as his body's response to nervous situations. He'd done it at dinner the other night at Theo and Kate's when Archie had asked him about his family and he'd been jiggling away today in Katrina Berry's office as he'd gone over the financial aspects of our rescue plan. Clearly he was working up to telling me something but I wasn't in a rush, I would wait for him to find the words.

I turned my gaze away to look across the harbour to the other side of the cove. The blue sky was mostly hidden behind big snow-white clouds today, but every so often the sun would break through and dazzle us with a big 'ta-dah!' before disappearing again.

Jude took a deep breath and braced his hands on his thighs. 'Nina, I just want to say that meeting you has become just as important – no – make that *more* important than the boat house.'

'Oh Jude,' I whispered. 'Thank you.'

My heart skipped a beat; that was the nicest thing he'd ever said to me.

'I don't think you realize how much you've already done for this community,' he continued. 'Look at the impact you've had on Theo. He and Kate now have a thriving business because of you.'

'I don't know about that,' I said. 'I was just in the right place at the right time.'

'You were the catalyst,' he insisted. 'It wouldn't have happened without you. Look at Eliza, she's another one. Storming ahead with her mermaid business after you got her that publicity. And Raquel here at the pub had a record month last month, due in part to you and all the extra booze for that hen party, and even Jethro's singing your praises.'

'Stop,' I laughed, feeling faintly embarrassed. 'You'll be wanting me to stand for mayor soon, although actually I think you should have a crack at that. You'd be brilliant.'

His eyes crinkled with a warm smile. 'There you go again: bigging other people up. But what about you, Nina? Where are you in all this? What makes you happy?'

The breath caught in my throat. That was easy: Jude Trevone made me happy. I gazed at him. Could he really not tell? But before I could answer his phone buzzed into life on the table.

He read the screen and stared at me. 'It's her. Katrina Berry.'

'Already?' I whispered. 'That was quick.'

'Hi Katrina, I'm sitting here with Nina, you're on speaker.'

'Oh, hi, both of you. Right. Okay. Where do I start? Phew.'

Jude and I glanced anxiously at each other. Katrina

seemed flustered; her voice was more jittery than normal. I wasn't sure whether that was a good or a bad thing.

'Have you spoken to your boss?' Jude asked, taking control.

'Yes! Just got out now. Gosh, what a morning; my feet haven't touched the ground. What with sureties from banks and solicitors' letters, etc.'

The sun, which had made one of its brief appearances, slipped behind a cloud and I found myself shivering.

Jude looked at me grimly. We hadn't been in touch with any banks or solicitors. I reached for his hand. He squeezed back and cleared his throat.

'Would that be *your* solicitor, Katrina?' His voice was so heavy with fading hope that I thought my heart would break.

'No, not ours.' There was a pause on the line. 'Oh gosh, Jude and Nina, I wish I could tell you more, but I can't.'

'So what can you tell us?' I said, fighting to keep the frustration from my voice.

'I can say that the auction is cancelled and—'

'Yes!' Jude grabbed hold of my face and kissed my cheek and in his haste we almost missed Katrina's next words . . .

'And I can tell you that the Brightside Cove lifeboat house has been sold.'

I froze. Jude's face drained of colour. 'But . . .' His eyes narrowed in confusion. 'I thought you liked our idea, I thought you were on our side.'

Katrina made a small whimpering noise. 'I did. I do! But an offer came in unexpectedly this morning. It's too good to refuse. Or rather, it's too good for my boss to refuse. It's this year's budget, you have to understand,' she said beseechingly. 'Things are really tight.'

'So we lose a treasured landmark, a building that has sat at the heart of this community for over a century, because of *this year's budget*?' Jude shook his head in disgust. 'To some rich developer? How short-sighted.'

'I know you're disappointed, but try to stay positive,' Katrina began, 'you don't know what will happen next.'

The offer would have come from Campion Carmichael, I realized with a jolt. He knew we were meeting with the council today. Jude's little damp trick yesterday had clearly not been enough to put the surveyors off. The thought of Mr Carmichael's smug face at getting one over on us made me feel quite ill. And the second thought – of him spending time in Brightside Cove on a regular basis – made me feel even worse.

'I'm afraid we've got a pretty good idea,' I said with a sigh.

'Please sit tight and don't do anything rash.' Katrina apologized again and then rang off, claiming she had another call waiting and wishing us the best.

Jude and I sat in a despair-filled silence for a few seconds.

'Oh, Nina,' he groaned.

'We could try to find out who's bought it,' I suggested. 'On the off-chance it isn't Mr Carmichael.'

'We could,' Jude agreed. 'But right now I can only concentrate on one thing.'

He fixed his eyes on me and tucked a breeze-ruffled strand of hair behind my ear.

'What's that?' I said softly.

'That you'll soon be leaving Brightside Cove for Scotland. I'll wake up one morning and you'll be gone and this . . .' He waved a hand between us. 'This will all be like a dream. I suppose it always felt as if it was too good to be true. Like the sort of happy ending that happens to other people.'

I swallowed a lump in my throat. He seemed to be dismissing us. Not even giving us a chance. And the sad thing was that I knew he was right. I would be at least five hundred miles away. Maybe if we'd known each other longer we'd have had a more solid foundation on which to build a strong relationship. But we'd barely even kissed. And I'd be leaving in a matter of days for the rescheduled press trip and to shoot my last scene for *Victory Road*. There was no time. No time for us.

There seemed to be nothing else left to say. We finished our drinks in silence and gathered our folders with our rejected plans in them and prepared to leave.

Just then the sun came out and a shaft of sunlight touched Jude's face. His lovely face with his golden lashes and caring hazel eyes, which flashed with a strength of passion I'd never seen before, and that tiny silver scar above his ear. And I felt a sob begin to build in my chest. Forget everything I'd just thought. I couldn't give up on him. I couldn't walk away from the man who had begun to mean so much to me in a few short weeks.

'Jude,' I said in a shaky voice, reaching a hand to his chest, 'we might have lost the boat house, but there's no need to lose each other.'

He placed his hand over mine and slowly removed it. 'I put my heart and soul into that campaign and I lost. And when you go to Scotland I'll lose you too, whether you realize it or not. You're entering the next phase of your life. You're going to be a huge star, Nina, just as you deserve; I don't want to be the one to hold you back. I want to be the one who sets you free.'

I thought my heart would break as he kissed my cheek and scooped up his car keys.

'And don't I get a say?' I said, conscious of my knees going all wobbly.

He turned and gave me a smile tinged with regret. 'It's for the best, Nina.'

I said nothing. I watched him walk away and I said absolutely nothing. My mind had gone blank and I could think of no words that would make him change his mind.

It was only after I saw his van pull away from the side of the road that the words came. Isn't that always the way? I could have kicked myself. Why hadn't I remembered my mantra: be more Meryl? What would Meryl Streep have done? One thing was for certain, she wouldn't have let a man she loved walk away from her without a fight. And now I had a sinking feeling that I'd left it too late to say anything.

I paused outside the door of Beaver's Barn, key in hand. My plan was to go in and strip the beds ready for the next guests – two retired lecturers, apparently, on a walking tour of the south-west. But a wave of exhaustion hit me and I changed my mind. The Prosecco had left my mouth dry and I wanted nothing more than a cup of tea and a lie on my bed for half an hour to revive my spirits. But before I could make a move, the door to Penguin's Pad opened and Molly flew out furiously, wearing a Christmas jumper, a pleated tartan skirt and a paper crown, the sort you get from a cracker. My heart plummeted. Today was the Christmas photo shoot. Theo had asked Archie to help out, modelling as part of a happy family with Molly and Ellis. No prizes for guessing what had happened . . .

'Have you heard from Archie?' she called, storming towards me.

I shook my head. 'Not since yesterday.'

Actually, I thought with a niggle of guilt, I should have called him this morning, to check he was okay, but what with Phil Turner arriving and then the council meeting, I hadn't had a moment to stop and think about Archie.

'Me neither.' She came to a halt in front of me, her eyes blinking with unshed tears. 'You told me to give him a chance. Well, that worked out well. Last time I listen to you.'

She folded her arms, her ribs rising and falling with emotion.

I rubbed a soothing hand on her arm, feeling responsible for Archie's behaviour.

'I'm sorry, Molly. He had an email from a competitor and it seemed to upset him. He dashed off saying that something had come up and he was going to deal with it once and for all.'

'Something's come up?' She fumed. 'Something's come up? Well, you can tell him from me that when I see him there'll be something else coming up: my boot up his backside. I've had it with him. He has had his last chance. I need someone who means what he says, who keeps his promises, who is prepared to actually spend time with me. And Ellis. In fact, no that's not true, I don't need a man at all. I have had it with men. Knobs, the lot of them.'

It was all I could do not to burst into tears myself. What a mess. What a bloody mess.

'You're quite right,' I managed to say. 'I don't blame you.'

My head felt all muzzy and Molly's red hair and flashing brown eyes kept going out of focus. I staggered towards the picnic bench outside Beaver's Barn and let out a big sob.

'Oh bloody hell, Nina!' She rushed over to sit beside me and flung her arms around me. 'I'm sorry, I didn't mean to take it out on you. It's not your fault. It's just I get so protective of Ellis. He's in there sitting under the Christmas tree trying not to rip into the pretend presents that Kate has wrapped up. And he was so looking forward to having his picture taken with Archie.'

'Oh no, that's terrible,' I wailed, letting my tears drip on to my lap.

'Exactly.' Molly's chin was trembling with the strain of not letting her own emotions out. 'That's why I get so upset. He's been through a lot in his four years and I'm constantly feeling guilty that we're not living the life I planned.'

I cried quietly into her shoulder, feeling overwhelmed. So much had happened over the last few days, it was no wonder I was over-wrought. From landing my dream role, albeit at the price of leaving Brightside Cove, to finding out about Dad and Tim, to fighting and losing our battle for the boat house. And then letting Jude slip through my fingers. I knew exactly how Molly felt: there seemed to be no plan, no structure to my existence either. It struck me suddenly that I wasn't the leading lady in my own life and perhaps it was time I did something about that.

The thought was so ridiculous that I felt a bubble of hysteria rise to the surface.

'Planning is overrated,' I said, wiping my tears away and squeezing out a hint of a smile. 'Perhaps we should take a leaf out of Eliza's book and just be mermaids instead.'

'Yeah, Siren Sisters unite.' Molly sniffed and a smile spread over her face. 'Perhaps I'd be better off with a merman.'

'It would certainly solve the knob issue,' I said with a snort.

We both laughed loudly then and only stopped when we heard the rattle of an engine, followed by the sound of a handbrake being applied roughly.

'I'd better go and see who it is,' I said with a sniff. 'How red is my nose?'

'What did you say, Rudolph?' Molly grinned. 'I'll come with you. Between my Christmas jumper and your red nose in early May, we should see them off quickly.'

Together we walked around to the front of the cottages into the courtyard to find Archie banging on the front door of Driftwood Lodge. His Range Rover wasn't here, though, which was odd. He seemed to have arrived in a beaten-up old Ford Fiesta the colour of mud.

'Shit,' Molly muttered. She smoothed her hair down and rubbed a finger under each eye. 'Now what do I do?'

'Up to you,' I said with a smile. 'You said you weren't going to listen to me again.'

He turned at the sound of our footsteps on the gravel and bounded over, a huge smile spread across his face.

'You're late,' Molly said flatly. 'Ellis had given up hope.'

'I'll make it up to him. Don't be mad at me, please,' he said, wincing. He dropped to his knees in front of Molly, clasping his hands together. 'It couldn't be helped, I promise.'

She folded her arms, doing her utmost to stay cross. 'Not that old chestnut. Get up, you fool. I know you're only trying to look up my skirt.'

He grinned and got to his feet. 'Okay, Neen?'

I shrugged. 'I've had better days, to be honest.'

He wrapped his arms round me. 'Bear with me; I just need to talk to Molly in private.'

I started to move away, but Molly grabbed my arm to force me to stay. 'You might be a nice guy but I don't need this, Archie. Why are you in that old car, by the way?' she added, wrinkling her nose.

He looked over his shoulder and beamed proudly. 'I sold the Range Rover and the vintage Triumph I had restored and I sold some other things too. And I feel . . .' He puffed his chest out. 'I feel on top of the world.'

I gasped. 'You sold your business, didn't you?'

Archie grinned. 'Yep. Time for a new challenge. Someone wanted it more than me, made me an offer I couldn't refuse and I thought, *Why not?*'

Molly looked confused. 'Hold on. You sold two cars and a business and all you bought was that old banger?'

'For now, yes.'

'Why?'

I suppressed a smile. That was our Molly, direct as ever.

'Well,' Archie began nervously, 'my thinking was this: you want to learn to drive and the Range Rover is far too big for a beginner.'

She shook her head. 'I don't want you to pay for driving lessons for me. I thought you understood.'

'I'm not. I'm going to give you one. A lesson! I'm going to teach you a lesson. Oh damn.' My poor brother looked to me for help. 'I am so useless at this.'

'I think Archie is trying to offer you driving lessons.' I laughed, looping my arm through both of theirs so we could all go and examine the little brown car.

'I bought it because it matches your eyes,' said Archie.

443

'Not because it matches your bullshit, then?' Molly retorted. Then instantly blushed. 'I'm sorry, that was rude. I'm useless at this too. I'm seriously touched that you'd want to spend your time teaching me to drive.'

'I can't think of anything I'd like more.'

I looked away discreetly while Molly and Archie fell into each other's arms and kissed. And managed to squash a mild pang of envy that mine and Jude's encounter this morning hadn't ended so romantically.

A downstairs window at Penguin's Pad opened and Kate's head popped out, followed immediately by Ellis's below her. Kate quickly slapped a hand across Ellis's eyes and stuck a thumb up at me.

'Okay, okay,' I said, tapping Archie's back. 'I think you've got me back for that nude scene in *Silent Witness* now. I've had enough of the floor show, thanks.'

'And there's some plastic mistletoe in here for you to canoodle under,' Kate put in from across the courtyard. 'Come on, I can't hold off from letting Ellis tear into the mocked-up parcels for much longer.'

'Oh heavens,' said Molly, adjusting her skirt. 'I do hope he understands that they're not really presents or this could get very messy. Let's get it over with.'

'Before we go in . . .' Archie reached into the inside pocket of his jacket and retrieved a small package wrapped in red paper. 'I do have a real present. One he can open.'

Molly's face went all gooey. 'Oh, Archie. He'll be chuffed to bits. Shall I put it under the tree?'

She went to take it off him, but he held on to it.

'It's a Mickey Mouse toy,' he said.

'He loves Disney!' she beamed.

'I know.' Archie swallowed. 'Nina told me. The thing is, Mickey isn't the actual present. It's to represent something.'

I felt a surge of joy, guessing where this was going. I was so proud of my brother; only I knew how hard it was for him to make this sort of gesture.

'Is it me, or are you talking in riddles today?' Molly wrinkled her nose and looked from Archie to me.

He let go of the parcel. 'I hope you aren't cross. Again. But I've booked a trip to Euro Disney in June. For you and Ellis.'

'Oh, Archie.' Molly's eyes brimmed with tears. 'Just me and Ellis?'

'Well.' He ran a finger round his collar. 'I could come along too? If you like.'

She nodded, her eyes shining. 'I like. We'd both like that.'

They kissed again and Archie said he'd be in in a minute after he'd had a quick word with me, and Molly ran back into Penguin's Pad.

'So.' I pulled my brother into a hug. 'You've sold up completely?'

He nodded. 'I could have kept part of it: the guy who bought me out suggested I keep the medical cleaning side as they don't have any experience in that industry. But I decided against it. I think I'd be constantly looking to see what they were up to with my old business. I decided a clean break is better. And also – doctor's orders.' He looked at me sheepishly and held his hands up at my horrified expression. 'The hospital picked up a heart murmur. Don't panic. As long as I make a few lifestyle changes, I'll be fine.'

'That's as may be, but I think you should tell Molly before you go any further.'

Archie blushed. 'She knows. We were chatting and she told me that her father had heart problems, and before I knew it I was confiding in her.'

My throat thickened with emotion. Amazing. I grinned at him. I could tick him off my worry list. He was going to be fine. *They* were going to be fine; another match made in Devon.

'You'd better go in and play happy families under the Christmas tree, then,' I said, forcing a smile. 'While I go in and book my train to London next week to go and film my final scene in *Victory Road*.'

'In a sec. But first I want to say something. All my life at the back of my mind there's been this feeling that I had to do better than Dad. I was going to behave better, look after my family better, and never run away from anything. But actually I have been running away. I've thrown my all into my career, used my hectic life as a way of keeping relationships at arm's length. And I think you do the same.'

'Me?' I retorted. 'That's not true.'

'So you're going to make a go of things with Jude, then?' he challenged. 'Even though you've lost out on the boat house?'

'I . . . well, it doesn't make sense,' I said, flustered. 'We don't really know each other that well and everyone knows that long-distance relationships are hard to maintain.'

'One thing I've learned from Dad and Tim is that what life comes down to at the end of the day is love. Nothing else matters. Nothing.' He stared at me earnestly.

'Hold on.' I frowned. 'How did you know we'd lost the boat house—' I interrupted myself with a gasp. 'Did you . . . ? Are you the one who bought it?'

'No.' He pulled a large old-fashioned key ring out of his pocket, hung with two pewter-coloured keys and handed it to me. 'You are. Or rather *we* are, I bought it with part of your pension fund and some of the proceeds from the sale of my company.'

I gawped at him. 'It's ours?'

'A joint investment.' He nodded. 'Penhaligon's Properties. I thought we might start by offering the village first dibs on a twenty-year lease.'

He gently pushed my mouth shut with his finger. 'Now go on,' he said, laughing at my astonishment. 'Go and give Action Man the good news.'

Chapter 40

The mobile phone mast up at the farm was obviously already working because when I got my phone out to find Jude's number I found I had a generous three bars of signal. My fingers were trembling so much I could barely tap in a text message to him.

Meet me at the lifeboat house. Three o'clock. Bring a towel.

A reply pinged back immediately.

What are you up to?

My fingers hovered over the touch screen while I tried to think of a suitably cryptic reply, a reason he wouldn't be able to resist.

You made me a promise, it's time to deliver.

At three o'clock, I was waiting for him. Not outside the boat house as he was expecting, but inside. When I heard the telltale sound of Mabel barking with her usual joyousness as she no doubt capered towards the waves, I quietly opened one of the doors to find him just a few paces away on the slipway, scouring the beach for me.

I crept up behind him. 'Looking for someone?'

Jude whirled round and stared at the open boat-house door, a bemused smile on his lips. 'What . . . ? How . . . ? Did Ned give you that key?'

'No,' I said chirpily, 'and officially I suppose he should surrender his key now that there's a new owner.'

He scowled. 'Don't remind me.'

I looked at his empty hands and sucked in air. 'You didn't bring a towel. You might regret that.'

Jude's face twisted into a smile and his eyes twinkled with curiosity as he folded his arms. 'You're very cheery this afternoon, given the news we've had.'

'I'm standing in front of a very lovely man who's about to go skinny dipping. What's not to be happy about?'

'What? Me? I'll take the lovely man bit, but . . . No way,' he said, shooting a worried look at the waves, which to me looked perfect for a dip – a very chilly dip.

'Oh, but you promised,' I said wide-eyed. 'What were your words?' I scratched my head, pretending to remember what he'd said. 'Oh yes, "If we can pull this off, I'll strip off, run down the beach and go skinny dipping." And guess what?' My eyes glittered as I held up my key ring complete with a full set of boat-house keys. 'We pulled it off.'

For a moment Jude just stared transfixed and then as the penny dropped, his face spread into a slow smile. 'Did we?'

'We did.'

'So it's not going to be an art gallery?'

I shook my head. 'Nor a posh boutique. It's going to be anything and everything we want it to be.'

'Really?' he said, and with a whoop of delight, he scooped me up into his arms and swung me round and I felt the tension of the day drop away like grains of sand on to the beach.

'That's amazing! I'm not sure how you've managed it, but you're amazing too.'

'Well,' I tipped my head to one side, 'it was a team effort.'

Mabel, sensing our mood, ran over and dropped her rope

toy at our feet, and after he'd set me down again Jude picked it up and threw it into the waves for her. We slipped off our shoes and rolled up our jeans and began to walk through the edge of the surf, letting foamy waves wash over our feet.

'So come on,' Jude grinned, 'put me out of my misery, who is the new owner?'

'The leading lady in a new drama series set in Devon. And her brother.'

'You? But . . . ?' Now it was Jude's turn to gawp. 'I don't believe it,' he said in a voice not much stronger than a whisper.

'Believe it,' I said solemnly. 'But there's one thing.'

'Right.' He ran the tip of his tongue around his lips, his eyes riveted to mine. 'I'm listening. Whatever it is, we can fix it between us.'

My eyes pricked with tears. We could. Him and me, between us, we could fix anything.

I thought back to earlier today when I couldn't think of the right words to say. Now was my chance. This was my Meryl Streep moment. I took a deep breath.

'Okay . . .' I began.

'Wait.' Jude stopped, ankle deep in the water. 'Please let me. There's something I need to say before we go any further.'

He rubbed a hand through his hair and looked down at his feet. 'What I said to you today. About setting you free. That was the hardest speech I've ever had to make. I said it because . . . not because I didn't care but because I do, very much. What I should have said was that whatever you do, wherever you go, given the chance, I'll be here waiting for you. For ever.'

I swallowed hard, unable to speak, my heart thumping like a drum.

'I nearly drove over this afternoon to tell you I'd made a mistake,' he continued, his words tumbling out over each other like the waves. 'I don't want to hold you back, that

449

much is true, but I was wrong not to give us a try. And the reason I'm saying this is because if I tell you now how I feel about you, I don't want you to think I'm only saying it because you're staying in Brightside Cove. Does that make sense?'

I nodded. 'I think so, but just for the record, how *do* you feel about me?'

Jude smiled a smile that lit up my heart. 'I love you.'

I'd never heard such wonderful words in my entire life. 'If you shout that out loudly, I might just let you off the skinny dipping.'

He cupped his hands to his mouth and bellowed. 'I LOVE YOU, NINA PENHALIGON.'

My heart might have just burst with joy.

'Excellent voice projection.' I nodded, impressed. 'Thank you, you are officially absolved.'

He took my hands and brought them to his lips. 'I've never felt like this about anyone. Until I met you I didn't even know I was capable of feeling like this. I've avoided love, I guess.'

'Same,' I said, beaming. 'But not any more. I love you too. Very much. I've hidden behind my career, using my job as a way of keeping myself at arm's length, but really I was too afraid to love. My mum found it hard to show emotion and if I'm honest I'm better at acting love scenes than coping with the real thing.'

Jude shook his head in amazement. 'I don't believe that for a moment. When I look at you, I see a beautiful girl so full of love it shines from her like the sun.'

'Oh Jude, that is a lovely thing to say.'

In that moment, he was probably right; my entire body felt as if it was glowing with love for him.

He stepped closer until our feet were touching, my small feet between his. He released my hands and touched my face, stroking my cheeks and brushing hair from my face.

'And when I look at you,' I murmured, 'I see a strong, wonderful man whose heart is big enough to care for an entire village. And, I hope, big enough to care for me too. So back to the thing I mentioned.' I placed my hands on his chest, feeling the solid wall of muscle beneath his T-shirt as I slid them up around his neck.

'Oh yes?' Jude was all ears.

'Will you be my leading man?'

He grinned. 'That is the best offer I've had all day.'

'All *day*! Cheek!' I stepped back, my eyes dancing with happiness as I skimmed the water with my foot, sending a huge arc of water in his direction.

He gasped as the cold water splashed his stomach. 'Right, this means war.'

I screamed as he dived at me and together we fell into the shallow water. The icy water took my breath away for a second and my lungs contracted with shock. And then Jude's lovely, smiley face was in front of me and we staggered to our feet laughing and gasping for air.

'Say it,' I laughed, 'say that thing again.'

He didn't shout it this time but pulled me into his arms and whispered softly, 'I love you, Nina Penhaligon. Have done I think since you mistook me for a stripper at the hen party and you were all stroppy and stressed.'

'What? Not when you saw me in my mermaid outfit being carried over the waves?' I said, pretending to be insulted.

Jude grinned. 'I admit you did do something for me then, but the feelings were a bit more lust-based, especially when you did your juggling act with your bikini top.'

'I'm happy with lust.'

'Good.'

'Then that's another match,' I murmured.

He raised his eyebrows questioningly and I smiled.

'A match made in Devon.'

And he kissed me very thoroughly. I closed my eyes and lost myself in the kiss, my body tingling as a response to his touch. I thought about Maxine's wise words: *always make room for love, dear heart.* I was making room and it felt like the

451

most natural thing in the world. I was in Jude's arms where I was meant to be and as the sea swirled around our feet, the seagulls wheeled overhead and somewhere in the distance Mabel signalled her presence with her ever joyful bark, I was sure my life had never been more perfect.

'Excuse me, are you Nina Penhaligon?' a small voice said somewhere close by.

I broke away from Jude's embrace to find a girl of about twelve or thirteen holding a pen and blue piece of paper out to me. She was panting from exertion and her trainers were wet from having waded up to us.

'Yes.' My voice came out a bit post-kiss husky so I tried again. 'Yes, I am.'

'Can I have your autograph please? I heard someone shout your name from over in the harbour and I came running. I really love *Victory Road*. Nurse Elsie is my favourite character.'

Jude looked on amused as I scrawled my name on the back of what I now saw was a Siam Palace takeaway menu, the place where he'd bought our hen party dinner from all those weeks ago.

The girl walked away, pink cheeked, and Jude wrapped his arm round my waist as we made our way back to where we'd left our shoes.

'I'll have to get used to the fame thing.' He grinned, and then stopped. 'Hey, will you still love me when you're a Hollywood legend?'

'Even then,' I confirmed solemnly. 'And if I do have to work away in LA or New York or somewhere exotic, I'll always come home.'

'Home?' Jude raised a hopeful eyebrow.

I filled my lungs with the fresh clean air and took a sweeping look at the beach before returning Jude's loving gaze.

'Yes, home to Brightside Cove.'

The Thank Yous

Thank you to Francesca Best, Hannah Bright, Julia Teece, Candy Ikwuwunna, Janine Giovanni and all the wonderful team at Transworld who add the sparkle and magic to make my books the very best they can be. Thank you to Hannah Ferguson, Joanna Swainson and Thérèse Coen at Hardman Swainson for waving the Team Bramley flag here and around the world.

Thank you to my wonderful writer chums who are always there with a word of encouragement and their cheerleading pompoms: Miranda Dickinson, Rachael Lucas, Jo Eustace, Lisa Dickenson, Alex Brown, Lizzie Lamb, June Kearns and Milly Johnson.

Thank you to the fabulous women I've met through my writing; they always make me feel a million dollars: Jane Streeter, Kim Nash, Harriet Bourton, Sharon Moore, Tracey Tyrell and Jackie Buxton.

Thank you to Lucy Salmon, whose cat, Mittens the kitten in the book is named after and thanks to the Lucas family whose dog Mabel is Jude's much loved Springer Spaniel. Thanks to Ken and Mandy Buxton whose South American adventure inspired Kate's trip. Thanks to Christie Barlow for her help in finding out from *Emmerdale* how top-secret storylines are handled by the cast and crew – all inaccuracies are mine! Thank you to Cath Cresswell whose love of a rock-solid itinerary inspired Catherine, the chief bridesmaid.

Thank you, and much love to my family: Tony, Phoebe, Isabel, Mum, Roger and Mary Monica for all the love, help and support you give me each and every day; I couldn't do this without you.

Escape to the serenity of Cumbria with Cathy
Bramley's heart-warming novel . . .

HETTY'S FARMHOUSE BAKERY

Thirty-two-year-old Hetty Greengrass is the star
around which the rest of her family orbits. Marriage,
motherhood and helping Dan run Sunnybank Farm
have certainly kept her hands full for the last twelve
years. But when her daughter Poppy has to choose
her inspiration for a school project and picks her aunt,
not her mum, Hetty is left full of self-doubt.

Hetty's always been generous with her time and until
now, her biggest talent – baking deliciously moreish
shortcrust pastry pies – has been limited to charity work
and the village fete. But taking part in a competition run
by Cumbria's Finest to find the very best produce from
the region might be just the thing to make her daughter
proud . . . and reclaim something for herself.

Except that life isn't as simple as producing
the perfect pie. Changing the status quo isn't easy –
and with cracks appearing in her marriage and shocking
secrets coming to light, Hetty must decide where
her priorities really lie . . .

Hetty's Farmhouse Bakery is available now in paperback

Discover a little bit of Mediterranean flavour
in the English countryside with
Cathy Bramley's gorgeous novel . . .

THE LEMON
TREE CAFÉ

When Rosie Featherstone finds herself unexpectedly
jobless, the offer to help her beloved Italian grandmother
out at the Lemon Tree Cafe – a little slice of Italy
nestled in the rolling hills of Derbyshire – feels like
the perfect way to keep busy.

Surrounded by the rich scent of espresso, delicious
biscotti and juicy village gossip, Rosie soon finds herself
falling for her new way of life. But she is haunted by
a terrible secret, one that even the appearance of a
handsome new face can't quite help her move on from.

Then disaster looms and the cafe's fortunes are
threatened . . . and Rosie discovers that her *nonna* has
been hiding a dark past of her own. With surprises,
betrayal and more than one secret brewing, can she
find a way to save the Lemon Tree Cafe and help
both herself and Nonna achieve the happy
endings they deserve?

The Lemon Tree Café is available now in paperback

Indulge with an extra slice of
Cathy Bramley in her delicious novel . . .

Verity Bloom hasn't been interested in cooking
anything more complicated than the perfect
fish-finger sandwich, ever since she lost her best
friend and baking companion two years ago.

But an opportunity to help a friend lands her right
back in the heart of the kitchen. The Plumberry School
of Comfort Food is due to open in a few weeks' time
and needs the kind of great ideas that only Verity
could cook up. And with new friendships bubbling
and a sprinkling of romance in the mix, Verity
finally begins to feel like she's home.

But when tragedy strikes at the very heart of
the cookery school, can Verity find the magic
ingredient for Plumberry while still writing
her own recipe for happiness?

The Plumberry School of Comfort Food is
available now in paperback

WIN £500 TOWARDS A DEVON COTTAGE GETAWAY

To celebrate the publication of

A MATCH
MADE IN DEVON

we have teamed up with holidaycottages.co.uk to offer you the chance to win a £500 voucher to spend on a Devon holiday cottage escape!

PRIZE INCLUDES:

A £500 holidaycottages.co.uk voucher

A set of Cathy Bramley books to read on your holiday

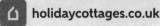

holidaycottages.co.uk